hey Barb ♥

heavenly bodies

ROCHELLE ALLISON

much love! xoxo
Rochelle allison

Publisher's Note: This is a work of fiction. Names, characters, places, and incidents are a product of the author's imagination. Locales and public names are sometimes used for atmospheric purposes. Any resemblance to actual people, living or dead, or to businesses, companies, events, institutions, or locales is completely coincidental.

Book Cover © 2016 Lauren Zuppo
Book Layout ©2016 Beth Bolden

Heavenly Bodies/ Rochelle Allison. -- 1st ed.
ISBN 978-1540772572

Dedicated to my father,
who spent hours with me beneath the night sky.
Thanks for introducing me to the stars, Dad,
especially Rigel and Orion.

1.

In the fifth grade, Benson Reid stuck a glob of ABC (already been chewed) gum into my ponytail, resulting in a hideous haircut for me and detention for him. I hated his guts. In the seventh grade, he and Gregory Hernandez got suspended for setting off stink bombs in the boy's bathroom during lunch. No one was surprised they were the culprits. They were usually the culprits, but Benny was clever and his good grades kept him in good graces.

In the tenth grade, he came back after a summer in Florida with muscles and a tan. Now, instead of cooties, Benny had sex appeal. He joined student government and started running track. His glasses, which I'd secretly found cool, got tossed for contacts, and I realized his eyes weren't just blue: they were the bluest eyes I'd ever seen.

I realized, during Spanish class one day, that I liked him. And I found out, via the Grady High grapevine, that he liked me too. But for some reason, we always dated other people. We even kissed sometimes, like once during a movie in Greg's basement, but nothing ever came of it.

My best friend, Sage, has been saying forever that I should make the first official move. "This isn't the fifties, Isla."

On Fridays, a lot of kids go to the skate park around dusk. We're sitting on the wall, discussing the merits of local fast food, when Benny and his friends show up.

"I'm not saying Sonic isn't good," Sage says, frowning at her chipped nails. "I'm saying nothing's better than Chick-Fil-A sauce. And you only get that at Chick-Fil-A."

"True, but you can always do what my mama does and take extras. She uses that sauce on everything," I say, watching to see who Benny's with. "And anything."

"So do I," says Sage. "But..."

Glancing over at me, eyes like cloudless skies, Benny gives me the confident little smile I've come to know so well. Returning it with a smile of my own, I wave back. And then Stella Conti materializes, shampoo commercial hair shimmering like an auburn waterfall.

"Hey Benny," I hear her coo, and just like that, he's distracted.

2

"Ugh. Never mind." Rolling my eyes, I grab Sage's arm and change directions. "Let's go get some fries."

Now Sage is the one rolling her eyes. She squints across the park, where Benny and his friends are talking, Stella hovering nearby. "What, because of that skank? Go get your man, Isla."

"My man? Does he know that?" I sweep my thick, curly hair into a bun. It's long overdue for a trim, the frizz made worse by Atlanta's legendary summer heat.

But Sage is already pulling me away, flagging down our friends. Peeking over my shoulder one last time, I catch Benny watching us leave. Our eyes meet and he smiles, lifting his hands: where ya going?

Yeah. Maybe he is mine.

There's a free, end-of-summer music festival in Piedmont Park. I hear Benny and Greg will be there, but we'll see.

"You're smiling," says Sage, slicking lip gloss on. Smirking, I hold my hand out for the tube. She hands it over. "What, Isla? Damn."

"What do you mean, what? I'm thinking about popsicles. Haven't had one in a while."

"Yeah, right." She snorts. "You're thinking about Benny."

"Maybe." I glance at her as I switch lanes.

Parking in downtown Atlanta is tricky on the best days. It's especially obnoxious on the weekend, though, when kids are out of school and tourists are tourist-ing and entire families clog up the Beltline. Today the fates smile upon us: we snag a spot seconds after it's vacated.

"Benny's here." Morgan barrels into me, hugging me so hard I squeak. She's tiny, her head fitting just under my chin. I squeeze her back, lifting her off the ground.

"Already?" I look around as we start walking, scanning the crowd for a fresh undercut and a tall, lanky build. Half the crowd fits this description, unfortunately. It's Atlanta.

"Stella was trying to talk to him but he totally ignored her. I almost felt bad for her." Morgan grins, tucking her bobbed hair behind her ears. "Almost."

Wandering through the crowded park, we find a popsicle stand and load up. Seems like everyone's out, enjoying the last few nights of summer. After watching a set from some band Sage likes, we find a bunch of kids from Grady fooling around by the 10th Street entrance. Morgan takes our picture with her phone...and then Benny's beside me, his arm around my shoulders.

The way he smells make my nose tingle in the best way, green and outdoorsy, fresh air and just-cut grass.

"Hey, Isla Grace," he drawls, grinning down at me. He's got pale, creamy skin, the type that burns before it tans.

I slide my arm around his waist. "Hey, Benson."

He pulls me even closer and yells something to somebody passing by, and I think maybe—finally—we've turned that corner.

The sun's gone down, but it's not quite night. Streetlights flicker on at random like firefly soldiers coming to attention in the dusk. A mosquito drones lazily by, fat off the sweet summer air. Swatting at it, I relax against the side of Benny's car, watching him watch me as the rest of our friends chase each other up the street, voices rising and falling with the relentless energy of being seventeen.

We're parked a few blocks from my house, tucked into a wooded cul-de-sac that backs up into a park. I've always loved it here. If you're quiet, you can hear the rush of the creek, which swells and recedes depending on how much rain we've had. Further inside, there are picnic tables and walking paths, and a playground we abandoned years ago when it became more fun to just hang out.

Greg Hernandez struts by, doing a silly but uncanny impersonation of the way Sage walks, and she jumps on his back, covering his eyes. I can't help but laugh as they stumble away, barreling into everyone else.

Benny's laughing, too, but it fades when our eyes meet. My stomach flips, and it has nothing to do with the milkshakes we had on the way home. Nervous energy crackles between us, more electric than it's ever been.

He comes closer, leaving just a breath between us. "You going to homecoming?"

Most of Grady's is going to homecoming, so I doubt that's what he's really asking. "Maybe."

"You wanna go with me?" He takes my hand, tangling our fingers.

"Maybe," I tease.

He smirks, because he knows I'm full of it, and kisses me.

My street is quiet and dark when Benny follows me home. Now that we're finally together, the last thing I want is to go inside, but I can't pull a Morgan and spend the last week of summer on lockdown.

At my door, below the porch light and its flutter of moths, he takes my face in his hands. We kiss until my phone goes off, reminding me it's nearly twelve. After he's gone, and I'm safely inside, I'm physically incapable of normalcy. Grinning like a goon, I tiptoe to the kitchen and grab a glass of water while texting Sage, who responds with all of the appropriate emoji.

heavenly bodies

I float upstairs, caught between memories of Benny's kisses and fantasies of how great senior year will be. But when my mother meets me at the top of the stairs, I falter.

The euphoria of the day drains out of me like a tired sigh. "Hey, Mama."

"Hi, baby." She pats my arm. "Let's talk."

"Right now?" I check my phone again, though I know exactly what time it is. "What's wrong?"

"Grandpa Harry's not doing too well."

"What happened?"

"Come." With a jerk of her head, she retreats back down the hallway. I follow her into my parent's room, where Daddy's sitting on the bed. He's disheveled and tired looking, and the old anxiety that accompanied his heavy drinking days bubbles in my gut. It's like muscle memory. I lean against the dresser, careful not to upset the coterie of perfume bottles and makeup.

"I spoke to Aunt Greta. They…think he might've had a minor stroke. He's in the hospital for now, where he can be monitored, but he'll have to go home soon. Isaac and Greta and the kids usually help out, but Greta's going to be busy with school starting." Mama sighs, pressing her fingers to her eyes. Her eyes are red; she's been crying. "And he needs more than what they can give him, anyway. He needs a nurse, and he needs someone to help him take care of the house."

A fuzzy memory of my mother's childhood home whispers through me: sitting on the floor in the kitchen, tiles cool against my skin, watching Grammie peel potatoes at the table. It was summertime, and we'd come to visit. Gran died a few years later, when I was thirteen. We went down for the funeral, but haven't been back since.

It has to be hard for Mama, watching Grandpa Harry get old like this.

"Are you guys going to hire someone?" I ask.

"It's a possibility, but—"

"We can't just bring him up here for awhile?" Although, I doubt he'd come. He's old school West Indian.

She shakes her head. "He can't travel, not at this point."

"So, then..."

"The best option, at this point, is to go to him."

"To St. Croix?"

"Yes."

"You're going to St. Croix?"

"You and me," she says. "And Alex." She looks down at her lap, to her motionless hands. One thing about my mother: she's calm. Always. It's predictable and safe; it's what makes her a good nurse. But I guess it can be frustrating, too, like right now when I want a reaction. Because right now, there are a hundred different emotions rippling through me, none of which are calm.

I stand a little straighter, bracing myself. "For how long?"

"For a while, honey." It's Daddy who speaks this time, and there couldn't be more resignation in his voice—or his eyes—if he tried.

I stare back at him, trying to wrap my mind around what my parents are saying. "Wait...we're moving?"

"In about a week," Mama says, unable to meet my eye now. "Dad's going to stay behind. For now."

Shocked, I shake my head. "But...what about school?"

"We can enroll you..."

Their words fade. I can barely even look at them. This is about more than just Grandpa Harry, that's for damn sure. This is about my parents, too. I see them differently now, sitting stiffly on opposite ends of their own bed. Definitely not a team.

Closing my eyes, I catalog the past few months. What else have they kept from me? What have I chosen not to see? "Are you getting a divorce?"

"No," Daddy says quickly.

I look up in time to see them share a look. "What're you going to do, then? If you're not coming?"

He shifts. "I'm gonna keep on working with John. Business has been good, so, there's work for me."

"Why can't you just do construction down there?"

"Maybe I will at some point." He nods slowly, patiently. They've gone over this a lot, I can tell. "But for now I need to stay and take care of things."

No, Mama needs him here so they can take a break. They don't say it, but that's what they mean. It's been a threat for a long time, but I guess time has made me complacent. I thought we were past this, that we were okay, but I was wrong.

"I'm sorry, baby," Mama says in that infuriatingly calm voice.

The weight of it comes down on me at once, and my chest tightens. Panicked, I shake my head. "This is not happening."

"Isla—"

"You can't be serious." My voices quivers.

"Isla—"

"You can't possibly think it's okay to move now!" I cry. "Everything is here! My friends are here!" My mother opens her mouth, like she's going to speak, but I steamroll right over her. "I only have one year left."

"Yes. The timing is awful," she says. "But—"

"I'll stay here, with Daddy." I don't know if I even mean that, but I can't leave. Not now.

"You're not staying here."

"Well, I'm not going."

She sighs, like this is such a hassle, and my God it really is. The biggest freaking hassle of my entire life. Overwhelmed, I go for the door.

"Isla," Mama says.

"Can you just...leave me alone?" I bite viciously at my lip, trying to keep the tears at bay. "Please."

Daddy stands. "Isla girl."

"Isla girl what?" My vision blurs. "This sucks! What do you guys want me to say?"

"It doesn't have to be a bad thing," Mama insists, pleading.

Incredulous, I raise my eyes. "You're kidding, right? You guys are basically splitting up. We're moving, like, days before senior year...my life is shit."

"Isla Grace!" Daddy says. "I know you're mad. I'm mad. Okay? But you can't talk to us like that. Not now, not ever."

I know I can't. I never do. But it doesn't matter. Pushing past them both, I escape to the safety of my room, the room I'll have to give up soon, and cry.

2.

Yawning, I snuggle deeper beneath the covers, staring at the moonlight shining through the divide in my curtains. The house is quiet, as it should be around three, but I can't sleep.

I guess I'm not the only one, because there's a soft knock and then my door opens. "You up?" Daddy whispers.

"Yep."

He comes in, sitting hesitantly on the edge of my bed. "Hey."

"Hey," I croak, picking at loose string on my blanket.

We sit in the dark for a minute, and then I click on my lamp. My dad and I have the same grass-green eyes, the same nose. I see more of myself in him than I used to. When I was little, people thought I was a light skinned version of my mother. I have her full mouth, her smile, the same smattering of freckles across the bridge of my nose. I even got her booty, which is good because it would've been a travesty had I inherited Daddy's. I mean, he's flat as a board back there.

"Isla..."

I list my head, letting him know I'm all ears.

"Talk to me."

Shrugging, I swallow the thickness in my throat. I wish I was asleep, but the knots in my stomach won't allow it. Reaching for my phone, I see several missed texts. Sage, probably. Maybe Benny.

Daddy pries the phone from my fingers and sets it on the nightstand, exhaling. "I know this is hard. I know," he insists, when it looks like I might speak. "I don't want y'all to go."

"Then why are we going?"

"To help your grandpa."

"I just don't see why this is the only option. It's crazy."

"It's crazy, but life's crazy sometimes."

Wrinkling my nose at his platitude, I lie back. "There's got to be another way."

"Even if there is, this is probably best. Grandpa Harry gets a live in nurse and your Mama gets a job. And they get each other." He pauses. "That's important. We don't know how much time he has left."

A stab of guilt pierces my anger, but I shove it away, irritated. "Sounds like a real win/win."

"You make it sound like we want to do this. You think we want to be apart right now? Make you start school someplace else?" Daddy stares at me, shaking his head. "Being an adult means making the right decisions, not the feel-good decisions."

My cheeks burn. I'm angry as hell, called out. But I'm right, too. "You've always said to exhaust every option."

"We have, Isla."

"And you can't come along because..." I know it's fruitless. When parents decide stuff like this, that's it. There's no discussion, really.

"Because your mama has a job there, and I have one here." Daddy squeezes my shoulder. "It's a rough time, I know it, but we'll get through. We always have."

I don't know that there's ever been anything quite like this, but I keep that to myself. My father's hurting enough as it is. Thing is, I'm hurting too, and it's making me less than charitable.

We look at each other and the urge to cry comes back with the force of a tsunami. My face crumples as I lean into him, and he holds me tight.

"I'll come to see you guys for Thanksgiving," he promises, and that just makes me cry harder. I hadn't even considered the holidays. What's it going to be like in a place where it doesn't even get cold? Any romantic notions I've ever had of this tropical paradise are evaporating in the face of actually living in it.

Grabbing a tissue from beside my bed, I blow my nose. "Can't I just live with you?"

"Even if you could, would you really want that?" he asks, regarding me seriously. "To leave Alex? To leave your mama alone?"

"She'll have Grandpa —"

"No, Grandpa will have her. She won't have anybody to lean on. I'm trusting you to help out."

"Why can't you help out?" I hear the words as they leave my mouth, unfair and unyielding, but I can't stop. "Isn't that what marriage is all about?"

"Of course it is. But it's also about doing whatever it takes to make things work, and right now, we're going through a rough patch. "

"She wants to split up?"

"Neither of us want to split up. Which is why we're taking a break."

"But—"

"I need help, Isla," he says. "Medical help."

My stomach ties itself into a knot. His drinking is getting worse, is what he's saying. How can I argue with that? The fight inside leaves me, and I wilt into the blankets. I feel, suddenly, like a stranger in my own family. There are all sorts of things I don't know. "I...didn't realize it had gotten that bad."

"It comes and goes, but I'm tired of doing it on my own. I'm tired, Isla girl." His eyes fill, and he looks away. "I just want to be who your mother needs me to be. Who you and Alex need."

And that's the crux of it. It's growing up; doing hard things. Mama has to help Grandpa Harry, I need to help her, and Daddy has to stay and work. Get better. The selfish part of me wants to plead with time, begging it to just stop, or rearrange itself, to let me finish out my school year here and go to college. Let things get real after that.

"I'm here if you want to talk," Daddy says after a while, standing up.

"What's there to talk about?" I scowl. "It's not like I have any say. My friends get to have senior year without me, and by the time we get to St. Croix, my new school will have already started so I'll be behind."

"Actually, no." He shakes his head. "Your new school starts after Labor Day. You'll be okay."

"Thank God for small mercies," I mutter.

"You might like it," Daddy says, giving me a small smile." It's a great school. Mama loved going there."

"Of course she did. It's the only school she ever went to."

"I'm sure you'll fit right in."

"Daddy." I groan. "Don't make it awkward."

"Love you." He bends, kissing my hair.

"Love you, too." I watch him leave, closing the door quietly.

Resignation creeps in, replacing the sadness I've been cocooned in. It's almost worse. I've spent my entire life in this house. I look at my room through fresh eyes, wondering what will come to St. Croix. My clothes, my books, my pictures. My first camera, a classic Minolta gifted to me by Grammie. It was one of many things she passed on to her kids and grandkids, but it kindled in me a love of photography.

Tucked into the border of my mirror are dozens of pictures. Me, as a toddler in dance class. Sage and me, the first day of freshman year at Grady. Waving sparklers at a sleepover. In a photobooth with my grandmother. Tubing down the Chattahoochee with my parents, right before we found out Mom was pregnant with Alex. He's four now. Almost five.

My favorite is the one of my parents, around the time they started dating. They're at the Varsity on a game day, sharing shakes and being all nauseatingly in love. The way they look at each other in that photo? They still do it today. They almost broke up when I was seven because of my dad's drinking, and then again at ten, but in the end they stuck it out.

Because of that look—the way they look at each other. The way they love each other. Mom says he's the love of her life. He says she's his reason. So why are we moving?

I've got to call Sage.

18

And what will I say to Benny? I can still feel his mouth on mine, still see the look on his face when he asked about homecoming. Are we going to miss each other? Or will it be like we never happened?

My phone buzzes from my nightstand. I glance at the screen, squinting at the incoming text.

It's Sage, of course: *back to school shopping. Mall of Georgia?*

Instead of messaging back, I call her. I need to hear her voice when I tell her what's going on, even though I know she's going to be as upset as I am.

"Mornin', homeslice," she drawls, laying that accent on thick as maple syrup.

"Hey, Sage."

"You just wake up? Damn, how late did you and Benny get in?" She snorts. "I must be the only good girl left—you know Morgan's mama caught her with a guy in her room last night?"

"What?" I crack a smile, despite. "That girl is crazy."

"Grounded til school starts."

"That sucks." I chew anxiously on my thumbnail. "But listen, I have news."

"Good or bad?"

"We're moving."

"No way," she says. "Like out of town? Are you guys losing the house or something?"

Anguish washes over me. "No, like out of state. To St. Croix," I explain, voice thick with tears.

"St. Croix? Your mama's St. Croix?"

"Yes."

"What?"

"Yeah. My parents told me last night...they were waiting for me when I got in."

"Isla," she chokes out, and I can just see her face.

"I'm coming over," I cry, yanking a dirty pair of jeans from the floor.

"Okay," she says, sniffling audibly. "Hurry up!"

Curled up in Sage's blankets, a bag of Whoppers between us, we reminisce about the way things have been and how they're about to change with The Big Move. Talking about it aches, but it makes things better, too, like Sage is sharing the weight of it.

"I'll write," I promise.

"Like with a pen?" Sage scoffs. "Just text me! Or email."

heavenly bodies

"Well, obviously." I laugh a little, feeling raw around the edges. We've cried a lot today. "But I like writing, too, you know. And sending packages. I don't care if it's old school."

"Packages full of treats I will accept. I'll even send you some. From home." She peeks over at me. "You think they have funnel cake down there?"

"Don't send me funnel cake."

"Now you have to keep me updated on Snapchat," she says, absently twirling one of my curls. "Do stories and stuff."

"Okay." I scroll through my phone, updating the app so I don't forget. Sage and Morgan are more into it that I am.

"What should we do today?" she asks, turning on her side and staring at me. "I mean, it's different now. Every day counts. We should make a bucket list or something."

"Yeah." I nod, but I don't know what I want to do. My brain feels like it's filled with cotton balls.

"We have one week," she says, voice wavering. "I can help you pack. Morgan too; her Mom'll let her out for this."

That makes me giggle, but it makes me want to cry again, too.

3.

Mlittle brother has gone into hyper-speed, thoroughly overstimulated by the early morning hustle and bustle of the airport. Alex was six months old the last time we flew, so all of this is very novel to him.

Normally I like traveling too, but today is different. I've been dreading this trip, and now that it's here, I'm sort of hovering between disbelief and numbness. Going through the motions. It's all I can do to help my mother navigate the airport with our oversized luggage and an effervescent four year old. I'm grateful for Alex, though. Focusing on him keeps me from thinking about Sage crying last night, or Daddy crying this morning, or my mother trying not to cry right now.

The depth of her sadness is the only thing that keeps me from drowning in mine. In some ways it pierces me, like we're grieving together. But mostly, I just feel betrayed.

"Come on, Al," says Mom, tightening her grip on Alex as he strains toward a nearby pretzel stand.

Standing, I take his hand. "I'll take him."

She nods, smiling gratefully, but I just pull Alex to my side and start walking. He acquiesces, excited to explore.

We make an adventure of it for awhile, visiting shops and watching planes take off. It's impossible to shake the detached feeling. It's as if I've already left, like I'm neither here nor there: in between. In one shop, an old fashioned globe beckons from between expensive pens and crystal chess sets. Keeping one eye on Alex, I wander over to it, searching for North America, Georgia, and then Atlanta. And then I trace my finger south, down to the Caribbean. St. Croix is tiny—a dot. I'll be living on a dot.

My last days home were spent judiciously not thinking about my soon-to-be island life, and I did pretty well until late last night when Sage and I gave into temptation and Googled my new school. It looked pretty rustic for a private prep school, a hippie commune of narrow, one story buildings and palm trees. Hence the name: the Palms. I can't decide if that sounds snooty or just islandy. Maybe a bit of both. I've gone to public my whole life, so I can't say I'm looking forward to spending my senior year with the entitled brats of St. Croix's privileged.

The one bright spot in all of this is my cousin Camille. We're awful at keeping in touch, but when we're together, we're thick as thieves. I haven't seen her since she came up with her parents for Thanksgiving two years back, but we're both seniors at the Palms now. I fully expect her to keep me from going crazy.

Mom says Camille's over the moon we're coming, that she can't wait to show me around. At least someone is excited.

A muffled announcement crackles over the loudspeaker, and I hurry Alex away from the display of Georgia Bulldogs plush toys. Mom is already standing, gathering our bags as she shoulders her phone.

"Yes. Yes, I know. I love you too. I will." She hangs up and pockets the phone, glancing at me. "Ready?"

"Who was that?" I ask, sliding Alex's little knapsack on to his back.

"Daddy," she says.

I don't know what I was expecting, but it wasn't that. Frowning, I grab Alex's hand and follow my mother onto the plane.

The tears come when we take off. I stare out the window, weathering the small wave of panic that washes over me as the ground disappears. This is it. We're really leaving. Alex sits between my mother and me, quiet for the moment as he leans over my lap to look at the sky.

"I want to," he murmurs after a while, eyes glazed at the beauty of the great blue beyond. "I wanna sit here, Isla, I want to."

"You should've said so before takeoff," I chide, rolling my eyes. He always does this. "I told you you could..."

"No Isla," he whines.

"Shush."

"Mama," he cries, scowling.

My mother quiets him with a pretzel she bought him in the airport. "Quiet down, buddy. Isla tried to give you that seat but you didn't want it, remember? I'm sure you can take turns." Alex fusses a little more before absorbing himself into a coloring book, gashing his new crayons across the pages with glee.

Turning my attention back to the window, I retrieve my phone from my bag and take a couple of sky shots. This, at least, never gets old. And then, because I like to torture myself, I open the photo gallery on my phone and reminisce.

4.

The first night is the hardest.

My bed is too soft, and the blankets smell vaguely like moth balls. And it's surprisingly loud. Crickets, a neighbor's dog barking, the constant rustling of a million trees...thank God for my ceiling fan. On high, its whirring drowns out most of the nighttime cacophony.

In the morning, I'm awoken by Alex climbing into bed with me. I reach for him out of habit and then freeze, because he's soaked.

"Alex, did you—"

"I peed," he whispers, kissing my cheek.

Groaning at the damp spot he just left on the already musty sheets, I wrangle him into the shower.

"Mom!"

"What?" she yells back.

"Alex wet the bed again."

She appears in the bathroom, drying her hands on a towel. "All right. I'll deal with the sheets."

"Is there a washing machine?" I call after her.

"Out back."

Of course it's outside. Still, that's preferable to the laundromat. Our washer bit the bullet once, and we had to lug our dirty clothes to Bobo's Bubbles for about a month. I must have watched a lifetime's worth of talk shows.

I rinse Alex and wrap him in a towel, passing Mom in the hallway as she carries the wet sheets outside. "No more water before bed," I say, toweling Alex's curls.

"But I'm thirsty."

"Yeah, but...just a sip, then. You don't want to pee the bed again, right?"

He shakes his head, then wiggles from my grasp and runs, naked butt disappearing around the corner. Yawning, I toss his towel over a chair and return to my room. Even without Alex's pee spot, this mattress could use a good scrub.

"We'll get you a new one," Mom says during breakfast, when I complain about the softness and the smell.

I've been texting back and forth with Sage, but this gets my attention. "Really?"

"A lot of the stuff here is ancient, Isla. Some of it is fine but other things, like the mattresses, can go. And the sheets. The ones in my room are from the eighties."

"No they're not." I laugh, stirring honey into my tea.

"They really are." She grabs Alex as he dances by and plops him into a chair at the kitchen table. "Anyway, Grandpa needs a new one, too."

"But Mom," grumbles Alex, driving a little yellow car across the placemat.

"Eat." She pries the car from his fingers and sets a bowl of sliced bananas down in front of him. Grandpa Harry's dog, inexplicably (or maybe ironically) named Larry, collapses at his feet, eyes shining hopefully up at the table.

"When's Grandpa coming home?"

"Probably tomorrow."

I nod, blowing the steam rising from my mug. "I can't wait to see him."

"Oh, you'll be seeing plenty of him," Mom says, jotting something into the little notebook she keeps in her purse.

"Why do you say it like that?"

"Well, his doctor has high hopes for full recovery— the stroke was minor—but it'll take time. And besides that, he's just...particular. Been living alone for a while now. Greta says he has his moods." She shakes her head. "And his pride."

"I can understand that," I say, remembering the Grandpa Harry of my younger years. Tall and gruff, with a voice that boomed across the house. He'd had a soft spot for me and Camille, though. And Grammie. When he wasn't working or fishing he was in the garden, tending to his plants. Eggplants, tomatoes, pumpkins, sorrel, and squash—dozens more. Herbs like peppermint and basil. I can't imagine being physically held back from doing the things I love.

"I understand it, too," Mom says. "But it doesn't change that he isn't where he used to be physically and his stubbornness could get him hurt. So just...be prepared for a lot of adjusting."

Because life has been such a cakewalk lately.

"I might need you to help out, especially with Alex," she continues, leaning against the counter. "At least until I can get him into preschool."

"I'm used to watching him," I remind her.

A warm breeze blows through the kitchen window, lifting the hair from my neck. The lack of air conditioning is taking some getting used to. This from a Georgia girl, used to swampy summers. I feel like I'm always sweating here.

Alex, finished with his bananas, pushes his bowl away with a soft belch. "Can I have a snack, Mom?" he asks.

"You just had a snack. Two snacks."

"But I need a yogurt."

"We don't have any. I need to go to the store," she says, springing one of his curls. She looks at me. "I thought we could go shopping today, grab what we need. Maybe even order the mattresses because once Grandpa's home it'll be harder for me to get out and do stuff like that."

"Sounds good, Mama."

She smiles, but it doesn't quite reach her eyes.

I join Mom and Alex in the car. It's a rusted green Explorer, and it was Grandpa Harry's before he stopped driving.

"A true island car," Mama says fondly as we bounce down the dirt road.

"Is this what I'm going to be driving to school?" I ask, already envisioning my entrance on the first day of school, the ancient Explorer farting my arrival.

"Either this or your cousin's car," she says, pulling out onto the main road.

"Camille?"

"Teddy."

Teddy, Camille's older brother, is in college now. All I remember about him was his merciless teasing and propensity for Barbie dismemberment.

"What kind of car? Is it as old as this?" I'm grateful for any set of wheels, really, but I miss my Maxima. It was old too, just not island-car-old.

"I don't know, Isla." She shrugs and turns up the music.

Shopping for mattresses is about as glamorous as it sounds. I choose my mine immediately, sucked in by the appeal of memory foam, but Mom takes way longer, considering adjustability and inner springs.

"Alex!" I grab his skinny little arm as he sprints by the Sleep Numbers. This is the third time.

"Stop," he cries, writhing melodramatically in an attempt to escape. The irritable looking lady at the other end of the display pins us with a frosty gaze.

"No," I whisper, yanking Alex close. "Mama's almost done. Can't you chill for like, five minutes?" Thing is, it's been an hour. I'm surprised he's lasted this long.

"Islaaaaa," he whines, seconds from crocodile tears.

Rolling my eyes, I pull him over to Mom, who's still talking to the salesman. "Mama, we're gonna go wait in the car."

"Oh, okay. I'm just about done." She tosses me the keys, and I bring Alex outside into the blazing midday sun. The Explorer, thankfully, has air conditioning.

We return to the house a couple of hours later with a trunk full of groceries and the promise of a mattress delivery by the end of the day.

I'm about to ask whose blue car is idling in the yard when its driver's side opens and a slender girl with cinnamon skin leaps out. It's my cousin Camille, barefoot and in a bikini. I remember her having curly, black, waist-length hair, but it barely skims her shoulders now. This is surprising; her hair was one of the reasons I grew my own out over the years.

"Finally!" she cries, jogging over. "I thought you'd never get back!"

"How long have you been waiting?" I ask, hugging her.

"Five minutes, maybe? But it felt like a hundred." She gives me another squeeze and skips over to my mother, who she embraces just as tightly. "Hi, Auntie Charlene."

"Camille, you're as tall as me," Mama says. "How have you been?"

"Good, good. Wait, is that Alex?" she squeals, bending to look inside the car as I release the car seat's buckles. "Hi, baby! Do you remember me?"

"I'm not a baby," he says, sliding out of the backseat. He allows her to hug him before running off, chattering about a lizard on the porch.

"He is so big," Camille says, eyes like saucers as we help my mother carry groceries inside. "He was tiny the last time."

"Well, it's been a while," I say, smiling. "You're taller, too."

"I know," she says, making a face. "I had a random growth spurt last year. Had to get a bunch of new jeans." She pauses, grinning. "Actually, I didn't mind that part."

"I bet." I laugh a little, remembering what it was like to hang out with Camille. "I can't believe you cut your hair, by the way."

Shrugging, she nods. "Sophomore year. I got tired of it."

"I like it." Camille's long hair was enviably beautiful, but I understand the need for change.

"Definitely easier."

"So, are you going to the beach or something?" I ask, gesturing to her skimpy choice of clothing.

"Yeah, babes. I wanted to snatch you up and show you around," she says, putting a carton of milk into the fridge.

"Oh..." I'm not really a beach person, but that's probably all there is to do here. Besides, I'd be lying if I said I wasn't ready to spend some time with people my own age. "I'll ask Mama."

"Auntie Charlene," Camille calls, darting off to find my mother. I shove the cheese and fruit I'm holding inside the fridge and follow her to the porch. Alex is on the steps, draping towels across Larry's furry back.

"I hope you weren't planning on using those," I say, making a face.

Mama waves me off. "They're ratty and old. Ready for the trash. Anyway, go ahead with Camille." She scoops my brother up and kisses the top of his head. "I was going to put Al down for a nap, so it's good timing."

"Are you sure? When are they delivering the mattresses?"

"I'll deal with that." She gives me a wry smile, shaking her head. "Go on. Have fun."

This is obviously her way of getting me to go make friends and be social, but whatever. Hanging out with my cousin certainly trumps moping around the house, which still feels more like Grandpa Harry's than ours.

Camille follows me into my sadly impersonal bedroom, watching as I rummage through a bag for my swimsuit. I might as well be living in a hotel. I have furniture and clothes, but my personal effects are somewhere between here and Georgia. "Do you need help unpacking?" she asks after moment.

"Uh...not really." I glance around, noting the wobbly towers of books near my bed, the clothing oozing from suitcases. Whoops. "I'll probably deal with it tomorrow."

"Isn't this bed the best?" she asks, running her hands over the intricately carved mahogany headboard.

I find a basic black two piece from last summer and pull it free. "Yeah, it is. All the furniture in this house is incredible."

"I know. It's been in the family forever. You're lucky."

My heart squeezes. Turning my eyes to the knot in my bikini, I focus on working it free. I definitely do not feel lucky. I'd take my old stuff over the cherished antiques in this house any day.

Camille exhales quietly. "I'm an idiot."

I shake my head. "It's okay.'

But she nods, coming closer and grabbing my hand. "I can't imagine having to leave home the way you guys did. You probably really miss it."

My throat thickens, and I give her a wobbly smile. "I do miss it."

Camille nods solemnly. "I know. I can't wait to get off St. Croix for college, but when I think about leaving everybody, I just..."

We fall quiet. Camille looks over my books, reading the back of one. "So you'll go to the mainland for college?" I ask, peeling off my cutoffs. They came to St. Croix as old jeans, but I suspected they'd be more comfortable as shorts—and they are.

"The States, yeah," she corrects, amused. "Mostly everyone does."

"That's cool. Where do you want to go?"

"New York, I think. I'm looking at fine arts programs."

"Oh, cool." She'd been into sketching way back when, always doodling in notebooks and giving me tattoos with markers. "You'll have to show me your work these days."

"I've got a ton of it. My mom said you're into photography now? The Palms has a dark room and stuff for yearbook."

"Really?" I wiggle into my bikini, relieved it still fits. I'm spilling out on top a little, but it's not like I'll be swimming. "I think I need a new suit."

"I can probably lend you one, but I think you look fine."

I've forgotten how easy going Camille is. I appreciate it. Once we're in the car, she blasts the a/c and plugs in her phone. "Ever heard of First Kings?"

"Is that a band?"

"Yeah. Out of St. Croix, but they're big all over now. Roots reggae."

She puts on a song and drives leisurely out of the yard, bumping along the gravel. Deep pink bougainvillea line the gate outside our property, punctuated by pops of yellow Ginger Thomas. Sunlight shines through a dozen shades of green. The sky's look-at-me blue, so pretty it makes my heart ache.

My gaze is drawn up as we turn onto Centerline Road, also known as the Queen Mary Highway (according to Aunt Greta). Tall, solid trees cluster along the roadside, branches wide and reaching, meeting and tangling in a canopy over the road.

Camille slows after a minute, flicking on her indicator. "I've gotta stop for gas," she says, pulling into a small, dusty station. Strings of faded pennant flags stretch across the lot, fluttering in the breeze. She reaches into the backseat, grabbing her sundress.

"I'm going in," I say, getting out when she does. "Do you want anything? Snickers bar?"

Camille climbs out of the car, tossing me a grin. "Good memory."

Door bells jangle as I walk into the otherwise quiet convenience store. Squeezing between the cramped aisles, I locate the candy bars and make my way up to the counter. The cashier, who looks completely stoned, smiles at me. "Good afternoon, miss."

I smile politely. "Good afternoon."

"Three dollars," he says, resting his elbows on the counter. "Want a bag, sweetness?"

I hand him a ten, wrinkling my nose at the endearment. "Sure. Thanks."

"It's my pleasure," he croons, winking like the lecher he probably is. He counts out my change, handing it to me as I turn to go.

The door swings open before I can touch it, letting in a blast of hot air and obscenely loud bass. Trying to avoid a collision I step aside, but he almost walks into me anyway: a tall, deeply tanned boy in faded jeans and a bright, white t-shirt. I grab the door handle, tensing when I catch him staring back. His eyes are unexpectedly light—hazel or gold—as are the curls peeking from beneath his hat. He gives me the once over as we squeeze

by one another, and then he's inside and I'm outside, re-turning to Camille.

Well, damn.

"How was the beach?" Mom asks, kneeling beside the tub as she scrubs Alex down.

I linger in the doorway, staring at my reflection in the little mirror over the sink. I'm already much darker than I was, sun-kissed into the best tan of my life. I'll never be as toasty as Camille, but this will do.

"It was fun. I met some of her friends."

"Did you go in the water?"

"No."

She glances back, a small, sleepy smile on her lips. "You will. Eventually."

"I know." Peeking at myself once more, I stifle a yawn and turn to go. "Thanks for setting my room up, Mama."

I returned from the beach to find my bed made and clothes put away. The louvered windows had been treated to sheer, white curtains, and there were hibiscus in a jelly jar beside the bed. It made everything feel more real, more permanent, but not in a bad way. If anything, it made me look forward to getting the rest of our boxes so I could finish what my mother started.

"Sure." She shrugs, squeezing water over Alex's head. He grabs at the sponge, chortling as sudsy drops hit him in the face. "It was the least I could do."

I lean against the wall, a bit contrite. This move ranks up there with Worse Times in My Life, but it's probably been just as bad for my mother. She's practically a single parent down here, and, even though they're dealing with his drinking and their separation, I know she really misses Daddy. Alex finally got that our father wasn't going to be around and he's become uncharacteristically clingy, begging Mom or even me to stay with him until he falls asleep at night.

None of us want to be here, not really. Not like this.

"Well, thank you," I say. "I appreciate it. A lot."

"Let me see your room," Sage says, stirring a spoon around her bowl of yogurt.

"I will, once it's fixed up a little." I pause, watching her add walnuts. Now I'm hungry. "My new bed's really pretty. It's an antique four poster."

She beams. "You could totally do that canopy we saw!"

"I was thinking that." I love that, even with an ocean between us, Sage and I are on the same page.

heavenly bodies

I adjust my pillows so I'm lying flat. We're on FaceTime, and it's so late I can't stop yawning.

"I'm getting you those lights we saw at IKEA," she continues. "For now you can use normal Christmas lights, though, the white ones...and that white gauzy material. Ya know."

Eyes closed, I smile. I can see the bed she's describing in my mind's eye. "I love that stuff. It's so pretty."

"Speaking of pretty." She clears her throat and my eyes pop open. "Your tan is incredible. I hate you."

"I went to the beach with my cousin today."

"Oh, Isla. Was it so blue? Was it beautiful? Was it paradisiacal?"

"Yeah." I laugh. "It was all of that."

"Pictures, girl. Pictures. I can't believe you didn't Snapchat me right from the beach."

"I'll send you some. Listen, I'm like, falling asleep. Talk tomorrow?"

"Okay." Sage pouts, blowing me a kiss. "Love you."

"Love you too." I blow a kiss and disconnect, making sure to text several beach photos her way. I feel warmer after talking to her, like I always do, but a little sad, too. She's looking forward to homecoming, maybe going with Gregory Hernandez—which I did not see coming—and pumpkin spice lattes, and back to school shopping at the Mall of Georgia. That's always been our thing, but she and Morgan went this year.

I fall asleep wondering how I can get back for Spring Break.

5.

My mother fusses into my room around eight. Swear to God, I'm never going to sleep in again at this rate.

"Isla, I'm headed to the hospital now to pick up Grandpa Harry."

Sitting up, I run my hand over my face and stifle a yawn. "Okay. Should I—"

"Just stay here with Al. It'll be easier. Call me if you need anything." She takes a deep breath and nods once. "Okay. I'll be back."

"I'll make breakfast," I say, relieved I don't have to go.

"Alex ate already," she calls, halfway down the hall. "Cereal."

Stretching, I ease out of bed. Might as well take a shower and get ready, because there's no telling what'll be expected of me once Grandpa's home.

Alex is in his room, zoning out with Mom's iPad. I watch him for a moment. "You okay, buddy?"

"Uh huh." He presses something, smiling faintly.

"I'm gonna take a shower. Come get me if you need me," I say. "Okay?"

"Uh huh."

"Alex."

He looks up, blinking.

"I'm taking a shower. Come get me if you need me. Okay?"

"'Kay."

Rushing through a shower, I dress and do a quick check of the house, making sure nothing needs to be done. Seems as though Mama's already done that, though. Sheets have been changed, floors mopped, fresh coffee brewed; she must have been up with the sun. My heart squeezes with the knowledge of it. She wants so badly for this to work out.

I'm standing at the counter, browsing Tumblr from my phone and eating toast, when I hear the Explorer rumble back into the yard. Wiping my hands on my shorts, I call for Alex and we make our way to the front porch together.

"Isla," Alex says, patting my thigh. "That's my grandpa."

He's never actually met Grandpa Harry, but we've been talking about him nonstop.

"Yeah, it is, buddy. You want to go say hi?"

Frowning, Alex shakes his head but then steps forward anyway, regarding Grandpa Harry with no small amount of suspicion.

Our grandfather looks nothing like I remember. He seems smaller, his stature compromised by significant weight loss and a stoop. Mom helps him step down the passenger side, placing his cane in one hand as she holds on to him.

"Hi, Grandpa Harry," I say, coming forward hesitantly.

He looks up, squints and then smiles. "Isla. Hello, little girl."

The endearment coaxes a smile, and I close the distance between us, kissing his smooth, dark cheek. He's got freckles across his nose like Mama and me, barely visible. "It's good to see you."

"Well, I doubt that," he gripes, shuffling along, "but it is certainly good to see you. And this fine young man here." He pauses, looking over Alex. "He needs a haircut."

"Dad." Mama sighs, rolling her eyes, and for a second she reminds me of me. Smothering back a smile, I scoop Alex up and sort of present him.

45

"Oh, no, his hair is pretty awesome, Grandpa Harry."

"Yes, well. Good morning, Alexander."

I pinch Alex's butt, making him jump. "Mornin', Grandpa."

"How you do?" he asks, accent coloring his words.

Alex looks askance at him. "How I do what?"

"He means, how are you," Mama says.

"Oh. I'm good."

"Good." Grandpa nods briskly. "Let's get inside. Between meh knees and meh back I don't know how you expect me to stay standing."

Putting Alex down, I grab Grandpa Harry's bags from the backseat and shut the doors. Larry, who I assumed was decrepit due to his general state of lethargy, bounds joyfully down from the porch. Grandpa chuckles, bending carefully to pet him before continuing on, Larry trotting dutifully along as his side.

Mama's been so worried about Grandpa Harry, about his health and her ability to take care of him, about his pride and stubbornness, that no one's surprised when he retires to his bedroom after only an hour of dinner and conversation.

"The worst place to get rest is the hospital," he says, sitting on the side of his bed. Mom helps him ease against the pillows while I shut his blinds. "I'll be right as rain in the morning."

I'm in the kitchen, loading the dishwasher, when Mama joins me. She sets Grandpa's tea cup down and pauses, leaning against the sink.

"Well...that went well," I say, making space in the top rack for the tea cup. "I mean, he's feisty but not incorrigible."

She nods, still standing at the sink, eyes trained on the window.

"Are you okay?" I ask after a moment.

Her cheeks are wet with tears. Closing the dishwasher, I dry my hands and hug her, really hug her properly, for the first time in weeks.

"I'm fine," she whispers, shaking her head. "Just a little overwhelmed. I'm okay."

"I'm here."

"I know you are, baby."

The first of our boxes arrive two days later. There are seven—four of which are mine. They're too heavy to carry, so I slide them across the tile, down the hall and into my room. I've got the box cutter in hand, but I hesitate, knowing stuff from back home is going to make me emotional.

I'm eager to finish my room though, too, so after a minute I go for it and rip the packing tape, cutting through the seams holding each box together. There's clothing and books, photos and knickknacks. These are the things I deemed too precious to donate or sell or throw away, the things I spent years looking at. One of my daddy's football blankets is at the bottom of the last box. I don't remember packing it, which means he probably did. Lump in my throat, I close my eyes and touch my nose to the fabric, inhaling the scent of home.

And then I text him.

Just got the boxes. Thx for the blanket. It smells like you. Miss you so much.

His response is instant.

miss you too, Isla girl. more than you can even imagine. take care of your mama.

My friends in Inman Park have already gone back to Grady. Curled up in bed late at night, I pore over their social media feeds, stomach in knots at everything I'm missing. That used to be me, and now it's an empty space they probably don't even notice.

"Everyone notices, Isla," Sage says. "It sucks."

"I miss you guys."

"I know." She sighs. "I already asked my mom about Spring Break. She said she'll think about it."

"Really?" I sit up, excited. "I was thinking about Spring Break too, but it might be even cooler if you came here..."

"Yeah. I asked about Thanksgiving but she shot that down pretty fast." She snickers. "But whatever. We'll have Spring Break and then we'll have college. You're still applying to Agnes Scott, right?"

"Are you really asking me that?" I huff, making a face at the screen. Agnes Scott College is my mother's alma mater. I've wanted to go there my entire life.

"Well, yeah!" Sage sticks her tongue out. "I don't know...it seems like it'll be all expensive now that you're out of state."

"It was expensive even when I was in state, Sage. Only way I have a chance is with lots of financial aid. And a scholarship or two." I lean back, taking my phone with me.

"And anyway, there's always Georgia State," she says. "Half our class is applying there."

"Maybe I'll catch up with Benny then," I joke. "How's he been?"

"You guys really haven't been talking, huh?" Sage asks, examining her nails.

"Nope." Actually, we texted twice—my first couple of days on St. Croix. Part of me is bummed out about that, but if I'm being honest with myself, we were hardly together. No matter how much I liked him.

"He's taking Stella Conti to homecoming," she blurts.

"You're not serious." That girl's wanted Benny his whole life, bless her heart. Guess the shiny red hair and big boobs finally lured him in.

"Yeah, girl," Sage says, disapproval flickering across her face. "Apparently they hooked up at a party Friday."

My stomach knots up. It shouldn't matter, but it totally does—I had no idea I was so amazingly replaceable. "That was fast."

"No kidding." Her eyes soften in sympathy, and in this moment I despise the miles between us, the fact that I'm alone in my bedroom with nothing but a phone to link me to the people I love the most. "I wanted to tell you before you saw it on Instagram or something."

Mom appears in the doorway, knocking gently.

"Hold on, Sage." I set my phone down, swinging my legs off the bed. "What's up? Is Grandpa sleeping?"

"He's fine." She nods to my phone. "But you should call it a night. Big day tomorrow."

She's right, but still. All I've had lately are big days.

I wake up before my alarm, rolling over in the dark to preemptively turn it off. Giving myself a minute, I lie still and let my eyes adjust. I try to let my heart adjust, too: I've never been the new kid before, not since kindergarten. I have no idea what the day will bring.

I also have no idea how the kids here dress. After a shower, hair and makeup, I go with jeans and a printed, sleeveless blouse Mama got me before we left Atlanta.

The morning is sweet and cool, the sun only beginning to burn the dew from the grass.

A glance in the Explorer's side mirror shows me, to my dismay, that my hair is already getting frizzy. Regretting the time I wasted straightening it, I salvage my look by weaving it into a side braid.

Alex trots out, climbing into the backseat. "Can I hear my song, Isla?" he asks, barely understandable through the muffin he's crammed into his mouth.

"Yeah...which one?" The Explorer's old enough that I can't plug my phone in for music, and I don't own any CDs.

"The song. Mama's song."

I frown, securing him into his car seat with a little kiss. "I don't know what you mean, buddy."

"He means this," Mama says, popping a Bob Marley CD in. Three Little Birds comes on as I slide into my seat, filling the car with timeless good vibes.

"Ah, okay." I glance back at Alex, whose face is split into a smile bright enough to rival the sun. "You have good taste, brother man."

We ride quietly for a moment, enjoying the music, our coffee, and the banana muffins we made yesterday.

"Is it far?" I ask, gazing at the endless stretch of trees along the main road.

"About ten minutes. It's mid-island."

"So...I was on the Palm's website again last night, and..." I pause, placing my empty travel mug into the cup holder. "How exactly can we afford this?"

"We can't, really." We shudder to a stop at a red light. "But you qualified for a partial scholarship, and Aunt Greta used her clout to have most of the fees waived," she says, referencing my Aunt's twenty years of teaching at the Palms. "Grandpa Harry took care of the rest."

I had a feeling. We don't have the funds for private school, especially not one like the Palms. "Grandpa's paying for this?"

"It was part of the deal."

"The deal, huh?" I stare blindly out the window, wondering how long this move was in the works before I found out about it.

"Yes, the deal. He could have hired someone else, but good help is hard to find. And anyway, this killed two birds with one stone: he got his nurse, and I got a job."

"Perfect."

Mom sighs. We seem have this discussion at least once a day. Still. "It's not perfect, but it is the best option for now. Okay? Can you at least...try?"

I nod, crumpling my napkin and shoving it into the cup holder.

"Grandpa wants to do this for you," she continues. "Education's important to him."

My mother's family isn't wealthy, but they always worked hard and made a name for themselves on island. Grandpa Harry retired as a highly decorated colonel back in the early nineties. Grammie worked as a seamstress from home, specializing in wedding dresses. Self-sufficient and disciplined, they weathered rough times and shaky economies through hard work and thrift. That they managed to send two children to private school, and then to college stateside, says a lot about their values.

Sometimes I wonder what Grandpa really thinks about us being here now. I know he's glad for the help and the company—he never really got over Grammie—but how much does he know about my parent's separation?

Then again, how much do I know?

6.

The Palms is set way back from the main road. If it wasn't for the intentionally rustic sign, and my mother, I would have missed it completely. Flamboyant trees line the narrow, paved road which opens suddenly into a sprawling campus. There's a soccer field to our left and several parking lots up ahead. Mama pulls into a space near the office, twisting around to release Alex from his car seat.

Private and non-parochial, the Palms begins in preschool and goes up to twelfth. Yet, it doesn't feel that big. In fact, there's something low-key about it. I find myself fascinated by the mildly chaotic yet comfortable routines happening all around me. Back at Grady, car loop and bus drop off were handled with almost military precision. Here it looks pretty relaxed, parents and kids and cars and buses all coming and going fluidly.

I peek at my mother, wondering what campus was like when she attended in the late eighties and early nineties. She grabs a folder from the backseat and grins overtop of the Explorer. "Ready?"

Looping my backpack through my arms, I slam the door and give her what I hope is a convincing smile. "Yep."

Inside the office, the scene is as crazy as any on the first day of school. There's a small line of people at the receptionist's desk. Several students sit on leather couches, their conversations blending into a loud hum.

Alex zeroes in on a child-sized table and chair in the corner. It has blocks and books, and he yanks his hand from Mama's grasp with relish, hurrying over. I sit beside him on the couch, fiddling with the zipper on my bag, resisting the urge to comfort-text Sage. One by one, the students around me filter out until it's just us.

"Good morning! How can I help you?" The receptionist, whose name tag reads Margot Blackwood, looks expectantly at us. I urge Alex away from the blocks, promising we'll build a Lego city later, at home.

"Good morning." Mama smiles and brings me closer. "This is my daughter, Isla Kelly. She's a new senior."

"Wonderful! Hello, Isla." Ms. Blackwood smiles warmly. She has feathers for earrings. "Welcome to the Palms. Let me get your file."

heavenly bodies

The bell rings, startling Alex. He squeaks, laughing, and hides between Mama's legs. I give his hair a playful tug, half envious he gets to go back home with her after this.

"Don't even worry about the bell for today," Ms. Blackwood says, standing. "Things are always crazy the first few days of school." She opens a manila folder and scans the contents, plucking a thin packet of paperwork which she hands to me. "Here's your schedule, with a school map and a few other resources. I trust you were able to get everything else completed online?"

I nod. "Yes, ma'am."

"We went through it yesterday," Mama says, eyes flickering to my schedule. "If there's anything else you'll let us know?"

"Of course, Mrs. Kelly. If I could just have you sign this..."

I zero in on my schedule:

Homeroom - Miller

AP History

AP English

French

Lunch

Calculus

Physics

Physical Education - M/W/F

Art Elective - T/TH

I wrinkle my nose. "Physics? I thought I was done with that stuff."

Mama pokes me, but Ms. Blackwood just nods. "Seniors aren't required to take it, but you were most likely placed there as a result of late registration. I can check and see if there are available study halls that period...or perhaps an alternate elective, like theater or yearbook."

"I'd love yearbook," I blurt. Yearbook means photography, and that's right up my alley. "I was told there's a lab here?"

"There is, actually." She jots something on a pad of paper before returning her attention to me. "Do you develop film?"

"A little. I took a class one summer."

"Excellent!" She taps her pen thoughtfully. "I'm going to go ahead and place you in yearbook, then. I'm sure they can squeeze you in. My daughter takes it, and she's always complaining about the lack of sports coverage."

I nod, giving her a grateful smile. As long as I get to take pictures, I don't care really what I'm assigned to.

"That would be wonderful; thank you," Mama says. Alex squirms his way back to the Lego table right as Ms. Blackwood motions toward a door opposite the one we came in.

"We're all set then. Go on ahead, Isla; your mother and I can finish up."

"Cool. Thank you." Adjusting my backpack, I blow a kiss to Alex and give my mother a quick squeeze, anxious

to get going. Nerves prickle through me, making my hands clammy. The sooner I get through my new classes and meet my new classmates, the sooner I can get to the point where I'm no longer new.

Mama adjusts my collar, trying to hide her anxiety for me. "Remember, you'll come home with Auntie Greta..."

"Yes, Mama."

"She's in the Lower School." She points in what I assume is the general vicinity. "Third Grade. Her name should be outside the door, but if — "

I grab her hand. "I'm sure I'll see Camille right away. I'll be fine."

"Okay." She takes a deep breath, dark eyes suspiciously shiny. "Have fun."

"I will," I say, waving, stepping out into sunshine so bright my eyes water. Save for a few stragglers, the pathways leading to different classrooms are empty now. I peer down at my map, which, judging by the attention to the most minute details, looks like it was rendered by an enthusiastic art student. Locating the Upper School with ease, I pocket the map and start walking.

The school is built on a terraced hill, along a gradual grade. According to my map, the offices and Lower School are on the bottom, the Middle and Upper Schools are somewhere in the middle, and athletics, pool, music and art are up top. Stairways and sidewalks connect everything.

Butterflies and bees float around flowers in full bloom. Tall, leafy trees provide shade, and there are picnic tables scattered around. Each building is a different shade of pastel...it's like going to school in a garden.

I find Mr. Miller's room halfway down building twelve. To my dismay, he's already doing roll call when I pause in the doorway. He straightens up, pointing his pen at me. "Isla Kelly?"

Heart pounding, I nod and step inside. "Yes."

"Welcome. Find a seat. I won't mark you late this time." He gives me a friendly wink, gesturing to the desks.

"Thanks," I mumble, gripping my schedule like a life raft. A quick survey of the room tells me Camille is not here, which sucks, and also that the only available seat is front and center. Of course. I move toward it, keenly aware that literally everyone is looking at me. The willowy, dark skinned girl to my left appraises me briefly before whispering to the guy beside her, while goofy blond twins give me grins of approval. Not sure which is worse, I slide into my seat, resting my backpack on my desk.

My phone vibrates. I wait until Mr. Miller finishes with attendance and turns back to his desk before checking it, not wanting to get chewed out my first day.

It's Camille: *u here yet?*

I peek quickly at Mr. Miller.

Yes

60

heavenly bodies

whose homeroom?
Miller
boo. i've got chaudry. 2 doors down.
Ok :)
c u soon

Her texting shorthand might be worse than my friend Morgan's.

I hardly hear the rest of the announcements. These classrooms could not be more different than the ones back home. Like Grandpa Harry's house, there's no air conditioning, just fans and louvered windows. The breeze is sporadic, the fan lazy, and I'm wondering how I'm supposed to learn anything when I'm battling heat exhaustion.

Mr. Miller looks expectantly at me. I'm worried he's going to make me stand up and talk about myself, but he does it for me.

"So. Isla Kelly." He looks at something on his desk. "From Atlanta, right?"

I nod, swallowing. "Yes, Sir."

"Great city! My in-laws hail from Alpharetta." He smiles. "Like I said, welcome. You'll like it here. Fernando, would you be so kind as to show Isla around today?" He waves a paper around. "I believe you two have similar schedules."

"My pleasure, my man," Fernando says, earning a laugh from the rest of the class. I twist around to look at him, and he grins at me, giving me a wink much saucier than Mr. Miller's.

"That's Mr. Man to you," Mr. Miller says, not missing a beat. The chuckles continue, and even I smile, grateful for the levity.

Second bell rings, and everyone hustles to their feet. Fernando sidles up to me as I stand, an easy smile on his face. He's charming and cute, with light brown skin and black hair cut real short in a fade. "Hey, Isla. Welcome to las Palmas."

"Thanks...Fernando." I tuck my hair back behind my ears, hoping it's not frizzy.

"Nando." He grimaces, leading me out of the class-room. "Miller Man likes to keep it official, but we can chill."

I nod. "Nando."

"Yeah, lemme see your schedule," he says, taking my paper as we head down the hallway. Actually, it's not so much a hallway as it is a sidewalk. Kids crowd past in both directions, talking and yelling and laughing. I get a few curious glances, and I ache. I'm used to having friends, and being the odd one out feels strange. "Yeah, we have a lot of the same classes...except physics. And P.E."

"Oh, actually I'm not taking physics. They're letting me switch to yearbook."

"Yeah, have fun with that." He gives me back my schedule. "I'll be sleeping it off in study hall."

Mr. Miller couldn't have given me a better guide, because Nando knows everybody. People high five as they pass, clapping his shoulder, catcalling, asking who his new woman is. My face warms, but he just laughs back, knocking fists, telling fools to mind their own business. Some of the kids here have thick Crucian accents, while others sound totally American. Nando slides effortlessly back and forth between the two, depending on who he's talking to. He even speaks Spanish to one girl.

"Okay, we're here." He ushers me into another classroom, leaning close to whisper, "Ms. Franklin's a bitch, so you might wanna stay on her good side."

My heart drops to my shoes, but not because of Nando's silly warning. The cute guy I saw at the gas station the other day is standing just inside the door, talking to Camille. With no hat to hide his hair, I can see all of his curls, brown and blond and adorable. He's tall and lean, but he's built—his shoulders are exceptionally broad—making me wonder if he plays sports. He doesn't seem like a jock, but things are different down here.

He grins at something my cousin says, before squeezing her into a side hug and walking away. They're obviously friends, and I plan to pump her for info the first chance I get. Nando gently shoves me along, reaching for Camille, who squeals when she sees me, linking her arm through mine. "You're in this class?"

"Yeah." I nod, relieved to see her. "I was wondering when I'd get to see you."

"Wait, you guys know each other?" Nando asks, throwing one arm around me and the other around Camille.

"She's my cousin, Nandito." She rolls her eyes. "The one I told you about?"

"Oh, okay." He eyes me, making a point. "But I have to say...all you have some good genes in your family," he says, accent so exaggerated I barely understand.

"I know you're not surprised," Camille says, extricating herself from Nando's grip. "Anyway, come sit with me, Isla."

"But I'm her guide," he teases, following us.

Camille sucks her teeth, dropping her backpack onto a desk in the back row. "You can be her guide later."

With a dramatic sigh, he leaves us for a group of guys a couple of rows over, one of whom is the cute guy. I don't know if I made an impression on him the other day, but he sure made one on me. It's hard not to stare. The bell rings. True to Nando's word, Ms. Franklin runs her class like a drill sergeant so there's no chit chat. Camille manages to pass me a note halfway through class, though.

you trying out for anything?

I shrug, glancing at her before responding.

like theater?

Now she's shrugging at me, smirking. With a quick glance at Ms. Franklin, she jots a reply and tosses the paper back.

i meant sports, but theater works.

Probably not. I'm taking yearbook though.

good, you can make sure i look good in my pics

Biting back a smile, I stow the note before we get caught. Ms. Franklin's nasally drone fills the room as she explains the syllabus and what she expects from us.

"Not everyone is cut out for advanced placement," she's saying, eyes narrowed. "I'll be assessing each student at the end of the first quarter to ensure that everyone here, belongs here."

That's not worrisome or anything.

Meanwhile, I'm trying not to be distracted by the cute guy. The desks are set up in traditional rows in this classroom, and he's only a seat up and over. He twists to hand the person behind him more of Ms. Franklin's paperwork, and our eyes meet so suddenly that my stomach flips. Violently.

Startled, I avert mine, staring down at my desk. Faded pen marks and etchings of students past litter the surface, reminding me of Grady High. Same scene, different place. Guess not even private school is immune to student mischief.

He's returned his attention to Ms. Franklin so I return mine to the back of his head, wondering if he has a girlfriend. He must, right? Boys like that are either majorly attached or completely un-attachable, bouncing from one girl to the next. I peek around the classroom, checking the other girls out. Back home, the obvious head-turners were Marina Camp, graceful and princess-pretty, an actual ballerina, and Quiana Whitney, the enviably curvy head cheerleader and most likely this year's valedictorian. Me? I'm just glad St. Croix's relentless sunshine has made my skin darker and my hair lighter, making me a more exotic version of myself.

The bell rings. Camille darts out of her chair and slides a kiss across my cheek. "See you at lunch, okay? I gotta get across campus!"

Nando appears, hands in his pockets as he watches Camille leave. "Ready? Tardiness is a big deal here, nena."

I'm tempted to ask him what the cute guy's name is, but I refrain. High school can be brutal, and if gets around that I'm asking, people will think I want to hook up. And while that may or may not be true, I don't need the gossip, drama or possible rejection.

Also, though I'm loathe to admit it, I'm still pretty sore over Benny. Not just because we were over seconds after we began, but also that he moved on as quickly as he did.

"Isla like Ees-lah, right?" Nando quips, using the Spanish pronunciation of my name.

When I nod, he smirks. "La Isla Bonita."

"Like I haven't heard that one, Nando."

7.

I sit with Camille and her friends at lunch. They're mostly friendly, although her girl, Jasmine, is a little on the abrupt side. With huge, dark eyes, inky black hair and olive skin, she's undeniably beautiful—even if her personality leaves something to be desired. Camille's not the type to suffer bitches though, so Jasmine must have some redeeming qualities.

The Palms has an interesting scene. There are cliques here, but they seem less defined. A lot of people drift from table to table, and there are even a few juniors in the mix. It's not like Grady, where the delineations between jocks and hipsters and brainiacs are maintained and apparent. Nando arrives late, trailed by the cute guy.

They plop down across from us, someone's sneakers hitting mine beneath the table. My eyes shoot to Nando, but he isn't looking my way. Cute Guy is.

He smiles faintly, opening a can of soda. "Sorry."

In an attempt to feign calm, cool and collected, I just shrug. "It's okay."

"Ey, you meet Cam's cousin yet?" Nando asks him, belching as he polishes off a soda. "Isla?"

"Hi, Isla," he says, staring at me as he takes another sip.

"Hi. Sorry," I say, wrestling my PB&J from its cling wrap prison, "I don't know your name."

Putting down his can, he gives me a grin. Of course he's got dimples. "I'm Ri."

"Rigel," Camille corrects, scoffing. "He thinks he's hot shit because he got swim captain this year."

"Nah." He chuckles, turning those awesome eyes on her. "I knew I was hot shit before that."

She throws a handful of sunflower seeds at him, and he opens his mouth, managing to catch a couple as they sail by.

Loud and rowdy, easygoing and inclusive, the vibe here is warmer than I expected. It's easy to see who's closest to who, although these kids have known each other forever. Camille's been attending the Palms since kindergarten. She points out several students she's known since then, like Rigel and Jasmine. She's known Nando since fifth; they dated briefly in seventh.

"You guys are like family," I say, when a guy I haven't yet met passes by and kisses her cheek.

She snorts, side-eying me. "Yeah, kissing cousins maybe."

One of my last classes is Phys Ed, which I have mixed feelings about. On one hand, it's really hot and getting grossly sweaty is magnificently unappealing. On the other hand, I love being outside. It's a gorgeous day, the sky a cheerful, bright blue. A breeze picks up, breaking the stillness as it rustles through the palm trees.

I'm about to pop back into the classroom to look for my faithful guide when he appears with an apologetic expression. "Sorry, had to clear something up with the teacher."

"It's okay. You have P.E. now too, right?"

"Yeah, but I'm down in the gym," he says, looking at our schedules one more time. "You got Coach Lockhart. Opposite end of campus. I'll walk you, come on."

"Oh...no, Nando. You'll be way late."

"It's cool. Mr. Miller can get me a pass."

"Thanks, but I can find it if you just point the way," I promise, taking my schedule back.

"Okay," he says, shaking his head. "Follow this sidewalk all the way up those stairs. Pass the pavilion, pass the art center. Softball's on the Upper Field. You literally cannot miss it."

"Cool. Thanks," I say, touching his arm briefly. "I appreciate everything today."

"It's all good. Call me if you need me." Procuring a marker, he scrawls a number on my hand and leaves, instantly flanked by a pair of girls who'd been at our lunch table earlier.

I jog up the stairs, hoping I can make it before the next bell. Everything here is so spread out; I don't know how everyone else does it. But like Nando said, the Upper Field is easy to find. Shielding my eyes from the sun, I approach the short, rotund man with the clipboard and wait for him to finish his conversation. Everyone is in gym uniforms, reminding me I need to get one.

"Coach Lockhart?" I come forward as the student he was talking to steps away.

He smiles grandly at me. "Yes, hello dear. Are you in this class?"

"I think so," I say, holding up my schedule. "I'm Isla Kelly. It's my first day."

"Welcome, then. Let me just..." He scans the clipboard in his hands, frowning. "Isla Kelly, you say?"

"Yes, sir."

"Hmm." He puts his clipboard down and looks at me. "Your name isn't here, but if you give me a moment I can check."

"Oh, okay."

He gives his whistle a shrill blow, warning the boys horsing around near third base, before retrieving a walkie talkie from his belt. After a series of crackly back and forth messages, he comes back, smiling.

"There was a little mix up, my dear. You're over at the pool."

"Oh...are you sure?" The pool? Not that it isn't impressive there's a pool, because it is, but swimming is just not my thing. "Can't I just stay? Since I'm already here? I don't have a swim suit."

"All new students take swimming. It's right over there, see the flags?" He dismisses me with a pat on my shoulder, returning to his students.

Weighed down with dread, I walk back down the hill and over to the pool. Green, yellow and white flags stretch across the pool, rippling sharply in the breeze. The class is already assembled on the bleachers, listening to a petite blonde in a baseball cap and shorts.

She spies me immediately, stopping mid-sentence. "Hi! Lockhart just called. You must be Isla. I'm Coach Archer."

"Hi." I wave awkwardly, feeling my face flame as yet another class full of kids stares on. "Sorry I'm so late."

"No problem! Grab a seat; we just got started," she says, sunny as all get out.

"Okay." I shuffle over to the bleachers and sit, trying to ignore the scrutiny. I recognize some students from my classes today, but not others. Regardless, I'll have to tell Coach Archer as soon as she has a minute that I can't stay. There's got to be another P.E. class I can take, surely.

Coach Archer goes over the class rules, stressing the importance of safety before explaining what we'll be covering. Like any other class, we'll be taught and then tested on each skill—every stroke, every life saving technique. Overwhelmed, I glance around the rest of the group, freezing when I spot a familiar face.

Rigel is sitting near the top bleacher, arms and legs sprawled everywhere. The very picture of nonchalance...he doesn't even look like he's listening. It occurs to me that being in this class would mean seeing him shirtless and wet.

"So that about wraps it up," Coach Archer says eventually, checking her watch. "We have about twenty minutes left of class, so feel free to talk quietly amongst yourselves and make sure to bring swimwear next time." She taps her clipboard with a pen. "And, if I've said it once I've said it a thousand times—no cut offs. And no bikinis, ladies."

While everyone else is chatting, I ease back down the bleachers and over to Coach Archer. She smiles at my approach, tucking her clipboard beneath her arm. "So! How are you enjoying the Palms, Isla?"

"Oh, it's great. Everyone's been really nice," I say, and thankfully, I mean it. "But I won't be able to take your class, ma'am."

"Oh?" She furrows her brow. "Why not?"

I fidget with the zipper on my backpack. "I don't swim."

Understanding dawns. She leans closer, lowering her voice. "Don't or can't?"

"Can't," I whisper. "I mean, I can handle being in the water. A little. I just prefer not to."

"Honey, it's fine." She gazes so sympathetically at me I think I'm home free, but then she says, "That's why we're here. We'll teach you everything you need to know."

"Coach Archer, please. I— "

"Isla, you cannot graduate from the Palms unless you've passed this class," she says firmly. "Swimming, CPR, survival techniques...these are critical skills. Every student here has mastered them, and you will too."

She's so sincere I can't even be mad. I am, however, on the brink of panic.

"Did something happen?" she asks, touching my elbow.

"In the water?"

She nods, holding her clipboard to her chest.

"We were at the lake one time. I was seven. There were a ton of kids and I just...got shoved to where I couldn't stand." I exhale slowly, intentionally releasing the tension that comes with the memory. "It's stupid."

"It's not," she says firmly. "It's more common than you know. It's critical you learn." She grins, switching

73

gears. "Besides, you don't want to be left behind when your friends go to the beach."

Everything she's saying is true—I just don't want to deal with the process. Anyway, it seems I have no choice. "Okay, but...it's going to take me awhile. To get used to it."

"I'm more concerned with whether or not you have a one piece."

"I think I do." From ninth grade. Might be time for an upgrade.

"Great! Bring that and a towel next time, and and we'll take it from there." She cocks her head, studying me. "You know, the swim team practices here after school, but there are always a couple of lanes empty on the sidelines. If you ever want to stay after, we can work on it a bit. Just you and me."

I shift from one leg to the other, trying to gauge her sincerity. It seems like an awful lot of trouble. "You'd do that?"

"Of course," she says, gesturing to the pool. "I've tutored plenty of kids."

The idea is unexpectedly appealing. "I might take you up on that."

"You should," she says.

Everyone springs into motion as the bell rings. Rigel passes by, arm slung around a petite girl with light brown skin and almond shaped eyes. It makes sense to see him with someone like her. She's graceful and lovely, and she fits right into his side.

I follow the crowd back to Upper School, meeting Camille at her locker. "Hey."

"How'd the rest of your day go?" she asks, shoving several textbooks into her locker before slamming it shut.

"Fine. I'm in swimming, though."

"Aw, I love swimming. Especially when it's all gross and hot like this," she says, sliding her arms through the straps of her bag. "I got basketball. Blech."

"I thought you liked sports?" I chuckle.

"Sports like volleyball. I've played that since seventh grade. I suck at basketball and anyway Nando's in there, being a pain in the ass." She shrugs. "Be happy you get to chill in the pool."

Kids swarm to the long line of idling, yellow buses in the loading area. The car loop and parking lots are a maelstrom of activity, much like this morning. I follow Camille to a bench beneath a tree and we sit.

A group of older boys crowd around a silver SUV in the parking lot, their raucous laughter carrying over the music. Then someone moves and I see Rigel, arms folded, talking to the driver.

"Man, I miss my car," Camille complains, checking her reflection with her phone.

I drag my eyes from the scene in the parking lot. "What happened to it?"

"Battery was acting up. My dad said he'd replace it before school started, but you know how that goes." She pockets her phone. "He's dealing with it today."

Jasmine walks over, sitting on Camille's other side. "You come with your mom today?"

"Yeah, my battery remember?"

"That sucks. You want to just come with me?"

"Nah, I'm gonna chill with Isla for awhile."

"Cool, cool." Jasmine glances my way, flashing a fake smile.

"You can come, you know," Cam says.

"I'm good. Call me later, babes."

They kiss one another's cheeks before she leaves, something everyone seems to do here. I get that it's cultural, but it feels almost too familiar. I try to imagine myself kissing everyone and can't.

My phone vibrates. It's a text, from Sage:

what's up, buttercup?

Her words are old-school familiar, making my heart smile.

not a thing chicken wing, I reply.

Down in the parking lot, Jasmine's joined the boys. She pushes past Rigel and rests her arms in the SUV's open window, smiling. There's another buzz from my phone.

miss you much :'(

miss you more :'(

I swallow the lump in my throat, sending Sage a photo I took earlier of the campus. She sends back a picture of herself at our lunch table, surrounded by our friends. They're holding pieces of paper that spell I LOVE YOU. I laugh, wiping the tears before they fall.

"Isla! Are you okay, baby?" Aunt Greta cries, sounding horrified. She and Camille are standing over me, identical in their concern. I must look pitiful, with my frizzy braid and watery eyes.

I nod. "Got a text from my friend back home." I hold my phone up. "I'm just a little homesick."

"Oh honey," Aunt Greta croons, pulling me to my feet so she can hug me. Behind her, Camille is rolling her eyes but she's smiling, knowing her mother loves nothing more than to soothe the world's hurts. "I can imagine. Let's get you home."

I wrap my arm around her side, appreciating the warm mom-vibes.

"I hope your first day was good?" she asks, glancing over as we walk.

"It was. Camille introduced me to everybody."

"And Nando was assigned to show her around, Mom," Camille says. "So I'm sure she got more than she bargained for."

"Oh boy." My aunt laughs, shaking her head. "Fernando is a real character."

We head down to faculty parking, where her car is parked beneath a tree. Papers and snack wrappers litter the backseat, all of which she sweeps to the floor. "Sorry, Isla. This is disgraceful. I really need to clean this up..."

Mama's car is usually the same, but with the detritus of toddler life. "It's fine, Auntie."

We stop at the supermarket and then head west, toward home. Camille and Aunt Greta chatter nonstop, but I tune out after a while, soaking in the scenery. I'm still getting used to the bucolic feel of Centerline Road, of our neighborhood. There's something peaceful about it, even if it's a little rough around the edges.

It couldn't be more different than home if it tried.

Grandpa Harry and Alex are relaxing on the front porch with Larry when we pull up. Alex abandons his Legos the second we stop. "Isla!"

"Hey, bud!" We embrace in the driveway like it's been months instead of hours.

"I had to get the child off that friggin' iPad thing," Grandpa Harry says. "All he wants to do is play games and silly shit."

"Language, Dad." Aunt Greta wraps her arms around him, giving him a good squeeze. "And don't be grumpy."

I'm tempted to defend our family, as Mom's generally strict about screen time, but I let it go. We're adjusting. Instead I choke back a laugh, hoping Alex didn't hear Grandpa's "slip," and go inside. The house is dark after the brightness of outside, and much cooler.

"Hey! How'd it go?" Mom asks, emerging from the kitchen with a glass.

78

"It was good." I hug her. She smells like Grandpa Harry's mentholated rub.

"Your classes were okay?"

"For the most part. Definitely harder than Grady." I peer into the glass she's holding. It looks like sweet tea. "What is that?"

"Lemongrass. Neighbor brought some over earlier." She takes a sip. "You want some?"

Later on, after Camille and Aunt Greta have gone home and Grandpa Harry and Alex are in their respective beds, I join my mother in the living room. I'm on my third glass of iced lemongrass tea—I have a new favorite, I think.

"So you're really okay?" Mom asks, lying back on the couch. I settle carefully into a rocking chair, missing the oversized sofa we had in our old house. It sank in the middle, but it was comfy. And ours. It's hard to feel at home in a house full of someone else's things.

Setting my glass down, I loosen my hair. "Yeah, it went a lot better than I thought it would. The teachers are cool...mostly...and Camille's friends were nice." And then there's that lump in my throat, again. Sipping my tea, I shrug. "I miss Grady. I miss home."

She nods slowly, putting a little cushion in her lap. "I miss it, too."

"I wish Dad was here."

"Me too." She gives me a wobbly smile.

Sniffling, I consider that. She's got family here, and it's her hometown, but her whole life was back in Atlanta, too. "What about you?"

"Adjusting, like you." She sighs, settling back. "It's actually been really good, spending time with Grandpa Harry. I missed him more than I realized."

I try to imagine living my life far away from Dad and can't. Maybe it's different once you're actually an adult. "I'm glad you guys have this time."

"I'm glad you have it, too. I know he can be prickly, but he loves you guys."

"We love him, too." I do, anyway. Alex is more of a wild card.

She nods. "He's not as physically dependent as we initially thought...which is great. He still can't be completely on his own, so it's good we're here, but he's gonna be alright."

"Every little thing's gonna be alright..." I sing, and she smiles, clinking her glass to mine.

"Greta's thinking of getting him a life alert bracelet."

"Good luck with that," I joke. It took weeks to get him to agree to a cell phone.

"No kidding." Her face lights up suddenly. "Oh, I meant to tell you: Alex and I found a preschool today! It's not too far from here."

"Really? That's awesome!"

"Yes; a friend of Greta's recommended it, so we headed over around lunch to check it out." She nods.

"We'll probably start with half days, see how he does. He needs to do his own thing, you know?"

"And it'll give you a break. Kind of."

"Kind of," she agrees, tossing me a blanket. "So. Tell me about your day, and give me details this time. Did you start yearbook yet?"

I glance down at the afghan in my lap, which we've had forever. And then I look around the room, really seeing it. The Yoruba masks on the wall, between the windows; they were in our hallway the last time I saw them, back home. A photo of Alex and I, and then another of Mom and Dad, sits on the window sill.

I mentally rewind to homeroom this morning and start over.

I'm wrapping up a phone call with Morgan when Camille texts.

car fixed! want a ride tmrw?

I smile, knowing she's off-the-rails-happy about this.

sure :)

k! be there at 7:15

Mom's not too thrilled with the thought of my over-exuberant cousin as a chauffeur, but in the spirit of trust and adjusting, she agrees. Camille barrels into the driveway at 7:25, and we set out with matching travel cups of coffee, courtesy of my mother.

"Do you always drink coffee?" she asks, watching curiously as I blow on the steam drifting from my cup.

"Mhm. Since the summer before junior year." In an effort to curb my costly addiction to the neighborhood coffee shops, Mom began making her own versions of mochas and lattes at home.

Camille sniffs her coffee before taking a sip. "Oh, it's sweet!"

"My mom adds hot chocolate to it." I savor a sip of my own. "How do you drink yours?"

"I don't," she says, taking another sip. "But this is really good."

Pulling up to a stoplight, she turns to look at me. "So. My friend Antoine was asking about you."

"Antoine?" I think back, trying to place the name. "I don't think I met him."

"He saw you though," she says, arching an eyebrow. "He's cute."

Not interested but not wanting to be rude, I stay silent, sipping my coffee.

"Did you have a boyfriend back in Atlanta?"

I try hesitantly to pinpoint what Benny and I had. "Kind of. I mean. No."

"One of those, huh?" She smirks. "It's complicated?"

"Just this kid, Benny. I've known him my whole life and we finally got together, right before I moved. We had an amazing week, though..." A magical, perfect week where I kissed and got kissed more than I ever had. "But we were never official."

"That sucks, Isla. I'm sorry."

"Tell me about it. I almost wish we hadn't bothered." That's not quite true, but my heart's a little messy right now.

"I know all about that, trust me."

"Oh yeah? Anybody I met yesterday?"

"No; he goes to a different school." She shakes her head, dainty gold headband glimmering.

My own hair is back in a bun today. I took a little extra time with it this morning, running my flat iron through just enough to tame the curls into waves, but it didn't work the way I'd hoped. "How do you keep your hair so...healthy? Mine's a mess ever since we moved."

Camille smiles knowingly. "Let it be curly, for one thing."

I roll my eyes. "You sound like my mother."

"Yeah, she's always worn hers natural. She's right, though."

I touch my bun self consciously. "It'll frizz."

"It won't; you need better products. Come over after school."

83

At the Palms, she navigates the congested parking lot and squeezes into a space with a cheer. "Senior parking, Isla! I've only been waiting twelve years!"

Laughing, I climb out of the car right as a gleaming black pickup truck pulls up. Rigel and the pretty girl from the pool yesterday get out, chatting as they cross the parking lot.

"They're a cute couple," I say as Camille joins me.

"Who, Rigel and Brielle?" She squints. "They're cousins."

It's sad, the hope and relief that spark through me. "Really? Is everyone here related?"

"It would seem so."

"Are you related to them, too?" I'm joking, but that would be just horrible.

"No, girlie." She grins, linking our arms. "You think Rigel's cute, huh."

I shake my head. "He's all right."

"Isla. Your face. Please."

She's right; it's burning up. Grimacing, I stare at the ground. "It's whatever."

"Everybody likes Rigel Thomas. Black girls, white girls, Puerto Rican girls..." She side-eyes me. "Mixed girls..."

"Do you like Rigel Thomas?" I tease.

"He was my first kiss."

"No way." I'm so shocked I stop walking, but she yanks me on.

"It was in middle school. Truth or Dare. And nasty." She makes a face and I giggle-snort, covering my mouth. "So slobbery."

"Well. I doubt he's that bad a kisser now, Camille."

"Oh, I'm sure he's great now, but my point is he's just a friend. One of my oldest friends—since kindergarten, remember?"

"Benny and I were like that." I adjust my backpack. "But we did end up liking each other."

She frowns sympathetically. "Yeah, you guys didn't even get a chance."

"Not really." Shrugging, I wait a beat. Honestly, I'm burning to ask the question that's been dancing around my mind—whether or not Rigel has any entanglements. He's vaguely flirty, but that doesn't mean anything. I watch Rigel and Brielle separate as we approach Upper School. "So...does Rigel have a girlfriend?"

"No. He was with this girl Mia for awhile. They were always on and off, but they were together before she left for college, so, who knows."

That's almost worse. It's the in between stuff, the complicated, messy stuff that lingers.

8.

At lunch, Nando sandwiches himself between Camille and me, bearing gifts of peanut M&Ms. Rigel drops into the seat across from me again. He chucks a wadded up napkin at Nando and then tucks into the biggest sandwich I've ever seen. Not that I'm staring or anything. I think about this kid way more than I'd like to admit. Good thing no one can see those thoughts...except for maybe Camille.

With Benny, there was an element of familiarity, safety; we ran with the same people. I liked him, but I knew he liked me back. Here I'm an unknown, and everything is unknown to me. Navigating this social scene, as chill and welcoming as it's been so far, is like feeling my way through a dark room, trying not to bump into things.

So instead of staring like a creeper, I keep Rigel safely in my peripheral...the way he pushes his hair back and slaps on a fitted hat, how the stark white of his t-shirt contrasts against his deeply tanned skin. He jokes around with nearly everyone, and that just makes him even more appealing.

"You're like...a peach," Nando says. "A Georgia Peach."

Scoffing, I section my orange and offer him some. "Again with the cliches, Nando."

"What? You look good enough to eat, like a peach," he clarifies, shoving the orange into his mouth.

Rigel coughs, loudly, and Camille whacks the back of Nando's head, sucking her teeth. "You're such a manwhore."

"Everybody knows that, nena," he shoots back, grinning. "You're late."

The table erupts into laughter and banter, and while everyone's accents still take some getting used to, the sentiments are easy to understand. It reminds me of home. Nando throws his arm around me, proving some non-existent point to Camille while she playfully curses him out. I grab my juice before it spills and peek at Rigel, but he's completely elsewhere, distracted and texting and having about three different conversations with people I still don't know.

The end of the day finds me in yearbook. Being back amongst the nostalgic stench of processing chemicals

makes me giddy. It's a multi-grade course, so some kids are brand new to photography and film development while others, like me, are a little more seasoned. At the end of class, we're allowed to choose a school camera. Most of my classmates go for the DSLRs, but I take a manual camera and several rolls of film. It's a medium I don't get to use often, and I look forward to getting dirty in the lab.

"By the way, iPhone photography is a very relevant source of material," Mr. Barnes exclaims, waving his pencil around. "I know every one of you brings yours to school, don't tell me you don't. So use them! Take pictures! Capture the lives of your fellow students from moment to moment!" He gulps down the contents of his jumbo-sized coffee mug. "Your assignment, should you choose to accept it"—he pauses for effect, grinning—"is to put together a montage of the week. Each class, and the events that transpire between, should be represented..." He rambles on, giving painstaking attention to the most diminutive of details, but that's cool. I can't fault the man for having passion.

Wednesday.
Moment of truth.

Sitting at the edge of the pool, I dangle my feet into the cool, blue water. On the opposite end, everyone's easing in, shouting and laughing about how cold it is, but the temperature isn't what scares me. It's being submerged and not being able to touch the bottom.

Also, it's looking like an idiot around a bunch of kids who have probably been swimming since birth.

Ms. Archer smiles encouragingly, squatting at my side. "Just sit here for a minute, get your feet wet. When you're ready go on in—this is the shallow end, so you'll be fine."

Eventually, I psych myself up and go for it, slipping into the water inch by inch until it comes to my elbows. Thanks to the rest of my class, the water's rough and it jostles me, sloshing around my midsection as I press against the wall. Back home, I was usually content to sit on the sidelines of pools and lakes while my friends swam. I didn't mind, and no one really bothered me about it. I saw how people horsed around, how they dunked each other and swam out to where I could barely see, and I could envision myself sinking, no one realizing. I'd remember being little, floundering beneath the surface, and seeing sunlight above the water but not being able to get to it.

Coach Archer's whistle snaps me back to attention. She returns to my side of the pool after calling out a set of instructions to the rest of the class. "How is it?"

Well, I'm not too cold. There's that. "It's okay."

"Get over here, Stanley," she yells suddenly.

A tall, gangly boy with a milk bottle complexion and bright red hair jogs over, much to Ms. Archer's chagrin. "No running by the pool, Stan, come on."

"Sorry, sorry," he mutters, flicking his hair from his face. He's okay looking, but he's got a great body, so I'm not surprised when Ms. Archer explains that he's on the Palms' swim team, the Stingrays.

"Stan's going to work with you today, all right?"

My heart sinks. I'd hoped, perhaps naively, that she'd be the one working with me. "Oh, okay."

"Stan's got the patience of a saint, dontcha, buddy?" She chortles, slapping his back as he drops down into the water.

He rolls his eyes and sighs. "So, yeah. I'm Stan. You're Isla, right? New girl?"

"Yup." I smile, nodding, though I'd rather hide beneath my towel and never emerge.

"Cool. Well, let's get started I guess." He squints down to the other end of the pool for a moment before returning his focus to me. "Can you tread water?"

"Not really."

"Okay...we'll start with that, then. It's important you learn."

We work on treading water for most of the class, which is more exhausting than it looks. True to Ms. Archer's word, though, Stanley is patient. Professional, even. He doesn't get frustrated and won't let me get embarrassed, which helps.

"You're a good teacher," I admit as he helps me out of the water after class.

"I teach little kids sometimes," he says, shrugging. "You did good."

"Thanks," I say, blushing. Despite my overall lack of skill, I did master treading water.

"We'll probably work on floating next. Archer's big on survival techniques."

On Friday, I have swimming again. For the first time since school started, I'm not dreading it. Stanley was really nice, and it's reassuring to know that he won't laugh at me when I goof. I don't see his shock of red hair when I arrive at the pool, but I'm early.

Fifteen minutes later, though, he's still nowhere to be seen. Coach Archer gets the class to warm up by swimming laps, and then she rushes over to me. "Sorry, Isla! Busy day," she says. "Stanley sprained his ankle, so he's out of commission for now."

"Oh no," I say, genuinely sorry.

"Yeah, poor kid. Fell off his skateboard again. Anyway." She blows her whistle abruptly. "Rigel! Let's go."

Wait, what? Horrified, I watch as Rigel swims over. He's sickeningly graceful, of course, like he was born underwater.

"Ri's on swim team too, Isla. He'll help you out today, okay?"

"Are you sure?" This is just...not good. At all. The one person I don't want to look like a idiot in front of is about to watch me flounder like a dying fish.

Rigel pops up, water sluicing down his face. Smiling politely, he rubs a hand through his curls, scattering water everywhere. I glance up at Archer but she's already striding back toward the other end of the pool, where everyone else is goofing off.

"Hey, Isla."

Hearing him say my name is weird—in a good way. "Hi, Rigel." Saying his is weird as well. Weird and beautiful.

"So, what'd you and Stan work on last time?"

"Treading water?"

"You asking or telling?" He cocks his head, teasing.

I fold my arms, staring back. "Telling." The sky is overcast today, and while it's anything but cold, the sun's absence is felt. A brisk wind skitters over the surface of the water, giving me goosebumps.

Rigel nods, running his hands through his hair again. I wonder if he wears a swim cap when he races. He must. "Okay, so you guys worked on treading water. Show me what you got."

I don't want to, but I do, treading for about thirty seconds before he nods and waves me back.

"Good. How about floating?"

"Like on my back?"

He nods.

Face burning, I lean against the pool wall. "I've never really tried."

"All right." He nods, then suddenly lies back in the pool, the way I'd lie down in bed. He does it so effortlessly, it's hard to believe there's nothing but water supporting his body. "See how I keep my body straight but not rigid?" he asks. "Look."

Oh, I'm looking, I want to say, but I just nod. "Got it."

"Arms at your side, out a little...the most important thing is to keep air in your lungs. Think of them like balloons, floating."

"Yeah," I agree, amused at the thought of it.

Grinning, he lets himself down so he's standing again. He gestures for me to come closer, and, heart lurching, I do. "I'm going to help you, okay?"

He puts his hand on my back and I stiffen. It's not that I don't want him to touch me, it's that I really, really do. I'd just fantasized about different circumstances.

"Is this okay?" he asks, peering at me.

My nerves are out of control. Between my anxiety with water and my attraction to Rigel, I feel like I'm going to puke.

"It's fine." I clamp my mouth shut to keep my teeth from chattering.

Giving me a dubious look, he proceeds, bending so that he's got one hand on my back and the other grazing behind my knee. I think I might die, right here, in this pool. And not from drowning. He tries to urge me back, but my body resists, flat out refusing to do what I want it to.

"Relax," he says, his voice quiet and close. "Lie back."

"I can't — " I start to say, but he's already trying again, attempting to scoop me into his arms which sounds a lot more romantic than it actually is. Panicking, I smack him in the face. He quickly puts me back on my feet.

"Oh God, I'm so sorry!" I cry, mortified.

Grimacing, he wipes the water from his face and regards me. "You know I have you, right? I won't let you go under."

"I know."

"So..."

"So, I'm just not used to all of this."

"Is this a can't swim thing, or an afraid to swim thing?" he asks.

"Both, I guess."

His eyes track over me. "Did something happen to you?"

"Just drop it, Rigel. I'll try again."

"Nah." He shakes his head. "You almost took my eye out."

If there's anyone I should share my issues with at this point, it's him. I can see he's getting frustrated. Taking a deep breath, I say, "I almost drowned when I was a kid."

"That sucks." He takes a deep breath, too. "But you need to get over it."

I narrow my eyes, surprised at his directness. "I know."

"Okay, so let's do this." His tawny eyes bore into mine, challenging me. I can't figure out if it's some weird motivational act he's got going or if he simply doesn't have the patience of Stanley.

It takes a few tries, and I stay stiff as a board, but Rigel manages to float me on my back while he supports me. He talks the entire time, encouraging me and tossing out pointers. And then it occurs to me, as he rambles, that maybe he's as self conscious as I am. That's oddly comforting.

By the time the bell rings, I'm nowhere near being able to float on my own. I'm frustrated, in more than one way—teaching someone to float requires touching. So much touching. I swear I can still feel his fingertips even after we've quit for the day.

Rigel seems unaware of my inner angst, though. Satisfied with our progress, he escorts me to the side of the pool. "It's like riding a bike...it's a feeling. Once you get it, you get it."

"I hope so."

"That's the spirit," he says, waggling his eyebrows. Foregoing the ladder, he plants his palms on the concrete and hoists himself out of the pool. Standing there

for a moment, he shakes out his hair, skin glistening with water and sunlight.

I take a second to appreciate, and I'm not the only one. A trio of towel-wrapped girls ogle him as they pass. "Hey, Ri," the blonde croons, punching his arm.

"Oh, hey Becky," he says, throwing her a lazy grin. He's gotta know.

Snapping out of my daze, I climb up the ladder and drip my way over to the bleachers where we keep our towels.

"Well...thanks, Rigel," I say over my shoulder. "I appreciate your help."

"Til next time," he says.

On Fridays, my Uncle Isaac picks Grandpa Harry up on his way home from work. They used to go fishing by the wharf in Frederiksted, but they're taking it easy now because of the stroke. They went back to Greta and Isaac's for dinner tonight, and the house feels quiet without him.

"What time is Uncle Isaac bringing Grandpa home?" I ask at dinner.

"Probably around nine," Mom says, glancing at the wall clock. "Greta said she was sending some fish and fungi back with him."

Wrinkling my nose, I say, "That's all you, Mama."

"Hmph." She purses her lips. "So how was swimming today?"

Swooping a green bean through my mountain of mashed potatoes, I make sure to skim the gravy lake on the way to my mouth. "Eh, it was okay I guess. The guy who helped me last time has a sprained ankle so I had to work with the swim team captain." I roll my eyes. "And we worked on floating, which everyone but me can do."

"It'll get better," she says, nodding in approval. "About time, right?"

"I guess."

"I want to swim," Alex announces. "Camber swims. Camber has a pool."

"Maybe we can put you in classes," Mama says, tapping his fork. "Couple more bites, Al."

Mama enrolled me in swim class one summer, but I begged out, going to a soccer camp instead. I was nine.

"Do they have swimming classes at the Palms, you think?" Mom asks, turning to me. "After school, perhaps?"

"I'll ask Coach Archer."

"Ask your friends, too. Might as well."

"My friends?"

"Yes." She nods, wiping her mouth with a napkin. "Like the one teaching you to swim."

Camille comes over after dinner, picking through my closet until she finds a dress she likes. She slides into it, examining her butt in the mirror. "Thoughts?"

"You know it looks good on you." I fix her tag, tucking it in. "Everything does."

"Not too short?"

Smirking, I eye the hem. "You're taller than me, so yeah, it's a little short."

"But not too short." She nods. "Let's roll through town. I'm bored."

"If you're changing, I'm changing. Give me five minutes."

We're halfway to "town" when I realize Camille meant Christiansted, on the east side of the island. Unlike quiet Frederiksted, which is closer to us, it's lively and loud, streets lined with all manner of restaurants and bars.

Cam parks in the Market Square, which is crowded but well lit. Like a lot of Christiansted, the surrounding buildings have maintained their original, Danish architecture from the 1700s. It's like stepping back in time, if you can ignore the music, the cars, and the hole in the wall restaurant boasting Bachata and fried chicken. A group of guys posted up on the wall watch as we pass, catcalling their appreciation: *psssst...hey, girl. Lookin' sweet...*

"Do you like karaoke?" Camille asks, linking her arm through mine.

"Not really." I snort. "I'm the worst singer ever."

"That's the whole point," she says. "There's this little place we go sometimes. It's fun." We stroll a couple blocks, chatting as we near the wharf. It's quieter on the side streets: less bars, less action. A rogue wind kicks up, sending several empty cups scraping down the street.

There are sounds of a scuffle between buildings as we pass, cursing and then broken glass. Startled, I grab Camille's arm. She glances back, urging me close. "Come on."

We cross over to the other side of the street, but not before a heavyset boy comes barreling out of the alley. He shoves roughly by, nearly knocking us over in an effort to get away. A lanky guy with a blond fade chases after him, yelling and cussing.

"Hey!" cries Camille, tightening her grip on me so I don't fall. "Watch it!"

"You alright, Camille?" A low, smoky voice drifts from the silver SUV idling at the curb. It's a Tahoe, and I feel like I've seen it before.

"Oh. Hey, Orion." Flustered, she pauses near the open door, looking at the driver. "I'm fine, but what the hell? Was that Drew just now?"

"Yeah. He was just dealing with that dirty lil' fucka."

Curious, I peek over my cousin's shoulder. With cafe-au-lait skin and bright green eyes, Orion is certainly not unfortunate looking. But he's got the driver's seat pushed back all the way, and he's rolling a blunt from

the mountain of weed in his lap. I avert my eyes and step back, scandalized he'd do that out in public.

"I don't even want to know," Cam says. Up the block, Orion's friend Drew is walking back.

Orion pauses, glancing at me as he reaches for the beer in his console. "Who's your friend?"

"My cousin," she says. "Isla. We're gonna go sing karaoke."

"Hi, Isla," he says, cracking a smile. He's gorgeous, but his eyes are hard.

"Hi." I give him a wave, but the whole situation makes me nervous. Between the shadiness in the alley and Orion's apparent apathy toward marijuana laws I feel like I've entered a parallel universe.

Cam must feel the same, because she leans in and gives him a quick kiss on the cheek. "We'll see you around, okay?"

"Who is that?" I whisper as we walk away. "He's a little intense."

"Orion Thomas." She gives me a knowing look. "Rigel's brother."

9.

On Saturday, Camille picks me up around noon. I'm a little groggy from our late night karaoke shenanigans, but that's what coffee is for. Now that I know people—kind of— I'm anxious to go out again...even if that means going to a beach I'll never swim in.

According to Camille, Sunday's the biggest beach day around here, but we're heading out today because a storm off the coast of Puerto Rico is creating larger than normal swells. I don't know if there's a surf culture here, but I'm looking forward to finding out.

My enthusiasm wanes when I find Jasmine sitting shotgun, but then she gives me a friendly wave and I have to wonder if maybe she was just having a crappy week at school.

"Gonna go say hi to your mom," Camille says, jogging past me. Tossing my beach bag in first, I climb into the backseat. "Hi, Jasmine."

"Hi Isla," she says, examining herself in the mirror. "What's up?"

"Not much."

She gives me a perfunctory smile, filling the car with the scent of peaches as she slicks lipgloss on. Camille jumps back into the car, cranking the a/c higher. "Okay, let's go!"

"So where are we going again?" I ask.

"Sandy Point. It's a really cool, hidden away spot," Camille says, turning toward the highway. "It's just kind of a pain in the ass getting there."

"Kind of? It's the longest road ever. And bumpy," Jasmine complains, tossing her purse aside. "You'd think they'd take some tax money and pave it, but no."

"Yeah, it's a national park," Camille says, eyes meeting mine in the rearview mirror. "At certain times of year, sea turtles lay their eggs here. It's really cool. We used to come on these special field trips for biology class, at night."

"Oh wow," I say. "That is cool."

"Hey," Jasmine says. "Remember the time Kendrick lost his shoes and spent like an hour searching the bush?" They dissolve into giggles, leaving me to my thoughts in the back seat. Sandy Point sounds great, but I've had a total of three swim days this week, only two of

which were spent in the water. Today will be my second time at the beach, and while I know I can just sit it out, part of me yearns to be like everyone else.

And who else will be there? Camille said everyone, but she exaggerates sometimes.

From the highway we take a dusty, deeply rutted dirt road, so rough Camille drops to molasses-like speeds. Jasmine wasn't lying. We rattle along for what seems like miles before finally pulling into a shaded grove packed with cars.

"It's not usually like this," Camille says, parking. "Way too remote, you know?"

"So remote it's creepy—unless you're with a group," Jasmine adds.

We grab our bags and lug out a giant cooler, dividing the weight between the three of us. There's a well worn path through the trees that opens up onto an immaculate beach, and my breath catches with the splendor of it. The sand is whiter than any I've ever seen, water and sky an endless blend of blues.

And there's no shade near the water, but no one has umbrellas.

"Because of the turtles," Cam explains, when I mention it. "Anything that goes down into the sand is prohibited."

"This...is amazing." I shade my eyes, looking down the length of the beach. "I'm going to take a thousand pictures."

"Knock yourself out." Camille laughs.

"Ugh," Jasmine grunts, hosting her end of the cooler a little higher. "Damn. Can we just drag this thing the rest of the way?"

"Seriously. What's in it? Bricks?" I ask as Nando jogs over with another kid from school. Maurice, maybe?

"Drinks and stuff," says Camille. "I'm just trying to avoid dehydration and starvation—we're in the middle of nowhere. Jeez and bread."

The boys catch up, and Nando lays a wet one on Camille's cheek. "We got this, mama."

When we finally make it to the shore, Camille and Jasmine procure a huge blanket, pinning the corners down with our bags. I strip down to my bikini, eager to work on my tan. Down at the water's edge, a pack of boys is playing touch football. It's music video worthy, especially when I spy Rigel leading the pack, muscles stretching as he reaches for, and catches, the ball.

There are several coolers scattered around, so it's not long before I'm offered a beer. The legal drinking age on St. Croix is eighteen, but no one seems to abide by that. Things feel more relaxed here than they did in the states, though. Especially with alcohol.

I take pictures of everyone and everything, inspired to capture the beauty and good vibes. And while I try not to be so aware of Rigel, it's kind of impossible. He is so obviously loved by everyone else. I see how close knit the boys are, how they tease each other. I also see how some

106

of the other girls look at him, and I wonder if I'm one of them. I hope my feelings aren't as naked as theirs.

The hours melt by. The park closes early in the afternoon, prompting everyone to race to the water for one last dip. Well, everyone but me. I watch, admiring how they become silhouettes against the blazing sun, how the waves shimmer and shift around them. It's like a dream. I take my camera out and snap a series of pictures, unable to just let it happen without attempting to capture it.

"You going in?" Rigel asks.

I look up, surprised to him standing so close. "I'm okay here."

"Are you afraid?" he asks, staring out at the water.

My stomach flutters, partly from his proximity, but partly because he really sees me. "Yes," I say. He already knows I am.

"Come on. I'll be right there."

I'm so surprised at his offer I actually bag my camera and stand up, following him hesitantly down to the shore. The sand is soft and hot, the water warm as it laps at my toes. I'm content to stay right here, but that isn't what Rigel has in mind. He marches right in, returning to his natural element, as I walk carefully behind, staring at my feet, grateful the water here is so clear. Once it reaches my elbows, my comfort level, I stop. There's a pretty strong current, but I can weather it as long as I stay where I am.

Rigel looks back at me, hand outstretched, summoning. "Just a little deeper."

"No." I shake my head. "I'm okay."

"You'll float," he promises. "The salt water helps."

"Come on," sings Camille, popping up out of nowhere. She has no idea I can't swim. "Get your hair wet! Beach hair is the best hair."

"This is good." I smile nervously, trying to enjoy it.

Rigel wades back, grabbing my hand. Admittedly, it feels good to touch him—even if this is how he touches me during swim class. Still, the pool at school is a lot different than the open ocean, and I feel myself seizing up. "Please, Rigel," I plead, pulling back. I don't know why he's so insistent. Can't he see I'm trying? This is plenty of progress for me.

Camille stares curiously, and I just know she's dying to ask. There are a couple of people watching, actually, though that's likely due to Rigel's holding my hand. He pulls me so that I'm right beside him, and then he goes further. We drift out. I feel the ground leave my feet and automatically start treading, the way Stan taught me. There's nothing graceful about it, but I'm able to keep my head above water.

"See?" he whispers, cocking his head. His mouth curves into the tiniest hint of a smile. "You freak yourself out, Isla."

Camille swims closer, clearing her throat. "Um...you guys okay?"

108

"Rigel's teaching me how to swim."

"What, like right now?" she squeaks, pushing her hair from her face.

"Like at school." I laugh, splashing her. I pull away from Rigel, not wanting him to feel like he has to stay here with me, and he takes the hint, swimming out deeper. When he's gone, I ease back to where I can stand, and on Camille's prompting, plug my nose so I can douse my hair. Being out in the open water isn't comfortable, but knowing I can do it at all feels good.

"You didn't tell me you couldn't swim, " Camille says quietly, steadying my arm as a small wave rolls in.

I squint at the horizon. "It's not something I broadcast, Cam. It's kind of embarrassing."

"Well, you couldn't have a better coach. Seriously." She eyes me. "And I'm here if you need help, obviously."

I give her hand a squeeze. "Thank you."

"For real, though. Ri's perfect for you."

I know she's talking about swimming, but her words spark other scenarios in my mind. Fantasies. I like Rigel, damn it. A lot. Boys who look the way he does usually have big egos and even bigger followings, but Rigel's not like that. He's charming, but his popularity seems to stem from genuine niceness.

"...you know?" Camille's saying with a snort.

I glance her way, cringing inwardly that I just missed half the conversation due to my obsessing. "Totally."

She ties her hair back. "I'm gonna swim out real quick before we go, okay?"

"Sure. I'll go pack up."

She disappears beneath the surface of the water, popping up several feet away. For a moment I envy that freedom, and it's then I realize I'm determined to do what she just did.

Even if it takes me till the end of the school year.

I lie in bed, running fingertips over slightly sunburnt forearms. Today was the best I've had yet, and tonight I'm tired in that well worn, sun drenched sort of way. Dozens of tiny, perfectly pink shells litter my desk, and sand is still falling from my hair, despite a thorough wash earlier.

Sleepy, I let memories of the day wash over me...swimming, the weightlessness and warmth of the water. The scorch of sand beneath my too-soft feet. The summer time scent of suntan oil. The crisp, hoppy taste of beer and the gem green glimmer of the empty bottles afterward. Camille's laugh, her perfect beach hair, and Jasmine, truly happy for once, propped up on Maurice's shoulders while they played chicken fight with someone else.

And Rigel. He made sure I felt safe and then disappeared, cutting through the water with practiced ease. Watching him swim, I could totally imagine him competing. I wanted to see it, wanted to cheer for him even if it was just silently and in the safety of my own mind.

The breeze picks up outside, rustling the leaves and stirring my curtains. Camille says that St. Croix's winters are much cooler, that sometimes she has to use a light comforter. I find this hard to believe, but if it's true, then I can't wait.

I wake up the next morning to the sound of heavy rain. I lie still for a while, listening. I've always loved rainy days and here the raindrops bang against the roof like tiny drums. A rush of cool, clean air sweeps through the house, billowing the curtains with a damp breeze.

Because of this, the sun never gets a chance to burn off the night's chill and the result is a pleasantly cool morning. I pack my swimsuit, hoping that the weather holds up so that I don't have to swim. Rigel said that as soon as I master floating we'd be moving on to breaststroke. I can't say I'm too excited about that.

Unfortunately, the rain tapers off right after lunch, leaving the ground as soggy as my spirits. Still, I head to the pool when it's time for PE, determined to put forth my best effort. Rigel's already doing laps when I arrive. He's got a small group of admirers it seems, younger girls hanging around from last period. They stare boldly as they get ready to leave, whispering every time he passes.

I spy Stanley on the bleachers, a pair of crutches propped at is side. Figuring I have a minute, I hurry over.

"Hey, Stan. How's the ankle?"

"Oh, hey, Isla." Smiling wryly, he unwraps his brace. His ankle is no longer swollen, but it is black and blue.

Wincing, I shake my head. "Ouch. I did that a couple years ago."

"It isn't my first time, either, but it's messing with swimming and that's not okay."

"That sucks." I watch him re-wrap the brace tightly around his ankle, giving it an experimental roll, obviously uncomfortable. "Hopefully you'll heal up fast, right?"

"Hopefully." He sits up, nodding toward the pool. "How's it going with Ri?"

"Rigel?"

He chuckles. "Yeah."

"Oh. It's okay. We're still working on floating." I roll my eyes. "I pretty much suck at that, too."

"You'll get it," he says, shrugging. "You better go change, though, before Archer...well. I guess she can't

punish you with swimming laps. She'll figure something out, though."

Before long everyone's in the water. Rigel ducks into my lane and swims over. "Hey, Isla. You all set?"

"Yes," I lie, smoothing my hair back.

This time, I'm able to relax as Rigel talks me through the exercise. He keeps telling me to visualize myself floating, until finally I'm unable to keep from laughing out loud.

"What?" he asks, grinning like he already knows what I'm going to say.

"It's just funny, you talking about visualizing. Is that how you win races?" I tease.

"Nah, I win races because I'm the best," he says, smirking. My stomach does a little flip. Yeah, he's being cocky, but it's appealing. So appealing. "But visualizing helps, too. My mom's into that. I was telling her about you, and she suggested I teach you about visualization."

My stomach flips again. He was telling his mom about me?

I step a little closer, nodding. "Then I'll try."

By the time PE is over, I'm able to float on my back for short amounts of time. I get the giggles, from nerves probably. Rigel watches my progress with smug satisfaction "See? Visualizing."

"Your mom's a genius."

Coach Archer blows the whistle, calling the end of class. Scaling the ladder, I look back to Rigel. "Hey, did you..." He's behind me, waiting to climb up.

And he's totally checking me out.

On Tuesday, Mama takes me to the DMV to get my local license. It takes forever, although she assures me Public Safety is a lot more efficient than it used to be. That's a frightening thought.

Once I make it through the testing and paperwork, I'm awarded my license, complete with a mug shot style photo. "Now you can drive to school," Mom says, giving me a nervous smile as we head home. I'm driving now, attempting to get used to being on the left. I just have to keep my turning lanes sorted.

"Yep. Maybe Cam and I can take turns."

Mom roots around her purse, pulling out her phone. "Which reminds me, I need to call Greta about Teddy's car. She said it was ready."

Camille comes by later on in her brother's old, maroon Nissan Sentra. It's rusted out near the back left tire, and there are rips in the front seat, but it runs and that's all that matters.

"I got you this, to christen it," Camille says, hanging a slender blue crystal on the rearview mirror as I drop her back home. It's similar to the one she has in her car.

"That's pretty. Thanks."

"My pleasure." She winks, propping her bare feet up on the dashboard.

"Your car working yet?" It conked out yesterday. Again.

"No," she whines. "It's not."

"Want me to pick you up tomorrow?"

"Is the Pope Catholic?"

We start off the same as always, doing a few underwater stretches before Rigel has me tread water for five minutes. He then makes me stand against the wall as he swims exaggeratedly slow laps in front of me, explaining how to do the breaststroke. I try to mimic what I see him doing, first with my arms, then with my legs, but my lack of coordination is truly sad. He must think so too, because after one particularly horrid attempt, he practically chokes holding in a laugh.

Caught between cracking up and crying, I splash him viciously. "Oh, shut up."

"You get so frustrated," he says, pushing his curls back. "But it takes time."

"Maybe it would help if you weren't laughing at me."

"Aw, come on — "

"Where's Stan? He'd never laugh at me." I make a point to look around, finally locating Stanley on the bleachers.

"Probably not," Rigel agrees, finally splashing me back. "Too bad I'm not Stan."

I fold my arms, giving him a dirty look.

"Let's try again," he says.

I try, and try, and fail. Miserably. Across the pool, everyone else is whooping it up, having blast like always because swimming is fun for everyone but me. It's drilled into my head every freaking time I take this class, and while I know self pity is unattractive it's so hard not to just marinate in it.

"Come on, Isla. Try again."

"I am trying," I mutter.

"Try harder."

By the end of class, though, I'm at wits end. Even Rigel seems to have lost his sense of humor. "Hey, you said Archer offered to help you after school right?"

"Right."

"Take her up on it. She taught me to swim when I was little."

"Really?" I glance over to Coach Archer, trying to imagine her ten or fifteen years younger.

"Yeah. Anyway, she's good. Way better than I am at teaching."

116

"You've been okay," I murmur, staring down at the glossy surface, wondering if he's over it. "I'll talk to her."

But then he splashes me again. "Good. Then we can move on to the other strokes."

Coach Archer agrees to start our after school sessions, so at last bell I head back to the pool and wrestle my way back into a still-wet bathing suit. The swim team is congregating near the deep end, so Coach Archer meets me near the shallow. A tropical storm is moving in overnight, and the sky looks already angry and sullen, dark clouds the color of soot.

Coach Archer's more methodical than the boys. Once she's satisfied that I can tread water and float on my back, she teaches me to tuck myself into a ball and float that way.

"It's for survival," she explains. "Expends the least amount of energy. Okay, now raise your chin and take another deep breath..."

I master that with surprising ease, which is encouraging.

"Good! Now we can move on to the breaststroke. I know you and Rigel have been working on that." She motions me closer and then shows me the stroke, although I've seen Rigel do it so many times it's burned into my brain.

A couple of lanes away, Rigel and one of the girls on the team are racing one another. It looks like a relay, because when they hit the opposite wall other swimmers dive in and take over.

"Isla." I look guiltily at Coach Archer, who's watching me with a mixture of amusement and exasperation.

I smile sheepishly. "Sorry."

We work for about forty minutes. By the end, I'm exhausted but I've gotten the hang of breaststroke. It's not pretty, but I can perfect the details later—I'm just glad I have the method down.

Sage grins giddily at me from my computer screen. It's a smile I know well, and one that usually means one thing: boys.

Eyeing her knowingly, I tear open bag of Goldfish I stole from Alex's snack stash. "Okay, Sage. Spill it. What have you been doing since we talked? Or should I ask who?"

It's a silly question; we talk all the time—but I know there's still plenty I'm missing.

"Yeah, definitely more like who." She coyly raises an eyebrow.

"What?" I draw closer to the screen as if she's actually sitting on my desk. We used to do this back home, too;

homework is way less of a drag with Facetime. "Who? Not Gregory Hernandez! "

"No. I'm done with him." She bites her lip, trying to contain a smile. "He's a little older. Do you remember Marshall? Brody Kowalski's older brother?"

"Marshall Kovalski? He's in college!" I gape at her.

"We're about to be in college too, silly," she says, laughing. "But anyway...we started hanging out the other night at roller rink."

"The rink?" I giggle. The rollerskating rink was our jam—in like, the seventh grade.

"Shut up, yeah." She giggles back, eyes shining. "I was babysitting for the Millers, so I brought the twins and...Marshall was there with his younger cousin. He's back home, taking the semester off before doing a year abroad."

"Sounds very serendipitous." I'm a little envious, but I'm happy for her. She's been on and off with Greg for a while, and while he's nice enough, I always secretly felt like she could do better. Marshall is cute, from what I remember. "Send pics when you can?"

"I will." She sits back in her chair, twisting her blonde hair into a topknot. "So how's swimming going? That hottie still tutoring you?" Smirking, she crooks her fingers into air quotes.

I arrange several Goldfish into a line on my desk. "He teaches me every other day during P.E.. And Coach Archer's helped me after school a couple times. I'm not as scared anymore, which is good, but it's just really hard. I feel like there's a disconnect between my mind and my body."

"I was so tiny when I learned to swim. My mom took me to Swim Atlanta." Sage smiles, remembering. "You'll get it, Isla. I know you're having a rough time, but once you catch on that's it. It's like...riding a bike."

"Have you been talking to Rigel?" I ask, giving her the side-eye. "Because you sound just like him with your bike analogy."

"Rigel is a sexy name. Kinda weird, but I dig it," she says, a thoughtful expression on her face. "I think that was a simile, by the way."

"Whatever."

"Speaking of pics," she says, leaning real close. "You need to send some. Of him."

"I can't just snap a random shot, Sage," I say, amused. "It's not like that."

"You're a photographer." She shrugs. "It's what you do."

Mama pops her head in. "Isla, can you set the table? Oh. Hello, Sage!"

"Hi, Ms. Charlene," Sage responds, waving from the screen. "How've you been? We miss y'all!"

"We miss you too," Mama says. "You'll have to come for a visit."

"Already on it," Sage says. "I'll let you go, Isla girl; I have a bunch of reading to get through."

"Okay. Talk soon."

"Yeah yeah. Love you."

"Love you too."

10.

"**C**an you get Alex's shoes on?" Mama asks breathlessly, disappearing back down the hall before I can respond.

It's Sunday. I'd love to laze around the house and catch up on TV, but Mama's intent on the "island tour" she's been talking about since the day we stepped foot on St. Croix. Grandpa Harry is coming along, too. I don't mind forced family fun, as long as Alex doesn't start self-destructing. He's sitting patiently now as we maneuver his feet into sandals, but after a few hours in a carseat he's been known to go Hulk. I make a stop in his room before we leave, grabbing his backpack. It's full of activities and books in case we get desperate.

I also pack my Canon Rebel; this is my chance to take pictures. We've been on island for awhile now, and if it wasn't for Camille, I'd know little else but the route to school. I want to see where my mother grew up, her favorite beaches and stomping grounds. I want to get to know her through the island that raised her.

Maybe I need this for me, too. I've been chillin' with one foot in St. Croix and the other back in Inman Park, living vicariously through my friends' social media accounts. I hate knowing that everyone's hanging out and having fun without me, that I'm missing senior year with kids I've known forever. I'm missing pumpkin-flavored-everything, shopping for scarves with Sage and Morgan, the way autumn sets our street on fire.

Maybe I'm so busy missing my old life that I'm completely missing my new life, too. Palm trees that frame postcard perfect beaches, and sea water that's as cozy as a bath. Roadside fruit stands and food trucks parked beneath the shade. New friends, new skills. Yearbook. Conquering swimming...spending time with Rigel Thomas. Thank you, P.E.

I'm staring at his Instagram, trying to muster the courage to follow him, when the car stops. We're in downtown Frederiksted, near the shops. Alex is already straining at his straps, fumbling with the buckle.

"Let's walk around a little," says Mama.

Jabbing at my screen, I hit follow on Rigel's account before I can chicken out.

"I'll sit here," Grandpa Harry says, pointing his cane at a bench overlooking the water. "You all take your time."

"You sure, Daddy?" Mama asks, squeezing his shoulder. "I just want to show them the wharf...maybe the pier."

"Go on ahead," he insists, waving her off.

"I'll bring you a guava tart from the bakery," she promises. "Maybe coconut."

"Fair enough." He winks at me. "Watch the boy. He likes to run, eh?"

We walk around, Alex trotting ahead on the uneven cobblestone sidewalks as Mom and I follow. There's a lot of history in this little town, from fires and slave revolts in the 1840s to the slightly less dramatic shenanigans my mother's crew engaged in as they ran the streets in the 1980s. She talks and talks, eyes bright as she gets lost in it.

"And then he tried to kiss me there...right in that doorway." She frowns as we approach, her story fading to a close. "But it was a scuba shop back then. Not a tourist trap."

"Mama," I whisper, pulling her along.

"What? It's true." She scoffs, catching up to Alex before he darts into the empty street. "It's too quiet these days. Frederiksted has always been a lot sleepier than Christiansted, but this is something else."

According to Grandpa Harry, the economy has gone to shit. He talks about it all the time.

"Let's walk over to the bakery," Mama says. We hold Alex's hands between us, and he screeches with laughter as we swing him up in the air. "Grab a few of those tarts for the road."

We drive for hours. I hear more from Grandpa Harry than I've heard from him my whole life. He talks about his childhood, fondly reminiscing as Mom loops around the island, returning west by way of the North Shore. We drive through a rainforest, several degrees cooler and overflowing with lush, green foliage of every shade. It's the kind of place I'd love to just chill in, and I make a mental note to ask Camille if they ever go there. There are curving roads and scenic routes and little beach bars. Everything here is a photo waiting to be taken, and suddenly I can't wait to go adventuring in my little Sentra.

We stop at Villa Morales for an early dinner. Baked chicken and fried golden bread called johnny cakes, seasoned rice and red beans, fried kingfish and bright, fresh salad. Tostones, which are flattened, fried plantains, and baked macaroni and cheese round out the meal. It's a total carb fest, and I'm in a food coma by the time we leave. I can't even force down dessert, which is sad because I love flan.

"We'll come back for that another time," Mama promises, rubbing her belly as we get back into the car.

Home's only five minutes away, but Grandpa Harry and Alex both fall asleep on the way.

The next morning, I receive a text during homeroom. We're not allowed to use our phones during school hours, so I wait until Mr. Miller's distracted before peeking at mine.

It's Camille, of course. ***beach today?***

On a Monday? I guess this is how island kids do high school.

I'll ask my mom.

ok. Let me know.

Sending back a thumbs up emoji, I stash my phone before it gets confiscated.

After school, Camille, Jasmine and I drive to the North Shore, to a beach called Davis Bay. One of the fancier 5-star resorts is located there, but the beach is public, a local favorite. We park and make our way down to the sand, where Rigel and Nando are hanging out with a couple of other boys, skim boards at their feet.

I've never actually seen anyone skim board. Nando is playful—like always—but Rigel's board is like an extension of himself. He coasts up and down the sand, the muscles in his stomach, shoulders and back flexing with his movements.

I splash around with the girls for a bit, but when we get hit by a sneaky wave, the bottom of my skirt gets drenched and I beg out. Wringing salt water from the fabric, I return to the beach chairs we adopted and grab my camera. I take a couple of test shots, adjusting the settings until the light's captured the way I want. It's not quite the magic hour yet, but the colors of the day are vivid; deep blues and warm golds. Tall, skinny palm trees tower above us, some bending so low their fronds tickle the sand beneath.

The boys are silhouettes when the sun is directly behind them, and I capture that, but their faces come into sharp relief when they change angles. Having switched into burst mode, I shoot indulgently, entertained by their shameless peacocking. Rigel looks up suddenly, and before I can stop myself I've taken several photos of just his face. I drop the camera to my lap, cheeks on fire as he lopes on over, droplets of water glinting off of his skin like jewels.

"Can I see?" he asks, hand outstretched. I toss him a towel so he doesn't get the camera wet, and then I give it to him, a little nervous of how he'll receive the shots. At first he's impassive, but then a smile grows until it takes over his face. If Rigel is hot when he's serious, he's a heartbreaker when he smiles like that. I shove my hands beneath my thighs to hide the trembling.

"These are so good, Isla," he says, gold eyes bright as they catch the sun.

128

"It's for yearbook," I say, trying to save face. And, I mean, it is. Sort of. "But thanks."

His lips curve into a tiny smile, and he cocks his head as he returns the camera. "Guess it's easy when you have a good subject."

I roll my eyes, appreciative of the levity his cockiness brings. "Yeah...Nando's pretty amazing."

Grinning, he roughs his hands through his hair. "These are seriously good, though. You could do sports photography for games."

"I'll be at your swim meet, actually."

"Yeah? Maybe I could use some of the shots for my applications."

"For college?" I ask, surprised he finds my work that good.

He nods, watching me closely.

"Well, I'll be there," I say softly, fingering the dials atop the camera. He smiles faintly, eyes searching mine. "For yearbook."

Nando yells his name and he's gone without another word, wild and free as they slash up and down the beach, laughter and shouts carried on the wind. I snap a couple more pictures, with my phone this time, and text them to Sage with a note:

i think i'm in love.

I'm the first one to arrive at our lunch table. Sliding onto the bench, I peek into my bag, hoping my mother remembered to toss in some of the guava tarts she picked up from town last night. I'm unwrapping my sandwich when Rigel wanders up and claims his spot across from me.

"Hey," he says, flashing me a quick grin before he goes to town on his sub.

"Hey." I follow suit, taking a more reasonable bite of my tuna-on-wheat. It occurs to me I might need to take over lunch-making duties to ensure non-stinky sandwiches in the future. I love tuna, but come on.

"So," Rigel says, swallowing another bite. "What's it like in Georgia?"

Pausing, I shake my head and stare at my sandwich. "It's...completely different. Culturally, socially...we lived just outside downtown Atlanta, so it was densely populated. My high school had just under fifteen hundred students."

His eyes widen.

"Yeah." I laugh. "This is a change."

"Do you miss it?"

"Every day," I say, popping a carrot stick into my mouth. "I grew in the same town, same house, my whole life. I didn't want to leave." Frowning, I shrug. "I'm getting used to this, though."

"I've lived in the same house my whole life, too," he says, nodding. "Can't imagine being anywhere else." He pauses. "Nah, that's a lie. I can't wait to get out of here for college."

"That's different, though. College is when you're supposed to go."

Wiping his mouth with a napkin, he leans closer. "You don't think you were supposed to come here?"

The table's filling up quickly now, but it feels like we're in a bubble.

"I...don't know."

We look at each other. I drop my eyes first, grabbing my stinky but delicious tuna sandwich.

"You miss your friends," he says, not questioning.

I nod, chewing.

"What else?"

I glance down the table, wondering where my cousin is. "The weather. It's fall right now, so the leaves are changing. It's my favorite time of year." Grabbing my phone, I scroll through the camera roll until I find a photo from last year. "This is my street." Was my street.

He takes the phone, nodding. "I've only seen that once, visiting family in Vermont."

"You have family in Vermont?" I never would've imagined. He's an island boy, through and through.

"My mom's from there."

Nodding, I reach for my phone. He leans away though, scrolling quietly through the photos. I'm slightly terrified he'll somehow see evidence that I like him—for the love of God, don't open my messages—but

131

he just goes through old pictures, pointing and asking questions. He pauses for a while on one, and I almost climb over the table to see which.

Of course, it's Benny and me. I look damn good in that one, with straightened hair and a cute little dress. "That your boyfriend?"

"Was," I half-fib. "We were never that serious."

"Oh no?" He holds the phone up. This one's of Benny and me wrapped in a football blanket on the field at school. We sneaked out there a lot toward the end of summer, hanging with friends. Thinking about it makes me feel wistful, so I shove emotion aside.

Giving Rigel what I hope is an enigmatic smile, I take the opportunity to retrieve my phone.

He smiles back at me, eyes narrowed. I wish I could see inside his head, but I can't, so I offer him a carrot stick instead.

"Rabbit food." He scowls, grabbing it anyway. "So...we have a meet here this Friday. Four p.m."

"Okay." I nod, typing that into my phone's calendar. "You might want pictures, right?"

"Right." He chews thoughtfully, glancing back at someone who's passing by. They bump fists. "If you want to. I know they belong to you."

I laugh, shaking my head. "I do want to."

"Want to what?" Camille squeezes in beside me, un-characteristically ruffled. I frown at her messy hair, smoothing it down for her.

"Take pictures at the swim meet."

Her deep brown eyes search mine, and she smiles a little, nodding. "Oh, that's cool. For yearbook?"

"Yeah." I crumple the last of my sandwich in a napkin. "And maybe his college applications."

Rigel stays quiet, drumming his fingers on the table. There's a slightly awkward silence, and I glance up in time to catch the tail end of a look between him and Camille. I don't know what that's all about, but I pretend to ignore it. Half the time I don't know what's going on; these kids have a dynamic all their own, forged by years of relationships and memories and inside jokes.

Whatever. I finish lunch quickly, eager to stop at the photo lab to drop off my used roll of film and grab a new one. I normally just go the digital route, but there's something appealing about the old-school flavor of film. It's satisfying to work through the process myself, from snapping a shot to unspooling the finished roll in the dark to developing prints from it. It's magic.

11.

Cutting the music, I pull into our driveway. The sky is beautiful this afternoon, and I suspect it's going to be a killer sunset. I have a ton of homework, but I just can't bring myself to stay cooped up in my room when the afternoon is as pretty as this.

I've been toying with the idea of going to the beach, even by myself.

Especially by myself.

"I'm home," I yell, kicking my shoes off at the door.

"We're in here," Mama calls back. She side eyes me as I join her. "You know I hate when you yell like that, Isla."

"Sorry." I kiss her cheek to make up for it, earning a swat on the behind, and then bend to snuggle Alex, who's making a mess of play dough at the table. "Hey, bud."

"Hi, Isla," he says, shouldering my kisses off. "I had fruit pizza today. At school."

"Oh, that sounds good. I love pizza."

"Yeah. I love pizza too," he says, spinning off into one of his preschool monologues. There's a kid named Camber and tomato plants outside and Ms. Rebecca and nap time, which he hates, and yummy Fridays, and, and, and...

I grin helplessly over his head at my mother, who smirks back before returning to her notebook, where she's writing busily.

"You need my help tonight?" I ask, sliding my backpack off. "With dinner and stuff?"

She looks up. "Not really. Why?"

"I was thinking of going to the beach for a little while. Not to swim," I add quickly. "Just to take some pictures. Get fresh air."

"Isla," Alex huffs, smacking his fist onto a ball of hot pink play dough. "You aren't listening!"

I squeeze his shoulder. "I was. You were talking about Camber."

"And Jamal."

Mama sets her pen down. "Which beach?"

"Rainbow?"

She looks like she's battling herself, but she gives in. "All right. Don't stay long, though. I don't like you being out there when it gets dark, especially when you're by yourself."

136

"I want to go!" Alex cries, squirming in his chair.

"Not this time, Al," Mama says.

"I'll be back in an hour or two," I promise, kissing her again before darting out. The day is suddenly that much brighter, brimming over with adventure and possibility. I snatch my purse from my room, making sure everything I need is inside, and leave.

Rainbow Beach is on the very west end of the island. We've driven past it a couple times, but I haven't had the chance to spend time there. It's a popular hangout, and Camille and I have plans to go soon, but for now, I want to go simply because I can.

It's just as I hoped: serene and tranquil, soft strains of reggae floating from the restaurant down the beach. Several kayakers make their way lazily out to sea, and in the far distance, the oblong shape of a cruise ship smudges the horizon. Kicking my flip flops off, I venture closer to the shore. I snap several shots of the ocean and sky, intrigued by the prismatic color play on the water.

"Isla?"

Whirling around, I nearly drop the camera in surprise. Rigel's beside me in a pair of boardshorts. "Hey, what're you..." I drift off, noticing a pair of goggles in his hand. "You swim here?"

"I swim everywhere," he says. "I like to mix it up, especially before meets."

"Makes sense."

"You coming in?"

"Haha, Rigel."

"What?" he says. "I'm serious."

"No, I'm not going in!"

"Come on." He makes like he's going to reach for me, but I duck away.

"I'm not even wearing a swimsuit."

"You came to the beach with no suit?" He squints out at the water. The sun hangs low in the sky, reflecting on the water in deep orange ripples.

"I really just came to hang out." I hold up the camera. "And take pictures."

Taking a step back, I slide into my flip flops. It's probably time to head home now, and anyway...I don't want Rigel to think I'm stalking him, even if I was here first.

"Camille here?" he asks, looking around.

"No, I drove." I gesture toward the water. "I'll let you go."

He nods, snapping his goggles on as he steps into the water. "Drive safe, Georgia."

I'm strangely anxious as school winds down on Friday, which is ridiculous because I'm not the one competing later. Rigel is, and besides wanting to get good pictures, I want him to do well. It's like an acute case of second-hand nervousness.

The day passes quickly, even PE. I half expect Rigel to hand the reins to Coach Archer so that she can work with me, but it's business as usual as we work on the freestyle. The good news is that I can stay afloat. The bad news is that I splash so much it's a miracle there's any water left in the pool.

I pop up, wiping my face only to find Rigel trying desperately to straighten his face.

"You're laughing at me!" I accuse, shoving a wave of water at his face. "Again!"

He holds his hands up, full on guffawing. "I'm not!" I don't think I've ever seen him this amused, and I don't know whether to feel embarrassed or delighted.

"You are," I say, scowling. "Don't talk to me."

"Aww, I'm sorry," he says, coming closer.

I splash him again, but he grabs my arms, containing me. Squirming and stomping on his feet, I try to get away...but not too hard. "You're meaner than you look," I say, cringing inwardly at how flirty this has become.

He grins down at me, water glinting off of his stupidly perfect cheekbones. "You just looked..so..."

"Yeah, yeah. Shut up, Rigel."

"Such aggression," he teases, accent creeping out.

"Not exactly what I had in mind, Rigel," Coach Archer yells from the sidelines.

139

We jump apart. Heart skipping, I swim quickly to the side of the pool. Archer rolls her eyes and strides back to the class, which is learning flotation techniques. Rigel runs a hand over his face, wiping water from it.

"You swam just now."

Frowning, I let go of the wall. "I did?"

"Yeah. When Archer called us out"—he averts his eyes—"you swam to the wall."

Taking a deep breath, I swim back to him. It's not graceful or fast, but it's swimming. I pop back up and give him a smile, unable to believe I actually did it. After all of this time, I'm finally making progress.

"Kind of a cross between breaststroke and freestyle, but I'll take it," he says, nodding in approval. "If you keep working on it, you'll be able to pass like that." He snaps his fingers.

"Cool." I bite my lip, amazed I actually did it."Thanks, Rigel."

"So I'm not mean, then?" he asks, grinning devilishly.

He tries to avoid my splash, but he's not fast enough.

The bleachers are packed when I return to the pool later on. Coach Archer made it sound like it was our civic duty to show up because the meets don't always have much support, but it's so crowded I can't find a seat.

Eventually I spot a girl I know from yearbook, Megan. She's got a spot right up front.

"Hey, Isla," she says, eyeing my camera as she scoots over. "You covering this for yearbook?"

"Something like that," I say, squeezing in beside her.

The first time I see Rigel compete, I get so into it I almost forget to take pictures. He cuts smoothly through the water, barely keeping up with the pack until they hit the wall and flip and then he kills it, out-swimming them all. There are several matches he competes in: freestyle, butterfly and relay. He wins every one, to the delight of the crowd, who scream his name like we're at a football game.

I manage to snap some good action shots, especially when he swims the butterfly. He dominates in that race, muscles in his back spread like angel's wings. I can imagine the hysteria that would ensue if he ever tried to teach me that one.

Camille joins me during the last heat, waving at me from the sidelines until I see her. Grabbing my stuff, I hurry over to her.

"Hey, I thought you had study group?" I say, carefully replacing my camera's lens cap.

"Yeah, we just got out. Brielle had to go home early," Camille says with a shrug. "So how was it?"

"Great." I shake my head. "I had no idea Rigel was so fast."

"I know!" She nods emphatically. "Rigel's a beast in the water. He's gonna have scholarships coming out his ears."

"Wow." I glance back at the pool, where the crowd is beginning to disperse now that the meet is over.

"That's his dad," Camille says suddenly, grabbing my elbow. "There. In the red t-shirt."

I don't know what I thought Rigel's dad looked like but it isn't this. He's tall and thin, with dark skin and dreadlocks wrapped in a knot behind his head. Handsome. I guess that part isn't really surprising. He lopes on over to the locker room, disappearing inside.

"I had a crush on him when I was little," Camille whispers, giggling.

"On his dad?" I laugh, poking her belly. "Crazy."

"Oh, come on. He's still hot."

We walk down to the parking lot where Jasmine and a bunch of other kids are standing around.

There's a celebratory feeling in the air, and when Rigel hits the parking lot people catcall and whoop it up, clapping him on the back. Swimming isn't exactly as thrilling as football or something, but he's got this undeniable hometown hero thing going on: the kind of face and talent that force people to watch.

Jasmine walks over, sighing loudly as she leans on Camille's car. "It's gonna take forever to decide where we're going."

142

"There's no plan?" I secretly love this; it reminds me of my friends in Inman Park.

"No. They"—she nods to Rigel, Nando and their boys—"want to go to Grassy Point up east. But they"—now she nods to another group getting into their cars—"want to hit up a party on the north side."

"Well, what do you want to do?" Camille asks, yawning.

"Eh, probably the beach. I'm in the mood to chill."

I nod. "Me too."

"Good luck getting this one to agree," she says, cutting her eye at Camille.

Cam chews her bottom lip. "Well, Nico's probably going to be at the party."

Jasmine looks at me, eyes wide in exasperation. "See?"

"What?" Camille says. "It sounds fun."

I scratch my arm. "Who's Nico?"

"It'll be the same as always," whines Jasmine. "A bunch of stupid, drunk boys and—"

Camille waves her off. "How's that any different than Green Cay?"

Jasmine and Camille tend to bicker like an old married couple, so I've learned to ignore it when they get going. I glance over to Rigel, only to find him already looking at me. He doesn't look away when our eyes meet, and, no matter how it makes my heart race, neither do I.

Then he smiles faintly, and I just know he knows I like him.

But I suspect the feeling is mutual. Before I can melt into a puddle, I'm grabbed into a bear hug by Nando. He lifts me off the ground, squeezing a laugh out of me.

"Isla," he sings, obnoxiously close to my ear. "You're coming to the beach later, right nena?"

"Well, I'd like to, but..." I turn to ask Cam, but she's making a beeline for Kyle, one of the juniors who sits at our lunch table. I don't know much about him, other than the fact he's good at math—he's in my calculus class. But he's cute in a quiet way, with cocoa brown skin and a dreamy smile. Standing with his hands deep in his pockets, he watches Camille as she approaches, smiling at something she's saying. They wander off, talking closely, and I randomly remember Camille showing up to lunch looking rumpled.

"We'll most likely stop by after, okay?" Jasmine's saying to Nando. "Isla doesn't wanna go to that party either, so we won't stay long."

I look around for Rigel, but he's in his truck. Music comes on seconds later with a deafening burst of bass. Kyle walks away, yelling for Nando. They get into another car and leave, trailing behind Rigel.

"So," Camille, who's back, begins. "I think we should hit up the party first and then meet them at the beach. Later on."

Pursing her lips, Jasmine looks at me "See?"

I love a good house party, but Jasmine was right: this place is crawling with vapid, drunk boys—and girls, to be fair. St. Christopher's is a Catholic school with a different scene, so maybe it would be different if I knew more people. I end up with a bottle of beer and Camille's purse as she twerks her way into oblivion. Jasmine's curled up on the couch beside me, texting. We've been fending off the manscaped and over-gelled since we got here.

"So, you gotta boyfriend?" the latest asks.

I shake my head. "Nope." Camille makes a face at me from the dancefloor, wrinkling her nose before one of her dance partners spins her around.

"You always this quiet, or...?"

"I'm just waiting for my cousin."

He follows my gaze. "Who? Camille?" Laughing snidely, he pushes off from the wall. "Well, don't let me bother you."

Grossed out and a little confused, I turn to Jasmine. "Who the hell was that?"

"Camille's ex, Darren," she says, without missing a beat. "He thinks he's God's gift to women."

Cam never does find the mysterious Nico, so we leave soon after that. Jasmine takes the wheel when it becomes obvious that Camille's too tipsy to drive. "This is why I didn't drink," sniffs Jasmine, putting the car in reverse. "Because I knew this shit would happen."

"Shut up, Jas," Camille says, emptying her purse on the back seat. "Hey. Hey, Isla. Did I give you my lip gloss? The glittery one?"

"This isn't the first time," Jasmine continues, waving her hand. "She did this twice last summer and Nando had to drive us home. Both times."

"Yeah, because you were drunk, too!" cackles Camille. "Isla...my lip gloss..."

"I don't have it, Cam," I say.

"Because you said you weren't gonna drink," snaps Jasmine.

Camille pouts. "You're killing my buzz."

"Good! When we get to Green Cay I'm gonna get my drink on, so don't bother asking to drive again," Jasmine says, turning the radio all the way up.

Guess that makes me the designated, which is fine. Warm with anticipation, I'm sitting up front. I've kept my little crush close to my heart, but I'm really hoping Rigel's at the beach. His black truck is in the lot when we pull in, making my heart flip flop. Rolling my eyes at myself, I pop a stick of gum into my mouth and check my hair in the mirror. The girls have settled back into their usual camaraderie, chatting nonstop, and I follow them down the rocky, overgrown path to the beach. The moon is just shy of full, illuminating the soft expanse of sand with diaphanous light. Its reflection ripples on inky

black water, and, if I listen closely, I can hear the waves breaking on the shore.

Music and voices drift with the wind. My eyes alight on the bonfire further down, at the curling smoke, how it barely takes shape before the wind snatches it. Breathing in the fresh, briny air, I stow my flip flops and walk barefoot. The closer we get to the fire the more people I recognize, and I relax into the warm feeling of finally being where I want to be tonight.

"The Three Musketeers!" Nando shouts drunkenly, flopping back in the sand.

Jasmine glances back at me, rolling her eyes as a few people crack up.

"You're so dumb, Nandito." Camille laughs, tossing her bag onto the sand.

Breaking away from the group, Kyle strides over and throws her arm over his shoulder. She squeals, flailing as he carries her off. Jasmine and I edge closer to the fire before she plops down beside a girl I don't really know. I set my bag next to Camille's and look around, wondering if I should say hi to Nando. He's pretty wasted.

Then three shadows emerge from the dark, and Rigel's among them. He's barefoot, in a faded red hoodie and baggy, blue shorts. His hair, covered mostly by his hood, looks bronze in the firelight. I wonder how much of that is natural and how much is from the sun and chlorine.

Smiling when he catches sight of me, he drops his empty beer bottle into a plastic bag in the sand. "Hey, Georgia."

"Hey, Rigel." The wind picks up, blowing my hair around.

He nods toward a cooler. "Want a beer?"

"I'd better not." I pause, tucking my hair behind my ears. "I think I might end up being the designated driver."

He cracks a smile, nodding. "I know how that goes. Although, designated usually implies it was planned..."

"Tell me about it."

Rigel closes the cooler without taking anything out.

Surprised, I blurt, "I mean, you can have one."

"Nah, I've already had one," he says. "I'm good."

I narrow my eyes. "You're just being nice."

"I just know how Cam gets when she drinks," he says, steering me away from the cooler. "Come on."

We start back toward the bonfire, where a sloppy-drunk Nando is holding court. "Speaking of how Cam gets when drunk..."

"Yeah, this shit is ridiculous," Rigel says, shaking his head. "He's upset over a girl."

My eyes widen. "Are you serious?"

He nods. "Unfortunately. Anyway, you guys just get here?"

"Yeah. We were at a party."

"By David Lee's house?"

148

heavenly bodies

"I don't even know," I say, shaking my head. "I think they go to St. Christopher's?"

"Yeah." Rigel heads for an empty spot by the fire. Hesitating, I look for Camille, but she's still wrapped up in Kyle. Hoping I'm not misreading the situation, I sit beside Rigel in the sand.

"So where's the camera?" he teases, knocking his shoulder against mine.

"Were you hoping for a photoshoot?" I laugh, turning my face toward the fire so he doesn't see it flush with pleasure.

"Only if you're offering."

"I'm not."

We share a smile, and I'm hot all over.

"You swam great today," I say, though the last thing he needs is a fangirl.

"Thanks." He shrugs, flipping his hood back. "I've been swimming as long as I've been walking."

"It shows."

"You've been improving," he says, turning to look at me.

"Yeah, you better watch out," I joke, picking at a loose thread on my shorts. "Maybe one day I'll be competing against you."

"It's entirely possible."

Nando and Kyle start wrestling across from us, Camille and the others egging them on from the sidelines.

"Look, I'll be happy when I can get from one side of the pool to the other," I say, staring at the flames. "That'll be huge for me."

"It'll happen. You're already progressing."

"I know. I just wish I could fast forward past the learning part."

"Come on...it's not that bad, is it?" He cocks his head, watching me with a little smile.

Realizing he means our P.E. sessions, I shake my head. "It's just frustrating sometimes."

"No, I hear you. I've always been able to swim, for as long as I can remember. I can't imagine not swimming," Rigel says, shaking his head.

"I guess that's how I feel about photography."

"Yeah," he agrees. "You're definitely a natural there."

The music shifts from rap to reggae. Camille and Kyle disappear down the beach, fingertips entwined. Nando's nowhere to be seen. I hope he's not going for a swim.

Feeling Rigel's gaze, I ask, "So what else are you into?"

"Music."

"You play an instrument?"

"Nah." He scoffs, shaking his head. "And I don't sing, either. I like sound systems, tech. Losing myself in the beat, especially when the system's on point."

"Ah." I nod, sifting sand through my fingers. "The truck."

"My cousins got me into it from young. I used to help them work on their cars, so they helped me install my first system when I got my truck." He shifts his eyes back to the fire. "It's just a hobby."

"Hobbies are important. They help you learn who you are."

"Oh, yeah?"

"Think about it: it's the stuff you choose to do when you could be doing anything. The stuff you're drawn to. I guess the people who can get paid for their hobbies are the lucky ones."

"That's true, though I wouldn't mind getting paid to swim," he says, nodding. "What do you do when you're not taking pictures?"

"I like to read. And I love music, same as you. My best friend..." I pause. "My best friend back in Inman Park, Sage, plays like, everything. Started with trombone in fifth grade and now she's a beast on the drums and piano, too. It's insane."

"That's tight."

"It is. She wants to attend Juilliard."

"So does my cousin Brielle. She's a dancer," says Rigel. "Do you know where you want to go?"

"Probably go back to Georgia. There are a lot of great schools there." I'd always thought I'd get the Hope Scholarship, no question, but now that we've left the state, it's no longer on the table. I'll have to meet with the guidance counselor at the Palms, find out what I might be eligible for.

"We have family in Vermont, so my Mom kind of wants me to apply to schools there, but I don't know. I like Florida. North Carolina's got some prospects."

"Florida's cool, but I like seasons. I miss fall."

"I remember that," Rigel says. "From your phone."

My stomach flips, and I start babbling. "I miss sweater weather, when it's just cold enough to see your breath. And it's like the trees are on fire, they're so vivid and red and orange. "

Rigel shifts closer. "You'll have to show it to me one day."

Shadows and light play across his face as he gazes at me. Someone throws a handful of tree branches into the fire, and the flames roar. Embers fly like flammable confetti and I inch back, giving it all a respectful space.

Camille sits abruptly down beside me, grabbing an empty beer bottle from the sand and turning it upside down. "You didn't even get me one?" she asks, tisking. "Hoes before bros!"

Vaguely mortified, I glance at Rigel, but he just smirks and turns to the girls that sat nearby while we were talking. Sighing, I give Camille a look, waiting until she makes proper eye contact. "That's not mine, and the beer is right there."

"No more beer. She's cut off," Kyle says, pulling her ponytail as he passes.

"Shut up," she breathes. I've never seen Camille anything less than one hundred percent, so this is amusing. Still, she's a handful when she imbibes, so I'll be keeping an eye on her. Jasmine's bitching in the car earlier makes sense now.

"What's up?" I ask quietly, poking her thigh.

"Nothing," she says, but her eyes flash to Rigel, and I know she wants to say something about him. Maybe he's a heartbreaker, or maybe he's between girlfriends, but the last time I checked it wasn't a crime to talk to somebody.

Standing, I brush sand from my bottom. "I'm going for a walk."

"Yay! I'll come." Beaming, she offers her hand so I'll help her up.

12.

Standing at the window, I gaze out at the motion-less trees in the yard. Macho, the guy who takes care of Grandpa Harry's lawn, halfheartedly pushes an ancient lawnmower, wiping sweat from his brow every couple of steps. It's not even eleven o'clock, and already hot as Hades. There's a tropical storm out at sea, and Mama says that means two things: one, that the hot spell is normal, and two, that the whole island is watching to see if it becomes a hurricane.

"It'll be nothing," Jasmine said in the car, late last night. "We go through this every year. Watch."

Mom's gone by the time I make it to the kitchen, her note letting me know she took Alex and Grandpa Harry to an open air market in La Reine. Relieved she didn't

155

spring another family outing on me, I take my time, sipping on lemongrass tea while getting dressed. And then, camera in hand, I hit the road. A car equals freedom, and I'm basking in mine, purposely exploring some of the longer westward routes. By the time I make it to Frederiksted, the sun's high in the sky. Wandering around town, I snap pictures at whim. It's nice not having anywhere to be.

After ordering a sandwich from a deli near the waterfront, I wander down the pier, people watching. A group of older men are fishing in one spot, quiet as they cast their lines. Further down, kids leap off the pier into the choppy, blue water. I watch for awhile, envious of their freedom, their courage. I'm sure Rigel, Camille and Nando all did this as children. According to Mama, jumping off of the pier is a rite of passage on St. Croix.

Maybe, when I learn to swim, I'll jump too.

My phone rings, and Cam's face pops up on the screen.

"Hello?"

"Hi, cuz. Where are you?"

I frown. "I'm on the pier. Where are you?"

"Your house."

"That's what you get for coming without calling," I tease.

"Oh, I didn't mean to offend your Southern sensibilities!"

"Bless your heart, Camille." I laugh. "I'll be home in a minute."

When I pull up to the house, still eating my deli sandwich, Cam's on the porch.

"Finally! Leh we go limin'!" she cries, springing up.

"You mean you wanna chill?"

She gives me the stink-eye. "When in Rome, Isla."

I don't even go inside; I just climb into Cam's car. Once we're on the road, I turn the music down. "So what's on the agenda for today? I thought you had chores."

"Girl, I got that done early." She scoffs, making a face. "My weekends are too precious for drudgery."

"I hear that."

"I was going to stop at Rigel's for a minute."

I roll my eyes. "Shut up."

"No, I'm serious. Nando's working on something in Mr. Thomas' garage, so I told him I'd stop by."

My heart slams in my chest. "Really?"

"Yeah." She smirks. "Try not to cream your panties."

"Camille!" I pinch her arm, hard.

"Ow, bruja..."

"You better not say anything in front of him," I warn. "And why are we going to see Nando? Weren't you with Kyle last night?"

"Because why not," she says, turning the volume up. "Hey, I love this song!"

Rigel's turn is only a few minutes after mine off Centerline Road, but it's long and speed-bumpy. We pass a few houses before the street narrows and the pavement ends, giving way to a dusty dirt road sheltered by the ubiquitous Crucian bush. It's about 95 degrees out, and Camille's a/c is on the fritz, so I'm grateful for the shade. A sturdy wooden gate comes into view, and beside it, nailed to a tree, a small sign: Thomas.

To the left sits a sizable, two story house—the first I've seen since living on St. Croix. Made of wood, it's tall and wide and sort of irregular, as if it's been continually added to over the years. Windchimes and potted plants hang around the wraparound porch. Across the yard, near the property line, several rusted out cars are tucked against a freestanding garage. Camille parks there, honking her horn just once.

Two Rottweilers come bounding out, barking exultantly. I hesitate inside the car, but Cam jumps out and runs over to them. Confident they aren't going to maul anyone, I join her, petting them as they sniff and nuzzle me. One of them jumps up, putting his paws on my shoulder as he licks my face.

"Clyde!" yells Rigel, startling both me and the dog.

Clyde lopes off sheepishly while I wipe slobber from my cheek. "Uh, hey."

"Hey, Isla," he says. He's in just basketball shorts, a t-shirt tied around his head. "Sorry about Clydie."

"Nice turban," I say, choosing not to focus his golden-toned swimmer's bod.

"I was cutting the grass," he says, grinning as he unties the t-shirt. A mess of curls falls free.

Camille passes him, patting his shoulder gingerly. "I'd hug you, but...ew, you're sweaty."

He lunges for her and she shrieks, dashing into the garage. I follow, slowing as Rigel falls into step.

"So you're doing yardwork today?"

"Yeah. I'm about halfway done."

I glance back at their property. "You have a lot of lawn to mow."

"No kidding."

Camille's in the back with Nando, who's working on a car. A smile spreads over his grease-smudged face as we approach. What is it about dirt that makes boys so cute?

"Two out of three musketeers," he says. "Not a bad way to start the day."

"Ugh, don't start with that again," groans Camille.

Ignoring her, he leans over and kisses my cheek. "What's up, nena?"

"Nothing, just hangin' with Cam."

"Going limin' later?"

Camille smiles smugly, pleased she can reinforce her Crucian lingo. "Why, what you got in mind?"

"You want something to drink?" asks Rigel, touching my elbow. "My dad keeps a fridge out here."

"Sure." We leave Cam and Nando and return to the front, where he roots through a mini fridge by the door.

"Water, lemonade..."

"Lemonade sounds good."

Clyde and the other dog, Guapo, trot alongside us as we stroll out into the yard. It's later in the day now, and not as brutally bright, but the heat seems to have gotten worse, like it's been simmering all day and has finally reached a boil. A chain link fence, rendered nearly invisible by overgrown guinea grass, lines what I can see of the Thomas property.

"You like horses?" Rigel asks.

"I love them." It's been years, but Sage and I used to ride them on her grandpa's ranch in Blue Ridge.

"My little sister does, too." He leads me to a small grove behind the garage where two horses, one blond and one brown, are grazing beneath the trees. "These belong to my uncle, but he brings them by most weekends so she can ride."

"Oh man —I would've loved that as a little kid." I run my hand over the female's flaxen mane, delighted when she raises her head to look at me. "I'd still love it."

"Her name's Nadine."

"Hi Nadine." I trail my knuckles gently down to her nose, tickled when she nickers softly. "She's sweet."

"The sweetest. Rory rides her all the time. Kasha is more like his name, prickly and temperamental." He nods at the other horse, who's ignoring us in favor of continuing lunch.

I look blankly at Rigel. "Okay?"

"Kasha? It's a thorny bush. It's everywhere."

"Oh." I shake my head. "I guess I haven't seen any yet."

"You will," he says, giving Nadine's rump a smack. She ambles over to a patch of little yellow flowers, tail swishing. "So what are you and Cam up to today?"

"I don't know, really. She just picked me up and said we were coming here."

His eyes flicker toward the garage, and he smirks. "I'm sure she did."

I laugh, a little uncertainly. "What?"

His eyes crinkle as he laughs, too. "What?"

"Come on," I say, giving him a little push. "You can't just say stuff like that and not explain!"

"I have no idea what you're talking about," he says, putting an arm up to defend himself.

He's full of it, but it's easy to forgive when he smiles at me like that.

Rigel's not in school on Monday.

It's not until AP History, when his seat remains empty long after the bell rings for class to start, that I realize. I turn to Nando during small group discussions. "Hey, is Rigel sick or something?"

He looks up from his notebook. "Not that I know of."

When I get to the pool later, I remember in the locker room that Rigel's absent and it sucks all over again. Stanley's back, but Coach Archer opts to work with me herself.

"You're doing great, Isla," she says, timing me as I tread water.

"Thanks," I pant, careful to keep my head above the surface.

"Okay, time. Get to the wall."

Then we work on the backstroke, which, oddly, I'm able to pick up by the end of class. Go figure.

Meanwhile, Camille's in a mood. She blames her period, which is so cliche I can't even, but I'm with her after school when Kyle leaves without saying goodbye. "What's up with you and Kyle?" I ask, going for the kill. Camille's more honest about her feelings if I can catch her off guard.

"Whatever." She shrugs. "He's young."

Kyle's only a year behind us, but I know what she means. Some guys act young, flashing hot then cold, playing games. Still, I have to wonder what changed between Friday, when they were all over each other, and now.

Oh, well there was Saturday when she went to see Nando.

"Talk to me."

"There's nothing to talk about," she says, waving me off. "Trust me."

"Fine. Let's get ice cream, then," I say. "From Armstrong's."

We get our ice cream to go, and then I drop Camille home. She says she's okay, but she keeps checking her phone when she thinks I'm not paying attention. Meanwhile, I have a ton of homework—the Palms is more intense than Grady ever was—and I want to get started.

A couple of hours later, I'm slipping right out the door again, promising Mom I'll be back in time to set the table. I want to catch another beach sunset, using a different camera this time. Grandpa Harry slips me a twenty on my way out, asking me to grab him a lottery ticket. I do that first, stopping at our usual gas station, and then continue on to Rainbow Beach. I tell myself I'm just going to watch...but there's a bikini beneath my cutoffs and t-shirt and if the right person encouraged me, I might just go in.

I'm in the zone, playing with the depth of field, when a shadow falls across the sand. Rigel's at my side, smirking down at me. He's in board shorts and an old t-shirt. "Hey, Georgia."

"Hey"—I replace the lens cap—"island boy."

"That's kinda cool," he says, nodding toward the camera in my lap. This one's a personal favorite, the old Minolta Grammie gave me a couple of years ago. It's quirky and square and uses real film, but I whip it out when I'm feeling sentimental. "Going old school today?"

"You could say that."

He nods, looking out to the sea.

"You weren't at school today."

"Nah." He toes his shoes off, old Adidas that have seen better days. He even wears bumminess well.

I look up at him. "How come?"

"Missed my alarm, and then I just...didn't want to deal with it."

"Are you serious?"

He nods, shrugging.

"Do you do that often?" I laugh, a little incredulously. That would never fly at my house.

"No," he says, eyes crinkling at the corners. "You coming in?"

"To the water?" I glance at the calm, glimmering sea, as if I hadn't noticed it before.

"Yeah, to the water," he says, voice muffled as he peels off his shirt.

My heart gives a little skip and I look away, not wanting to be caught staring. "Are you, uh, training today? Or just going for a swim?"

"Both. Got two meets this week."

"At our pool?"

"Tomorrow's is at our pool, Thursday's is at McKinley." He drops the shirt in the sand, next to his shoes. "Anyway, you're at the beach so I think you should come in. You can put your stuff in the truck. " He stretches his arms back, linking his hands behinds head. "I'm parked right there."

I look over at the road where Rigel's truck sits. If he's actually encouraging me to go swimming with him, how can I refuse? "Just for a few minutes...I'm not really supposed to stay out late."

He's already headed back toward his truck, keys in hand. "You came to hang out, right?"

I did, but damn if he didn't just call me out! "Yeah."

He smiles over his shoulder at me. Unlocking the cab, he stuffs my camera and phone into the glove compartment and grabs a couple of towels. Back on the sand, I leave my clothes besides Rigel's before venturing in. The water is a little cooler than I'm expecting, and I shiver as my arms goosebump.

"It's because the sun's almost down," he says, noticing. "But I'm sure it's worse in Atlanta."

I smile, because there's no comparison. "I wouldn't know. There aren't any beaches there."

His smiles drops. "No beaches anywhere?"

"Well, in Savannah. There are beaches, just not where I lived."

"I'd feel landlocked."

"I never thought about it, I guess." I wade a little deeper. "Okay, the water's not so bad now."

"When we have two-a-days, I have to be at the pool by five thirty to practice before school. It's freezing."

"Sounds awful." I tip my head back, wetting my hair. It helps me adjust, and I relax.

"It is, but it's over the second you start swimming." He drags his hand through the water, creating ripples. "Give me a minute, okay?" He puts his goggles on and dives beneath the surface, re-emerging when he's far away. I back up until it's shallow enough to sit, and then I watch him swim laps, back and forth, alternating strokes each time. Something brushes my thigh and I glance down, surprised to see several little fish swimming around me. Tiny and silver, they dart like they're made of light. I watch them, slowly lowering my hands to play with them.

The sun is a gold coin turned copper, minutes from dropping beneath the horizon. It's probably time for me to go. If Rigel doesn't swim back soon, I'm going to have to get his attention somehow. But, as if he senses it, he makes his way back, cutting rapidly through the water. I think he's going to swim right up to me, but he keeps his distance, treading water as he wrestles the goggles from his face. He wipes water from his eyes before running a hand through his hair, the setting sun shining through his darkened curls.

"Swim out," he calls, tossing me his goggles.

I reach out instinctively, not wanting them to sink. "I'm okay here."

"Come on," he urges, coming a little closer.

"Nope."

"Isla."

"Why are you always pushing me?" I'm not really complaining, though. I like that it matters to him.

"Someone has to, city girl," he says, splashing water my way. "You'll be fine. It's not that deep."

I wrap the goggle straps around my wrist, considering.

"I won't let anything happen to you," he says.

"I know you won't."

The sun is behind Rigel, so it's hard to see his face, but I know mine is clear to him. I wonder what he sees. A girl that's brave? Taking a deep breath, I leave the safety of the sand. I panic for a second as the salty water closes over my face, but then my lessons kick in and I resurface, paddling my arms and legs. I close the distance between us quickly, surprised when his arms close around me. Catching my breath, I squeeze the water from my eyes.

His skin is so soft. When he tutors me at school he has to be close, obviously, but this is different. We're not at school; we're alone at the beach. It's seconds from dusk, and the last of the sun casts everything in bronze. Shivering with nerves, I almost ask if the girl Camille told me about is someone I should consider before doing what I really, really want to do...but I chicken out. I'll ask later, because I'm selfish and all I want now is to kiss him.

Rigel floats us back to where we can stand, his arms tightening around me as my feet hit the sand. "Hey."

Resting my hands on his shoulders, I stare at the freckles on his neck. I can't look at those eyes, not this closeup. But he ducks down and kisses me, pressing his lips gently to mine. "I have to know," he whispers, mouth so close I feel his breath. There's a tiny, curved scar right above his mouth, marring his smooth skin.

Everything else fades: the music down the beach, the sway of the warm water, the squishy, wet sand beneath my toes. Clasping my hands around his neck, I kiss him back, letting him in when his tongue touches my lips. His kisses are slow, like he's taking his time and memorizing my mouth. And then he switches gears, trailing his lips over my jaw and down my neck. It feels so good that I know we need to stop; I can feel myself tightening up with feelings way too intense for kisses on the beach. I run my thumb over his cheek and his eyes open.

He blinks, looking at me. The lust fog clears.

"We should go," he says quietly, nodding.

"Yeah." It's the last thing I want to do, but I let go of him as he lets go of me. Newly aware of how public the beach is, I peek around, but we're alone. We walk out of the water together, as if we're leaving the version of ourselves who kiss behind.

My mind races as we towel off on the beach. I think again of his ex, and how she'll probably be around at some point, and does she even matter to him? Are there other girls he likes? He could have anyone. Is my appeal in my new-ness? Am I the shiny new toy?

But, oh man. My lips still tingle. I stifle the urge to touch them, anxious at how much I want this. How much I want him. His eyes flash to mine, and we share a smile. If there was any doubt in his mind before, it's gone now. I obviously like him. But he likes me too, enough to make a move the way he just did.

"You gonna get in trouble?" he asks as we walk to his truck.

"Maybe. Probably." I shiver as the breeze picks up. It's almost dark. Whoops.

"Here you go," he says, handing me my camera and keys. The branches he's parked under shift restlessly, leaves whispering as they touch.

"Thanks." I immediately text my mother, letting her know I'm on my way, and then drop the phone into my bag. I don't need to see her response to know she's annoyed. Sliding into my flip flops, I peek at Rigel. He's brushing sand from his feet, quiet. I try, but it's hard to control the inner crazy: does he regret it? Did we rush? Are things going to be awkward now?

It occurs to me that I'm so lost in my own thoughts that I'm being just as quiet as he is.

"Well," he says, straightening up. "Sorry I kept you so long."

"It's...quite all right." I laugh a little, shaking my head. "I'll see you tomorrow?"

"You asking or telling?" He comes toward me, towel slung over his shoulder.

"Asking," I say. "You tend to skip sometimes."

"Naw, I'm going." He rests his hand on my hip. My heart skips. "Where did you park?"

I jerk my thumb over my shoulder. "In the lot."

"I'll walk you."

Sleep is a hard won battle. I lie awake forever, mind running wild with possible scenarios. What'll it be like at school tomorrow? At the meet? Does Rigel expect me to photograph all of his meets? Just when I'm feeling warm he'd want me to, I have a paranoid thought; what if he thinks I'm stalking him? I should probably veer on the side of caution and have Megan cover a couple meets.

I go through my morning rituals in a daze, eating oatmeal and brushing my teeth by rote. I kiss everyone goodbye—Grandpa Harry and Mama and even Alex, who clasps my cheeks with sticky fingers—and head to school, my stomach a knot of nerves. Camille pulls in right after I do, sticking her tongue out at me, and we walk in together, chatting about a quiz we have in history. She's in a way better mood than yesterday, but she never mentions Kyle. I suppose we all have secrets this morning.

Nando talks my ear off during homeroom, trying to get advice on a girl he likes, and then we're walking to history. Seconds later Rigel breezes in. He's perfect in jeans and a black t-shirt, eyes downcast as he takes off his hat. I expect him to drop into his usual seat a couple of rows up, but he gives me a lazy little smile as he taps Nando's shoulder.

"Hey, man," Nando says, looking up. "'Sup?"

"Let me sit here," Rigel says, dropping his backpack.

A look of confusion crosses Nando's face for about a split second before he glances at me. Smirking, he shakes his head and moves. Rigel takes the seat beside me, resting his feet on the rung of the one front of him.

Relaxing back, he aims his gaze at me. "What's up?"

"Nothing, just getting ready for this quiz."

"Did you study last night?" He smiles suddenly, dimples and all. "When you got home?"

My heart stutters, and I grin back reflexively. "A little this morning. I feel good about it."

He nods, tapping his pencil against the desk.

I lean closer, wanting to ask him about his meet later, but the bell rings with finality, ending the conversation. We get our quizzes right away, and I breeze though, glad I took a moment to go over the material at breakfast. I steal a peek at Rigel, remembering with great clarity his lips parting mine, his tongue sweeping my mouth.

The thought of it nearly steals my breath, and when he looks back at me, his gaze darkens, like he knows.

13.

The sky is cloudless today, as clear and blue as the pool. Sunlight ripples dreamily through the turquoise water, reminding me of one of my favorite photographers, a girl who creates stunning underwater vistas. I'm lost in thought, wondering how much underwater housing costs for cameras, when Rigel eases into the water beside me.

"Hey, sorry I'm late."

Before I can even respond, Archer is looming above us. "You're late, Rigel."

"Sorry, Coach. Had a phone call."

"Not my problem," she says. "The only reason I'm not making you swim laps is because that would waste Isla's time."

Rigel nods. "Won't happen again."

"I hope not."

"I really am sorry," Rigel says to me once Archer's gone.

I turn to him, hiding a smile. "Phone calls at school?" I tease. "Tsk, tsk."

"Yeah, I'm a real rebel." He comes closer. "I thought we could work on diving today."

Guess we're getting right down to business. "Diving?" I echo, cracked skulls and bloody water coming to mind.

"Diving down from the surface, like this." Taking a breath, he ducks beneath the surface and kicks off, propelling himself down until he touches the pool floor. Then he floats slowly back up, wiping water from his eyes. The whole thing takes maybe ten seconds.

"Is that part of Archer's curriculum?" I ask, shading my eyes from the sun's brightness.

"No, it's part of mine." He sweeps his hair back, squeezing water from it. "If you can master this, the rest is cake."

That makes sense. It's being submerged, not swimming along the surface, that sets me off. Still, having a panic attack in front of Rigel isn't something I feel like going through. I can't say for sure that won't happen if I go that far underwater. "I'm gonna have to put my foot down and say no."

"You have to face it eventually," he says.

"Eventually is not today, Rigel."

"At least try," he says. "You need to conquer this."

Leaning against the side of the pool, I fold my arms. "Maybe, but not to pass this class."

He folds his arms, too. "You're seriously not going to try."

"No."

"Isla."

"I said no!" I send a wave of water his way, splashing the incredulity off his face.

"You sound really Southern right now," he says, wiping water from his eyes. "You must be really vexed with me."

I cut my eyes at him. "Vexed?"

"You're bigger than your fear, Georgia."

"And you're a swimmer, not a psychologist."

Our classmates are running drills now. I watch them for awhile, wondering how long we're going to go without saying something. But when I sneak a peek at Rigel, he's floating peacefully, staring at the sky.

Eventually Coach Archer walks over. "Everything okay?"

I begin to explain, but Rigel beats me to it. "Everything's great. Isla refuses to do anything, so I get to relax for the rest of the class."

"That's not true," I say, pushing off from the wall. "He's deviating from the curriculum."

She looks from me to him and back to me. "What?"

175

Rigel gets to his feet, pushing his dripping hair back. He looks the way he did at the beach yesterday, and my breath catches. "I'm just trying to teach her how to dive down. You know? Basic."

Ouch. "Basic? For you, maybe."

"You won't even try."

Archer clears her throat. "Isla, he's right in that you should try, but you're right in that's it's not part of the curriculum." She pauses, looking regretful. "Just stick to the strokes, Ri."

"All right." It's a victory I guess, but it feels crappy. "Thanks."

"Got it," says Rigel.

"We still have twenty minutes," she says, pointing to her watch as she leaves. "Get moving."

Rigel and I look at each other. "Backstroke," he says. "You know how to float, so we'll start there."

"Oh, is that basic enough for me?"

His face falls. "You know I didn't mean it like that."

"Just...teach me the backstroke, Rigel." Without waiting for a response, I ease onto my back and float.

Today's meet against Hamilton High, one of our main rivals, is well attended. Camille, Jasmine and I sit

176

squashed together near the front, chatting as I ready my camera.

I haven't seen Rigel since the end of our awkward swim session. We separated on good terms, and by good I mean bullshitty and polite. I'm a little embarrassed I freaked, but mostly, I just wish he hadn't pushed me. I'm well aware of my inadequacies in the water, and no one's as bothered by them as I am.

"I need a swimmer in my life," Camille announces. The smell of her popcorn is making my mouth water. "I mean...look at them."

"Trust me, girl, I'm looking." Positioning my camera, I take a couple experimental shots before adjusting the settings.

"Yes, I know you are," she whispers, tapping my knee.

Camille's not stupid, so I decide not to insult her by feigning ignorance. Instead, I simply shrug and nod, squinting through my viewfinder. Rigel's zoomed-in gaze stares back at me, and I lower the camera, caught. He gives me the subtlest wink before getting into position up on the starting block.

Not subtle enough, though. Camille sighs, leaning into me again. "Mhm. What was that?"

I'm surprised by how relieved I feel that Rigel and I are okay. "What was what?"

The race starts with a bang. Camille passes the popcorn to Jasmine. "You know what."

I smile. The swimmers reach the wall and flip; I snap a picture of Rigel in the lead.

"Looks like we have some catching up to do, *Georgia,*" Cam says.

Rigel's nickname for me. I blush. "Maybe we do."

Mama's not around when I get home.

"She took the lil one to the store," Grandpa Harry says. He's in his Lazy Boy today, bush tea at his side as he keeps an eye on the weather. "Wanted to stock up before the storm."

As Jasmine said, the storms seem to come and go with little consequence. The latest one has been worrisome, though. "Has it gotten a lot worse?"

"Well, it's been upgraded to a Category 1."

"Oh, no." Dismayed, I look past him to the TV where the Weather Channel is discussing several of the storm's potential paths.

"Don't vex yourself, dahlin. That ain't nothing," he says, patting my arm. "We've had much worse around here."

I'm not sure if that makes me better or worse. We can't even evacuate if things get bad. Dropping my backpack on the couch, I lean in to give my grandfather a hug. "How was your day?"

"Not bad. Helped Macho put away the patio furniture, get the place ready." He sighs, settling back. "Doesn't take much wind to make a mess."

"I thought you were supposed to be taking it easy," I tease.

"All I do is take it easy," he says, glaring at me over his glasses. "I can't stand around picking my nose when there's work to be done."

"That's true." I pick up his empty mug. "Did you want more, Grandpa?"

"Thank you," he says, nodding. "You going out to-day?"

I know why he's asking; he's got quite the penchant for lottery tickets. "I was thinking about it," I say, smiling slyly. "Need me to pick something up?"

"Look in the drawer beside the bed, take a twenty. Keep the change."

"Thanks, Grandpa." I give him a hug, careful not to squeeze too hard. He's frailer than he was. I suspect, also, that he's much more indulgent with me than he ever was with my mother or Aunt Greta. "Powerball, right?"

Trading my backpack for a purse, I head out. Because of the swim meet, I'm heading to Rainbow a little later than usual. The bar beside the beach looks about half full, buoyed by a reggae cover band. Ignoring the dusty parking lot across the street, I pull up to where Rigel had his truck yesterday. If he doesn't come within the half hour, I'll grab my grandfather's lottery tickets and go

179

home. There are plenty of reasons I shouldn't be here: homework, an overdue Facetime session with Morgan, the storm...

...and Rigel might not even show up. For all I know he's at home, celebrating his wins with his family.

I climb onto the trunk of my car, swinging my legs as I look around. Down on the rocks, jutting into the water, sit the silhouettes of two men fishing. I watch them for awhile, thinking about my father, wondering what he's up to today. I text him: I miss you!

The far-off rumble of bass jostles me from my thoughts, growing louder and louder as a black truck comes down the road. Parking behind my car, Rigel steps out, fixing his baseball cap. I slide my phone into my purse as he approaches. "Hey."

"Hey." He stops inches away, playing with his keys. "I knew you'd be here."

"I'd knew you'd be here, too."

He smiles and comes closer, his jeans brushing against my legs. "Predictable, huh?"

"Well, it is your spot..."

"We can share." Another step brings him between my knees.

My stomach dips. "I wanted to talk to you."

"I wanted to talk to you, too. Be a lot easier if I had your number, though," he says, retrieving his phone from his back pocket. "What is it?"

I tell him, and seconds later my phone buzzes in my purse, letting me know I have a new message.

"I take it you're not swimming today?" I ask, nodding toward the water.

"No way." He looks at me like I'm nuts. "I'm tired as hell after that race."

"I got a lot of good shots today; I'll have to show you."

"You brought them?"

I shake my head. "My camera's at home. I'll email them."

He nods. "You want to go somewhere?"

I still my hands, wishing I could still the flutters in my belly, too. "Is it close?"

Backing up, he nods toward his truck. "You okay with leaving your car here a minute?"

"Just a minute?"

"Twenty minutes," he amends, cocking his head. "Thirty." He knows I'll agree.

And I do. Sliding off the trunk, I grab my bag and climb into the cab of Rigel's truck. It smells faintly of incense. A slim stack of books sits on the console, his phone on top. There's sand on the seats and a fishing rod in the back. Getting in beside me, Rigel reverses out, the music I've quietly obsessed over from afar booming to life with a flick of his wrist. We drive with the windows down, the salty sea breeze playing with our hair.

He rides the way boys do, one arm framed in the window, the other resting on the steering wheel. I keep my eyes on the road but I feel everything he does, tensing every time he reaches over to switch gears. We ride along the main road for a few minutes before turning down into the rainforest, where the trees grow so thick they seem to close in. Verdant and lush, it's noticeably cooler the deeper we go. After passing a couple of cars on the twisty road, Rigel pulls off, turning the music down.

"This is Creque Dam. It's pretty empty in the summer months, but come winter it'll be full of water."

"The rainy season, right?"

"Yeah." He gets out and I follow, swinging my purse over my shoulder. The dam's spillway is a long, narrow walkway made of concrete. The right side is filled with overgrown brush and plants, but the other's a sheer drop of bare concrete. It's at least thirty or forty feet. "I hope you're not afraid of heights," Rigel calls over his shoulder.

"Not really," I say, supremely grateful for the rusty, metal handrail lining the walkway. I have good balance, and there's enough room to walk safely, but it's still a little precarious feeling.

Rigel walks slowly, leading me further along until he stops, sitting down. I sit beside him, and we dangle our feet over the edge.

"This is amazing," I whisper, compulsively snapping a couple of photos before putting my phone away. Straggles of sunlight shine weakly through the tangled canopy of trees, and with the exception of the occasional bird, it's still. Reverent.

"We used to hang out here a lot...still do, sometimes," Rigel says, looking up at the sky. "Mostly I come by myself, though. I like the quiet."

"We drove through a rainforest, but I don't remember this." Two of birds dart by, chasing each other up into the trees.

"You probably came down Mahogany Road."

I look around, eyeing the dam. "So do people swim? When it's full?"

"No," he laughs, wrinkling his nose. "Not up here. There are waterfalls further down; people swim in those. They'll probably surge tonight with the all rain we're going to get."

"Grandpa Harry said the storm got upgraded to a hurricane, but you'd never know it by this weather." It's still as a tomb, the leaves motionless.

"It's always like this right before," says Rigel. "Wait until midnight. You'll see some serious wind then."

We still in silence for awhile, soaking in the tranquility. "So, about today."

He smiles, staring out into the darkening wilderness. I narrow my eyes. "What?"

Twisting around to face me, he throws one leg over and straddles the spillway. "I didn't bring you here to talk about how stubborn you are"—I try to butt in, but he barrels right over me—"or to explain that I pushed you today because being afraid of touching the bottom is a hundred times worse than actually touching the bottom."

I feel convicted, called out. Seen. It doesn't hurt like I thought it would, but it's not pleasant, either. Swallowing past my thundering heart, I look away. "Then why did you bring me here?"

"Because." Rigel touches my chin with his thumb, tilting my face back to his. It's different this time, slower. His hand is at the nape of my neck, fingers in my hair, and I lean in, high off the feeling of being wanted by someone I want so badly. He kisses me, parted lips and a tentative tongue. I close my eyes, giving it back to him a little deeper.

"Come here," he says, turning me to face him. Moving carefully, we arrange my legs over his, so that we're sitting interlocked, and then he comes in for the deepest sort of kiss. There's something raw and honest about Rigel, like he's not afraid to show me that he wants me. I slide his hat off so I can touch his hair, tangling my fingers in his curls.

"You're a beautiful girl, Isla," he whispers against my mouth. "That's why."

He's the beautiful one.

heavenly bodies

It gets dark faster here, I've noticed, probably because we're so far south.

We get back to my car in a way different headspace than the one we left it in. I manage to wrench myself from the giddy pull of Rigel's sideways glances and secret smiles long enough to send my mother a message. She's texted twice, and though I know Grandpa Harry told her where I went, she's pissed I'm still out.

Her response comes a millisecond after I hit send: *Just get home. Now.*

Cringing, I put my phone away. Rigel turns down the volume and looks my way. "Everything okay? She flipping out?"

"Yeah. It's the storm, I think."

"Can't blame her, I guess." He frowns, pulling up behind my car. "You guys gonna be okay tonight?"

"I think so." I pause, hand on the door handle. "Do you really think it's going to be that bad? Jasmine said storms pass by every year, no big deal."

"That's true, except for the times it is a big deal."

Nodding, I open the door. "I'd better get home, then."

"I'll follow you."

Warmed, I smile at him through the open window. "Thanks."

His headlights keep me company until his turnoff, where they flash twice and disappear as I continue on home. My mother's on the porch, arms crossed, when I

185

pull up. Bracing for the storm, pun totally intended, I gather my things and get out.

"It's almost seven o'clock, Isla Grace. Even if there wasn't a hurricane coming our way"—she glares at me—"it's a school night!"

"I know." I hug my bag to my chest. It's bad enough getting in trouble; knowing you deserve it is the worst. "I'm so, so sorry. I—"

"It can be dangerous at night, especially on the beach," she continues, turning to go back inside. "You still don't know the island that well."

I follow, pulling the door shut behind me. "I know. I'm learning, though."

Alex races by, saying something about turtles.

Mom eyes me, washing her hands. Dinner looks half made, like most of the prep work is done already. "That's not the point," she says. "I think I've been pretty lenient with you, letting you come and go as you please, but you need to respect the boundaries I've set, okay? Seven is too late. I didn't think I'd have to give you a curfew during the week, but..."

"No, I know. I'm really, really sorry. I totally lost track of time."

"Doing what? Taking pictures?" Arching an eyebrow, she looks skeptically from me to the window. "At this time?"

Fighting the urge to be bratty, I decide to make my escape. "I'm going to go take a shower, okay?"

186

"You should. The power will probably go out later and the water pump won't work."

I'm halfway down the hall when she suddenly asks, "Who were you with tonight?"

"A kid from school, Rigel."

"Rigel? The one teaching you to swim?" she says, closer than I realize when she touches my hair. "You weren't swimming tonight."

"No." I rest my hand on the door to my room. "We were just hanging out."

"Hm." She looks me up and down, pausing at my neck. "Go get cleaned up."

In the bathroom, I rest my warm cheek against the cool door. The mirror above the sink shows me a flushed girl with a shiny eyes and faint marks along her collarbone. Also? Her hair looks like she's already been through a hurricane.

No wonder Mom was giving me the serious side eye.

We rush through dinner, eager to clean up in case we lose electricity. Grandpa Harry turns in soon after, tuckered out from his day. I spend the evening watching the Weather Channel with Mama and texting my friends. When Alex falls asleep beside me on the couch I carry him to bed, tucking him in and checking the windows. It's ten thirty, and the wind is picking up. My phone vibrates with a message from my father.

How's my Isla-girl? I miss you too. Y'all doing ok with this hurricane?

187

I think it's a little one, don't worry.

Mama said that. Still wish I was with you.

Me too :(

Keep me updated. Mama's not as quick with texting as you are.

Haha. Will do.

Made my reservation for Thanksgiving.

My heart leaps. *Really? How long?*

Four days. Mom and I are worked something out.

My chest hurts. I hate not having Daddy around. I hate that some days pass where I don't think of him at all. I hate that at a time where he and my mother should be leaning on each other they're an ocean apart.

Love you, Daddy.

Love you too.

14.

"I t's like a freight train," Mama says. Hurricane
Carmen is passing over St. Croix, bestowing
upon us howling wind and relentless rain. It's two in the
morning, and the power just went out. I'd just dozed off
sometime around one only to have Alex climb into bed
with me, frightened of the thunder and lightning...and
that damn wind.

Cocking my ear toward the window, I listen. "It is.
It's kind of eerie."

She nods, rubbing my brother's back, though he's
long since fallen back asleep.

Yawning, I pull my blanket up.

"I'll bring him to my bed," Mama says, standing and
stretching.

"Just leave him," I say. "I don't mind."

189

Nodding, she leans to kiss me, covers Al with the blanket, and leaves. I settle back, closing my eyes. The storm is fierce, but I'm not afraid. Grandpa Harry's house is a fortress.

In the morning, I wake up sweaty. The power's still out, so my fan's at a standstill. Alex is already gone, his portion of the blanket crumpled on the floor. Climbing blearily out of bed, I peer out the window to a calm, grey morning. There's debris in the yard, but it looks like mostly tree branches. Some of Grandpa's plants have been destroyed, though.

My phone still has some battery left, but there aren't any new messages. I text both Camille and Rigel, letting them know we're ok, asking how they fared, but neither of them respond.

"Cell service might be down," Mama says. "With everyone on the phone, calling the states..."

Startled, I spin around to find her at the kitchen table. "Are you serious?"

She smiles. "No electricity? No big deal. But no phone? Isla's got problems."

"Haha," I say, sticking out my tongue.

"Best keep that thing in your mouth; you're never too old for a spanking," she says, Crucian accent making a comeback. Over the years, I only heard it when she spoke to Aunt Greta or someone from here, but it comes out more frequently now that she's back.

Moving from room to room, Mama and I open all of the louvers we cranked shut last night. Weak, watery sunlight and a gust of fresh air come in, making the mood a little less gloomy.

"Charlene, the generator," Grandpa Harry calls, shuffling into the living room. "Macho left it in the shed."

"Why didn't he just bring it onto the porch?" Mama says, sucking her teeth. "That thing weighs a ton!"

"Didn't want it to get wet during the hurricane."

Mom stalks off to her bedroom, muttering.

"I can help you carry it," I offer.

"Go put your shoes on," she says. "God knows what's in the yard today."

Minutes later, Alex and I trail dutifully after Mama through the saturated grass while Grandpa Harry yells directions from the porch. The shed's not as much of a pig-sty as it was when we first got here, thanks to Mama's diligence, but it's still a little gross. Between the cobwebs and bugs, I generally steer clear of it. But today we have to lug Grandpa's enormous generator out so we can set it up behind the house.

Mom peeks through the shed's tiny window. "You expecting someone?"

My heart leaps, because if it's who I hope it is, I can't believe he's here. Sure enough, Rigel's truck is coming through the gate. He pulls up next to my car and gets out, adjusting his hat.

"Hey! What are you doing here?" I go over to him, my sneakers squelching in the mud. "How'd you even know where I lived?"

"My dad knows your grandparents, so he told me how to get here." He glances at the house. "And you didn't reply to my text, so I came to check."

I fumble for the phone in my back pocket. "You texted me?"

"Yeah."

"It didn't come through," I say. "My mama said cell service might be down, though."

"Probably." He nods. "Is there anything I can do? Did you guys have any damage?"

I fumble for words, still surprised he showed up. "I don't think so, but you can help us with the generator."

Grandpa Harry's suddenly nowhere to be found, but Mama comes out of the shed just then. Before she can embarrass me, I grab her arm. "Mama, this is Rigel. Rigel, my mother."

"Hi, Mrs. Kelly." He extends his hand. "Nice to meet you."

"Ah, Rigel," she says. I cringe as they shake, hoping she doesn't say anything weird and/or parental. "So you're the one teaching Isla to swim."

"I'm trying," he says, smirking at me.

~

heavenly bodies

I oversleep the next morning, exhausted from the roughing it that is post-hurricane life. Rigel stayed for a little while yesterday, helping with the generator and some cleanup before returning home. In the end, we went to Camille's for dinner. Uncle Isaac didn't have much faith in the local power company to get its act together anytime soon, so he opted to grill most of the meat in his fridge before it could go bad.

The lights came back on halfway through dinner. We now have enough steak and drumsticks to last the apocalypse.

"Camille needs a ride," Mama says, leaning in my doorway as I scramble into my favorite pair of Adidas. "Says her car's acting up."

"Probably her battery again," I say, standing. "Tell her to be outside. Please."

"Where's your phone, Isla?" she asks.

"Charging."

I slide silver hoops through my ears and grab my phone, shoving it into my bag. Camille picked a crappy day to need a last minute ride; I'm already behind. Grabbing a granola bar, I kiss my mother as she tucks two coffees into my hands. "Thank you! Love you!"

"Drive carefully," she yells as I rush out the door. "Don't be crazy, Isla!"

Camille's waiting outside when I pull up, bless her.

"You're lucky I'm running late, otherwise I'd be gone already," I say as we reverse out of her driveway.

"Everyone's late today," she says. "There was a damn hurricane."

"Well, that's true." I gaze at the roadside as we fly past. Other than a few downed branches and a lot of water, St. Croix seems to have fared well. "Your mom went in already?"

"The whole faculty went in early. They had meetings this morning about water damage and stuff."

I hand Cam a coffee. "Sounds fun."

"Speaking of mothers, I love yours," she says, a beatific smile gracing her lips as she sniffs her cup. "Her coffee is a God-send."

We drive in companionable silence, waking up to caffeine and good music. About five minutes from school, though, boy-related anxiety kicks in, making the last of my coffee taste like tar.

"So I like Rigel."

"I know."

"I mean, I really like him."

"Oh, I know," Camille says, turning the music down. "It's all over your face whenever he's around."

"Shush." There's no good parking left, so I head for the end of the lot. "He kissed me."

"What?" Gasping, she jabs at the radio until it's off. "When? Isla!"

I turn the a/c vent to cool my face. "I see him sometimes at Rainbow Beach. After school."

194

"Where he goes to train," she murmurs, nodding. "How'd you find that out?"

Bristling at the almost accusatory undertones of her voice, I pull into a spot. "It was by mistake. I started going there to take pictures the day I got my car, and we ran into each other."

"And every day after, huh?" she teases, poking my side.

"There was only one day after that, and that's when he kissed me." I glance her. "And we went to the rainforest once."

"I thought it was kinda suspect he went by your house yesterday." She sits back, a thoughtful look other face. "Maybe it really is over with Mia. They were on and off for so long, you know? Have you asked about her?"

My stomach knots up at the thought of that conversation. "No."

Camille nods, shifting her eyes away.

"Just...what?" I ask, exasperated by her weirdness. "Is there something you need to say?"

"Look, I love Rigel. I really do. But be careful."

"Careful in what way?"

"Just talk to him, okay? Get to know him for real." She looks at me. "Because he knows he's cute, and he definitely uses it."

"What does that even mean?"

"It means there's a lot more to Rigel than what meets the eye." She frowns thoughtfully.

The anticipation that's been bubbling all morning sours into anxiety. Turning the car off, I reach into the back seat and yank my backpack out. "Well, Camille, you know him better than I do."

"Don't be mad," she says, sighing. "I just don't want you to get burned."

"I don't want that, either. But I can't help how I feel." Climbing out, I lock the door and start walking. "Is this about Mia?"

"No." She catches right up, bumping her hip to mine. "I'm sorry if I'm being judgy. It would just really suck if you guys had a bad break up. Things would be so awkward at lunch."

"Camille," I say loudly. "Slow down. We can't break up if we're not even together."

"Okay, okay." She links her arm through mine, lowering her voice. "Anyway. I got my own drama to deal with, namely Kyle...and Nando."

"Nando?!" I squeal, stopping short.

"Shh-shh," she says, squeezing my arm. "No one knows."

Except maybe Rigel. His cryptic comments over the past few days suddenly make sense. "My lips are sealed."

The Upper and Lower school fields are soaked, and there is minor water damage to some of the classrooms, but other than that everything's copacetic. I feel like I've found my groove in the weeks I've been at the Palms. I know which teachers to joke around with and which ones to avoid, which spots are the quietest for study and which are the most fun for hanging out. I'm newer than most, but I'm no longer The New Girl—and that's, perhaps, the best part of all. I have a place here.

Rigel's the same as always, playing footsie with me during lunch, sneaking peeks in history. I'm equal parts bummed we're not more after the past week and glad nothing's changed. Because the pool is still undergoing post-Carmen scouring, we spend P.E as a free period on the bleachers. Rigel sits beside me, but he's elsewhere, messing with his phone every time Archer walks the other way.

"Are you nervous about the meet later?" I ask eventually.

"A little. Not really."

"So what's up?" I ask him, shading my eyes. "You seem jumpy."

Smiling a little, he shakes his head. "Nothing."

After school, Camille and I run to the store for my mama before heading east. McKinley's parking lot is packed by the time we arrive, and I'm forced to circle a couple of times before a minivan vacates a space in the back.

"This is going to be intense," Camille says, making a face at a group of girls in McKinley colors. "Whoever wins competes against St. Thomas in a couple weeks."

Inside, we find a group of seniors from the Palms holding down a row of bleachers. They scoot over to

197

make room for us, and then Jasmine, who shows up with Brielle. Before long there's a bunch of us representing the Palms, mostly upperclassmen.

I spy Rigel's father in the first row down front. He's with a tall blonde and a slew of beautiful, mixed kids with hair like Rigel's. It's cool to see them here as an entire family, supporting their own.

Camille elbows me, pointing when I look up. "There's your boy."

Following her gaze, I find Rigel and the rest of the Stingrays making their way to the pool. With those broad shoulders, toned abs and tapered waists, their bodies are hard-won, sculpted and lean from years of training. Rigel's v-lines alone are paradigms of perfection.

"Make sure you take pictures of everybody, not just the captain," Camille whispers, grinning impishly.

"Shut up, I will." I lean against her, glad we talked. I never really kept secrets with my old friends, and I didn't like doing it with Cam.

Once the heats start, I move closer to the edge of the pool to improve my angle. The energy that crackles through the crowd is electric; it's hard not to get caught up in it. I manage several stellar shots, and I can't wait to get home and check them out on my computer. Coming to St. Croix rejuvenated my love of photography; yearbook has made me realize I can make a career out of it.

By the time the meet wraps up, the Palms is dominating. Everyone clamors off the bleachers to mill around the pool, spilling into the parking lot. Brielle, after talking to Rigel's family—which, I suppose, is her family—wanders over. "Get any good pictures?"

"I think so," I say, nodding.

"Can I see?"

"Of course." I turn the camera back on and hand it over, looking around for Rigel.

"Ooh, this is a good one," she exclaims, pointing to a shot I got of him on the starting block.

We're discussing her senior portrait when movement near the changing rooms catches my eye. I'd hoped to see Rigel, but the rest of his team has filed out and he's not with them. I refocus on Brielle, agreeing to a tentative "photoshoot" one weekend.

Jasmine clears her throat, touching Brielle's arm. "Hey, I have to get home."

"Okay; I'll see you guys," Brielle says, kissing my cheek. "Bye!"

And then it's just Camille and me in the dwindling crowd. Rigel's family is gone, so perhaps he left with them.

"Ready?" I ask Camille, securing the camera back into its case.

"Yeah, girlie," she says, fingers flying busily across her phone as she texts someone.

McKinley is about as far east as we live west. Camille and I chat the whole way home, stopping only to get milkshakes from the McDonalds drive-thru. I don't mention Rigel, because I don't need an *I told you so*, but he's definitely running through the back of my mind. I mean, I'm a little confused. Maybe I shouldn't be. Years of back and forth and *does he or doesn't he* with Benny should have taught me that there's no certainty with boys.

But it's a nice afternoon, the heat of the day fading with the light. The sky darkens rapidly, ruddy oranges and pinks cooling into navy and purple. I'm home in time to get Alex into his bath, where we splash and play until the water turns cold. Grandpa Harry makes his famous saltfish and dumplings for dinner, and we linger around the dinner table, talking until both he and my little brother are close to dozing.

Before falling asleep, I go online to see what sorts of liberal arts programs schools like Agnes Scott and the University of Georgia have. Minors in visual arts and film studies are compelling, and I read until I'm dozing off to fantasies of campus life.

15.

Rigel doesn't bring up his disappearing act the next day, and neither do I. It's one of those things that seems bigger than it is, inflated by over-analyzation. It's not like we're dating.

We're just friends...who kiss sometimes.

When I get to the pool later on, Coach Archer meets me by the locker room with a grin. "How're you feeling today, Isla?"

"Pretty good." I nod, returning her smile.

"Glad to hear it, because I'd like you to take your test today."

My heart sinks. "I thought I had another week."

"You do, but I think you're ready." She shrugs. "And I'd like to integrate you into the regular class for what's left of the quarter."

Chewing the inside of my cheek, I peek at the pool. The sun is blinding today, making the bright blue pool seem almost welcoming. I take a deep breath. "Okay. Can I take it again if I bomb?"

"Sure. But you'll be fine."

Archer dismisses Rigel a while later when he tries to get into my end of the pool. "She's testing today, Ri. You can join the class."

"Oh. Okay." He glances down to me. "Good luck."

"Thanks," I stutter, teeth chattering despite the warmth. I'm jittery from nerves now, so the faster we get this over with, the better.

In the end, my fretting is for naught, because all the time Coach Archer, Rigel and even Stan have put into my lessons pays off. There's no style to my strokes, but there is proficiency.

"That about does it," Archer says, jotting something down on her clipboard. "You've demonstrated each survival technique and swimming stroke required of you. You've passed."

Surreal. I can swim, well enough to pass a class. Relief, and a deep sense of satisfaction, wash over me. I can't wait to tell my mother. Hoisting myself out of the pool, I wipe water from my face and glance at Archer's clipboard. "Really?"

"Really. I'm proud of you, Isla." She gestures to the deep end, where everyone else is swimming laps. "Feel free to join the class."

Rigel's eyes meet mine as I ease into the water beside him. "You passed."

I can't believe it. I'm buoyant, in more ways than one. "I passed."

"I knew you would." He smiles, hand brushing my thigh underwater.

It's subtle, but the weather does start to cool some as the end of October draws near. It's most noticeable at night, and really early in the morning.

With the end of first quarter comes mid-semester exams. I'm confident in most of my classes, but I attend a couple of after school study sessions anyway. The Palms has proven itself to be much more rigorous than what I'm used to, and I don't want to fall behind. Between that and my mother's insistence I stop visiting Rainbow Beach so late in the day, I don't see much of Rigel outside of school. Not that it matters much. He's been training almost non-stop, two-a-days that start with pre-class practice at the pool and end long after his teammates go home in the afternoons. I get that he's driven, and that this is his future, but I wonder sometimes if there are other reasons behind the laser focus. Family stuff, maybe. Or school. No one trains like he does.

Late at night, we text. It started with a homework question, which I think we both knew was bs, and evolved into conversations that stretched over hours. It's both better and worse: better because I'm getting to know him without being distracted by all the physical stuff. Worse because I really, really enjoy the physical stuff.

Still, I like putting the pieces of Rigel Thomas together. He's squarely a middle child, with not just one older brother, but two. I remember Orion—how could I not? He made quite the impression—but I'm surprised there's another one.

Really? I text.

yeah.

Is he around?

he lives in St. Thomas now. he has a different mother.

Interesting. I wonder what this brother looks like, if he's anything like the genetically blessed brood I saw at the McKinley meet. Rigel's father, so tall and lanky, with dreadlocks tucked up in a hat I now know is called a tam. His mother had seemed his opposite, curvy and blonde, her skin as fair as his was dark.

Rigel's fallen quiet. It's nearly ten, and he gets up early for morning sessions, so I know he's tired.

are you close to him? I ask.

not anymore.

heavenly bodies

"Do ya'll dress up for Halloween?" I ask, examining the scrap of fabric Camille just called a dress. "Is this from junior high or something?"

"Or something," she says, snatching it back. "And I haven't dressed up for Halloween since I was twelve."

"Really? But Halloween is so much fun," I say, eyeing the hemline on Cam's dress as she pulls it on. "Damn, girl."

"It's a beach dress," Cam says. "You know if I tried to wear it anyplace else Mom would lock me in my room."

It's true. As feisty as Aunt Greta is, she's old fashioned when it comes to things like manners and dress. My mother's not much different; it's how they were raised.

"There is, however..." Camille's muffled voice trails off as she disappears into her closet.

I follow her, watching her hang freshly laundered clothing. She's got an outfit for every day of the year, I swear. "There is what?"

"A dance." She glances back at me. "Not a school dance. A jam, at a club downtown."

"And we can get in?"

She hangs one more blouse and pushes me out of the closet with a scoff. "Five dollars at the door, ladies half off until midnight. They do it every year."

I've hung out downtown with Camille and Jasmine a couple times, but not to go clubbing. I'm surprised Aunt Greta is even letting Cam go, seeing as it's a school night. Hopefully that'll grease the wheels when I ask my own mother.

Halloween falls on a Thursday. A parade of little kids from Lower School wends through the Palms for most of the morning, showing off their costumes as they collect candy. Stunned by Cranky Franklin's downright gooey niceness as she bestows Skittles on a tiny mermaid, I can't help but wonder what it would have been like growing up here.

"So you guys used to do this, too?" I ask Camille.

"Camille always wanted to be Barbie," snarks Nando, grinning when she narrows her eyes at him. "Always. Some things don't change, right, muñeca?"

"Twice, Nando. I dressed as Barbie twice, and at least I didn't moon the school when my clown pants fell down!"

Laughing at their increasingly hostile banter—the sexual tension is so apparent I don't know how I missed it before—I peek over at Rigel. He's already looking my way, and he leans forward when our eyes meet.

"You doing anything later?" he asks, inclining his head toward me.

"I might. Cam says there's a party downtown?"

"At Baobab Club." He nods, chewing his pen. "Nando wants to go...we might pass by."

Of course Nando wants to go. He and Camille probably agreed to meet up. They're stealthy, but they're con-
sistent—unlike Rigel and me; I don't know what we are.
I can't say I wouldn't love to kiss him again, because I
would, but there's something intimate about our late
night messaging, too. We talk about our families, growing up, siblings and irritating things mothers do. Little
things, big things. Pancake syrup. College.

We talked more last night about his oldest brother,
Daniel, and how close they'd been when he was younger
despite the eight year age difference.

why aren't you close now? I'd asked. *because he
moved?*

because he changed.

He's chatty today, telling me about his dad, and the
truck, and how they're fixing something that's gone
wrong with it. I like who Rigel is, not just the way he
looks, so I try to be a friend and not just a girl crush-
ing...but it's a tricky balance. It's hard to play cool when
he turns those tiger eyes on me, or when he steals chocolate from Ms. Franklin's Halloween stash and stuffs
some of it into my pocket.

And especially when, on the way to lunch, he slides
his arm over my shoulders as we walk.

My mother is not impressed that Camille is going to a bar on a school night.

"It's...not a bar, really. It's more like a party," I mumble, chewing on my lip.

She gives me the side-eye, barely missing a beat in the rhythm of her laundry folding. In the next room, Grandpa Harry curses at the television, berating someone for being an idiot.

I pick up a towel and fold it halfheartedly. "I always did stuff back home on Halloween."

She opens her mouth and closes it, and I think maybe I've won. But then she shakes her head. "Isla, you went trick or treating back home. Or to a friend's house. I know what the Baobab Club is. It gets a little wild, even when they aren't catering to your age group."

"Can I just go for a little while? I'll drive, so I can come home early," I plead. "Please?"

"If I let you go, I'd actually prefer you rode with your cousin." Sighing, she reaches for her phone. "Let me call Greta, okay?"

I immediately send a text to Camille: *looks good! fingers crossed she lets me go.*

In the end my mother relents, assuaged by Aunt Greta's reassurances that we'll be home no later than eleven, and that we're riding together. The good old buddy system.

"No drinking, Isla." Mom watches as I get into Aunt Greta's car, which Cam has borrowed for the evening. "I mean it. That goes for you too, Camille!"

The Baobab Club is bigger than I expected, though there are so many people milling around it's hard to move. It's also mostly outdoors, a bar tucked into one side and a massive courtyard in the middle. Jewel toned twinkle lights are strung across the dancefloor, tiny rainbow stars beneath the open sky. There's a DJ in one corner, and people both in and out of costume, dancing. I adjust my brown bunny ears, which I'm using as a headband. They're my little brother's, but he generously lent them to me for the occasion.

Jasmine and Brielle meet us near the door. We weave through the crowd, looking for people we know. Camille loves being the center of attention, so she and Brielle go dancing while Jasmine and I hang back, chatting with kids from the Palms.

The DJ announces a break and a slow reggae song comes on, mellowing the mood. Camille joins us, sweaty from her dance-a-thon and complaining about the heat. "Do you want something to drink?" she asks, nodding toward the bar. "I'm dying over here."

The crowd surrounding the bar is about three deep. We join the mob, waiting impatiently until we're finally at the front, where we order a couple of sodas. Jasmine gets a beer before wandering off. I'm guessing she doesn't have a suspicious mother waiting up for her.

A familiar face materializes from the crowd. "Where's your costume, Camille?" Orion grins, kissing her cheek. Unlike the last time I saw him, he seems friendly tonight. Relaxed.

"Hey, Orion," she says, kissing him back. "What're you doing here?"

"You know. Some old, same old." He winks, taking a sip of his drink. Now that I know he's Rigel's brother, it's hard not to search his face for similarities.

Camille rolls her eyes, but it's indulgent. "Slumming it with the peasants?"

"You again," he says suddenly, throwing me a wolfish grin. "Isla."

"Good memory," I say, nodding.

"Pretty faces are easy to remember," he says, eyeing me intently as he clasps my hand. What a flirt! Startled, I glance at Camille, who just shakes her head and whispers something to him.

"Seriously?" Orion says, visibly amused as he lets go of me. "I just saw him." He looks around, searching the crowd.

"You did?" Camille frowns, pulling her phone from her pocket. "Where?"

"Hey." I sip my soda, watching as she texts. "What am I missing?"

Orion cocks his head, watching me. "So, you go to the Palms?"

"Yes, I'm a senior."

Camille holds up her phone. "Nando and Rigel are here."

"Where are you from?" Orion asks, touching my elbow.

Distracted, I force myself to look at him. "Atlanta."

"Yeah? A friend of mine lives out there."

Everyone knows someone out there, but I nod politely. Glancing around, I search for the boys but the crowd's thickened since we first arrived. Orion takes my hand. "We should dance, Isla."

Tickled, I finally focus on him. "Why's that?"

"Because everyone wants to dance with me."

And then, in an alcove near the back, I spy Rigel leaning against the wall. My heart leaps...and then it sinks. He's with someone. And it's not that she's slender and tall, or that her glossy, black hair is so long it almost skims her butt. It's the intimate way she leans into him, touching his face and hair. The affectionate way he smiles down at her.

When she stretches up and slowly kisses each of his cheeks, I freeze in disbelief. He doesn't push her away. Stricken, I turn, swallowing back the burn in my throat. "Camille."

"What's up?" Her expression darkens as she takes in mine.

"What does Rigel's ex look like?"

"She's Puerto Rican. Lighter than me; long, black hair." She frowns warily. "Why? Did you...see her?"

211

I point to where I saw Mia and Rigel. They're back to talking, thankfully, but they're still way too close.

Camille follows my gaze, her eyes narrowed. "That's definitely Mia."

Meanwhile, Orion's standing between us, running a hand over his closely cropped hair. He touches my shoulder, and I turn blindly his way, trying to process what I just saw. My heart hurts; my stomach hurts.

"Forget him," he says. "He's full of shit."

I suppose he means well, but it's too soon. Wishing I could teleport home to the comfort and safety of my bed, I shake my head. "I'm okay."

"I mean it," he says. "I know him better than anybody...trust."

Camille takes my hand, but she's looking at Orion. "No offense, Orion, but this isn't about you and Ri's brotherly drama."

"What drama?" he asks innocently. I've seen that look on Rigel's face a dozen times, usually in the pool when he's teasing me.

"You even look like him," I mumble.

"You mean he looks like me." He smirks. "Come on. One dance."

Camille pries my cup from my fingers, giving me a little push. "Just go."

Orion takes my hand, pulling me to the center of the floor. Everyone seems to know him. He's quite charismatic, but maybe a little conceited, too. Still, he's a great

212

dancer, and despite the sting of betrayal, I force myself to enjoy the moment. I'm grateful he's around to keep me from crying. Honestly, I'm not sure who I'm more disenchanted by: Rigel, for being that kind of guy, or myself, for being the idiot that fell for him. I hate that Camille was right.

"Hey," Orion says, flashing a familiar dimple. "Stop thinking about it."

"Easier said than done," I say, wishing he'd just stick to dancing.

Keeping his eyes locked on mine, he swings me out and then pulls me close. "Don't let little boys get so close to you. They never know what they want."

"Little boys, huh?"

"Little boys." I must look dubious, because he adds, "I know," before spinning me so fast my stomach flips. A laugh escapes. I've never danced like this with anyone, and it's fun.

"That's better," he says, tucking me in close.

Orion keeps his word, walking me back to my friends as soon as the song is over. He's hard to figure out: I can't tell if he's flirting because he likes me, or because that's just how he operates with women.

"Thanks for the dance." He kisses my cheek. "Don't let him ruin your night, okay?"

"I'll do my best."

"I'm serious. You seem like a sweetheart, and he..." A shadow passes over his face. He shrugs, squeezing my shoulder.

Camille wanders over, holding Nando's hand. Guess they're on again. "You should just dance with Orion all night," she says, scowling. "Rub it in Rigel's face!"

"Nope." Orion grins, holding his hands up as he backs away. "Not going there."

Meanwhile, I'm wondering how much Cam's told Nando. It's not a secret, exactly, but talking about stuff with Rigel's friends is different than girl talk with my cousin.

"You should, though," Jasmine stage-whispers to me. "Orion's hot. And I hear he's amazing in bed."

"Don't listen to these two," Nando says, leaning in to give me a quick hug. "That's going from the frying pan into the fire."

"Why?" I ask, confused. These kids all know each other, sharing histories and secrets, but I'm still unraveling all of that. Times like this my newness to the scene is irritatingly apparent.

"Orion's trouble," Nando says, cocking an eyebrow.

"Right, because Rigel's such a goody two shoes." Jasmine rolls her eyes so hard I'm surprised they don't stay that way. "Come on."

Nando glances at me, scratching the back of his head. "Yeah, well."

"Yeah well, what?" Jasmine sips her beer.

214

"You really bringing up old shit?" he snaps.

Taken aback, I look at Jasmine. But instead of letting Nando have it, she just makes a face. "Whatever."

"What are y'all talking about?" I ask, confused by the turn the conversation just took. "If he's a player just say it. Damn."

"He's not." Camille cuts her eyes at Jasmine. "Not really. That, though?" She points toward the alcove. "Some cojones."

"We didn't know Mia was going to be here!" Nando says, taking a step back. "She was on Ri like white on rice as soon as he walked in the door."

"He doesn't really seem to mind," I say.

Camille's eyes go soft with sympathy. "You want to just go?"

I glance down at my phone. It's barely nine thirty, but I'm over it. "Okay. I mean, if you really don't mind."

"I don't." She whispers something to Nando, kissing his cheek before pulling away. "Come on."

Sliding my bunny ears off, I follow her through the crowd. A fast song with a driving beat starts up, hitting so hard I feel it in my chest. I look back at Jasmine and Nando. Rigel's with them now, his eyes following me as I leave.

There are almost as many people outside the Baobob Club as there were inside. Traffic clogs the street, music blaring from several cars. Camille steps off the curb and I follow, crossing between cars.

"Isla."

I ignore Rigel until he grabs my hand, and then I shake him off. I can't look at him right now.

"How's it going with your boy?" I ask Sage later that night. It's late, and we should both be asleep, but this FaceTime session is long overdue. She's still in her Halloween costume, some literary heroine I'm not familiar with.

"He's all right," she says casually, the pink on her cheeks letting me know he's so much better than that. "What about you?

"I'm...okay."

"What about that guy? The swimmer."

"Rigel." His name puts a stone in my stomach. I shrug. I'd half hoped he'd text me tonight, even after that mess at Baobab, but he didn't. Not that I'd have answered. "I don't know. I think he might have a girlfriend in college. They were off, apparently, but she was at the party tonight and they looked pretty 'on' to me."

"Wait." Sage frowns. "Are you serious?"

"Yeah." I close my eyes, yawning. "It's whatever."

"Really?" She's doubtful, probably remembering how starry-eyed I'd been about him the last we spoke.

"It'll have to be. I have enough on my plate without worrying about the hot island boy with wandering eyes."

"He's not coaching you anymore, right?"

"Right, but I still have swimming until second quarter starts next week." I yawn again. "Maybe I can convince Coach Archer to let me skip. I'll tell her I have my period."

Sage smiles sympathetically. "I'm sorry, baby."

"Me too." I look down, picking at the duvet on my bed as my eyes burn. I'm more let down than anything, but it's a crappy feeling nonetheless.

She nods once, and the way I miss her wells up so much that tears spill over after all. She bites her lip and leans forward, her own eyes shiny. "Isla girl. I wish I was there! I hate this. I hate it."

"Me too." Sniffling, I give myself a moment to regain my composure. "Maybe you could come around the holidays. For New Years?"

"Yeah." She nods quickly, wiping her eyes. "I have money saved up. I'll tell my parents I don't need anything for Christmas, just a ticket."

"Just a ticket." I laugh. "It's expensive. Maybe we can go halfsies."

"We'll figure it out."

16.

Despite our late night, I get up an hour before my alarm. After putting on a cute skirt I haven't worn since my Grady High days, I take a little extra time on my hair. I even put on mascara. Nona—Daddy's mother—used to always say that when she felt bad she made sure she looked good. It's become something I do, too. I need to feel confident today.

"You're up early," Mama says, looking up from her devotional and coffee when I hit the kitchen. She's had this routine as long as I remember. It's comforting and familiar, and for a moment I'm so grateful for that I hug her extra long.

"I know." I drop a kiss on her cheek. "But I have to pick up Camille, so it works out. I hate rushing."

"Did you call her to make sure she'd be ready?"

219

"Check." I hold up my phone.

"You look pretty today," she observes as I pour a bowl of cereal.

"Thanks." I catch the tail end of her private smile and sigh inwardly, knowing she thinks I'm dressing up for a boy. And in some ways I am, though not for the reasons she thinks.

Alex saunters in, climbing onto the seat beside me. Like every morning, his hair is a magnificent mess of knotty, bed-head curls. He unfists a small assortment of Legos onto the table and points to a long abandoned bowl. "Isla. I have cereal, too."

"I know, I saw that."

"Look!"

"I did, dude!"

He eyes my bowl. "That's my cereal."

"That one's yours, this one's mine." I tip the bowl back, finishing my milk.

"It's mine," he says, following me to the sink.

"It's ours."

"No," he says, but he's got the sauciest grin ever. Little imp.

Knowing well the futility of arguing with a four year old, I let him have his win. We share chewable vitamins and then I ruffle his hair. "Have fun at school today, Al."

"You have fun!" he commands, hugging my thighs fiercely before disappearing again.

Wanting to make sure Camille's ready when I arrive, I send her another text from my driveway. She tends to procrastinate, and we've already had a couple of close calls with the tardy bell at school. She's waiting on the porch when I pull up.

"Morning," she says, handing me an oversized chocolate chip muffin. Despite the fact I just ate, my mouth waters. "Oh, hey, I like your skirt."

"Thanks, I've had it forever." I sniff the muffin. "Mmm...chocolate. My kryptonite."

"Figured it would go good with coffee." She sighs happily, snatching up the cup I brought for her.

"You figured right." I cram a mouthful as I reverse out, reveling in the chocolatey goodness. "Thanks, Cam."

Waving me off, she washes down her bite with a gulp of coffee. "Okay, so, I was talking to Nando last night."

"After you dropped me home?"

"Yes," she says. "Anyway, he said the thing with Mia was a fluke."

"Ca-mille!" I moan, crumbs flying. "Why are you talking to him about this?"

"What? It's just Nando."

"Yeah! Rigel's best friend!"

"Jeez and bread, Isla, he knows you guys like each other. It was kind of obvious, even before last night."

I shoot her a look. She's probably right, but still.

"Listen, I don't know what it was like in your old school, but here, everyone knows everyone's business. If you're going to be hooking up with someone like Rigel, expect people to hear about it."

"Well, they don't need to hear about it from you." I'm whining, but I don't care.

"Nando. Already. Knew," she says, extra slow to make a point. "Maybe Ri told him, did you consider that? Anyway. After what happened at Baobab he wanted to know if you guys were actually a thing, and I said you kind of of were...and that Rigel's a dick for doing that with his ex, especially right where you could see." She sucks her teeth in disgust. "Nando says they're not like that, but what does that even mean?"

Indeed. What does that mean? Finishing my coffee, I pop a piece of gum into my mouth and park. Camille jumps out, but I fiddle with my phone, pretending to answer a text.

"I'll be up in a sec," I promise, giving her a small smile.

If she thinks I'm stalling, she doesn't show it. Closing the door, she hurries over to Nando, who's waiting by the steps. I check Instagram, killing time until first bell's about to ring, and then get out. Satisfied no one's around, I hurry to homeroom.

I can't avoid Rigel forever, though. I make it to history first, begging Camille to switch seats with me when she walks in.

"I love you," she whispers, obediently sitting in my seat, "but this is stupid."

"I'd do it for you," I whisper back, cracking open my notebook so I can scan my notes one last time before the exam. The test takes all of class, so it's easy to stay in a bubble.

Lunch is another story, though. As usual, Rigel sits right across the table, and from the second he does I feel him looking at me. I ignore him. Maybe I am being dumb, but avoidance has always been my preferred strategy. Seeing predictably gorgeous Mia all over him last night sucked. It was worse than finding out Benny was with Stella. Way worse.

Rigel's shoe bumps mine under the table. Twice. I look up involuntarily, making eye contact. He raises his eyebrows. Before he actually says anything, I cram the rest of my PB&J into my mouth and climb off the crowded bench. Camille and Jasmine scramble out after me.

"I heard Lower School has a bake sale today," Jasmine says. "Wanna check it out?"

They've probably talked about this, about how best to keep from losing me to the dark side of boy drama. It reminds me of something Sage and Morgan would've done, and I kind of love them for it.

"Muffins and now bake sales?" I shake my head. "You trying to get me to eat my feelings?"

"Hey," Camille says, dead serious. "It works for me."

"I completely understand, Isla. I have a really, really heavy flow at that time of the month, too." Coach Archer says, cringing with compassion. "And the cramps!"

I'm cringing, too. There's such a thing as too friendly, and this conversation just crossed that line.

"So you don't mind if I sit out, then?" I ask, gesturing toward the bleachers.

"No, of course not. It's the last day of class, anyway." She cocks her head. "Do you need to go to the nurse?"

Feeling guilty as hell because I'm lying through my teeth, I shake my head. "No, that's okay. I'll be fine."

Patting my shoulder, she walks away. Climbing to the top of the bleachers, I rifle through my backpack, content to use the time as a study hall. I've just started when there's a creak and then someone sits beside me. I don't have to look to know who it is. Rigel always smells like essential oils (his mother's into it), peppermint chewing gum, and chlorine. It's a clean, appealing scent, the sort you want to snuggle in.

"Hey," he says, elbows propped on the bleacher behind.

"Hey."

We're quiet for a long time. I work steadily on calculus, channeling all of my energy into completing each problem. Because, you know: math problems < life problems.

"I wanted to talk to you," he says.

"Okay." I move on to the next question.

There's a beat of silence, and then, "I didn't know Mia was coming."

"Yeah, Nando said." My voice is sharper than I intend, and I bite my tongue before I say something I'll regret.

Rigel exhales, tossing his hat onto the bleachers.

Finally, I look at him. He's eyeing me, his face hard. It's the same look he gets before a race. "It's all good," I say. "Camille said you kind of had a girlfriend, so..."

"No." He shakes his head. "I don't."

Oh, here we go. Scoffing, I shove my schoolwork into my backpack.

"We broke up last summer, before she went to college." He pauses so that I'll look at him—and I do. "Last night was...Mia catching me off guard. We were together for a while, and we've stayed close."

I nod slowly. "That's apparent."

"I know what it looked like, Isla—"

"Yeah, it looked like y'all are still together."

"We're not," he says. "At all."

I shrug, watching an ant crawl across the bleachers. "I'm sorry, okay?"

"Sorry for what, exactly?"

"For not being more upfront with her before she got that close." He folds his hands behind his head, closing his eyes. "And that you saw that shit."

"So it would have been better if I hadn't seen it?"

"You know that's not what I mean." He looks at me. "It just, it wasn't what it looked like. And I know that sounds like bs, but it's true. Mia's used to picking up where we left off, and she had no reason not to think that. Until now."

He's probably telling the truth, but it doesn't make me feel any better. Camille said Rigel and Mia were on and off, so it sounds like college is what broke them up. Do they miss each other? Am I a rebound? I look away, squinting at the sunlight glaring off the pool.

"But there are still feelings."

He hesitates, and my chest squeezes unpleasantly. "On her side, yes."

The afternoon light hits his eyes, making them glow amber. My chest squeezes again, but for other reasons...like relief.

"We talked about it last night, though," he continues. "She knows what's up now."

"Really?" I blurt. "Because I don't even know what's up."

Genuine bemusement passes over his face. "What do you mean?"

He's told me with kisses and touches, conversations and flirting, that he likes me, but we've never defined things. I thought I could keep up, that I didn't need labels for this maybe-relationship, but I deluded myself. It was easier to go with the flow when there no one else was threatening it.

"I mean...we've never really...decided." Ugh, why is discussing the relationship harder than actually having it? "I don't know what we're doing, Rigel."

"I like the way you say my name."

"Yeah, I like how you say mine, too." It's true. The way his accent wraps around my name gives me chill bumps. "But you're changing the subject."

He sits up so we're shoulder to shoulder. "I'm not with anyone else. Haven't been since..." Since we started kissing, I suppose. But his vagueness is annoying.

A huge cheer erupts from the pool, where everyone else is playing water polo. The one day I skip class, and they play a game.

Rigel flips his hat back on. "Are you?"

"Am I what?"

"With anyone else?" He's teasing now, the tension gone from his voice, and it loosens something in me, too. A little.

"Yeah, I'm secretly dating Stanley," I say, biting back a smile when he presses his thigh to mine.

He chuffs quietly, taking my hand. "You still mad?"

"Should I be?" I ask, staring at our hands. "You could totally be playing me right now."

"You think I'm like that?"

"I don't know."

"I'm not." His hand squeezes mine. "I'm not playing you."

I think back to what I've heard about Rigel Thomas. There's never any context, so I never know what to make of it. "Okay. But I think there might be things I don't know about you."

He narrows his eyes for a second. "There are things I don't know about you, too."

"That's true." I pause, choosing my words carefully. "I don't want to be mad at you, but last night sucked." And it really did. I hate that I feel this much for someone I've only known a month, but it is what it is.

"Yeah." He sighs, looking away. "It did. I messed up."

We sit quietly for a minute, watching the class. Or, pretending to.

"You gonna give me another chance?" he asks.

I smile, despite.

He leans over, kissing my cheek. I squeeze his hand, surprised he'd do this at school. "That a yes?"

"Well, I'm not with anyone else..."

Bright eyes like little suns, he smiles slowly and kisses me again, on the mouth this time. Stars shoot across the universe of my skin.

"Rigel Thomas!"

Archer's voice snaps across the pool like a whip, but Rigel just melts back, adjusting the brim of his hat. "Sorry, Coach."

"And Isla." She stands aghast at the bottom of the bleachers while our class looks on, snickering and whispering from the pool. "That is...not the kind of physical education we're doing, here!"

Jasmine crosses her legs, tilting her face toward the sun. "I heard from like three different people you and Ri were making out during PE."

My face burns, but not just from embarrassment. I feel warm every time I think about kissing him. "I wouldn't say we were making out."

She opens one eye and peeks at me. "Would've paid to see it, just saying."

"We barely kissed." I laugh. "Not that we should have been doing that at all."

"Not that anyone even knew you guys were like that!" Jasmine says, ditching her faux nonchalance to gape at me. "How long?"

"Few weeks." I shrug, brushing imaginary lint from my skirt.

Camille walks over, handing Jasmine a bag of jellybeans so she can finger comb her hair and stuff it into a sloppy bun. "Soccer tryouts are today. Nando's staying so I might just ride home with him."

Now that exams are over, I don't have after school study sessions. Reveling in my freedom, I take a few jellybeans. "I'll hang out for awhile, too."

Bass rumbles from the parking lot, low enough that the administration will likely let it slide. Nando and Rigel are parked beneath a tree, socializing with a few other guys. With a start, I realize the person Rigel's talking to is Orion. I can only see part of his face, but I know it's him. Side by side, they look so much alike.

Rigel's tense as he listens, one sneaker anchored on the ground. He says something and then Orion stalks off, getting into the Tahoe parked a few feet away.

Nando comes over, meeting us halfway. "Hey, nena," he says, throwing his arm around me. "You coming to watch tryouts?"

Rigel's reclining now, back to messing with his music. He summons me when our eyes meet. I guess we're really doing this. "I don't know; maybe," I tell Nando, kissing his cheek. "Good luck, though."

With a murmur of thanks, he leaves for the field. Rigel sits up as I approach, legs open, and I step into the space he's created. His hands settle on my hips. I rest mine on his knees. "What're you up to right now?"

"Nothing...you staying for soccer tryouts?"

"Do I look like I need another sport?" he teases. "I used to play, you know. Up until ninth grade."

heavenly bodies

"I meant for Nando. But soccer and swimming?" The breeze picks up, blowing my hair around. "Sounds exhausting."

"It was," he says, hands falling away even as his stare deepens. Something shifted at the pool today. Knowing Rigel wants this is exhilarating, but it's scary, too, like we're at the edge of a precipice. Anything could happen.

His song ends, and so does the moment. I glance around while he goes through his phone, noticing that Orion hasn't moved.

"So that's your brother," I say, watching closely for a reaction.

"Yeah." His eyes flicker to Orion. "Who told you? Camille?"

"I met him with Cam once, and then again last night." He frowns.

"He asked me to dance," I add, biting back a smile.

"Did you?" he asks, looking legitimately put off.

"I did." I decide to go for broke. "I think he was trying to distract me from...you."

Remorse flickers over his face. "Great. I can only imagine the bullshit he spewed."

"Why do you guys hate each other so much?" I ask.

"I don't hate him," Rigel says, yanking me closer. "But promise me you'll stay away from him, okay?"

I frown, glancing surreptitiously at Orion's ride. "I don't exactly go looking for him, but okay."

"I mean it. He's into a lot of shit." He tilts his head, squeezing my hips. "But that's another story for another day."

"You'll tell me, though?"

Giving me a kiss, he turns me so that my back is to his chest. "Mhm."

Orion's leaving now, his obnoxiously loud music drowning out everything else. Some of the crowd has moved to the sidelines of the soccer field, waiting for try-outs to start.

And there's Mia, presiding over a group of senior girls. She was a student here as of last year, so it makes sense she'd visit her friends. Still, her presence is un-nerving. I peek over my shoulder at Rigel, but he's talking to Maurice about car parts.

Mia scans the crowd, her gaze skipping over as if she doesn't see us at all. And I'd believe that was the case, if she didn't then fold her arms and turn the other way.

"Want to go somewhere?" Rigel whispers, resting his chin on my shoulder..

"Like where?"

"There's a beach..." He sits back and I turn around, creating some space. "I can bring you back later if you want to leave your car."

There's always a beach. Luckily, Camille rode in with me today so there's no need to come back. "I'll let Ca-mille take my car," I say, brandishing my keys.

heavenly bodies

She and Jasmine are sitting on the grass beside the soccer field, watching the players warm up. "Hey." I drop to my knees beside her, sliding my keys to her lap. "I'm gonna go with Rigel. Do you want to drive my car home? I can just pick it up later."

Her eyes light up as I knew they would. She's hated not having wheels. "Sounds mutually beneficial."

"Okay." I smile, handing her my keys. "Thanks, Cam."

"Oh no, thank you," she says, pinching my cheek.

I give Jasmine a friendly wave and return to Rigel, who's closed his door and looks ready to go. Retrieving my phone, I toss my backpack into the back of his truck and climb into the cab. He turns up the music and eases through the congested parking lot, stopping only to stick his head out the window. "Good luck, Nandito!"

We pass the Frederiksted Pier as we drive through town. It's a different scene than on the weekend, when families are out and kids are jumping into the water with ecstatic screams. Today just a few fishermen stand along the sides, setting out lines.

Rigel turns down the music, following my gaze. "When are we jumping off?"

"The pier?" I give him a wry smile. "What do you think?"

"It's a little scary the first time, nothing you can't handle."

I nod. "I saw kids diving off back there a few weeks ago."

He pauses at a stop sign. "You can't live here and not do it at least once."

"So I've heard."

"I'll go with you."

"Not today!" I say, grabbing his arm.

"Not today," he agrees. "But soon."

We pass Rainbow Beach and the rainforest road, heading further west than I've ever been. Less houses, more trees, the road hugs gently the coast, revealing flashes of water through gaps in the bush. Eventually Rigel pulls off onto a barely visible dirt clearing on the side of the road.

I unbuckle my seatbelt. "I don't have a bathing suit." The one I usually wear for P.E. is in my locker, still dry as a result of begging out of swimming earlier.

"Me neither," he says, sliding out of the truck.

I cock an eyebrow. "I find that hard to believe."

Grinning, he locks up and leads the way. "Come on."

Nestled behind the tree line is an almost hidden cove. Rocks jut out on either side, isolating a stretch of sand from rest of the coast. St. Croix never fails to enchant me. Every time I think I've found the prettiest, the most magical, something even better finds me.

We could be on a deserted island right now. I'd take a picture or ten, but Rigel's already pocketed his phone and keys and is starting to strip. He's welcome to—I'm certainly enjoying the view. I just have little desire to join him.

"Come on," he says again, a mischievous smile stretching across his face when he gets down to his underwear.

"You've got to be kidding me."

"Nope." He leaves his boxers on and struts into the water, looking every inch the swim star that he is.

I, on the other hand, have underwear that don't match my bra. Leaving my skirt and camisole on top of Rigel's clothes, I hurry into the water, grateful it's so warm.

"Does it ever get cold here?" I ask, wading toward Rigel.

"Define cold," he says, reaching for me as soon as I'm close.

The sun is still pretty high in the sky, but when it starts to sink, it'll go quickly. Vibrant and sunny one minute, leached of color the next. Right now it's postcard-perfect, an aqua lagoon framed by curving palm trees and fuller, denser brush. Prisms of sunlight dart beneath the surface like fish. The water is so clear that its depth is deceptive, seeming shallower than it is.

With a squeeze of his hands, Rigel hoists me up, wrapping my legs around his hips. Flattening his palms against my back, he brushes his thumbs just under my shoulder blades and brings me in for a kiss. I run my hands over his arms, his neck, the muscled curvature of his shoulders and back, touching him the way he's touching me. Being this close, wet, with so little between us, I feel everything.

My legs tighten around him. His hands slide, almost reflexively, down until he's cupping my bottom. Our kisses deepen until I'm lost in the slide of his tongue against mine, the way he tastes. I could do this all day, but eventually the fire calms and I pull back, hands linked loosely around Rigel's neck. He's breathing hard, Adam's apple bobbing as he catches himself. And then, because he's a guy, his gaze drops to my chest. I kept my bra on, but it's probably see-through by now.

My heart thumps. "I'm starting to think you just bring me to these beaches so we can...do this."

"I can't lie."

"I bet you bring all the girls here," I joke, watching as he tries valiantly to keep his eyes on mine.

"Just the special ones."

"Easy, cheesy." I roll my eyes playfully. "Who'd fall for that?"

"Hey, you're here." He leers, tickling me beneath the water.

heavenly bodies

Laughing, I shove off from him and swim away, not getting very far before he grabs my leg and pulls me back. We cavort around, splashing and chasing each other until I'm begging for mercy, giggling so hard I can't breathe. "Stop," I gasp, holding him at arm's length.

We float over to where it's shallow enough to sit and settle on the sand, bodies shifting back and forth with the current. After a while, Rigel lies back. "I used to do this thing when I was little, where I'd listen to the underwater. It's loud under there. Sometimes, if you do it on the right day, you can hear sonar signals from navy ships off the coast."

"Really?" I stare at the horizon, imagining.

"Mhm." He rests his hand on my thigh. "Come here."

I glance down at his peaceful face. His eyes are closed, and only his ears are submerged. Slowly, I unfurl myself and lie beside him, staring up at the deep blue sky. At first, the crush and fizzle of sand and rock caught in the tide are harsh, but as I listen I start to anticipate its rhythm. I find Rigel's hand, and we zone out for awhile, listening to the sea.

Rigel touches my stomach. I open my eyes, only just having realized they drifted shut. "Isla."

His voice sounds muffled, far away. I hear him, though, and I emerge, resting on my elbows.

"Let's go under," he says. "Together."

My heart skips a beat, but it's not romantic. I gaze at the surface, how it glimmers and gleams in the sun.

"You were telling me about that photographer you liked." His fingertips circle my belly button. "The one who takes pictures underwater. You could do that too, you know."

I don't admit I've thought the very same thing. I catch his hand and sit up.

"We'll go slow," he says, smirking.

"Okay. But the second things go south I'm done."

"Isn't that the point, though? To go south? Underwater?" he teases.

"I'm serious," I say, letting go of him.

"I know. I got you." He leads me into slightly deeper waters and goes first, sinking just below the surface.

I mimic him, going under for just a second before popping back up. Each time we go a little further, a little longer. I can't touch the bottom, I won't. Not today. But every time I go under the discomfort lessens. A little.

Later, we watch the sun as it melts down, hoping to see the famous green flash. Apparently, on clear days when there are no clouds, a burst of green light glints on the horizon the moment the sun sets.

"I didn't see it," I murmur, disappointed.

"Me neither. Next time."

"Have you ever seen it?"

"Couple times."

"Is it rare? Like seeing a comet?"

"More like seeing a shooting star. Not that rare."

I nod, taking one last look at the fuchsia sky before turning my attention to my hands. "We've been in here so long I'm wrinkly."

"Let's go," he says, running his hands through his hair. It's even blonder and curlier today, thanks to the sun and salt. "I have some towels and stuff in the truck."

A few months ago, I never would have imagined myself at the beach for hours, let alone in the water. Rigel pulls me up, and I follow him out of the water. "Thanks for teaching me to swim," I say, pulling on his hand.

He stops, and I walk into his arms. "Teaching the new girl how to swim..." His hands skim down my back, staying just above my behind. "Wasn't exactly a chore."

17.

"I'm guessing you've never been on a jet-ski," Jasmine muses, shading her eyes as we watch the boys race over the surface of the water. We're on the east end, hanging out at Cramer Park. I haven't spent too much time on this part of the island, but Nando lives close by. These beaches are his stomping grounds.

"You'd be guessing right." I slather sunscreen onto my arms, my second time in hours. It's a scorcher of a day, and the beach was already packed when we arrived, leaving no shady spots.

Nando's Uncle Manny passes by, gnawing contentedly on a chicken leg. "All you sure you ain't hungry?" He gestures to the grill, where they've been barbecuing all afternoon. "Don't play cute, you know. There's plenty."

241

We've already eaten—twice. If I consume any more potato salad I'm going to have to wear a shirt to hide my gut.

"You must want us to get fat," says Camille, accent deepening to match Manny's.

Scoffing, he ambles down to the shore where he flags Nando and Rigel down.

"It's about time." Camille jumps up, throwing her hair into a ponytail. It's getting long again, undertones of red in her dark waves. "I want to go for a ride before Manny brings them in."

From the depths of my beach bag, my phone emits a muffled beep. After a fair amount of searching, I find it, warmed to see a text from Daddy. We try to talk every couple of days.

Isla girl. What should I bring Mama when I come down for Turkey Day?

Happiness pulses through me. Wiping my hands on my towel, I reply.

Cookie butter! Lots!

perfect.

can't wait to see you!

me neither! gotta go back to work. love you.

love you, too.

Beaming, I tuck my phone back into my bag and poke Camille. "My daddy's bringing cookie butter when he comes for Thanksgiving."

"Oh, good." She grins, adjusting her bikini top. "I can finally taste it."

If my father was here, I think I'd be okay with staying. Like, one hundred percent on-board. Talking with Sage and Morgan always brings measures of wistfulness and nostalgia, but as the months go by, I find myself pining over their social media accounts less and less. It's hard to feel lonely when I'm never really alone...and anyway, I like it here. At first this made me feel slightly guilty, like I was cheating on Atlanta. But as the days go by and I settle deeper into island life, the thought of leaving makes me sad. Life here is unexpectedly full, not the hollow, pre-college placeholder I'd feared it would be.

The whine of jet-skis grows louder before cutting off abruptly. Propping myself up on my elbows, I watch Rigel wade out of the water, dragging his jet ski to the sand. He makes a beeline for our blanket, wiping the water from his face.

"It's now or never, Isla," he announces, panting slightly from his shenanigans on the water. "Manny wants to start bringing these in, so..."

Battling uncertainty, I get to my feet. Hurtling across the bay at sixty miles per hour is definitely daunting, but it can't be that deadly if Camille and Jasmine are already at the water's edge, vying for turns. "I'll go if you take it easy on me."

"Promise." Dimples flashing, his grin turns devilish. Oh, Lord. "Come on."

"Okay, okay." The jet-skis bob expectantly in the warm, shallow water. Uncle Manny tosses us an extra vest that Rigel helps me fasten, and then we clamor aboard.

"Ready?" Rigel squeezes the throttle and we start to move, rumbling slowly toward the horizon. Nando passes us, flying so fast over the surface he barely touches it, Camille hanging on behind him. I'm pretty sure the shrieking we hear is hers.

"You better not do that to me," I warn playfully, tightening my grip.

He guns it for just a second, making the jet-ski jerk ahead. "Like that?" he shouts, barely audible over the overzealous squeal of the engine.

Loosening my grip long enough to find his thigh, I give him a vicious pinch. Laughing, he heads for Nando, who's slowed enough for us to catch up. Camille wipes her face of saltwater, her gleeful grin speaking volumes. "Let's race!" she shouts, bouncing in her seat.

One of Nando's cousins races by with Jasmine on the back, creating enough wake to rock both our jet-skis. Nando responds reflexively, not even waiting for us to answer. He catches up quickly, and they speed toward the beach's natural curve, where the land juts far out into the water.

"Which way do you want to go?" Rigel asks.

"It doesn't matter." I reach back, tightening my ponytail. "This thing has enough gas, right? We're not gonna break down out there?"

Leaning to the side so I can see, he taps the gas gauge and then glances back at me, probably wondering why I'm such a worrywart.

Yeah, I'm being a killjoy. Grandpa Harry probably has more guts than I do. I point to the tiny silhouette of a far-off sailboat. "Go that way."

He starts slowly, gradually picking up speed, and when I don't protest, goes a little faster still.

"Okay, okay—just go for it," I yell. It's all the permission he needs. No sooner do the words leave my mouth we bolt ahead, gunning over the water so rapidly all I can do is hold on. I'm laughing and screaming, arms and legs clamped around Rigel like my life depends on it—because it does—and it's glorious, way more fun than I thought it would be. We ride out far, leaving the calm of the beach for the choppier waves further out.

Rigel releases the throttle, allowing us to drift with the current. The water is clear but indeterminately deep, shadows of coral and rock barely visible on the ocean floor. I've never been this far out, and I'm both fascinated and intimidated by the hugeness of the open sea.

"Lean that way," Rigel says, pointing. I do, and he stands, turning and sitting so that we're facing one another. "So what do you think?"

"I love it."

"I knew you would." He rests his hands on my thighs. I'm almost as brown as he is now. "You worry too much."

"I know." It's beautiful and wild here, the restless water a hundred different shades of blue. "It's not as scary as I thought it would be."

Nando and Camille ride by, waving. "Heading back in," Nando shouts.

Rigel nods, motioning for them to go on ahead. "We'll follow."

They leave, and he brings his attention back to me. "My sister's birthday is tomorrow."

"Little sister? The one who likes horses?"

"Only sister. She's turning seven."

"I remember being seven. I was into unicorns."

"That's funny; she likes unicorns, too," Rigel says. "And pegasus. Pegasuses. Pegasi?"

I laugh, because who knows? "So, anything even vaguely horsey."

"Pretty much." He plucks a piece of seaweed from the water, only to toss it again. "She likes gardening, too. Dad gave her a couple of rows to herself and they planted a bunch of stuff. She's always in the garden with my parents."

"I think that's a really cool thing to share with your mom and dad."

He nods. "We have an acre. The backyard stretches all the way back to the tree line and most of it's a garden...my dad grows everything. My mother doesn't buy produce."

"Because y'all have it already," I say, impressed. "My grandfather's got a garden in the back, too, fruit trees mainly." I pause, staring at our entwined fingers. "Someone else takes care of it now, though. He's not as active as he used to be."

"He had a stroke, right?"

I look up. "How'd you know?"

"My dad knows him, remember? Your grandfather used to bring his truck by to get serviced."

I smile a little. "I forget everyone knows each other here."

Rigel shrugs. "Well, yeah. We're practically neighbors. I think..." He bites his lip.

"What?" I ask, sitting up.

"He and my grandmother had a thing. Back in the day."

"What?" I gasp. "For real?"

"For real." He chuckles. "They went to school together."

I blink at the news, trying to imagine Grandpa Harry with anyone other than Grammie. "That's so weird."

A series of shrill blasts—an air horn, probably—sounds from the beach. Several people, including what looks like Uncle Manny, are waving us down.

"Shit. They're ready to go. Come on." Rigel flips back around so he's facing front and pats my leg. "Hold on, okay?"

We're back to the beach in seconds, scenery whipping by in a salt-sprayed blur. Manny helps haul us to shore, and then I climb clumsily off, legs wobbly from holding on. Camille and Jasmine are back at the blanket, shaking out our towels and packing up. I give my life jacket to Rigel and ease back into the warm water, wanting one last dip before we go.

A minute later he joins me, pulling on my legs and wrapping them around his body. "So, do you want to come?" he asks, squeezing my thighs underwater. "Tomorrow?"

"To your sister's birthday party?" I ask, resting my hands on his shoulders. My heart beats a little faster. Something—warmth, anticipation—bubbles through me.

"Yeah."

⌇

I wince, easing into Camille's car. "My legs feel like jelly."

heavenly bodies

Jasmine pats my shoulder from the backseat. "A good ride'll do that to ya." Her tone, as usual, oozes with innuendo. I've never met someone with so much sex on the brain.

Groaning, I yank the door shut. "I can't tell if you need to get some, or you get entirely too much."

"Wouldn't you like to know?" Her eyes meet mine in the rear-view, and she purses her lips into a kiss.

Camille slides into the driver's seat. "She needs some." She turns the air conditioning to high, which, in her car, is feeble at best. "Jas had a stellar run when we were juniors, but Orion's ruined it for her."

"Orion?" I turn around, eyes bugging out. "Orion Thomas?!"

She shrugs, but there's a smug smile on her face. I don't even know what to think of that. Between sly comments regarding Orion's sexual prowess and rumors he's got a foot in the drug game, he's practically legendary. I can't take any of that as word until I hear it from Rigel, though.

The drug dealer gossip, that is. His sexcapades are probably real.

I think back to the Baobab Club when Jasmine had joked that he'd be good in bed. "Unbelievable," I say, laughing.

"What?" She grins, sitting closer.

"You're good. I never would've guessed you two were hooking up."

Camille pulls out of the parking lot. Rigel's truck follows behind us for a moment before passing on a double yellow line and speeding off. "Jasmine doesn't kiss and tell."

"I don't need to, obviously, not with you around," Jasmine says, giving her hair a playful yank. "Talking my business like that..."

"Ow!" Camille snaps, slapping her away. "It's just Isla."

They start bickering, which is my cue to pop a scratched, old CD into the equally decrepit sound system and settle into the long ride back west. When we're close to home, the munchies kick in, so Camille pulls into Armstrong Ice Cream. It's been around for generations, a consummate favorite of both Grandpa Harry and my mother.

I'm texting her, asking if she wants me to bring any home, when Camille sidles on over to me. "I have an idea."

I glance up at her. "What?"

"We should get Black Stallions and have a sleepover. At your house."

I peek up at the menu to see what she's talking about: a boozy milkshake, of course. "Let's get Grandpa Harry one, too."

She flips her hair over her shoulders. "You think I'm joking."

"You want to, Jasmine?" I ask, poking Jasmine. "Sleep over?"

"Sure, just have to let my mother know."

I send Mom a text, asking if it's okay for Cam and Jasmine to sleep over.

That's fine. Bring home a pint of banana while you're there. Use your debit card.

Grandpa Harry's on the porch when we pull up. He fusses at the kisses and hugs, but he can't hide the pleasure in his smile. "I have to put up with this noise all night?"

I squeeze his shoulder. Tonight he smells like lemongrass and Vapo-rub. "We'll try to keep it down, Grandpa."

"You forget, I raised girls," he reminds me, tapping my hand so I'll help him up. He's been more honest with his needs lately, and while I like that he trusts me with these vulnerabilities, it makes me sad, too. I wonder sometimes if he's living on borrowed time, if last year's stroke was just the beginning.

Mama says he's doing as well as can be expected. She's used to this sort of thing, having decades in the medical field, but I'm not. I try to spend time with Grandpa Harry when I can, but between school and friends, it's not enough. Not really. I hold his arm as we walk inside, fondly sniffing his familiar scent.

"You want to watch TV?" I ask as we enter the living room, grabbing the remote.

"Not now, dear," he says, waving me off. "I'm going to lie down awhile."

I find Mama in the kitchen, getting dinner ready as she listens to Camille and Jasmine prattle on. Accompanied by her favorite Charlie Parker album and an ice cold Heineken, she looks like she's in the zone. I hang back for a second, watching her. She's always liked to cook, but back home work took precedence. Down here, though, she's home so she's usually in the kitchen. I'm ashamed to admit I didn't know just how good of a cook, especially of West Indian food, she was until we moved.

"What's for dinner?" I ask, tucking myself into her side. "Smells really good in here."

"Stewed chicken," she replies, twisting to give me a quick kiss. "Rice and beans and fried plantains. Why, you want to help?"

Camille backs out of the freezer, where she's probably just stowed our Black Stallions. "No one makes tostones like me, Auntie Charlene!" she says. Uncle Isaac is Puerto Rican, so Cam grew up with a slew of aunts and cousins teaching her how to cook Spanish food. She loves bragging about it.

Mama chuckles, nodding. "Okay, okay. Get washed up and then feel free."

I throw a salad together and then sit with Jasmine, who's helping Alex build his latest Lego set. He's pleased with the attention, but bossy, overseeing construction with an entertaining degree of acumen.

252

"Isla, please get Grandpa," Mama says after a spell, interrupting the assembly of a drawbridge. "It's time to eat. Alex, go wash your hands, honey."

"Mommy," he murmurs distractedly, frowning at Jasmine's attempts to connect two pieces. "No. It goes here." He points to a block.

"No, man, it goes here," she argues, holding up the instructions.

"Alex." Mama sighs, gently pulling him off his chair. "We need to set the table. And you need to wash your hands."

He huffs, stomping off toward the bathroom in a display I know would've gotten me a swat on the butt as a kid. Jasmine sweeps the rest of the unfinished set back into its box as I leave to find Grandpa Harry.

He's in his room, napping in the flickering glow of the silent TV. I softly shake him, not wanting to upset him; he startles easily these days, a result of his hearing decline. "Grandpa," I whisper.

Opening his eyes, he stares blearily up at me. "I'm okay, Charlene."

"It's me, Grandpa Harry." I pull back, still holding his hand.

"Isla," he says, shaking his head. "Don't worry, I'm not losing it yet."

"I know," I assure him, rubbing his hand.

He nods briskly, pulling away. "Tell your mother I'll stay in here. I don't feel like getting up again."

"Shouldn't you eat?"

"I'm tired, dahlin."

Determined, I straighten up. "I'll bring you a plate."

"Fine."

Back in the kitchen, I grab a plate from the cupboard. "Mama, I'm just going to bring Grandpa dinner in bed. He's tired tonight."

She nods, setting napkins around the table. "He spent a lot of time outside today, in the garden."

The vague anxiety lingering in my gut dissolves. Glad to hear there's a tangible reason for Grandpa Harry's lethargy, I plate his food, adding extra tostones. And when Mama's not looking, I stealthily grab the extra Black Stallion milkshake from the freezer, as well. Back in the bedroom, I prop a few extra pillows behind Grandpa Harry and set his food down on a bed tray. Placing the milkshake in his hands, I give him a saucy wink. "Got you some dessert from Armstrong's earlier, too."

"Hmm?" He eyes it, and me, slyly. You don't live on St. Croix for seventy plus years and not recognize these particular styrofoam cups from Armstrong's.

"Taste it." I tuck an extra napkin beneath his plate, watching him.

He does, and his face smooths into the best smile. "Ah. That's good. Real good, girl."

Kissing his cheek, I leave him to enjoy his meal in peace.

heavenly bodies

Jasmine's in the shower and Camille's chortling over Youtube videos when I slip away to find my mother. She's in her room, typing furiously away on her laptop, but she looks up when I pause in the doorway.

"I can come back," I say, giving her a small smile.

"No, it's fine." She closes the laptop with a quiet click and pats the bed. "What's up? You have fun today?"

We regaled her and Alex with stories of barbecues and jet-skis over dinner, but I wanted to chat with her one on one. "I got a text from Daddy. I told him to bring a ton of cookie butter."

"Yeah?" She presses her lips together in an attempt to appear neutral, but she's so obvious that it's funny.

"You're excited," I accuse playfully, bumping her shoulder with mine. "You miss him."

"Of course I do." She nods, bumping me back. "He's my man."

Gathering my hair to the side, I stare at my lap. Despite their rocky road, my parents have always loved each other. Leaving Atlanta—leaving my father—seemed so fundamentally wrong, and even though I understood the reasons on a logical level, I could never fully accept them. It still feels wrong. So though I've come to love St. Croix, I find myself feeling ambivalent toward my mother at times like this. If she and Daddy speak every day, why can't they just be together? So we can be together?

"Hey." Mama grabs my hand, squeezing it. "I still love your daddy. I always will."

"I know," I say quietly, squeezing back.

"It was never permanent, this separation," she continues. "Never. It was...just, necessary. Sometimes we have to take things apart so we can put them back together better."

I nod. We've had this discussion a dozen times in a dozen different ways over the past months. She squeezes my hand again. Damn. This isn't why I came in here tonight. I didn't want to dredge up the bad feelings I've only recently been able to let go of. Exhaling heavily, I force myself to look at her, alarmed at the tears in her eyes.

"Mama, it's okay. I'm...okay."

"You don't hate me anymore?" she whispers, smiling thinly.

"I never hated you," I say, regretting the days I froze her out. She didn't just lose the daily companionship of her best friend, my father, she kind of lost me for awhile, too. "I was just...mad. Scared I'd hate this place, and that it would hate me."

"It could never hate you," she reassures me. "It's a part of you."

"No, it's a part of you. I barely know St. Croix."

256

"It is a part of you, Isla. It's a part of Alex. This is where you come from; it doesn't matter where you were born. I know there are aspects of it that still feel foreign, but it's in your blood." She lets go of my hand to dab at her eyes. "Look how easily you made friends. That doesn't happen just anywhere."

"That was mostly Camille."

Mama rolls her eyes in amusement, standing. "I'm sure it was."

Her ears must've been burning, because Camille chooses that moment to poke her head in, knocking belatedly at the doorjamb. "I was looking for you," she says, waggling her eyebrows at me.

"I don't even want to know," Mama says, sighing. "Go on. Let me finish up here."

I give her a kiss, pausing. "Love you."

"Love you, too." My mama's crows feet and laugh lines are deeper than I remember. And I realize that, despite Daddy's absence, we are, in fact, happy. Like it's far from perfect, but it's exactly where we're supposed to be. We share a smile. "You girls keep it down, okay? I don't want Alex getting up during the night."

Camille pokes at me as we walk back down the hall. "We forgot about the Black Stallions," she hisses.

"I didn't forget." I raise an eyebrow. "I was just waiting on Jasmine."

18.

Morning dawns fair and warm, the sky a muted grey-blue smudged with wispy clouds. Complaining about the glut of homework she's got waiting at home, Jasmine has her mother pick her up while Camille and I linger over breakfast on the porch. I tell her about the birthday party I'll be attending later on, and she smiles knowingly.

Today is pivotal, I think. It'll be Rigel's first time picking me up, the first time he brings me to his house. We hung around outside last time, goofing around with Cam and Nando in the garage. This time I'm meeting his family. His mother. It all feels very significant.

Mama drives Camille home while I get ready. I'm halfway through my shower when Alex decides to make a game of throwing little dinosaurs into the tub. It's cute for about five seconds, until I step on one.

"Alex!"

Giggling maniacally, he tosses another one in. It lands on my toe. Before I can rip the shower curtain open, I hear Grandpa Harry's voice telling Alex to leave his damn sister alone. The door closes, and things are quiet after that.

Rinsing my hair one last time, I hop out of the shower. Admittedly, longer showers are one thing I miss about the States. Here, houses collect rainwater in underground cisterns. If there's a dry season (or a crack in the cistern, like the house Jasmine and her mom used to live in) the water can run out, requiring a water truck to come and deliver more. Everyone conserves water here—which, logically, is great.

Selfishly, though? I miss longer showers. I tell myself this is better for the environment, but damn.

After rifling through my closet about five times, I spy a pale yellow sundress Camille convinced me to buy from a boutique in Christiansted. It's delicate and strappy and sweet, with eyelet detailing along the hem. Perfectly useless in general, but pretty perfect for a birthday party.

"That's gorgeous on you," says Mama, watching as I braid my hair into submission. I wanted to wear it down, but it's not cooperating. "Yellow's your color."

"Thanks," I mumble, frowning at my frizz. "Is there any leave-in conditioner left?"

"No, I used it on Alex's hair last night," she says, tucking one of my stray curls back. "I'll get more."

Out front, in the driveway, tires growl loudly over the gravel. Larry starts to bark, which is rare, so I'm guessing he doesn't know the vehicle. It's probably Rigel. Finishing a hasty fishtail braid, I grab my bag and head for the door, only to find that Grandpa Harry's beat me to it. He swings it open open boisterously, clapping Rigel's shoulder. "I knew I recognized that truck. How you do, boy?"

"Can't complain, Mr. Evans," Rigel says, grinning, his eyes flickering my way just briefly before giving my grandfather his full attention. "How have you been?"

"Good, good. Thanks for asking." He steps back, allowing Rigel inside. "First the hurricane and now this. Didn't realize you were so closely acquainted with my granddaughter."

"We go to school together, Grandpa," I explain, cheeks warm. "And he taught me to swim."

"Hmm." He gives me the side eye before returning to Rigel, who's watching the two of us with a faint grin. "How's your father?"

"He's great. Doing a lot of business these days. I was telling Isla about his crops."

"Let me know if he has sorrel come Christmas."

"Will do."

261

"Hi Rigel," says Mama. "Good to see you again."

"You too, Mrs. Kelly. Thanks for letting me take Isla out."

"Of course," she says, all charmed as she looks at me.

"Be on your best behavior," Grandpa Harry warns, and I can't tell if he's kidding or not. "And give your father my regards."

"I'll be sure to," Rigel promises, and Grandpa shuffles away, presumably back to his armchair.

I give my mother a look, and she snorts. "Welcome to my teenaged years."

"My grandpa's the same way," Rigel says. "I'm used to it."

Wearing Star Wars socks and matching underwear, Alex skids into the room. He stares up at Rigel, uncharacteristically shy.

"Al, this is my friend Rigel." I ruffle his curls. "Rigel, this is my brother, Alex."

"Hey, little man," Rigel says, bending down to bump fists.

"Hi." Alex reaches out, taps Rigel, and then hides behind Mom's legs.

"Not too late, okay?" she says to me, even though it's only two o'clock in the afternoon.

"Okay." I give her a kiss, and try to grab Alex, too, but he darts away.

"You look like your mom," Rigel says, once we're in the truck.

"You think so?" I peer at myself in the sideview mirror. "I used to hear that all the time. Now people say I look more like my dad."

"Guess I won't know till I meet your dad."

"He'll be here in a few weeks," I say, light inside at the thought. "For Thanksgiving."

Rigel nods, pausing to look both ways on Centerline Road before turning onto it. The truck is quiet without music. "I like this," he says, touching the scalloped hem of my dress. His hand lingers, and my stomach wobbles at the feeling of his fingertips on my skin.

"Thank you."

His eyes are off the road just long enough to look at me. He flattens his hand against my thigh, and I rest my hand over it, keeping it there.

There are at least a dozen cars parked in front of the Thomas house.

Now the nervousness comes. Rigel cuts the engine and gets out, and I scramble to join him, not wanting to get left behind in this sea of family and friends. When he said birthday party, I imagined seven-year-old girls and their mothers. This looks like a wedding.

Perhaps Rigel senses my hesitancy, because he slides his hand into mine and leads me inside. Right away, I catch a warm, cozy vibe, like this house is lived and loved in. There's art everywhere: paintings and tapestries, sculptures on ornately carved, wooden stands. Brightly colored rugs adorn the gleaming hardwood floor, and plants hang from corners and beside windows. Faint strains of incense mingle with the mouthwatering aroma of grilling from outside, and fans blow lazily in every room. It's easy to imagine Rigel spending time here.

A group of children runs by, barely avoiding us as they scream and laugh. A beat later Orion lumbers after them, hands clawed, roaring like a lion. Our eyes meet before he disappears outside, and there's a sparkle in his eye I remember from Halloween. Rigel ignores him, drawing me toward the kitchen. "My mother's probably in here," he says.

The only white woman in the room, Rigel's mom stands out. She's curvy and tall, with wavy, dark blonde hair tucked into a topknot and a freckled tan. At the moment, she's pressed against the kitchen island, deep in conversation with another woman. They're slicing mangoes, oranges and strawberries and tossing them into a glass bowl.

Rigel touches her arm to get her attention, as if he doesn't want to interrupt her. She looks up at him, and then at me. She's got Orion's catlike green eyes, and Rigel's mouth and smirk, and she's beautiful. "Just a minute Joycie," she says to the other woman, setting down her knife. She wipes her hands on a towel and comes around to our side.

"Mom, this is Isla, and...Isla, this is my mom, Diana."

"Hello, Isla," she says, giving me a hug. Her accent isn't Crucian, per se, but it's not quite American, either, as if years of living here have seasoned it into something her own.

"Hi, Diana," I say, her first name foreign on my tongue. It feels so casual. "Thank you for having me today."

"Oh, so polite!" she teases, eyes crinkling as she grins. Rigel looks so much like her in this moment. "I love it."

Shaking my head, I glance at Rigel. "Can't help it...my mama's brainwashed me."

"Good!" she says, patting my hand. "She's a wise woman."

"She's Harry Evan's granddaughter, Mom," Rigel says, his hand resting on the small of my back.

Diana's amusement dies down, and she cocks her head. "No kidding? Charlene's your mom?"

"She is." It's a recurring theme: everyone knows everyone in this intricately woven island society. "I didn't know you knew her."

"I know Greta better, but we've met a few times. Long time back." She nods, just once. "You look a lot like her."

Surprised, I laugh a little. "That's what Rigel said."

"Because it's true," he says.

"Family genes run strong, eh?" Diana pushes a few blonde wisps from her face. "Speaking of which, is Camille coming?"

"I don't know," Rigel says, before I can. "You don't have enough people here already? Jeez and bread."

Sucking her teeth, she smacks him with the towel. "Rude self. Go on, show Isla around. Have something to eat. Uncle Jimmy brought passion fruit juice...there's a cooler out back..." She's already back to cutting fruit, chatting with Joycie. Rigel steps around the island to give Joycie a half-hug and a kiss on the cheek, saying something to her that earns a swat, he barely escapes, and then we're outdoors.

People, old and young, mill around patio. Built beneath a copse of trees, it's the only part of the backyard that isn't the garden. It's well shaded and indulgently green, so the heat is kept at bay. Balloons and streamers play in the breeze, and there are tables and chairs scattered around.

"Is that a hot tub?" I ask, noticing a small, covered, above ground pool near the house.

Rigel shakes his head. "Lap pool. I use it for practice."

I frown. "Oh. It's so small."

"It's got jets that create a current for me to swim against," he explains. "I'll show you later. I want you to meet Rory."

"Rory," I muse, imagining a little girl who looks like Rigel. "That's cute."

266

"It's short for Aurora...but no one really calls her that."

"Aurora's such a pretty name," I say, following him as we wind through tables and people. "Like Sleeping Beauty."

"Sleeping Beauty?"

"Yeah. The Disney movie?" I frown, digging around my memory. "Actually, I think it predates Disney."

"I know what Sleeping Beauty is." He throws a smile over his shoulder. "But I can't say I remember any of the names. Guess I was more of a Nemo kid."

"Ah, Nemo...the ocean. Of course."

We find Aurora and her friends having a water balloon fight, party clothes damp and dirty. Barefoot and squealing, they chase each other around, grabbing water balloons from a giant bucket.

"Leo and I filled those up this morning," Rigel says, nodding at it. "Rory insisted."

"Is he here? Leo?"

"Probably in his room with friends, playing video games. Mom'll force them out eventually."

"How old is he, again?"

"Thirteen."

Just then, Rory spies us and jogs over, a water balloon in each hand.

"Don't even think about it," Rigel warns, holding out his hands.

"But it's my birthday!"

"Too bad." He grabs my hand, pulling me forward. "Come meet my friend, Isla."

I give her a wave. "Happy birthday, Rory. It's nice to meet you."

"Thanks!" She grins widely, showing off a missing tooth. With messy curls, round cheeks and eyes like her mother, she's pretty adorable.

Several of her little girlfriends teeter over, giggling and grass-stained. "Hiii, Rigel," one of them sighs. I look at him, holding back a laugh.

But he just gives the little brunette an exaggerated wink. "Hiii, Mariely."

Rory gives me the once over, eyes landing on our joined hands. "So, you're like his girlfriend now, right?"

And it doesn't even matter that she's only seven; her question so catches me off guard that I go red in the face. I'm about to stammer something out when Rigel scoffs, wrinkling his nose. "Man, you're nosy," he says, giving one of her pigtails a yank. "Go back to your games, birthday girl."

"That means she is," Rory informs her friends.

"We're gonna go eat," Rigel says loudly. "Don't do the piñata without me."

"We won't," she says as we turn to walk back.

I'm about to tease him about his pint-sized admirer when a red water balloon explodes on his back. Freezing, he closes his eyes and shakes his head. I look back just in time to see the girls running away, squealing giddily.

"You did let your guard down." I chuckle, eyeing his soaked shirt. "She's got good aim, too."

"I'll get her back later." He shrugs. "It feels good, actually. It's hot out."

"You want to talk family resemblance..." I raise my eyebrows. "She looks a lot like you."

"Yeah? I've been thinking about growing my hair out. So I can do pigtails."

We might all be here to celebrate Aurora's birthday, but this party is more than that. I'm introduced to so many aunts and uncles and cousins and friends that their faces start to blur. Distant cousin Junie, a Rasta, catches us beneath the mango tree, explaining to me why it's important to eat ital. "Good for your mind and soul," he says sagely, nodding. "And for childbearing," he adds meaningfully, eyeing Rigel.

"Thanks, Junie," Rigel says. "Not quite there yet, but I'll keep it in mind."

"What's ital?" I whisper, following him to a tiki bar set up on the patio.

"Eating clean. Vegetarian." He gestures to a nearby table packed with every meat known to mankind. It smells like heaven. "The opposite of that." On cue, a large woman waddles over, hands on her hips.

"You eat yet, dahlin?" she asks me.

"No, I—"

She clucks disapprovingly, leading me over to the food. "Come."

269

"We just reached, Auntie Estelle," Rigel says, following close behind.

"But you could have still offered her something," she chides, piling my plate with rice and beans, baked macaroni, potato salad, chicken and coleslaw.

"You like goat?" She pauses, ladle at the ready.

"Oh, no—this is more than enough," I assure her. "Thank you..."

She peers suspiciously at my plate. "Well."

"Thanks, Auntie," Rigel says, kissing her cheek with a loud smack. Weighed down by his own plate, he nods for me to follow, and I do, over to an empty table.

"I can't get over how many people are here," I say.

"Oh yeah?" he asks through a mouthful of macaroni.

"Well, yeah. Is seven a major birthday or something?"

"All our birthdays are like this." He shrugs, looking around as if just noticing the crowd. "My parent's anniversary was like this last year. I don't know. I guess we don't need an excuse to party."

"But you're related to most of these people!"

"More or less."

"My mama was telling me about some of the island's bigger families. It's not really like that where I'm from." And it isn't. Not this big. Families like Rigel's seem to rule whole parts of the island.

"It has its pros and cons." He wipes his mouth. "If one person gets in trouble...then, in a way, so does everyone else. It affects everybody. But on the flip side, someone always has your back."

I consider how Orion's lifestyle probably affects the rest of the family. Rigel's attitude toward his brother starts to make sense.

Reggae blends into calypso, salsa and meringue, inspiring a few couples to use the patio as a dancefloor. No one seems to care when Rigel and I switch from soda to beer, although as the day burns on I discover I really, really like passion fruit juice.

"Try this," Rigel says, handing me a plastic cup filled to the brim. It smells like passion fruit juice, but tastes a little different. It's got a kick.

"Mmm." I moan appreciatively. "That is so good."

"Guava rum," he says, mixing himself one. "Not that strong compared to regular Cruzan rum, but it has a nice taste. You'd like the mango, too."

"I didn't realize you were such a rum connoisseur," I tease, licking a sticky drop from my hand.

His eyes fall to my mouth. "I'm a connoisseur of tasty things." I open my mouth to respond, but he grabs my hand and turns me around. "Dad, this is my girl, Isla."

I stare up at Raymond Thomas. His mouth twitches, probably in amusement. "Hello, Isla. Glad you could make it," he says, as if we're old friends. He extends his hand, and I give it a firm shake.

"Hi, Mr. Thomas. Thanks for having me; your home is beautiful."

"Yeah, it's our little paradise back here," he says, grinning. "You like the passion fruit juice, eh?"

"I love it."

"Rigel will give you one to go home with," he says. His light brown eyes, which already stand out against the smooth darkness of his face, seem mischievous—like his son's. "Have fun, eh? I'd tell you two to behave but..." He shrugs, opening a bottle of beer with the back of a lighter. "I rarely do, myself."

~~~

My hair's not as wild as I'd feared, but it's getting there. Gazing at my reflection in the bathroom mirror, I quickly re-do my braid with wet hands.

It's just past eight. Most of the guests are gone, and those who remain linger around the fire pit in the backyard, voices rising and falling on the breeze. I send my mother a text, making sure she's okay with me staying a little longer.

The hallway is filled with family photos, and I study them as I pass by. In one Rigel and Orion sit amongst a sprawling group of blonds; their coloring is darker, but their features are similar. I assume that's Diana's side of the family. In another, the silhouette of a boy leaps from the Frederiksted pier. There are Santa pictures and wedding pictures, proms and birthdays and portraits.

Dozens of school photos, including a full set of Daniel, who I've never seen before. He couldn't look more like Raymond if he tried, right down to the dreadlocks.

Toward the front of the house, near the living room, there's a large, open study. One wall is filled from top to bottom with books. There's a laptop and a globe on the desk, and a stylized world map hung on the wall behind it. Upon closer inspection I see it's one of those really old versions, with loopy, antiquated spelling and edges curled by time. Beside it is a map of just the Caribbean. I trace my way down the Leeward islands, finding St. Croix with ease. Here it's of considerable size, even amongst larger islands, but on most maps it's a tiny dot.

On the wall opposite looms a colossal map of the night sky labeled *Heavenly Bodies*. Divided by the Southern Hemisphere and the Northern, the stars and constellations are vivid and clear, tempting me to go outside and see which ones I can identify. I'm familiar with a few names, like the Big and Little Dippers, but then I spy a star named Rigel. I lean closer, squinting.

There's a soft noise behind me. Before I can turn around, an arm snakes around my shoulder and Orion points to the constellation bearing his name. And then he reads it aloud, in case I can't, I suppose. He's a little close, which I suspect is intentional, so I squeeze out from between him and the wall and flash a polite smile. "Orion and Rigel. I didn't realize...that's cool."

"It is, isn't it," he agrees, giving me a little smile of his own as he half-sits on the desk. "How've you been, beautiful?"

It's such a generic line, and yet somehow, coming out of Orion's mouth, it works. It's a very nice mouth—I can understand Jasmine's obsession with him. "I've been good. How about you?"

"I've been great." He jerks his chin at me. "So I'm guessing Rigel finally got his head out of his ass?"

Folding my arms, I give him a blank stare.

He eyes me slyly. "What?"

"Do you say stuff like that just to get a reaction?"

"I think it's a fair question. Last time I saw you two in the same place you were about to cry."

"Not that it's any of your business, but yes. We figured it out."

He nods. "You're a good girl. He needs someone like you to take care of him, you know?"

"What do you mean?"

"Keep him straight, make sure he keeps his hands clean and all that."

What the hell? I narrow my eyes.

"Come on, Isla," he says, grinning. "Figure it out. You're a smart girl."

Rigel walks in just then, seemingly unsurprised to find us here. Giving no indication he heard Orion, though he must have, he takes my hand. "You ready?"

"To go home?" I ask, not really wanting to just yet.

"Do you...want to go home?" he asks, lowering his voice. "We don't have to—"

I squeeze his hand. "I don't want to."

He squeezes back. "Let's go upstairs. We have to be quiet, though; Rory's already passed out."

"She had a wild day," I say, but my heart's pounding to be alone with him again.

"You really gonna act like I'm not here?" Orion laughs. "No introductions, nothing? Mom didn't raise you like that."

Rigel shrugs, barely turning around. "You've already met Isla."

"That's true, I have." He smirks, pointing to the constellations. "I was just showing her how Rigel's a part of Orion."

"And yet Rigel's still the lucida," Rigel says dryly. He tugs me out of the room but not before I see something like regret pass over his brother's face.

"What's the lucida?" I ask, once Rigel's closed the door to his bedroom. "La lucida?"

"The brightest star in a constellation." He points to himself.

I grin, because that's random. Really random.

He grins, too. "I was just being a dick to Orion. He makes it easy."

"Maybe so," I say. "But I have never met a family so into astronomy."

"It's one hundred percent my mom's thing," he says, flopping back onto his unmade bed. It's huge, and it takes up most of the small room. "The rest of us just deal with it."

I laugh softly. "I think it's interesting."

"I guess." He shakes his head. "I don't think about it unless I'm explaining my name..."

"Like now."

"Right." He smirks. "But my mom...she's always studied astronomy, Greek and Roman mythologies. All that stuff. She wanted to teach at the University of Vermont, but then she met my dad, and that was that."

I sit beside him, resting my bag on a chair. "Is that her alma mater?"

He nods, moving a pillow so I can rest comfortably.

"But you don't want to go there?"

"Not really. I mean, it's nice up there. Really pretty." He smiles, tracing the zipper on the back of my dress with his finger. "Lots of leaves in the fall. You'd like it."

Goosebumps prickle across my arms. "I probably would. I've never been that far north before."

"You should go."

"You should come to Atlanta."

"Yeah? What's in Atlanta?" he teases.

276

Me, I'd like to say. At least, me next year. "Everything. There's a ton of stuff to do."

"Orion almost went to some college there because he'd heard so much about Swim Atlanta."

"Orion swims, too?" I twist around in surprise.

Rigel drops his hand, nodding. "Used to."

"Why'd he stop?"

He quiets, lying flat on his back now as he watches the blades of the fan spin in lazy circles. Easing down, I rest on my elbow so that I'm right beside him. "Are you ever going to tell me?" I ask, touching his hair.

His eyes move to me. "I will...but not now. I'm sick of talking about my brother."

"Oh," I say. "Sorry."

"I mean in general. He gets himself into trouble and then it's all we talk about. All my parents talk about. Everybody knows Orion, and everybody talks about him, and I'm just over it."

I don't know the specifics, but I get it. And if it's too sore to talk about, I'll just wait until he's ready to tell me. I'm not here for juicy family gossip, anyway. I'm here because being close to Rigel Thomas is becoming my favorite place to be.

A door slams downstairs, and outside there's laughter, a lot of it. The tinny soundtrack of a videogame seeps from the room next door. "Is that Leo?" I ask, glancing at the wall.

Rigel nods, touching the hem of my dress again.

277

"What does he play?"

"Right now, it's Legend of Zelda."

Letting my gaze travel the room, I take in Rigel's things: posters of musicians—mostly reggae, but some hip hop, and more medals than I can count—all swimming, I'm sure. A new-looking desk littered with books and papers, a stack of folded towels teetering off the chair. Goggles dangling from the doorknob. His open closet is immaculate, everything hung neatly, a row of sneakers below.

Rigel's fingers trace down my arm. Heart skipping like a stone, I lie back beside him. Before I can wish he'd kiss me, he does, coaxing my mouth open with soft lips and a sweet tongue. He tastes like passion fruit, and I smile.

He pulls back a little, biting my bottom lip. "What?" he whispers.

I can't talk with my lip between his teeth, and I start giggling. He grins, letting go.

"You taste nice," I say.

Moving us up his bed, he eases me over rumpled sheets and past pillows. Sandals fall from dangling feet, delicate slaps against the wood floor, followed by the muted thump of sneakers.

We're wearing more than we usually are while kissing—our makeout sessions seem to always be at the beach—but being in Rigel's room, on his bed, feels more intimate. We're utterly alone, finally, and our kisses consume, each one tangling endlessly into the next. He tickles his fingers beneath the underside of my knee. I hook my leg over him, giving his hand a reason to chase the hem that's been distracting him all day.

Everything dominoes after that: he squeezes my thigh, I tighten my grip around him, which brings him closer, letting me feel what this is doing to him, which steals my breath. He moves intentionally now, pushing against me in ways that whisper he wishes he was inside.

A sharp knock on the door startles me out of my lusty haze, and I jerk, knocking my chin against Rigel's forehead. He leaves my neck slowly, eyes closed, panting. "Shit."

"Rigel." It's his mother, and she's still knocking. "You'd better not have Isla in there with the door closed."

"I'm taking her home now, Mom," he says, rolling off of me. I smooth my dress down, hormones barely in submission to my mortification.

"All right. Come back soon, Isla..." Her voice fades as she walks away.

"Sorry," he whispers, his smile saying he's anything but.

"No, you're not." Grinning, I lean over and kiss his cheek before sliding off the bed. "But neither am I."

19.

With the new school quarter comes a slightly new schedule. The first half of my day remains the same, and I keep yearbook, but I trade art for a course on news through photojournalism with Mr. Miller. The fact he offers this class at all feels serendipitous, solidifying my desire to go into this direction in college next year.

As for Phys Ed, Camille and I sign up for volleyball. The class is made up of mostly girls, and it's loads of fun, but I miss swimming. I miss it because of Rigel, of course, but also because a little part of me wants to get better at it.

"We can swim anytime," he says, at lunch.

"Not really." I frown at my carrot sticks. "I don't have access to the pool like you do."

"So we'll go to the beach." Rigel shrugs, brushing his hands off on his pants. "I have a meet Saturday. How about Sunday?"

Because I still cover sports for yearbook, I'm at most of Rigel's meets. It's inspiring to watch someone like him do what he loves. Like the more serious kids on the team, Rigel's dream is the Olympics. I see it when he races, in the way he focuses when it's time—and even later on, looking over the photos I've taken.

It's hard not to obsess over the future, where we'll end up at college. I know I'll be in Atlanta, but Rigel can swim anywhere. He's said he likes the Southeast, but that does little to narrow things down, especially when common sense says he'll go with whomever gives him the best scholarships and financial aid packages.

"So talk to him about it," Sage says one night, over Facetime.

"We've been together for a month." I pause, mentally counting on my fingers. "I think."

"You mean like officially? That doesn't matter...it's obviously on your mind," she argues, wrestling her hair into a ponytail. It's a lot shorter than it used to be.

"Discussing college feels like jumping the gun."

"How is that jumping the gun? Don't you guys have guidance counselors talking to you about college already?"

"That's different."

"You're avoiding."

"Yep."

"You're being dumb." She yawns, flopping back into her blankets.

I stick my tongue out at her, but she's right. Maybe I am being kind of dumb.

Rigel grabs the last cookie, eyes closed as he pops the whole thing into his mouth. "Amaaa-fing," he mumbles.

It's Friday night and we're in my kitchen, eating the cookies I made earlier. My mother's usually the one doing the baking, but I took initiative tonight, wanting to introduce Rigel to the wonders of cookie butter. Dad, realizing how much I missed the stuff, priority mailed a jar so I wouldn't have to wait until Thanksgiving. I nearly cried, partly because I miss him and this was so sweet, but also because cookie butter is so damn divine. Rigel was a little confused as to why one would make cookies out of butter that had once been cookies, but he's a believer now.

"I'll keep in mind you like these," I say, eating a spoonful of the stuff straight from the jar. It's pretty much gone.

"I love them," Rigel corrects, patting his belly. "Feel free to make them, or any cookies, again. I'm an equal-opportunity cookie lover."

Alex shuffles in, rubbing his eyes. Unlike the last time these two met, he's clothed—in Star Wars Lego jammies. He pauses when he sees Rigel, eyes sliding to the crumbs on the empty cookie plate.

"Hey, Alex," Rigel says, taking a swallow of milk. I tried to give him sweet tea, one of my favorites from home, but he wasn't too into that.

"Hi." Alex yawns, leaning against me. "Isla, you have cookies?"

"I saved you some, buddy. For tomorrow, okay?"

He nods, pushing his face into my thigh. Bending, I pick him up and give him a good snuggle. He's always most compliant right before bed, all warm and sleepy. "Sweet dreams, little man."

Allowing himself to be kissed just for a moment, he wiggles promptly back to the ground. "Can I have water?"

"Magic word."

"Please."

"Sure." I pour him a small cup of water, which he sips carefully before disappearing again.

"You about ready to go?" Rigel asks, distracted by his phone.

"Yeah. I'll let my mama know."

I find her in Alex's room, helping him choose a book for bedtime. They look up when I peek in. "We're leaving now, okay?"

"You're going to see a movie, right?" She tucks Alex, settling beside him.

I nod. "And maybe Jump Up, afterward."

"Jump Up is always a good time." She beckons me closer and I go, hugging her. "Be careful downtown, okay baby?"

"I will." Biting my lip, I take a couple of steps backward. "Can I stay out a little later tonight?"

"How late?" she asks, raising an eyebrow.

"I want this one, Mamamamama," Alex butts in, squirming restlessly with his book.

"I...I'm not sure. But I just want to hang out with him." Cheeks warm, I almost whisper the last part. "I feel like there's never enough time."

Her face softens, and she smiles, scooping my brother into her lap to settle him. She always did that with me, too. "One thirty," she says. "Text me if you're running late, though."

It's a brisk evening, the coolest I've felt on St. Croix so far. It's no Georgia in November, but I bring a hoodie just in case. Rigel's got the windows in the truck rolled down and the music set low.

Hands resting on the wheel, he watches me mess around with my seatbelt and then my bag, searching for gum. "So what do you want to do tonight?"

"I thought we were going to the movies."

"I thought that was code for something," he says, features lit up by the electric blue of his dashboard.

"Yeah, code for there's a movie I want to see." I poke his thigh. "We don't have to go if you don't want to, though."

"We can go. I haven't been to the movies in a while," he says, tapping the wheel. "Let me see what my brother Leo's up to. He's always hanging out in Sunny Isles...he might want a ride."

"What grade is he in, again?"

"Eigth."

"Yeah. I remember doing stuff like that in junior high." I smile, remembering. "We'd tell our mothers we were going to see a movie, but then we'd hang out instead."

"We did, too." He smirks before straightening suddenly, phone to his ear. "Leo! Hey, want a ride to Sunny Isles?"

Back home, cinemas were a dime a dozen. Mainstream, artsy, independent, discount— from the Plaza

Theater in our neighborhood to the AMC in Buckhead where you could eat a meal while watching your movie. Moviegoing was a thing for my friends, and we went all the time—even when we got old enough to do other stuff.

This is my first time going on St. Croix, and while the theater is smaller than what I'm used to, it's no less crowded. After loading up on popcorn, candy and soda, we squeeze into theater seven to watch the creepy slasher flick I've wanted to see.

"Now this surprises me." Rigel chuckles as the previews start. "I never would've guessed you were into movies like this."

"Oh, really? Well. Looks can be deceiving." I grab a handful of the excessively buttery popcorn we're sharing. "I like scary books, too."

Sitting back in his seat, he grins smugly. "That's...interesting."

"Why?"

"You know," he says, reaching into the tub of popcorn. "The link between horror and sex?"

"Really, Rigel?" Our fingers slide together on their mutual quest for more popcorn. "Why do guys always have to go there?"

He smiles real slow, popping a kernel into his mouth. "I don't know."

Ugh, he's cute. Snatching the bucket, I turn my eyes to the screen. "While we're on topic, don't think I'm naive as to why we're sitting in the back row."

He leans close. "Yeah?"

"Mhm."

"Then I guess it's the same everywhere, eh?" He kisses my ear before stealing back the popcorn.

It's Friday night, so the theater fills to capacity fast. A couple of kids from the Palms pass on their way down front, and Rigel says hi to so many people I start calling him the Mayor.

"St. Croix is small," he says, opening a bag of Reese's Pieces. "You'll know everyone by the time you go to college, too."

"Maybe."

He nods emphatically. "Definitely."

The guy in front of us turns, bumping fists with Rigel. After a quick introduction—Taylor; he's one of McKinley's top swimmers— they talk college and scholarships. I half-listen for clues, wiping my hands on my jeans so I can reply to an incoming text from Morgan.

Eventually, the house lights go down as the movie starts. Putting my phone away, I tear open another bag of candy and start searching for reds and purples.

"No picking colors," Rigel says, leaning in again. "You'll ruin the ratio."

"They're my Skittles," I retort, eating a small handful before he deftly snatches the bag from me.

heavenly bodies

Despite my back-row observations, we make it through the movie with minimal kissing. The plot's good, juicy enough that we're actually paying attention. Besides, making out gets weird when there's screaming and savagery on-screen. Afterward, we find Leo in a crowd of middle and high school kids by the fountain. Though we met briefly at Rory's birthday party, I don't really know Leo. He seems like a cool kid, quiet and serious. At thirteen he's gangly and tall, sneakered feet so huge it's a wonder he doesn't trip over them.

In the truck, Rigel and Leo chat easily. It's obvious they have a close relationship marked by deep, mutual affection. I'm glad. That's real, and it's important, especially considering Rigel's strained relationship with Orion.

"Thanks, Ri," Leo murmurs before getting out of the truck. Hesitating just outside, he glances back at me. "Um, bye, Isla."

"Bye, Leo." I smile as I scoot back over. "Have fun."

"You got all your stuff?" Rigel asks as Leo makes his escape. "Your phone?"

Leo nods, patting his backpack before jogging up the driveway of a palatial blue house with concrete lions on either side of the front door. Waiting until he disappears inside before pulling away, Rigel drops his phone into my lap. "Will you text my Mom? Tell her we dropped Leo off at Ahmad's."

~~

We're running late because of the movie, but Christiansted is still crowded when we arrive. Jump Up is an official street party that happens four times a year—restaurants, pubs and shops stay open late, and there's always live music and street performers. I've never been, but it's all anyone's talked about lately, so I'm excited to go.

Rigel finally finds a parking space on a side street, and I shoot Camille a text, letting her know we're minutes away.

I receive a text back. "They're at...Mateo's?"

"A lounge." Rigel nods, locking his truck. "We play pool there sometimes."

The streets are jammed with food trucks, tourists, drunks and several exhausted looking parents carrying passed out children. Mocko Jumbies amble by on sky-high stilts, masks and costumes fluttering in the salty breeze coming off the wharf. Mateo's is a couple of blocks down on Strand Street. Like most of the establishments on Strand, it's dark and loud inside. A polished, wooden bar stretches across one wall, a row of booths along the other. Pool tables sit in the middle, all of them occupied.

Beneath the glow of dim, blue lighting, Jasmine and Kyle are in a booth with Brielle and Maurice. Camille's nowhere to be seen. After we say hello to everyone, Rigel turns to me. "You want anything from the bar?"

I squeeze into the booth, setting my purse down. "Are you having anything?"

"I'll probably have a greenie."

A Heineken. "Sounds good."

Jasmine puts her phone away, turning to me. She's rocking kohl eyeliner tonight, playing up the Indian in her Trinidadian blood. "So you guys just got to town?"

"Yeah. We went to the movies first."

"Oh, what'd you see?"

"*Obsecration.*"

"Ew! I heard that was so scary!" Jasmine says, eyes alight.

"It was," I agree. "But I like that kind of stuff."

"Not me," she says with a shiver. "I'd be up all night if I watched that."

I glance around, looking for my cousin. Why tell me to meet her if she was just going to dip out? I pull Jasmine closer. "Hey, where's Cam? I literally just talked to her, and she said y'all were here together."

"Oh." Jasmine shakes her head, disgusted. "She and Nando had it out."

"In the time it took for us to get here?" I ask, incredulous.

"Yes, girl."

Trying to keep things chill, I lower my voice a little more. "Was it about Kyle?"

Jasmine nods.

"Huh. I thought she would've figured it out by now." But an inkling of guilt squirms through me. I've been letting Cam put me off whenever we discuss boys, figuring she'd spill when she needed to, but now I feel selfish. I should've pressed her, made her tell me what was going on. I know how adept she is at playing things off, even when she's hurting.

"Nando's liked her for awhile. Not Kyle, though. He just wants to hook up." She pauses. "She was into it for awhile, but I think she's catching real feelings for Nando."

"Wow." I don't know what else to say. Camille and Nando have been close forever, but this aspect of their relationship definitely complicates things. Rigel returns with our beer, and I scoot over, making room for him. "Was Nando drunk?"

"Not really," Jasmine says. "Anyway—there's your girl."

Camille squeezes between Kyle and Brielle, giving me a quick wave. "You guys finally made it."

"Hey, Cam." I give her a smile, but she's obviously upset, lowering her eyes as Kyle whispers something in her ear. She looks seconds away from tears.

"What's going on?" Rigel asks, either not picking up on Cam's lame attempts at hiding her distress, or not caring. "What happened?"

"Nothing." Camille waves her hand, taking a long sip of her drink.

Considering how tight Rigel and Nando are, though, he probably already knows. "You want to play?" he asks me, looking the pool tables. Maurice is already over there, racking the balls.

Sipping the beer he brought me, I shake my head. I need to talk to Camille. "No, go ahead."

"You sure?"

"Maybe later."

"I can teach you if you don't know how," he offers.

Little does he know I'd probably kick his butt at pool. My friends and I spent many summers in Morgan's garage, being schooled by her older brothers. I smirk at Rigel's earnest expression. "Oh, I know how. But thanks."

His eyes widen. "It's like that? You definitely have to play me one day, then."

"I will."

"I'll play," Kyle offers. Rigel nods, grabbing his greenie, and they leave to join Maurice.

Brielle launches into a story of someone caught cheating at school last week. I'm seconds from demanding Camille fill me in on the Nando and Kyle situation when Orion saunters up to our table, flanked by three guys I've never met. He looks good tonight, his hair cut in a fresh fade. Jasmine's practically vibrating beside me.

"Ladies," he says, grinning at us. "How's it going, Bri?"

Brielle smiles, standing and leaning across the table to hug him. "Everything's good, cuz. You?"

"Can't complain," he says, he's already distracted by Jasmine. "Princess Jasmine. Where you been hiding?" She levels him with a glare, but he bends and kisses her cheek anyway, laughing when she shoves him off. Things must be sour between them at the moment. His eyes alight on me. "Isla."

"Hey, Orion." I fiddle with my purse, uncomfortable with the way his friends are watching.

Leaning down, he kisses my cheek. "My brother here?"

"He's playing pool," I reply, craning my head to see across the room. "Right over there."

Rigel's already looking warily our way as he rubs blue chalk onto the tip of his stick. Orion straightens, giving us a half-smile. "Thanks. See you."

Jasmine and Brielle resume their conversation, but I'm watching the group circled around the pool table. The Thomas boys stand closely, bodies tense as if ready to spring. It's obvious Orion's trying to convince Rigel of something, who remains impassive with the world's best poker face. I'm relieved when Orion and his friends stroll back out of the lounge.

"What did he want?" I ask, joining Rigel a minute later.

He shakes his head, hardening his jaw. "They're meeting somebody tonight...and he wanted me and

294

Nando to come. Told him Nando left already, and that I had you. So..."

"Why would he want you to go?" I ask, genuinely puzzled.

He sighs, facing me fully. "Back up."

"Back up?" A thousand thoughts flood my mind, none of them good. "For what? A fight?"

"A deal." His eyes burn into mine, searching, asking me to understand without further explanation.

And I do; I get it.

20.

East End is lovely by day, with rolling, green hills and peaceful ocean views, but at night the serpentine roads are so isolated that it's a little eerie. We're deep in the countryside now, where houses are few and far between, their lights so far away they might as well be stars.

My mind's wandering. I'm thinking about Camille, and how out of it she was when we'd said our goodbyes tonight.

you okay? I text. *let's talk soon.*

"There's this beach..." Rigel begins, turning down the music.

"There's always a beach with you," I tease.

He glances my way, eyes traveling over me, and my stomach flips at the intention in his eyes. His phone beeps. He glances down at it, and then, scowling, abruptly pulls off onto the side of the road. "You've got to be kidding me."

"What?" I ask, alarmed, although my gut is telling me exactly what before it even leaves his mouth.

"Orion." He slams his hand against the steering wheel. "I knew this shit was gonna happen. I told him." Furious, he types something back.

"Is he okay?"

"Hell no, he's not okay," he spits, dropping the phone on my lap. Taking a long look down either side of the pitch black road, he wrenches the truck around and starts gunning back the way we came. "Answer him for me, if he texts again."

This is a side of Rigel I've never seen, and I realize, thinking about the times I've seen him with Orion, that his brother seems to bring out the worst in him. By the way he's driving, whatever's happening now must be major.

Sure enough, the phone beeps again.

second to last building. txt when u reach.

I read the message aloud, looking at Rigel. "Where is he?"

"Down by Redbrick." We make eye contact, and he softens, squeezing my thigh. "Housing projects right outside town." He looks conflicted, as if he isn't sure whether or not he wants to fill me in. I think it's obvious he has to now, though.

heavenly bodies

"So Orion sells. I knew that. I mean, I've heard," I say, gazing out the window. Flickers of my reflection on the glass play against the dark, blurred landscape outside. It's just past eleven, and we're the only car on the road.

"He sells weed, sometimes coke," Rigel says.

I wait, and when it seems like he's not going to go any further, I touch his knee. "Tell me. How'd he start?"

"His senior year. He and Daniel were thick as thieves."

"Your half brother?"

"Yes. The oldest." He nods briefly. "The two of them would hang with guys from Marley—"

"What's that?"

"More projects, down west though. By Frederiksted."

I nod, listening.

"My dad had joint custody, so Daniel didn't live with us full time. His mother lived maybe ten minutes away, so he split his time between her house and ours. My parents are strict—especially my dad—but when Daniel stayed by his mom's, he was allowed to do whatever. He hated school, hated rules...ironically the only person he really respected was my mom, and that's because she expected more out of him. And because she showed him more love than anybody else did."

"Do they talk now? Daniel and your mom?"

"They keep in touch."

"But you don't?"

"Not really. I mean, when we were younger we were kind of close, but Orion was always his boy. When Daniel graduated and started living at the UVI dorms, Orion would drive down and hang out until my mom called him for dinner. We didn't know it then, obviously, but they were usually at Marley. They started having cash all the time, buying clothes, stuff for their cars...toys for Leo and Rory and Phoenix."

"Flaunting it."

"Like idiots. You can leave campus for lunch when you're a senior and Orion would go every day, bringing me back food from restaurants—it was ridiculous but I didn't mind it at the time." He cracks a smile. "Anyway, it took awhile, but my parents started to notice."

"What'd they do?"

"They thought it was mostly Daniel at first. I mean, Orion was on honor roll...swim team...all of that. But he started coming home late, sometimes missing swim practice. The casual cash...all the time. Things started adding up. Eventually Coach Archer called my mother to tell her he'd missed another practice. Mom tried calling Orion, but she couldn't reach him, and when he finally got home it was really, really late. My parents grounded him after that, but he'd find ways to sneak out, especially on the weekends. I thought my Dad was going to kill him one night."

"Did they fight?"

"Yeah. Orion came home drunk, acting like an ass, and my dad came this close to clocking him in the face. The next morning my mom was going through his car and she found a bunch of baggies and a scale. And that was it. They took his car away and grounded him. He couldn't go anywhere but school for awhile. Daniel's mom had moved to St. Thomas, so my dad arranged for Daniel to transfer to the UVI campus there. It was mostly to keep him away from Orion...and us."

"It didn't matter, did it?" I ask, thinking about the version of Orion I saw tonight. Hard, aloof.

"Not a bit." He chuckles darkly. "Daniel was gone, but Orion was already deep in the game."

I sit back, contemplating the story he's just told me. It's no worse than anything my imagination has conjured up, but I get why he was reluctant to share. The phone vibrates, this time with an unrelated message from Nando. I read it aloud, but Rigel motions for me to ignore it, slowing as we leave East End for the more populated neighborhoods outside town.

"But that's not why you stopped talking to Orion, is it?" I ask, wondering if something else happened.

"No." He stops for a light. "We were still really tight at that point. I was in tenth grade, and I still looked up to him. My parents would let him use the car to go to school so he could drive me. We'd stay after to swim, like old times." He smiles ruefully. "Everyone thought we'd end up in the Olympics together."

We drive back through town, which has emptied in the time we've been gone. A homeless man lingers beneath a streetlight, rummaging through his backpack as we pass by. Rigel continues, "Nothing had really changed, though—Orion just got better at living a double life. He still found ways to go out. Sometimes, I'd sneak out with him. One night, he got caught with a bunch of weed in town, and because I was there, we both got hauled in." He runs his hand over his hair. "Dad wanted us to stay the night, to teach us a lesson, but Mom couldn't do it, so they left the kids with the neighbor and came to get us. I'll never forget my mother's face. She cried and cried, Isla. I felt like shit. My dad knows everybody, so he was able to get me out. But Orion was already eighteen. They made him stay."

"Over night?"

"Until we could bail him out. And then he was sentenced with a second degree misdemeanor for intent to distribute. He was in Golden Grove sixty days."

"He spent two months in jail?" I whisper, shocked.

"Yeah. He was lucky—would've been longer in the States." Rigel glances at me. "All jail did was make him worse. When he got out, he went right back to it, even though he was on probation. He distanced himself because he didn't want me to get messed up in it, so I hardly saw him after that."

Another text comes through, Orion asking if we're close.

302

heavenly bodies

"Tell him we're five minutes out," snaps Rigel. I relay the message, tucking the phone beneath my thigh and the seat.

"So that's it? He didn't even go to college?"

"No, he went to school in Miami. Dropped out before the first semester was even over and came back home."

"Your parents must have been livid."

Rigel laughs harshly. "They didn't even let him come back to the house. He had to stay with my Uncle Chuck and get a job at the rum factory."

I can't imagine Casanova working in a factory. "Doing what?"

"Giving tours," he says. "He still does it, you know. He has a couple of gigs, all fronts for his real profession. Hey." He pats my knee. "Scoot over so he can get in."

"Oh—" Unbuckling my seatbelt, I slide over. Outside, darkened silhouettes of mostly abandoned buildings clutter wide, cracked streets. Rigel pulls over, and seconds later the door opens. Orion climbs inside, shutting the door quickly. No one else seems to be around, but adrenaline rolls off of him like fumes.

"Let's go," he says, bracing his arm against the closed window. "Hey, pretty girl," he says to me, serious as a heart attack.

"Hi." I adjust the way I'm sitting, self conscious of the gearshift between my knees. Rigel switches gears, knuckles brushing my skin, and I tense, wondering if he notices. And then I feel silly, because right now copping an involuntary feel is probably the last thing on his mind.

"Am I bringing you home?" Rigel asks, as we leave the silent streets of Redbrick. Up ahead, our headlights wash over a grassy area littered with trash that gives way to the beach. I didn't realize we were so close to the water. The juxtaposition is jarring: a rundown concrete jungle against the dreamy nighttime glow of the ocean.

Orion's fingers fly over his phone. "Yeah. Home."

"What happened to the Tahoe?"

"Drew has it."

We barrel down the main road, putting distance between us and whatever Orion wants to leave behind. The world is dead quiet; we pass just one car before turning onto a more residential street. Rigel's hand grazes my inner thighs again as he downshifts, but this time he pauses, tickling me. Grinning, I grab his hand.

We pull up to a gate and Rigel rolls down his window, revealing a keypad. "Code."

"2676," Orion says.

Rigel jabs the numbers in, and seconds later, the gate swings open. A security guard gives us a polite wave from his booth, and as we continue on, I can see how this neighborhood differs from others I've visited on St. Croix. Tall, evenly spaced palm trees line the main drive, and the homes are swanky and oversized, set back from the street by circular driveways and manicured lawns. We turn down several streets, venturing deeper into a labyrinth of wealth and tidy shrubbery, until Rigel pulls up to a darkened house on a corner lot. He cuts the lights as we park in front of the garage, and for a moment, no one moves.

"Thanks, Ri," Orion says eventually, reaching over me to slap Rigel's shoulder.

"Don't do this to me again," Rigel says, staring straight ahead. "You knew I had Isla with me."

"It wasn't by choice, trust that."

"There's always a choice. You just make shitty ones."

Orion doesn't even wait for Rigel to finish. "Bye, Isla. Take care of him, okay?" And then he's gone, pulling keys from his pocket as he disappears around the side of the house.

"Is there an apartment downstairs or something?"

"Yeah, but his landlords spend most of the year in New England, so he's hooked up."

"Lucky," I say, but it's thoughtless, because if there's one word I'd choose for Orion Thomas it wouldn't be that.

"Choices," Rigel says, reversing out. "My father always says we are where we are because of the choices we've made. No one wants to accept that, but it's true."

"It is true," I agree. I haven't heard it put that way before, but it resonates. "Do you think Orion blames other people for where he's at?"

"No. He'll tell you in a split second he's self-made, and proud of it. He owns it." Rigel snorts derisively. "He wanted this lifestyle, and he got it."

Instead of going back the way we came, Rigel heads in the opposite direction. We pass several more homes before the road darkens and starts to slant upward, the grade growing increasingly steeper.

"Where are we going?" I ask, moving back to my side of the cab so I can fasten my seatbelt.

"You'll see." Pulling to a sudden stop, he yanks the emergency break up and jumps out. In front of the truck, a thick rope hangs across an overgrown dirt road which is almost completely eroded. Rigel loosens the rope and eases the truck past, trading asphalt for dirt and rocks. At first it's a tight fit, trees and bush closing in around us, but then one side falls away, and I realize we're climbing another, steeper, hill by way of the questionable pathway carved into its side.

I'm starting to think we'll never emerge, when we reach the summit. Well, actually it's more of a bluff, flat and covered in a sea of long, wispy grass. It's like water, the way the wind pushes through it in waves. Rigel cuts the engine and slips out but I just sit, captivated. There's only a sliver of a moon, so it's impossible to see where the ocean meets the sky, but I can hear the waves throwing themselves against the rocks below. Far away, the lights of Christiansted and its harbor twinkle, giving me some perspective of where on island we are.

heavenly bodies

After a moment I shrug into my hoodie and open the door. The grass comes nearly to my waist, and I touch the tops as I wade through to where Rigel's sitting on the open tailgate. He helps me up and we settle in, arranging the bundle of blankets he's got back there.

"Were you planning on coming up here?" I ask, surprised at this foresight. We'd been en route to the beach when Orion's text had derailed things.

"Not tonight." Lying back, he rests his head on his hands. "Why?"

"You just had a bunch of blankets back here?"

"I wasn't sure what we'd end up doing, but I wanted you to be comfortable," he says. My eyes are adjusting to the dark, and I can sense him watching me.

With no moon and no light pollution, the sky is at its blackest, clear and strewn with so many stars it doesn't seem real. Shivering, I lie down beside Rigel and pull one of the other blankets over us. "Are you okay?"

"Yeah."

"I mean, with Orion."

He pauses, coming closer beneath the blanket. "I'm fine. I just don't like when he pulls me into that shit. He knows I'm not down."

I find his hand beneath the blankets. "He definitely knows," I say, remembering Orion's face the night we ran into him at Rory's birthday party. "I think he regrets it."

"Look at you, already believing his act," he says, playful but meaning it, too. "The only thing Orion regrets is that I'm not running the streets with him. That's all."

"You think he doesn't care?"

"It doesn't matter whether he does or not. I don't care." His tone tells me we're done talking about it.

I get why Rigel's fed up with Orion. He's wrong and strong, seemingly unrepentant about his lifestyle and the impact it has on the people who love him. Even so, part of me wishes they'd sort it out. They're blood.

Then again, my brother is five and our worst fight has been over what to watch on TV.

The starry dazzle above catches my eye, and I surrender, giving it my full attention. I haven't seen stars like this since camping at Cloudland Canyon two summers ago. Rigel points up to a constellation, waiting until I see it to whisper its stats in my ear. *Leo, Leo Minor. Perseus. Cassiopeia. Sirius,* the brightest star of all. It's First Date 101 meets the Astronomy club as Rigel seduces me with ear kisses and adorably geeky recitations of the heavenlies. We kiss and we stargaze, fingers tracing lines in the sky as our legs tangle beneath.

"Orion," I say, pointing. "*Rigel* glows blue, right?"

"Yeah. And see the red one on the bottom? *Betelgeuse.*"

I pause, smiling. "What, no sisters named after that one?"

"No sisters...maybe a horse."

"That would be a good horse name." A thought pops into my head and I close my eyes, shaking my head. "I just realized something."

"What?"

"Your sister is Aurora as in Borealis, isn't she? Not Sleeping Beauty."

His hands wrap around my waist as he presses close. "You would be correct."

There was something else I had to say, but we kiss and I forget.

21.

Ms. Torino is one of the younger advisors on staff at the Palms. With her strawberry blonde side bangs and trendy, rectangular glasses, she looks more like a Starbucks barista than our guidance counselor. She sings quietly to herself as she looks over my records, alternately scrolling on the computer and shuffling paperwork.

"So, Isla," she says eventually, catching me staring. Smiling sweetly, she offers me a stick of gum.

"Thanks," I say, taking my time unwrapping it.

Tossing the pack back on her desk, she leans back. "Photojournalism, huh? Must say, I'm really feeling that for you."

I sit up, surprised by her candor. "Yeah?"

She nods enthusiastically, turning her laptop around so I can see what she's looking at. Several of the photos I've taken at recent athletic events have been featured in the Palm's monthly e-newsletter, and one was even put on the school's site permanently. They're great shots, and I'm proud of them, but they're not exactly Pulitzer winning so it's surprising when she continues, "You've got a great eye, and from what Ms. Franklin's told me, a great mind for current events as well."

Hearing that Ms. Franklin holds me in such high regard comes as a shock. I'd never know it by the way she acts during class, and I almost feel guilty about adopting Nando's "Cranky Franklin" nickname.

"You have plenty of time to choose a major," Ms. Torino continues, pushing back from her desk. "There is, seriously, no rush. But I'd like to see you consider a school that can offer you a journalism major, photojournalism track. Or you could major in photography, minor in journalism, but..."

"I think I like the first option," I say, nodding. "It makes sense, and I really am interested in current events. It's a good fit."

"I know it," she agrees. "Okay. So, I know you've got your heart set on Agnes Scott and being downtown and all that, but how about the University of Georgia? Their journalism school was ranked one of the top three in the country a couple years ago. If you're serious about focusing on photojournalism, I think they're worth a look."

312

heavenly bodies

I've had my heart set on Agnes Scott my whole life mainly because my mother went there. While I'm not ashamed of that admittedly childish desire, I've outgrown it. "I agree."

It's six thirty on a Wednesday evening, and we're en route to the airport. It's muggy and close, Alex won't stop grousing—he skipped nap time today—and we're running late, but none of that matters because in about twenty minutes we'll be with my father.

I haven't been to the airport since the day Delta flight 1752 dumped us on St. Croix, and it looks different to me now. Feels different. I suppose I've gotten used to the heat, the open air buildings and melange of dialects.

Mom drops me off at the curb while she and Alex look for a place to park. Hurrying over to baggage claim, I look from face to face, wondering if Daddy's in this crowd. Multiple flights must have landed recently, because there are people everywhere. Grabbing my phone, I start to send a quick text only to see he's beaten me to it.

Just landed! It was sent five minutes ago. I look around again, noticing that the baggage claim carousel, which had stopped, has resumed. Another wave of people gushes over to it, and then I see him — he's gained a little weight since August. I realize it looks good on him, that maybe he was too thin before. Our eyes meet and he grins, eyes crinkling. I didn't think I'd cry when I saw him, but I do. He catches me up, hugging me, and I push my face into his shirt, inhaling the cologne he's always worn. It smells like familiarity, safety. It smells like the way things are supposed to be.

"I missed you," I say, wiping my nose.

"Missed you too, Isla-girl." He squeezes me until I can barely breathe, then sets me free, ruffling my hair the way he's done since I was a kid.

"Daddy," I complain, grabbing his hand as I smooth back what he's messed up. "Mama went to park."

"She told me," he says, holding up his phone. Suitcases and bags revolve sluggishly by on the conveyor belt, waiting to be plucked up. Daddy finds his right as Mama and Alex find us. My little brother yells and barrels into him, making Daddy drop everything and embrace him. Mama joins in, crying, and then we're all hugging and sniffling, our little group taking up room like a boulder in a stream, forcing people to go around us.

Having him here feels like the final piece of a puzzle, sliding into place. It feels like home.

heavenly bodies

On Thursday morning, I wake to the smell of roasting turkey and pumpkin pie. Other sweet and savory smells tickle my nose as I shuffle down the hallway, yawning, chest light with contentment. We stayed up late last night, talking way into the night—even Grandpa Harry, who usually passes out early.

In the kitchen, Alex sits on a high stool at the counter, helping my mother roll out pie crust. Daddy's making his famous cornbread, and Grandpa Harry's shelling pigeon peas, for peas and rice. I grimace, wondering how long they let me sleep.

"Mhm. And look what the cat dragged in," Grandpa says, eyebrows raised.

"Morning, everyone," I say, generous with kisses on my way to the coffee maker.

"Honey, huh? Just like your mother." Daddy chuckles, watching me stir honey into my mug.

I smile, nodding. It's true. I've picked up more than a few of her habits, I'm sure.

"There's bread and cheese from the bakery," Mama says, nodding toward the cutting board. I make a little sandwich and wolf it down, wanting to get to work.

"What do you need me to do? Chop vegetables?" I look around, trying to gauge. "I can get started on salad."

"Greta's bringing salad and baked macaroni," Mama says, wiping her brow with the back of her arm. She positions her hand over Alex's, helping him with the cookie cutters he's using to make little designs for the top of one of the pies. "You can...peel and core apples. That would be a big help."

Aunt Greta, Uncle Isaac and Camille show up around one, arms overflowing with food. I'm helping Cam bring juice and soda in from the car when a rental pulls up, and my cousin Teddy hops out. He goes to college in Maryland. I haven't seen him in years, but he's still as goofy as I remember.

"Hey, Isla." Giving me a side hug, he scoops the bags from my hands. He might be the tallest person I've ever seen. "How's the car running?"

"Running perfectly. I love it."

"She was a great car. Lots of good memories." Waggling his bushy eyebrows, he goes on inside. I don't particularly want to imagine what sorts of shenanigans Teddy got into in that car.

My phone vibrates against my thigh as we walk back inside.

happy thanksgiving, Georgia.

happy thanksgiving ;) how many people y'all have over there? 100?

haha. maybe 20. we're eating outside.

Is Orion home?

All of my brothers are home.

We message back and forth a bit until Mama smacks my butt and tells me to make myself useful. Camille and I set the table, going outside for fresh blooms to decorate

with. There's so much food my stomach hurts just looking at it, and everyone—even Alex McFussyPants—has
seconds. It's not until later I realize we don't have alcohol at dinner. No beer, wine or rum. Nothing local. Just
juice and soda.

I'm not a big drinker myself, but alcohol is woven so
deeply into the culture here. I've become used to seeing
it at most social events and dinners, but I know we're
abstaining because of my daddy. He looks better than he
has in some time, and I wonder again how blind I was
before.

"So you're able to stay longer?" I ask later on, curling
up beside him on the porch. Alex's asleep in his lap, curls
fluttering with our father's breathing.

"Five days," he says, giving me a quiet smile. "I
worked it out. Seemed a waste to come for just two or
three."

This gives us until Monday, plenty of time for the
beach and maybe the Rainforest. Armstrong's Ice Cream
and town and the bakery, and maybe I'll even take him
by the Palms, so he can see where I spend my days.
"Much better. There's so much to show you."

"I'll bet there is." He leans over, kissing the top of my
head. "Who knows? Maybe I'll just stay." He's being
lighthearted, but there's longing in his words. He's a
Georgia boy, born and raised, but home is where your
family is, and we're all here. I know, because having him

here makes this house feel more like home than it ever has.

"You should," I say.

In the morning, Alex and Grandpa Harry take Daddy around the backyard to see which fruit trees are flowering or bearing fruit. Grandpa lasts about a half hour, but Alex has much to say, so he stays outside with Daddy longer. They've got pink cheeks when they finally come back in.

When Alex goes down for his nap, I take Daddy on an exploration of my own, giving him the tour of Frederiksted as I know it. We take a leisurely drive through the rainforest, and I park on the side to show him Creque Dam. As Rigel predicted months ago it's now full of mossy green water due to the rainy season. There are a lot of people out and about today, so it doesn't feel as private, but my father doesn't seem to mind.

Back in town, I point out the convenience store where I buy Grandpa Harry's lottery tickets. Daddy's amused they sell tickets to me at all, and we buy a few since we're already there. After getting gas—which he pays for; score!—we stop at the bakery to get treats for everyone.

"We'll save Armstrong's for another day," he says. "Al would be upset if he missed out."

I've thought about Daddy's visit a lot, and I always assumed things would be as heavy and deep as they were when Mom and I left, but it's not. It's actually kind of like we were never apart. He asks about school and how the college application process is coming along, and even though I know Mom fills him him on every-freaking-thing, I indulge him and spill all.

"So, University of Georgia, huh? Mom said you were considering?"

"Yeah." I nod, pausing at a stop sign. "Athens is a little further from the city than what I wanted, but they've got a good journalism school."

"You know, I almost went to UGA."

"Really? I thought you were Georgia State, all the way."

"Oh, I'm Georgia State." He smiles. "It's what I could afford at the time, so that's where I went."

"That's what it all boils down to, I guess. They all have good programs...we just have to see who accepts me and what we can afford." I pause, ambivalent to the feeling this conversation is giving me. I'm conflicted, anxious even. "All I want is to be home again." That's not completely true, though. There are other things—people—I'm considering lately.

My father's still stuck on what I just said, though, seeing it through the lens he's always seen it through. "Your grades are good, and you're going to a prep school now. Things are a little different than they were back at Grady, honey. I wouldn't worry too much."

"Daddy." I give him a look. "Did you seriously not worry at all about college? About where you were going to go?"

He shifts in his seat, drumming his fingers along with frame of the open window. "A little bit. But you're smarter than I was. You'll have plenty of options."

We keep talking, but my mind wanders, drawn away by unresolved questions and decisions to be made. I wish I was the kind of girl who didn't let other people...like boys...factor into her decisions, but I'm not. And really, it's only one boy: if I'm going to have the college experience, I want to have it with Rigel.

On Sunday, my father's last night on St. Croix, we go out to dinner. Having only met Rigel once, Daddy suggests he come along. We choose a popular restaurant on the North Shore, resplendent with outdoor seating and an awe-inspiring view of the ocean.

Afterwards, I ride back with Rigel. Stuffed from the brownie sundae I polished off after dinner, I rub my stomach. "I need to swim laps after this weekend. It's been an eat-a-thon since Thanksgiving."

"Yeah, me too. Come train with me in the morning."

"No way." I laugh, shaking my head. "I'm not getting up at the butt-crack of dawn."

"Come on." He reaches over, squeezing my thigh. He knows I'm ticklish there.

"Stop!" I squeal, cringing away as I grab his hand. "I'll go with you another time."

"Lies," he says, raising his eyebrow.

"I'm going to be late for school tomorrow, anyway. We're dropping my daddy at the airport."

"What time's his flight?"

"Nine."

"Quick trip." Rigel adjust our hands, sliding his fingers through mine. "He coming back for Christmas?"

"I don't know yet." I shrug, a wave of sadness undulating through me. The holidays minus Daddy are a grim prospect, but quite possible. "Hopefully."

We're quiet for awhile, navigating the gentle slopes and curves of the North Shore. To our right the ocean ripples and glimmers darkly, whitecaps fluttering like mermaid's tails in the moonlight. I peek at Rigel, studying him as he drives. "Have you sent any more of your applications out yet?"

"A couple of colleges in South Carolina and two in Florida—UCF, USF."

"The University of Georgia has a really good swim team," I blurt out. "It's in Athens." Like he knows where that is.

Rigel brings his eyes back to the road, but his smile grows. If I didn't know any better, I'd think maybe he likes the idea. "I'll have to check it out."

"You should."

"That where you're going?"

"I don't know," I say. "Maybe."

⌇

I come home from school one day to find the house transformed into Santa's workshop. Between the decorations Mama had shipped down and Grandpa Harry's dusty relics, the spirit of Christmas is alive and well, right down to the Crucian carols blaring from the kitchen.

"Hi, Mama," I call out, attempting to get her attention as she fastens sprigs of fake holly to the corners of the windows. "Who is this?"

"Stanley and the Ten Sleepless Nights." Climbing back down the ladder, she gives me a quick hug. "I grew up listening to these guys!"

"Where's Al?" I ask, surprised he's not at her feet in a tangle of tinsel.

"Napping. He's got a little fever, so we skipped preschool today."

"Oh, no." Putting down my backpack, I go quietly to my brother's room, peeking in. He's fast asleep, thin blanket pulled to his chin. His cheeks are flushed, and I touch them, hoping he's not too hot. Camille, who dropped me home, tiptoes in behind me. She pouts down at Alex.

"Poor guy," she says, following me back down the hall.

"I know. It's weird when he's out of commission. The house is all quiet."

Camille snorts. "Or would be, if it wasn't for Auntie Charlene's jam session in the kitchen."

"For real." I laugh, pulling her into my room. We collapse onto my bed, sandals falling to the floor. It feels good to have nowhere to be for once, to relax with Cam. Most weekdays I stay after school to work in yearbook, while she tutors lower school kids in math.

"Did you paint?" she asks, pointing her toe at the far wall.

"I can't believe you can even see that," I murmur, squinting at the pale, pale sea green I was experimenting with last night. I've been itching to add color to these walls since we got here.

"I've got eagle eyes," she says, sitting up. "And it smells like paint in here."

"Yeah, it does," I admit, cranking my louvers wider for a better breeze. "So, what's going on with Kyle?" The last we'd talked, she'd been determined to break it off with him.

"I cut him loose. Tuesday night."

"For real?"

"We were on the phone."

"Does Nando know?"

"No." She shakes her head.

"Why?" I ask, but I suspect I already know why. Feelings are complicated, and Cam and Nando have been dancing around theirs even longer than Benny and I did. Things haven't been the same since their fight at Jump Up a month ago, and while they play it off at school, everyone feels the tension.

"Because I have feelings for Nando that go beyond good chemistry," she finally admits, pushing her hair back.

"But he has feelings for you, too."

She nods, tracing her finger along the pattern on my comforter. "I think, at this point, that Nando doesn't really trust me."

"Because of Kyle?"

"Yeah." She rolls her eyes, twisting her hair into a bun. "Even though I never lied to anybody."

"Not verbally," I say. "But you were being a little covert."

She opens her mouth, but nothing comes out.

"What if the situation was reversed, and Nando was seeing you and another girl?" I prod. "Even if he was honest about it, it would feel shady."

She pouts. "I guess."

I found out recently that Camille and Nando's "random" hookups have actually been going on for years. She made it sound before like things were platonic between them after their stint in middle school, but that's bull. Keeping this in mind, I say, "I think it's really hard to have repeated hookups without catching feelings, Camille. Kyle might be cool with it, but Nando's not like that. And neither are you."

She puts her face in her hands. "Jasmine said the same thing."

"Just my opinion. I'm here no matter what."

Sighing, she rolls onto her side. "I've never gone this long without talking to Nando. Kyle may have been the last straw."

I doubt that, but I can't speak for Nando so I keep quiet. Allowing the conversation to fizzle out, we lie side by side a while, scrolling through Cam's Instagram feed until it's time for dinner.

22.

The holidays, normally my favorite time of year, come with an emotional wallop I'm not expecting. One day I'm Christmas shopping in Christiansted with Camille and Jasmine, the next I'm bawling into my pillow, devastated with memories and nostalgia and the reality that I won't be home for any of my favorite things.

To make it worse, Rigel's mother decides the week before winter break to take him on a college tour, visiting campuses in Vermont—she's still holding out hope—South Carolina and Florida. He leaves the last day of school, missing the Palm's yearly school-wide sing-along in the Pavilion. It's a shame, because caroling with five hundred other kids of various ages is hilarious, and by the end I'm laughing so hard I'm crying.

I do, however, text Rigel halfway through Rudolph the Red-Nosed Reindeer, jokingly telling him to drive through Athens, Georgia if he gets the chance.

Tired of my unexpectedly blue mood, Mama finds reasons for me to come out of my room. Instead of the cookies we always made back home, I help her make tamarind stew and real ginger beer. We drive through town, looking at the Christmas lights strung along the streets. Mama, Alex and I go to Christmas Spoken Here, a festival held every year at the Botanical Gardens. We load up on homemade peppermints and guavaberry rum, and Alex gets his picture taken with Santa Claus. That reminds me of old times at the Mall of Georgia. It's bittersweet. How wonderful this moment is, and how wonderful it was when I was small.

I spend days at the beach with friends: always at the very core, me, the girls and Nando. He and Camille went from not talking to being attached at the hip. It's a relief they've gotten over themselves, but the frequent touching and flirting just reminds me what I'm missing.

I'm sitting outside at Jasmine's when Rigel messages me with an update.

flight is still delayed, so we're landing even later.

It's late in the day now, a hazy, languid afternoon fading into the soft blue-purples of dusk. I wish he was here to see it with me, although the sunset in Miami is probably gorgeous right now too. Snapping a shot of the sky, I send it to him with a message of my own:

:(

His response is immediate.

Wish I was back already. A photo of an overcast sky comes through seconds later, ominous grey clouds hovering above a row of planes ready to take off.

So much for the lovely sunset I envisioned for him.

You'll be here soon. say hi to your mom for me.

I will.

"Is he still stuck in Miami?" Jasmine lies back, stretching her legs and wiggling her freshly painted toes. Maybe I'll do mine—I won't be doing anything else tonight.

"Just boarding now because they were delayed. They're getting in late, so that sucks."

"Yeah, I hate that." She caps her nail polish, straightening up. "You wanna just stay the night?"

"Your mom won't mind?" I ask, curling up beneath the quilt. The apartment Jasmine and her mom share has air conditioning, so her room is always deliciously cold.

"Nope, Cam stays all the time. I'll ask her." Jasmine snatches her phone up and sends a quick message to her mom. Natalie's a full time nurse down at the hospital, so she's usually out when I come over. She's cool though, more like Jasmine's sister than her mother. "She's fine with it," Jasmine announces a moment later.

Camille comes in, suppressing a smile.

"You just spoke to Nando, didn't you?" I ask. She's been like this since she and Nando made things for-real-official, like life is one big giddy secret.

She nods, sitting beside me. "He wants to come by later."

"Stay over," Jasmine offers. "Isla's going to."

"Okay." Camille nods. "Your mom's working late, right?"

"Yeah."

"You're fine with Nando coming over?"

"Of course," Jasmine says, rolling her eyes. "It's Nando. Just make sure he parks at the end of the lot."

Her apartment is on the ground floor, a corner unit. Both bedrooms have sliding glass doors leading to little patios, making Jasmine's place the easiest to sneak in and out of. I'd be surprised if Natalie didn't know this, frankly. Jasmine doesn't even have a curfew anymore.

"I'll have to borrow clothes, Jasmine," I say, calling my mom to ask if I can stay.

"That's fine..." Her voice fades as I leave the room, phone pressed to my ear. Mama's phone goes to voicemail, but she calls back right away. "Hello, Isla?"

"Hey, Mama. Just wanted to see if I could sleep at Jasmine's tonight. Cam's staying."

"Did she ask her mother?"

"Yes, and Natalie said it was fine."

"And she's okay with it?"

"Totally fine."

She hesitates, and I know it's because she hasn't met Natalie yet. "Well, I guess so. Call me in the morning, though, okay?"

"I will. Love you."

"Love you too, honey."

Camille and Nando are sequestered in the living room, play fighting and making out. They're more than a little liquored up, thanks to the rum and cokes Nando's been mixing since he got here. Jasmine and I aren't too far behind, but we're watching a movie in her room, pigging out on pizza and popcorn.

"Drinking gives me the munchies," she complains, rubbing her stomach. "It's like I can't stop eating."

"I know. I'm putting this away." Standing, I scoop up what's left of our pizza and transport it to the safety of the kitchen. My phone vibrates on my way back to the bedroom, and I pause, checking it.

Are you home?

My heart leaps, because there is only one person I want to hear from and that's who this is.

at jasmine's. are you back?

Just got in, driving home w/ mom.

are you tired?

Yes

But not too tired

Those two texts come back to back. Grinning like a goofball, I respond.

you should come over. nando's here

Give me half an hour.

ok

Pocketing my phone, I join Jasmine, who's got the movie paused as she scrolls through pictures on her phone. "Hey...Rigel's back. Is it okay if he stops by?"

She smirks, glancing up at me. "Of course it's okay. Just don't defile my mother's room or anything."

"We won't be defiling anything." I laugh, embarrassment adding to the flush the rum's given me.

"Yet," she says.

Hoping I don't look as tipsy as I feel, I pull a hoodie over the pj's Jasmine lent me and duck into her bathroom. I wash my face and dry it, staring at my pinked cheeks and bright eyes. By this time of night my hair is hopeless, so I loosen it from its messy bun only to tuck it into another. I just want to see Rigel, and I'm glad that, despite being travel-weary, he wants to see me.

In the living room Camille and Nando are still going at it. I detour to the kitchen, wondering how wise it was for Jasmine and I to encourage them to finally get together. I mean, it's great but—

The doorbell rings, follow by three sharp knocks. I'm at the door before the lovebirds can even disengage, squinting through the peephole and throwing it open.

heavenly bodies

"Hey." I can't even temper my smile; I'm so glad he's here. Rigel lets me pull him inside, wrapping me in his arms as he kicks the door shut. Even after a day on planes and in airports, he smells so good.

"Hey," he says, brushing a kiss to my temple before letting go.

"Look what the cat dragged in," chortles Nando, who finally gets off the couch. Camille lounges behind him, fluttering her fingers in a wave. "Didn't think we'd be seeing you tonight."

"You and me both," says Rigel, shaking his head. "One delay after the next. Anyway, what's good?"

"Not a thing. You drinkin'?" Nando asks, sweeping an arm toward the kitchen. "We have rum, coke and rum-and-coke."

Cam tosses a throw pillow at Nando to shush him. "Was it cold up there?"

"Pretty cold." Rigel nods, glancing at me. "Your kind of weather."

We flop down onto the couch not disheveled from Cam and Nando's cavorting. Rigel looks at me, his eyes soft. "So what's up?"

"Nothing, really." I twist so I'm facing him. "I think I went to the beach every day this week."

"I'll miss that when I'm in the states."

"I'll miss it, too." I frown, realizing how true this is, and how different that is to how I felt a year ago.

"Ey, for real; you drinking, Ri?" Nando calls. Judging by the sounds of clinking ice and carbonation, he's back to bartending.

"Yeah, just a little bit though," Rigel says. "I'm tired."

"Hey, you." Jasmine strides in, giving him a quick hug before sitting. "How was it? Anything look promising?"

"Maybe," he says. "University of South Carolina has a nice campus...and a pretty good swimming program. But I liked Charleston better."

"The city or the school?" I ask.

"Both."

"Charleston's beautiful."

We talk college for a while. I'll be in Georgia of course, but all of the schools Camille's applied to have been liberal arts colleges on the east coast. Jasmine's top five are in Florida. "I have to be near the beach."

"You could just stay here," Nando jokes.

"Are you kidding? I can't wait to get off St. Croix."

Nando isn't sure he wants to go right away. "I mean damn. Thirteen years of school, if you count kindergarten—and I do—just to go for another four years? Or five, if you frig around. Naw, man. I need at least a year to recover."

"A lot of people who take gap years never go," Camille says, crunching on the ice from her cup.

Nando starts to answer, but Rigel turns to me, asking very quietly, "Want to go somewhere?"

heavenly bodies

The breadth of freedom we have hits me all at once, almost overwhelming with possibilities: I don't have a curfew tonight. I can go anywhere with Rigel, for as long as I want, without consequence.

And the way he's looking at me right now?

I smile, nodding. "Sure."

Patting his pocket for his keys, he stands and pulls me to my feet. "We'll be back."

Outside, the wind picks up, making the trees rustle in the darkness. "You okay to drive?" My pinky hooks his, and we swing our arms as we walk.

"We're not going far," he promises. "And yeah, I'm okay. I didn't even finish my drink."

"They were good," I say. "But not as good as passion fruit juice."

"Nothing's as good as that." He opens my door, and I climb clumsily into the cab of his truck, nearly missing my footing.

"How much did you have?" Rigel chuckles, watching me.

"Way more than you." I grin goofily over my shoulder.

"You're cute when you're drunk," he says, shutting the door.

"I'm not really drunk," I say the second he slides into the driver's seat. "Just a little buzzed."

"Listen to that accent," he says, putting the truck in reverse. "Such a Southern girl."

"Please!" I cackle, amused. "It is not that strong. You make me sound like Scarlett O'Hara!"

"Where was she from, again?" he asks. "Georgia, wasn't it?"

"My accent's nowhere near as strong as yours."

"I have an accent?" He's teasing me, but I play along.

"You do. It comes and goes, but you do—especially with Orion and Nando."

Rigel isn't joking about not going far. Ten minutes after leaving Jasmine's, the quiet neighborhood road we're following culminates in a grassy, overgrown dead-end. Rigel turns so we're facing out and then parks, cutting the lights. This isn't like the windy bluff he took me to before, in Orion's neighborhood. This reminds me more of the defunded, abandoned housing developments back home, where roads were built but never the houses.

"It's cute, though, your accent."

Rigel changes the song, turns it down. "Yeah?"

My gushing would probably be better off kept private, but the rum's got me talking. Getting tipsy was a great idea when my evening consisted of giggling with Jasmine in her room. But now Rigel and I are together in the dark, and attraction is coursing through my veins. I peer out into the inky dark, made bottomless by Rigel's extinguished headlights. "Where exactly are we?"

"Sugar Mill Cove. It's supposed be a neighborhood, but the developers left after a hurricane in the nineties."

"There's something like this near my friend's house back home. We used to play in it when we were kids, running around in the grass, exploring the roads." I sit back, shuddering. "Kind of creepy at night."

Rigel unbuckles his seatbelt. Our eyes meet. I'm trying to think of something witty to say, but all I can think about is how much I want to kiss him. "I remember the first time I saw you."

"I remember, too." He cants his head, eyes catching the small bit of light coming from the moon.

"At the gas station?"

"Was there another time?"

I unbuckle my seatbelt, too. "No, that was it."

"I could tell you were new."

"You could?"

"Yeah, I'd never seen you before."

"Come on."

"That's how it is here." He shrugs, resting a hand on my thigh. "But I saw you with Camille, so I knew it was a matter of time."

I rest my hand over Rigel's.

"It was pretty there," he says. "In South Carolina. Some of the trees still had red and orange leaves. Reminded me of you."

"South Carolina's like Georgia," I say, glancing at his mouth. "Mild winters."

"We went to Athens, by the way. It was cold enough for me." Before I can really process what he just said, he

337

curves his hand around the back of my neck and kisses me. It's slow and very thorough, and my eyes close as we float through a kiss so deep it almost puts me in a coma. One second I'm beside him, straining to be closer, the next I'm on his lap, my knees bracketing his thighs.

I'm lost in the taste of his mouth, the push and pull of his tongue as he unzips my hoodie and slides it off. Pressing his lips just under my chin, he trails kisses down the column of my neck and across my collarbone. I know he's leaving marks, because he usually does when we're like this, but it feels so good I let him do it. And then we switch, and I leave marks of my own on his neck until he groans and laughs and distracts me with more kissing.

Somewhere, in the heady rush of hormones and horniness and intense-like, I'm aware that we're ships at sea, rudderless and anchorless, nothing to guide us or stop us. No parents or friends, curfews or commitments...just us. No boundaries. I rock against Rigel, eager for the closest contact, and he inhales sharply, stilling my hips with his hands. He's hard and tense beneath me, and I imagine what it would feel like if there were no clothes between us.

He's thinking it too, because our kisses slow, and then he's looking up at me, playing with the hem of my shirt. "Can I take this off?"

He's seen me in bikinis, but this is different—I don't even have a bra on. I lift my arms, want and curiosity overriding self-consciousness. Rigel slides the thin shirt over my head and drops it to the seat beside us. I've never been so bare with a boy. My heart pounds so hard it hurts. Hands spanning my back, he brushes his lips over the contours of my breasts. The sensation steals my breath and, swallowing, I twine my fingers behind his neck. Then he uses his tongue, and goosebumps ripple over my skin because nothing has ever felt like that.

And then all I want is to feel his skin on mine. I tug the hem of his t-shirt until he gets the hint and peels it off. He's warm and smooth and I wrap myself around him, pressing my chest to his. He slides his hands down over my butt, drawing me closer still. The shorts Jasmine loaned me aren't that skimpy, but they're not substantial, either, and it doesn't take much effort for Rigel to get his hand inside...

...or for him to find what makes me feel good...

...or for me to find bliss.

23.

O n the last day of the year, I wake to rain. A damp, cool breeze lifts the curtains, making them billow and swell before sucking them back against the screens. Snuggling down beneath a blanket, enjoying the brisk morning, I think of last night, watching movies at Rigel's with his family. Orion was there for awhile, giving me a glimpse into what life might have been like for their family before things changed.

Diana Thomas' affection for her eldest was obvious, and he was unbearably sweet, too, hugging on her and teasing her. Raymond wasn't too physically affectionate, but he and Orion talked quietly for most of the movie. I'd like to believe that, beneath the bravado, he's just a guy who loves his family. One of the hardest things last night was watching Orion try to connect with Rigel. Rigel listens and responds, but there's this impenetrable wall between them. It's subtle.

Because he's far different with me. He's wide open, generous and easy with his words, whether they're face to face or via text message. His full attention, eye contact and conversation make it easy to give him mine. He gives me his pieces, even the parts that are hurt and bitter; the parts that worry Orion will be arrested again, that he won't be good enough to compete with the swimmers in the states, that finances might interfere with tuition if things don't change with his dad's business. Every time I'm tempted to freak out over my own stuff, like Daddy's absence and the hiatus of my parent's marriage, I remember that everyone's got their own mess. It's sort of reassuring in a depressing way.

Last night was an effort to spend time in what's been a frenetic holiday season. Christmas and its endless parade of parties, festivals, family dinners and church services have kept everyone busy. I've seen Rigel a total of two times, and neither time we were alone.

But tonight's New Year's Eve, and my parents have agreed—after an extensive long distance conversation—that I could celebrate by camping out with friends. It's tradition to party downtown and then watch the first sunrise of the New Year. When Mama and Aunt Greta were teenagers, people went to Grassy Point, an isolated bluff on the South Shore. Eventually, though, the land

was bought up by a statesider and developed, much to the dismay of, well, everyone. Camille says that by the time she was old enough to stay out, people had started going to Ha'penny, a beach further down the South Shore.

"It's one of the few beaches on St. Croix that occasionally has big swells," she says. "It's pretty far away, but sometimes the boys go to surf."

I'm glad my mother agrees to let me go. She did this when she was younger, and anyway, I turn eighteen in January. I'll be living parent-free by the fall. Mama's loosened up, ironically. We drink more here, socially, and I'm in the most serious relationship I've ever had, but my mother's trust in me seems to be growing. Maybe it's the environment she trusts.

The tropical rainshower shifts into a torrential downpour, raindrops coming sideways at the house. "Shoot," I mutter, tumbling out of bed to close the louvers a little. By the time I'm in the kitchen, trying to decide between frozen waffles and leftover Chinese food, the sun is out again, shining so brightly that the rain could've very well been a mirage.

"I was wondering when you were getting up," Mama teases, joining me in the kitchen.

The clock on the stove reads 9:57. Nearly ten. "It's not that late," I croak, giving her a sleepy smile as I fumble with my coffee.

She squeezes my shoulder as she passes. "Excited about tonight?"

"Really excited." I haven't been camping in forever. It'll be interesting to do it on a beach.

"I think you'll have fun. Greta says it's grown over the years. Not as big as Easter weekend camping, but still something."

I nod, wrestling a carton of milk from the overstuffed fridge. "Any suggestions? Grandpa Harry said he had a tent."

"That old thing?" She laughs, wrinkling her nose. "It's in the shed, if you want to venture back there and look for it."

"Gross. There are probably cockroaches and cobwebs in it."

"Camille's is probably big enough. Ask her."

I do, wiping my hands on my pajamas before typing out a text. And then, because he's never far from my thoughts, I message Rigel too, asking him the same question.

hey, how big is your tent?

Asking him feels way more brazen than asking my cousin, but at least this way, I'm covered. For all I know, Cam's already decided to have Jasmine stay with her. Or Nando. I close my eyes, shuddering at the thought of catching those two in an awkward position.

She responds first, though:

344

It's pretty roomy. You and Jasmine can both fit. We've had up to 4.

I pass this on to my mother, who seems gratified I won't be sleeping alone in the cold. Sweetening my coffee, I blow and sip on it as I return to my room to pack. My phone chimes with another notification.

It's Rigel this time:

big enough. stay with me.

There's a big jam in Christiansted with live music and free champagne for the ladies until eleven. We stay until midnight, ringing in the new year with confetti and kisses, snagging another bottle of champagne for the road.

Ha'penny Beach is a scene by the time we arrive. The parking lot, a space cleared of bush at the end of the road, is packed, forcing us to circle several times before finding a spot. Grabbing our bags and cooler, we join the steady stream of people trickling onto the beach. Nando and a bunch of his cousins already have a spot, and they're waving us down with the glow of their cell phones. Camille and Jasmine arrive with a huge group from the Palms, popping their tents beside ours while the boys fashion a makeshift bar.

"There are more people here than I expected." Shivering, I huddle against Jasmine. The late night wind coming off the water is brisk.

"Me too," she says. "Definitely more than last year."

"I heard they're doing it at Green Cay, too," Cam says, pulling cut-offs on up under her dress.

"I'm glad we came here though," Jasmine says. "It's still officially the first." Because St. Croix is technically the easternmost part of the United States, it's the first place the sun shines every new year. Beaches on the southeast are packed tonight for this very reason.

Everyone else is changing, so I trade the classy dress I wore out for a bikini and one of Rigel's hoodies, which is so long it nearly comes to my knees. A bonfire goes up at the edge of the gathering. We sit around it for awhile, talking and drinking with people from all over.

Rigel's cousin Junie, who I met at Rory's birthday party, pops up, giving me a hug...and a joint. "Happy New Year's, empress," he says, clasping my hand to Rigel's.

Chuffing quietly, I drop the joint into Rigel's hand once Junie leaves. "Here you go."

He looks down at it, unsurprised. "He grows it."

"Really?" I giggle, imagining Junie out in the field, long dreadlocks tied back as he nurtured his plants. It's not hard to see. "In the rainforest?"

heavenly bodies

"No, he has a place out west, up in the hills." He closes his hand around our contraband. "Close to the rainforest."

"Do you..." I trail off, realizing I'm unsure of his stance on the stuff. Even as we sit here, the smell of it is thick on the air. Someone around here is smoking.

"Nah. I mean, I have." He shrugs, looking over his shoulder. "Nando!"

Nando wanders over, staring down at us. "What's up?"

"You want this?"

Nando grins, plucking the joint from Rigel's fingers. "Maybe. Where'd you get it?"

"Junie."

Nando sniffs it, shrugging. "If you're gonna twist my arm..." He's gone before either of us can say anything else, absorbed by the darkness beyond the firelight.

Rigel looks at me, brushing his hands against each other. "Sorry...I didn't even ask you if you wanted it."

"I don't." Playing with the zipper on my hoodie, I shake my head. "I mean, I've never done it."

"Never?" He seems surprised.

"No. My friends weren't really into that scene back home." I glance up at him. "Everyone here does it though, huh?"

"No." He leans back on his elbows, and I follow, watching him. "It's like any place. There are the kids

347

who do and the ones who don't. I don't do it mainly because I swim. I have to take care of my body...my
lungs...and I can't afford to get in trouble. Not at this
point."

I nod, because that's smart.

"I don't even morally oppose it," he continues. "It's
just more trouble than it's worth."

"I think so, too." I laugh, tossing a twig into the fire.
"It was nice of Junie to share, though."

"Junie's always sharing. He'd be happy to have us go
completely veggie, live in the bush and start a family."

"At seventeen?"

"I'm eighteen." He jerks his chin at me. "And you
have a birthday soon, right?"

"This month." I press my lips together. "Still a little
young for kids."

He grins, raising his eyebrows. "Just a little."

We talk and dance, take quick dips in the cool water.
And then we dry ourselves by the fire, making s'mores
with the marshmallows Jasmine brought. One moment
I'm floating in the tepid water, watching stars wheel
through the sparkling sky. The next I'm looking at the
horizon as its edges start to go grey.

"You see that?" I ask Rigel, pointing. We're at the
shore, trying to dry off with damp towels.

He hangs his on his shoulders. "Sun will be up soon."

Word spreads, and people congregate on the sand,
mellowed out from a night of revelry. The water's calm,

a silver mirror reflecting the sky above it. At first, the sunrise is gradual, but then it explodes, melting peaches and pinks across the sky. By the time the sun itself comes up, I'm so overwhelmed I have a lump in my throat. Except for the push and pull of the tide, it's completely silent. Nobody says a word.

The crowd disperses bit by bit. Some start packing up, ready to leave, but most tuck into tents or blankets on the sand. Rigel nods for me to go on ahead into his tent. Early morning light glows cozily through the tent's red material, filling it with a warm blush.

"I haven't watched the sunrise in a really long time."

"We do it once a year," says Rigel, zipping us into our little cocoon. "At least."

"It's been years for me," I murmur. "But it's crazy how something that happens every single day can be such a miracle."

"It never gets old." Rigel joins me on the blankets, which are way more comfortable than they have any right being. "And it's always different."

"I'm glad I got to see it." Yawning, I roll on my stomach. Sleep is so close, maybe a breath away.

Other than the crashing waves, the beach has fallen quiet. I'm just starting to doze when Rigel runs his hand over my back, sliding his fingers beneath the string holding my bikini top. Shivering from the feeling, I turn my head. We share a smile, delirious from a lack of sleep.

And then he loosens the knot with a soft tug. I feel the slight pressure of it give, the fabric brushing the sides of my breasts. He unties the other knot, the one at my neck. I want whatever we're going to do, because I want him, but he's only ever seen me this way once before and that was in the darkness of his truck. This is nerve-wracking. But it's sexy, too. I turn onto my back, letting the top of my suit slide off. Rigel's eyes go right to my chest and I clap my hands over my face, laughing.

He pulls my hands down, grinning. "Hey."

Wrapping my fingers around his wrists, I pull him closer. "Hey."

Sliding his knee between my legs, he eases down and kisses me from my mouth to my neck, and down to my breasts. "No hickies," I whisper, gasping when his tongue begins to play.

"No hickies," he agrees, coming back briefly to quiet me with a small kiss before heading south again.

Running my hands over the smooth expanse of his back, I catalog by touch the angles and planes of his shoulder blades and spine, the way his hips narrow between my knees. He resumes his explorations, making my stomach flip with every kiss...and he kisses it a lot, teasing his fingers around the strings keeping my bikini bottoms together.

"Leave those on," I whisper, reaching down.

Climbing back up, he presses his body to mine and runs his tongue over the shell of my ear. "Probably a good idea."

I close my eyes, swallowing. It's hard to talk when he touches me like this. "Yeah."

We kiss, and I wrap my legs around him, letting his hands traverse the mountains and valleys of my hips and thighs. "I love the way you feel," Rigel says, and I press my lips to the curve between his neck and shoulders because I love the way he feels, too. He cringes like it tickles, coming back to bite my bottom lip. Our kisses coalesce, our bodies move, locked into a rhythm. He feels it, and I feel it, and my eyes close as we fall.

His breathing turns choppy and then pleasure ripples over his face. Relaxing, he pins me for a second and then rolls to my side. I watch him as he catches his breath, eyes closed, his warm, golden skin damp with exertion. Opening his eyes again, he gives me a dopey, satisfied grin. He leans over and kisses my breasts, blowing on the goosebumps that follow. I sink my fingers into his hair.

"You have to put on a shirt," Rigel whispers, "because I can't concentrate on anything else right now." My heart flip flops at the pink on his cheeks.

"I don't want you to concentrate on anything else," I say quietly, bringing his face up to mine. We kiss. "And anyway"—I let him sit up—"I'm not the one who took it off."

"Oh, I take full responsibility," he says, staring shamelessly at my boobs.

Leaning over, I grab the scrap of material that is the other half of my bikini.

"I need to go for a swim," he says with a yawn.

"Now?"

Gesturing to his lap, he nods. "Yeah. Now."

"Oh, right." I stifle a giggle. "I'll come with you."

I'm in bed, half asleep at nine p.m., phone pressed to my ear as Camille chatters about her adventures with Nando after leaving the beach today. She giggles hysterically, bringing my attention back and making me smile in the darkness. "Right?" she gasps.

"Right..." Suppressing another yawn, I readjust the phone so it doesn't slip.

"You're falling asleep," she accuses.

Letting my eyes close, I settle deeper into my pillow. "I am. Sorry, Cam...I'm exhausted."

"Yeah, me too."

"Did Jasmine end up staying by you?"

"Nah." Camille sighs. "She left the beach before we did."

"She did?" I pause, trying to remember when last I saw her.

"Orion came and got her."

"Oh. I didn't even see him." I have mixed feelings when it comes to Orion. He's good to me, but he and Rigel clash. He loves his family, but he loves running the streets, too. And he obviously has feelings for Jasmine, but he's a free agent. I suppose she is, too, but I think we all know she'd settle down with him if he was into it.

"He was at some house party up east, so he came right after sunrise. Jasmine called him."

I can't say I blame her; if everyone but me was coupled up, I'd probably leave too. "How's he doing?"

"Okay, I guess. He was in a mood, but that could've been from staying up all night."

"Well..."

"Isla, she's still there."

"What?" Shocked awake, I blink at the phone. "How'd she pull that off?"

"I have no idea!"

"Her mom—"

"Natalie had to go into work today, so she doesn't even know Jas is still out," Camille says. "But listen, she texted me earlier...they spent the day in his pool. And his bed."

Jasmine and Orion are both extremely attractive, but still. "Unnecessary visuals, Camille."

She titters, pleased with herself. "Anyway, I'm tired, too. Let's sleep."

"'Kay. Night, Cam."

"Night, Isla."

For a while after we disconnect, I float in the half-space between wakefulness and dreams, my mind drifting as it processes the day. Thinking about Jasmine and Orion and what they've been doing, reminds me of how Rigel and I started this morning, and now I'm achy and wistful, wishing he was here for me to wrap myself around.

My eighteenth birthday falls on a Thursday.

Mom makes pancakes, and then, while we're eating, Daddy calls to wish me a happy birthday. I get texts from Sage and Morgan as I run out the door, and by the time I'm on the road, my phone's bursting with notifications, gifs and messages. Camille catches me by my locker before homeroom, giving me a coconut tart with a candle in it.

"Happy birthday," says Rigel, placing a pink hibiscus on my desk before he sits down.

"Thanks." Warmed, happy, I put it in my hair, tucking it behind one ear.

Feeling his stare, I glance at him sideways. "What?"

"I've never really seen your hair like this." He reaches across the aisle, touching it.

It's straight. I haven't bothered in months, allowing it to be curly, but today I woke up in the mood for something different. Nodding, I touch it too. "I used to do it all the time, back home."

I want to ask what he thinks of it, but Ms. Franklin brings the class to order.

We're in the library later, taking notes for Ms. Franklin's history project, when I feel Rigel's eyes on me again. He's been playing with my hair since we sat down; I can't pretend like his attention doesn't thrill me. I look, first for the teacher—who's disappeared, thankfully—and then at the boy.

One side of his mouth lifts in a faint smile, triggering that dimple. Turning to a fresh page in my notebook, I scribble, *what's up?*

His eyes slide down to the notebook. Peeking at me, he pulls it toward him and writes something. When he's done I take it back, anxious to read.

You don't want to know.

Wouldn't have asked if I didn't, I scrawl.

He pauses, chewing on his pen before he responds. **Are you a virgin?**

Startled, I glance back at a sheepish Rigel. It's a valid question, just unexpected.

Is it that obvious?

Stifling a little laugh, he shakes his head and writes, **no.**

You're so full of it.

355

We look at each other. His little half-smile returns. *So is that a yes?*

Yes.

He reads that and nods, looking at me as he returns the notebook. Blushing, I snatch it up and write, **why, are you?**

No.

Ok then. Glad we cleared that up.

He gives me a sly, cheeky grin. **Is it something you want to do, or are you waiting?**

I blush so hard my face throbs with my heartbeat. Rigel snorts, squeezing my knee underneath the table.

Are you asking/offering???

I meant in general.

Yes, I'm waiting. And yes, I want to.

We stare at each other for a beat, and before he can say or write anything I write it again, to make sure he understands.

Yes.

Giving in to my desire for just a little more chocolatey goodness, I leave my bedroom and sneak into the kitchen. It's late, and the house is quiet and dark. My birthday cake—what's left of it— sits on the counter, beneath a glass cake dome. Quietly grabbing a plate, I cut myself a slice and pour a glass of milk. I'm about to make my escape when Mama wanders into the kitchen.

"Oh, you're still up?" She picks up the kettle, bringing it to the faucet. "I wanted to talk to you, actually."

"Uh-oh," I joke. But not really.

She smiles tiredly at me, filling the kettle and putting it back on the stove to boil.

"You okay?" I ask, giving in and taking a bite of cake.

"Just tired. Haven't been sleeping too well." She punctuates this with a yawn. "I'm going to bed in a minute. But listen. I just got off the phone with Daddy. He's found a realtor to help us with the house."

My heart sinks, the way it does whenever we talk about selling the Inman Park house. It's as if my concept of "back home" is starting to exist less and less, like slipping into a dream and then realizing there's no way to wake up, that the dream is now real, and what was reality is the dream. A memory.

For awhile, my parents had considered refinancing but in the end decided to just cut their losses. I guess I've still been hoping that some sort of miracle would allow us to keep my childhood home.

"Isla?"

I take a bite of cake. "I'm listening."

She leans against the counter, folding her arms. "I'm just trying to keep you abreast on what's happening. I know you get upset when we don't tell you things."

I nod.

She looks vaguely disappointed. I don't know what she wants me to say. I love the house in Inman park, and I hate that we have to sell it. Sometimes I miss my old life so badly it aches...but if going back means losing everything I've found here, I wouldn't go.

I'm not sure when I turned this corner, but I did.

The kettle whistles, and my mother whisks it from the burner before it starts to screech. I watch her make tea, recalling countless memories of this scenario over the years. Evenings she didn't have work, bustling around the kitchen while I chilled at the table. I always wanted hot chocolate. It's why she puts it in my coffee these days.

"So, long term. Would you ever go back to Atlanta?" I ask. "Or do you think Daddy would ever come?"

"I think we're both pretty flexible," she says. "But there are just so many variables at play right now. It's hard to make plans, but I'm trying not to worry too much about it."

I guess I've never thought about it that way before. Kids kind of just go with the flow; parents are expected to have it together. Not knowing our next step is scary.

"Daddy's open to coming down," she continues. "He loves St. Croix. It depends mostly on his job situation, how quickly the house sells...and it depends a lot on Grandpa Harry, too."

She doesn't say it, but she doesn't have to: it depends a lot on Grandpa's health, and, morbid as it sounds, how long he lives.

"I mean, that's what my staying here hinges on, too," Mama says, spoon tinkling gently against the side of her cup as she stirs.

I return to my cake, licking a glob of frosting from my fork. "Okay. Ideal scenario, then. Your deepest wish."

She smiles, tilting her head. "Living on island with your father. Staying here to take care of Grandpa, or..." She shrugs.

"This is home."

"Mm. I suppose so." She sips her tea.

"I hope Daddy does come, then."

"I do, too..." She reaches out, squeezing my shoulder. "But it wouldn't be for awhile, most likely long after you've graduated."

"I just want him with us." My throat thickens, and I swallow, trying to force the sadness back. Every time I think I've gotten used to this, to our family being split up, something knocks the scab off.

Mom sighs. "I know, baby. But Daddy's doing well and he needs to stay where he is a little longer."

My father started counseling sessions in Atlanta the week we left for St. Croix. It's something he talks to me a lot about, not the gory details of his depression, but the things he's learned while talking to someone. He attends

AA meetings, too, the same ones he's gone to on and off for years. I try not to get my hopes up. He sounds healthy and sober, and my mother seems cautiously confident about his progress, but relapses over the years have taught us to be careful.

The most recent relapse was the worst for me, because I didn't even see it coming. Part of me still feels guilty that I was so wrapped up in my own life I couldn't see the tell-tale signs of struggle in his.

"At least he'll be close by," Mom says. "You two can visit on the weekends sometimes."

I wash my cake down with milk. "Already counting on it."

"I know this is has been hard for you. Atlanta will always be home." Hugging me hard, she turns to go.

"Mama."

She turns in the doorway, glancing back at me.

"This feels like home, too."

24.

I'm lost down the rabbit hole of my Instagram feed again, obsessing over the kaleidoscopic blues and greens of my favorite underwater photographers. There's magic beneath the surfaces of oceans, lakes and pools: daytime, sunlight fracturing and rippling as it hits the water, and nighttime, spectre-like shapes and shadows telling stories.

Sometimes Rigel doesn't have practice after school, so we go to the beach to swim. He does laps while I wade around the shallow parts, dipping my hair and getting used to being underwater. I still don't love it, but at this point it's no longer scary. If I can keep it together long enough to master taking pictures while being underwater, I'll have achieved a personal best.

Sometimes we end up in the little lap pool at his house. There's barely any room there, though, and despite the constant threat of siblings, we usually end up making out.

"Have you been to Buck Island yet?" Rigel asks. We're at his kitchen table, pretending to do homework.

"Shhhh," hushes Rory, frowning as she points her pencil at him. "Some people are trying to study."

He scoffs, looking at her askance. "What could you possibly be studying for, little girl?"

"I have a spelling test!" she says, flipping her wild nest of curls back.

Making a face, Rigel scoots his chair closer to mine. "Anyway, have you?"

"Not recently," I say, remembering the island paradise turned national park just off St. Croix's east coast. It's surrounded by the clearest, bluest water ever. "We went during a trip when I was seven or eight."

"You want to go this weekend? My Uncle Jimmy's taking the boat out."

Turns out Uncle Jimmy has an old fishing boat that moonlights as a family pleasure craft. We leave the beach on St. Croix just before noon, when the sun is high in the sky. Salt sprays up from the boat's wake, coalescing nicely with the warm breeze. I close my eyes, enjoying the feelings and smells. In my bag is a disposable, waterproof camera I found at the dive shop last week. It's junk compared to the equipment professionals work with, but it's perfect for my purposes today.

My eyes snap open when Uncle Jimmy yells over the grind of the motor, instructing Rigel and his cousins to ready the anchor. Several other boats float along the shore. A small group of snorkelers lingers nearby, red and orange breathing tubes bobbing in the waves. Before we've even stopped anchor, most of the cousins have already dived in, slick as seals as they glide through the water. I watch with a frisson of trepidation, wishing we'd anchored closer.

"It's not as big a jump as it looks." Rigel kisses my neck. "Come on. We'll jump together."

"This is as bad as the pier." I stuff my clothes into a bag and straighten up, chewing nervously on my lip. "I thought we'd wait..."

"Not half as bad." He grabs my hand and brings me to the side.

"Wait, I need sunblock." Fishing the bottle from my bag, I slather the goopy wet mess all over my arms and face, asking Rigel to get my back.

"Want some?" I ask as he obliges.

Working quickly, he spreads goo all over my back and arms and tosses the bottle down. "No, I want to get in the water."

"You're being pushy again. Remember where that got us last time." My heart pounds and my insides liquefy. This might be worse than the Great American Scream Machine at Six Flags.

"On three," says Rigel, fingers tangling with mine.

Uncle Jimmy watches with interest from the wheel, shading his eyes from the sun. "You don't like the water?"

"I like it, just..."

"She just learned how to swim," Rigel says. "And anyway, she's a Statesider."

I roll my eyes as he grins at me. "Is that suppose to be reverse-psychology?"

"Yeah. Is it working?"

"Kind of." I look back at Uncle Jimmy. "Rigel taught me to swim, actually. At school."

"That's a real case of opposites attract," teases Jimmy, cracking a smile. "Go on, Isla. This boy won't let anything happen to you."

I don't know when I make up my mind, but I do, stepping off the edge and pulling Rigel down with me.

"I sent my last application in." I draw my finger through the soaked sand at the water's edge, idly crafting designs. We've been at the beach all day and, despite sunscreen, my shoulders and cheeks sting slightly, having borne the brunt of the sun. Rigel's slightly pink, too, and his hair blonder than ever.

"Yeah, me too. My mom was on top of me to get it done."

"Mine, too. And my dad." I sigh. "And my grandfather."

"How many did you send out?"

"Five. You?"

"Seven."

"Oh, wow." Nodding, I erase my sand picture and start over. "Which schools made the cut?"

He pushes his hair from his face. "UCF, USF, UF, SC"—he pauses, squinting—"UGA, UNC and the University of Charleston."

"Chapel Hill?" I clarify, but that's not what I'm really stuck on.

"Yeah."

"You applied to UGA." I peek up at him, smiling.

"Heard good things about it." He smiles and tugs one of my curls, still wet from our last swim. "You applied there, right?"

Nodding, I gaze out at the water. The sun is low in the sky, a ripe orange ready to be devoured by the sea. "So, I've figured out what I want to do for my senior portrait."

"What?"

"An underwater portrait. You know the girl I showed you online...the one I've been following....something like that." I toss the disposable camera back and forth between my hands, wondering how many of the pictures we took turned out. It'll be fun to see. I love the immediacy of digital, but there's something about the anticipation of waiting for film to be developed. "I want to play around with it...get underwater housing for my camera."

"Yeah, that sounds like you," Rigel says, sitting up. I brush off the sand that's stuck to his back. It's been an indulgent day of swimming and lazing around.

"I wish I could do it here. It's perfect."

"It is," Rigel agrees. "Park's closed at night, though. Even if we had a way to get here."

"Aw, really? No one ever comes out at night?"

"People do, they're just not really supposed to." He tosses a broken shell toward the water. "I think the Coast Guard might patrol at night. Make sure no one's doing drug runs and shit."

"For real?"

His eyes cut to me and then drift down to my chest. He touches my clavicle, pulling my bikini strap aside. "You got really tan today."

Pleased, I mimic his touch, tracing my fingers along the line left by his board shorts. "You, too."

The muscles in his stomach contract visibly, and he grabs my hand. "Easy."

"Don't tell me that turns you on." Biting back a smile, I lie down. I'll have sand in my hair for weeks but it feels so good, having been warmed through by the sun.

"Doesn't take much." Cool, gritty fingers dance across my belly. I catch Rigel's hand and hold it. "Listen."

I look at him.

"If you really want night pictures," he says, "I can get us into the pool at the Palms."

"Orion's talking about leaving," Rigel says suddenly, turning down the volume.

It's Tuesday night, just past twelve, and we're in his truck, zipping through the quiet dark. We're on our way to the Palms to test my new equipment, underwater housing for my Canon. Between sneaking out of the house and into the pool, I'm a little on edge.

But Rigel's comment distracts me from my nerves. I peek at him, trying to gauge how he feels. "For good?"

He shrugs. "I don't know. Some stuff's been going on."

"What kind of stuff?"

"You remember Drew?"

One of Orion's crazy friends; I nod.

"He was telling me about this run-in he and my brother had a couple months back with this crew from William's Delight," he says. "Thing is, they've had problems for a long time. Since...I was younger. Anyway, Drew heard one of them has it out for Orion now."

"Is it..." I fumble over my words. "Business or personal?"

"It's always personal, but yeah, it's some bullshit about turf. And I guess it's serious. And then last night at dinner Orion comes by and tells Mom he's thinking of starting over in the states."

"Where would he go?"

"Back to Miami, maybe, or Vermont. He knows people everywhere." He pauses at an intersection, making a right turn. "He asked if I wanted to get a place together next year. My mother almost chased him out of the house."

I shake my head, confused. "Am I missing something?"

He looks at me. "What do you mean?"

"Orion seems to be more into your relationship than you. It's like he doesn't take you seriously."

"I think he's waiting for me to come around," says Rigel, hooking his fingers into air quotes. "He misses the way it used to be, and doesn't understand why I'm over it."

"Or maybe he understands, he just really wants his partner in crime back."

Rigel's jaw hardens. "Sounds about right."

We turn into the Palms. Familiar by day, it's eerie at night. Bypassing the parking lots, Rigel continues to the other side of campus and parks as close to the pool as he can. Except for the yellow security lights scattered haphazardly around, it's silent and dark.

Unbuckling my seatbelt, I peer out at the shadows.

Rigel chuckles. "You look like you're about to walk the plank."

"I don't want to get in trouble!" We've been having this conversation all evening.

"We're not going to. I've done this a thousand times." Grabbing my camera bag, he hops out and leads the way, expertly navigating the unlit paths. Wispy clouds pass over a half-full moon, and the pool reflects that restlessness, wind rippling its surface. "You ready?" Rigel asks. "I'm going to turn on the lights."

"Go ahead."

He flips a switch, illuminating the water before jumping in. Meanwhile, I strip down to my suit and tiptoe into the water. It's freezing—Rigel's already swimming laps to warm up. Securing the equipment, which I tested in my bathtub earlier, I ease my camera into the water. And then, making sure the settings are where I want them, I take a deep breath and duck beneath the surface. I push past the momentary panic, coming back up for another breath. My heartbeat starts to calm. When Rigel begins another lap toward me, I capture several photos, using the built-in flash when he's close enough.

He pops up beside me, rivulets of water sluicing down his face. "Show me?"

"How to take a picture?"

He nods, holding his hand out.

"It's pretty much the same. I've already adjusted the settings, so..." Placing the camera in his hands, I point out the buttons and dials he'll need and then swim a couple of feet away. I'm still talking when I hear a click, and then another. "If these are horrible I'll just get a timer and do it myself next time."

"Nah. I'm good at everything, Georgia."

Placing my tablet on Camille's lap, I point to my favorite shots of Rigel moving underwater. "These two, especially. He said he might use this one for his senior page."

She nods, looking through the images. There were a few duds, but I got a great set of photos from my late night pool session with Rigel. "You rocked this little photo session," she says, smirking. "Rigel, not so much."

I snort; she giggles. Sifting through the blurry shots of bubbles and arms and walls, it seems we've finally found something in which Rigel does not naturally excel:

photography. At least, the underwater kind. "Oddly he did get one of me I really like, though." Reaching over her, I tap on my favorite: me, swimming up from the bottom of the deep end. We'd traded the lights inside the pool for the ones surrounding it, so the image is nearly leached of color, giving the faint shaft of light shining down an ethereal glow.

"Isla," she breathes. "Wow."

We look through the other photos, commenting on a couple. Rigel might not be too keen behind the camera but in front of it he's golden and now, I'd love to experiment on everyone else. Camille turns off the tablet, tucking it into my backpack.

"We might try it at the beach one night," I say. "If you want to come."

"Yeah, maybe. Let me know." She smiles, cocking her head. "Bet you never thought you'd be taking underwater pictures."

"Never."

25.

"**H**ave you seen the latest?" Megan chuckles, turning the screen toward me.

We're in the yearbook room, working on layouts. As the deadline looms near, senior portraits have been flooding our photo lab's email address. One of today's submissions is Stanley. He's skating down a crumbling stone staircase I recognize from a building in Christiansted, probably doing the same thing he was when he sprained his ankle last fall.

This is the third time he's submitted a portrait.

I turn the screen back to Megan. "Not even remotely surprising."

"He included a note saying this was his favorite. Like we have time to sift through his freaking portfolio!"

"Does he want a collage or something?'"

"Nope." She rolls her eyes, saving the photo. "Just this one."

My left buttcheek vibrates, courtesy of a silenced phone. Plucking it from my pocket, I peer at the message Mama just sent:

Grandpa's fine. Just left the doc, getting stuff for dinner.

I close my eyes, offering up a quick prayer of thanks. This morning, Grandpa Harry woke up crankier than usual and complaining of a headache. It was so bad by the time I left for school that Mama said she was bringing him to the doctor.

It's one thirty now. I message her back: ***Thank God. How long did you wait for an appt?***

He was seen at 11.

What did they say it was?

His blood pressure. They adjusted his meds.

While I'm glad it was something doctors could remedy this time, I can't help but wonder what other scares and complications lie on the horizon. Mama might have known what she was getting into professionally when she took on this role, but emotionally? I'm not so sure.

My thumbs hover over the screen as Megan calls over to me, asking for my opinion on a font.

Tell him I love him. Gotta go.

heavenly bodies

Except for the chatty clique of parents sitting at one end, the bleachers are mostly empty today. I'm finishing up French homework while the swim team practices. Palm trees rustle peacefully overhead, swaying lazily in the breeze.

Rigel walks over, toweling his hair as he drips all over the concrete. "We're done. I'm gonna go change."

"Okay." Nodding, I give him a quick smile and jot down the answer to number seventeen.

Leaning closer, he ruffles his hand through his hair, getting me wet on purpose.

"You're worse than a puppy!" Shielding myself from the onslaught, I hold up my French textbook. "Rigel!"

Laughing, he struts off toward the locker rooms. Dragging the books across my lap in an attempt to dry them, I return to my conjugations.

The Stingrays' morning practices are on hiatus due to scheduling conflicts with one of the coaches, so Rigel's been going in at a more humane time than usual. He picks me up most mornings and we ride in together, stopping at the bakery on Centerline Road for fresh titi bread and cheese. Sometimes, if I don't feel like waiting through afternoon practice, I ride home with Camille. But on days like today, when it feels good to be outside and my mother doesn't need me just yet, I stay.

On the way home, Rigel and I stop at the supermarket so he can pick up a few things for his mother. "She always forgets stuff when she has the kids with her," he explains, tossing a box of cereal into the cart.

"I bet Rory talks her ear off."

"She's the worst," he agrees, holding up two boxes of toaster pastries. "We go through five or six boxes a week."

"I didn't even know there were healthy versions of those." I grab a box, eyeing the ingredients. "The strawberry sounds amazing."

"So, Orion's leaving in a few days. He's staying with people in Miami and then maybe heading up to North Carolina."

Hmm, this explains why Jasmine's been MIA lately. She's probably hiding out at Orion's. "Wow. That's soon."

"Not soon enough—Orion's boys had a fight with some of the crew from William's Delight." He scowls at his phone before pocketing it again. "Playing with fire, man. He needs to leave today."

Unnerved, I stop where I am. "Does your mom knows why he's leaving?"

Rigel scoffs. "He plays her, and she wants to believe him, so she does. My dad's not as easy to fool, but who knows. I think they both just want to believe he's moving on."

heavenly bodies

I remember Orion at Rory's birthday, chasing that tribe of little kids around. "Maybe he is."

He just looks at me. Rigel thinks I can be naive when it comes to his brother. Maybe he's right.

I'm in the middle of dinner with my family when Rigel texts. My phone glows at me from my lap, silently beckoning, while Grandpa Harry glares at me from across the table, silently judging.

"Put it away, Isla," Mama says, not missing a beat as she coaxes a snow pea into Alex's mouth. He makes a face, letting it fall back onto his plate.

It's Rigel. My fingers hover over the screen, itching to respond.

She holds her hand out. "Isla."

"Okay, okay." Sighing, I hand the phone over and proceed to shovel the rest of my food. Mama gives me a look. "What?" I swallow. "I love dumplings."

"I love dumplings, too!" cries Alex, pushing the rest of his peas away.

The second we're done with dinner, I swipe my phone from the counter so I can read Rigel's message.

You still riding with me tomorrow?

Oui, mon petit chou.

Was that for Camille? Because I take Spanish.

Well in that case: yes, my darling.

377

I'm on the porch with Grandpa Harry the next morning, sipping tea and talking college, when Rigel's truck pulls into the yard. Larry gives a half-hearted bark before flopping back into the shade of Grandpa's chair.

Tipping the last of the tea into my mouth, I watch Rigel come up the steps. His hair, which has been growing longer and more unruly since we met, is knotted back into a bun. It looks good on him.

Really good. My stomach dips.

"Good morning," he says, winking at me. He goes for Grandpa first, shaking his hand.

Grandpa Harry sets his cup down, accepting the handshake. "Mahnin', boy."

"Morning, Rigel," I say, slipping back into the house for my bag.

He follows a second later, hooking his finger into my belt loop. "*Chou* means cabbage, by the way. Not darling."

"It's both." I laugh, trying to escape his tickling. "A pet name: *mon petit chou.*"

"For what? A poodle?"

"Hi, Rigel," Mama calls.

"Hi, Mrs. Kelly." Taking my backpack from me, he pops into the kitchen to see my mother.

Today is Senior Skip Day. It was kind of a legend back at Grady, a myth of cooler times, but at the Palms it's alive and well. Our class voted back in November to have it today, so instead of attending class we'll be partying poolside at Margaret Tancredi's, the class president.

"We don't have to be at Margaret's for a few hours," Rigel says, once we're on the road. "I was thinking we could just do our own thing for awhile."

"Did you have something specific in mind?"

"I do."

We pull into the bakery's gravelly parking lot. My mouth is already watering for a guava tart. Unbuckling my seatbelt, I follow Rigel inside. "Well, what is it? The suspense is killing me."

He grins. "I want to jump off the pier. It's the perfect day to do it."

Licking the last bits of sugar from my fingers, I gaze out at the water. It glitters brilliantly below the full morning sun, so dazzling it's hard to look at.

"You done stalling?" Rigel asks, peeling off his shirt. We're in his truck, parked beneath a tree near the pier. Frederiksted is quiet.

"No." Working beneath my clothing so I don't flash the world—or at least Rigel—I trade my bra for a bikini top.

"You ready?"

"Not really, but I'm sensing I don't have a choice." I gesture toward my backpack. "Is it okay to leave this here?"

"Better not to. Here, I'll carry it."

It's not heavy, but I allow him, going instead for the towels in the truck bed. We make our way down the pier, passing a lone fisherman. Within hours, he'll be one of many.

Rigel stops at a spot about halfway down. Dropping my bag, he tucks his keys inside and kicks off his flip flops. Wandering to the edge, I peer over the side, relieved to see a metal ladder leading up from the water. The water seems dark, though, and rough.

Without warning Rigel sprints off of the pier, flipping in mid-air before hitting the water with a giant splash. Seconds later he pops up, face split into a joyous grin. "Come on!"

"Show off."

"Isla..."

My insides clench. All I can think about are creepy sea animals, or getting dragged beneath the pier by a rogue wave. "You said you'd jump with me!"

"Okay, okay, I did," he says, scaling the ladder. Not giving me time to back out, he takes my hand and brings me back to the very edge.

Shivering, I stare down into the abyss. "I've heard there are barracudas around here."

"I don't know, but there are seahorses."

"Really?"

"You're stalling again. This is just like the boat," he says. "Remember?"

"Pretty sure you said that was nowhere near as bad as this," I say. "Remember?"

"One, two..." He glances at me, eyebrows raised. I nod, immediately regretting it. "Three!" We step off, plummeting so fast my heart's in my throat. My scream is cut off by a cold, salty slap of ocean water, and I tug my hand from Rigel's, propelling myself back to the surface.

It's scarier than I imagined, and also way more exciting. "Okay! Okay. I get it." I'm smiling so hard my face hurts.

Rigel laughs, treading water beside me. "You good?"

"Yes!"

"Want to go again?"

"I love that we have a legit excuse for skipping school." Polishing off the rest of my roti, I grab a napkin and begin the tedious process of cleaning curry-stained fingers.

As usual, Rigel's fiddling with his sound system. "You really didn't have Senior Skip day at your old school?"

"Not a sanctioned one. The kids that tried usually got busted."

"It's tradition here."

"So I hear," I say. "I wonder how it's going at Margaret's—I heard she got a DJ."

"Nando's been sending updates." He shows me the screen of his phone. "Almost everyone's there, but it's still pretty chill."

"Really?" I take the phone, skimming through Nando's messages.

"You want to head over?"

"I do, but...not yet." After a morning of pier jumping, and then lunch from a Trinidadian food truck, I'm satisfied and sleepy, wondering if there's a beach we can doze on.

He starts the truck and reverses back onto the road, leaving town to go further west. I check my phone. There's a text from Sage, talking about airline tickets for spring break, and several from Cam, asking where the hell I am. I send her a selfie with Rigel, which he ruins with his middle finger. When he pulls off the road again, just a minute later, it's a spot I remember well— the private cove he took me to when we first started making out on beaches.

That seems like forever ago.

The water is warm and clear, full of tiny silver fish like last time. We swim for a good while, Rigel getting in a few laps as I float and dip, but the midday sun is fierce. Leaving the water, I take my towel and find shelter beneath a cluster of sea-grape trees. Rigel joins me after a moment, dropping his towel alongside mine. I take a thousand pictures, drunk with the beauty of outside, grateful we didn't spend today trapped in a series of classrooms.

"I taste like curry," I say, when Rigel kisses me.

"A little." He licks my bottom lip. "I probably do, too."

"And salt water," I say, licking his.

We kiss until we're sandy and sweaty, and he won't stop poking me. I can't take it; I smile, and our mouths drift apart.

"What's up?" He smiles back, but he looks a bit dazed.

Pushing my hips up, I let him know exactly what.

"Oh. Yeah." Now he smiles for real, dimples and all. "Sorry 'bout that." Moving lower, he nudges the top of my swimsuit aside and kisses what he sees. His lips feel good, but getting this close outside gives me butterflies—and not just the good kind.

Bringing his face back to mine, I kiss the corner of his mouth. There's a smudge of sand on his cheek, and I brush it off with my thumb. "I'm freaked out someone's going to see."

"No one's going to see." But he pauses, fixing my suit. "Do you...want to come over?"

Everything else fades, then. Our eyes meet. His, this close up, are melty and warm, like honey. I feel melty and warm. Like honey. "To your house?"

"Yeah." He kisses my neck, my ear, and yes; melty.

"What'll we do there?" I hear myself ask, already adrift in the possibilities.

"Whatever you want." Another kiss. "I just want to kick it. Alone."

"To have sex?" I whisper.

"Yes." His breath comes out in a small whoosh. "No. We don't have to. We can just..."

But I want to. I've wanted to for quite some time. "Okay."

The Thomas house is, for once, quiet. No barking or scrabble of puppy paws across the tiled floors, no reggae echoing from the yard. No Diana singing, or Rory giggling, no Leo in the zone with oversized headphones.

I follow Rigel up a narrow staircase and down a dim hall, into his room where sunlight spills across the wooden floors. Locking the door, he turns to me and runs his hands down my arms. His fingers touch mine, and I tangle them together, my heart fluttering like a trapped bird. He brings me to his bed, where he sits, drawing me close so that I'm standing between his knees, gazing down at him as he gazes up at me.

I touch his face, his hair, closing my eyes when he responds by kissing my stomach. He unties the top of my bikini, letting it fall to the floor, and then he pauses, hands on the small of my back. "We can do whatever you want to do, Isla." He kisses one breast, and then the other.

"I know." My heartbeat is crazy, my stomach tight with anxiety, but there's nowhere else I'd rather be. I tug on one side of my bikini bottoms, loosening the knot. Rigel pulls on the other side, and then I'm naked. He wraps his arms around my waist and I wrap mine around his neck. Gentling me onto his bed, he kisses my thighs and my belly, my breasts and my neck, not holding back now, his hands everywhere. Making out this way is so different; I feel everything. He stands long enough to shed his board shorts, and then he's on top of me, skin to skin, every part of him touching every part of me.

"Do you"—pausing, I try to catch my breath—"do you have..."

"Yeah." He grapples around the sheets, holding up his wallet.

"Okay." We kiss; I come up for air. "Did you plan this? Because I want to— "

"Kind of...I wanted to...I hoped you wanted to."

Nodding, I clasp his face between my hands. His cheeks are flushed. "I want to."

He sighs, kissing me, reaching down between us. "You have to talk to me, though," he says, eyes searching mine. "I've never done this."

"Really?" I grin, raising my eyebrows. "That's not what you told me..."

"I mean"—he pauses, smirking—"I've never taken someone's virginity."

"Have there been a lot of someones?"

"Just two." Another kiss, on my neck. "And you."

I watch silvery particles of dust dance and float through the sunlight coming in the window. Looking around for Rigel's phone, I find it on the floor, beneath his shorts. It's two fourteen, but it feels later.

Two texts, both from Orion, come through. Not wanting to be a snoop, I leave the phone where I found it and tell Rigel when he comes back from the bathroom. Frowning, he responds to the messages and then tosses his phone aside.

"You okay?" he asks, joining me in bed. Beneath the sheets, his hand rests on my stomach.

I put my hand on his. "Just wondering if the school's gonna call my mother."

"Probably. She won't mind, though. Didn't she go to the Palms back in the day?"

"Yeah." I sneak a peek at him. He's got a peaceful vibe, probably staring at the same dust motes I was. It could be like this always, if we stayed together. If. Who knows what'll happen once colleges choose us and we choose them.

"What?" he asks, smiling.

"You've got sand in your hair."

"Yep." He nods, matter of fact. "And all over my bed. Nothing new."

"It's in my hair, too." I scratch my nails lightly over my scalp. "Which probably looks like a bird's nest by now."

"I like you like this," he says, mischievous. "You look well f— "

"Don't even!" With a quickness, I'm on my knees, bringing a pillow down on his head. I'm attempting to smother him when he flips me over, caging me in. Wrestling turns to kissing, but the distant sound of a car door slamming has us scrambling for our clothes.

Or, in my case, my swimsuit. Rigel's dressed in seconds, handing me the same hoodie I wore on New Year's.

"I can't wear this." I hold the hoodie up, helplessly. "It'll look like I have no pants on!"

Looking pointedly at my bikini, he says, "You don't have pants on."

"No pants because I'm in a bathing suit is totally different than a top and no pants in your house." My face flames in response to what I just said, and he grins, waggling his eyebrows. I cover my face, laughing. "I can't even look at you right now."

Wrapping my damp towel around my body, I follow Rigel downstairs.

"It's just my dad," murmurs Rigel, peeking through a window. "He's over by the garage."

Relieved, I sidle up beside him and take a look. Raymond Thomas is across the yard, opening the hood of a car. Reggae drifts over. "I'm going to grab my stuff so I can change."

Rigel nods, following me out the door. "I gotta talk to him...I'll be right back."

Once I'm dressed, I check my phone. Surprised there are no messages or voicemails from Mama, I give her call.

"Hello, Isla," she says, and I swear she sounds amused.

"Hi Mama!" I catch sight of my reflection in the mirror—I'm all pinked cheeks and messy hair. Smoothing the rumpled material of my tank top, I leave the bathroom. "We had Senior Skip Day today."

"Yes, I had a feeling," she says. "When the school called...and then Greta called about Camille..."

"Are you mad?"

"No, we did it too," she says, and I can hear the smile in her voice. "I knew you girls wouldn't just play hooky like that."

A pinch of guilt prickles through me: I haven't exactly been with the girls all day. Still, in this case, what my mother doesn't know won't hurt her. "No, we wouldn't. But listen, I'm just calling to check in. Is it okay if I hang out a little longer?"

Promising I'll be home for dinner, I pocket my phone and look for Rigel. Outside, I spot him talking to his father near the fence lining their property. I can't hear what they're saying, but the light heartedness of their conversation carries. Raymond glances over, waving when he sees me. "Afternoon, Isla," he calls.

"Good afternoon!" I wave back somewhat self consciously, wondering if he's wondering what we're doing here.

Rigel meets me at the door of his truck, smiling. He bends to kiss me, his hand on my hip. "Nando said Camille's mad you're not at the barbecue yet."

A burst of wind spins through the yard, lifting the hair from my neck. A half hour ago we were doing the most intimate thing we could possibly do, but it's the way his eyes track over me now that make me feel wanted. Seen. Maybe even loved. I tiptoe to kiss his cheek. "Then we should go."

He half-grins. "You want to?"

I give him a push so I can open the door and climb in. "Yeah."

26.

It takes awhile, but eventually I'm pulled from sleep, yawning as I reach blindly for the phone. It glows momentarily in the dark before blinking out again. Turning it back on, I see there are three texts from Rigel, all sent within the last ten minutes.

I peer at the time: it's just past two. Hoping nothing's wrong, I quickly scan the messages.

Isla Isla

Isla

You up?

Now I'm just wondering if he's drunk. The last message came through seconds ago—it was the one that finally woke me. Yawning, I peck out a brief response.

I am now. This better be good.

Can I come over?

kidding, right?

no

Did something happen?

can't sleep.

Climbing out of bed, I open my bedroom door and look down the hall. The house is silent and dark, although if I listen closely, I'm pretty sure I can hear Grandpa Harry's snores.

Come in thru front door. Be quiet.

Ok. 5 minutes.

Five minutes? He's close by. I tiptoe down the hall and through the darkened living room. Man, this is really brazen. My mother has insomnia sometimes, and even if she didn't, she's got mom-sense. Squinting through the window, I offer up a prayer of gratitude that Larry sleeps in Grandpa's room at night—otherwise he'd be barking hysterically at Rigel materializing like a wraith. The door squeaks as I open it, and I wince, pulling him inside.

He grins, squeezing my hip. His skin is cool to the touch. Locking the door, I lead him back to my room and plug in my fairy lights. Rigel sprawls across my bed, sneakers thumping to the floor. "Hi."

Nerves quicken my heart—what we're doing is dangerous—but that's nothing compared to the heat in my belly having Rigel here. In my bedroom. At two a.m. "Hi?" An incredulous laugh escapes me.

I didn't learn one thing at school this week. All I could think about was Rigel, and how we spent Senior Skip

heavenly bodies

Day. Of course, he hasn't been helping, with his lingering touches and private smiles reassuring me he's on the same page. We haven't really been alone together since last week, so I assume tonight's visit is one of desperation.

It's nice knowing I'm not the only one with feelings. Rigel hooks a socked foot around my calf the second I'm close enough. I climb onto the bed, intent on sitting beside him, but he brings me into his lap, squeezing my hips.

"So is this a booty call?"

"Only if you want it to be." He bucks for effect.

I laugh, smacking his chest. "I'm serious. What on earth is so important you couldn't wait til tomorrow?"

"I wanted to see you." He pauses, smiling and biting his lip. "You'd rather be asleep, eh?"

"Yep." I nod, yawning again. I can't stop.

"It seemed more romantic in my head."

"You sound like your brother with those lines," I say, arching an eyebrow.

"Real talk, then. I couldn't sleep. And you've been on my mind all day." He brushes the backs of his fingers along the inside of my thighs, but his eyes stay on mine. "All week."

I shift on his lap, delicately avoiding the situation in his pants. "I've been thinking about you, too."

His gaze is so heated, I think he's going to kiss me, but he brings his hands back to the safe zone of my hips.

"Orion called," he admits, sighing. "And I couldn't fall back asleep afterwards."

Orion's in the States now, apparently living by his own clock. This isn't the first time he's called Rigel at odd hours.

"So you want me to put you to sleep or something?" I tease.

Rigel draws me close for another kiss as his hands wander up my shirt and over my spine. "Or something."

"How's Orion doing, anyway?" I ask, once we break apart.

"He says he like it. Says he wants to establish residency in Miami and start going to school again."

Surprising. I wonder if Jasmine has any bearing on his decision to stay in Miami. "That was fast."

"That's Orion."

"Does he have a job yet?"

"Orion's a lot of things, but he's not lazy," says Rigel.

"Legitimately."

"He's an Uber driver."

I snort. "No he's not."

Rigel tumbles me onto my back, establishing control. "Yeah, he is. I'm serious." More kisses. Our shirts go. I hold him close, arching into his touch when he tickles his fingers down my ribs. "Making good money, too."

"I'm glad y'all are talking more."

"You really want things to be good between us, huh?"

"Don't you?"

"Yeah. I do. But it's easier having him gone." Wariness flickers over his face, like he expects me to judge him for the harsh sentiment.

I don't, though, because I get it. "My mama says some people are easier to love from a distance."

"She's right." Scooting down, he rests his head on my belly. Warmed by a rush of tenderness, I run my hands over his curls. Some are so blond, making me wonder what his hair would be like if he wasn't perpetually swimming in the sun. "You know he's still doing the same shit out there though, right?"

I haven't really given it much thought. "Yeah."

"Mom wants him to come back for graduation." He kisses my belly button. "I told him not to bother."

"Why?" I sigh, exasperated. "Why can't you just let him be your brother, Rigel?"

"It gets old, having unmet expectations."

"I know all about that. My daddy's an alcoholic."

Rigel halts his little foray into my underwear. "I didn't know that."

"He's in recovery, but there have been plenty of disappointments over the years. Believe me."

"Is that why..." He trails off, perhaps searching for the right words. "Why he stayed up there?"

"Partly. The house, though, too." I scrub my hands over my eyes, sleepy. "Which they're now selling."

"They're selling your house?"

I nod.

"Are you okay with that?"

"Not really," I admit, shrugging. "But it's not like I have a choice in the matter."

"You grew up there." I know he's thinking about his house, and how it's the only one he's ever known. We're alike in that way, I guess.

"I did, but..." I resume playing with his hair. "They're behind on the mortgage. My daddy's employment has been iffy. I get the impression this is the worst case scenario, you know?"

He nods, tracing his thumb around my belly button.

"And anyway," I continue. "So much has happened. I feel like things would be different if I went back now."

"Different how?"

"Different like I've missed stuff. My friends are living the life I would've been living, except I've had a life of my own down here. A parallel universe...where going home would feel like visiting."

"If it's visiting, does that make this home?"

"I haven't decided." Our eyes meet, and I smile. "This still feels new sometimes. Temporary."

"Is it? Temporary?" His tone is neutral, but he's stopped moving.

"I don't think so." I sit up a bit, balancing on my elbows. "Now when I think about coming home for Christmas, this is what comes to mind. My mama loves being back. She's got Grandpa Harry and Aunt Greta...and she loves that Alex is growing up here, and that I'm going to the Palms and hanging out with my cousin..."

"Is your dad planning on coming down, ever?"

So many questions. It's deeper, a little uncomfortable, Rigel asking me to put words to the stuff that's been floating around my mind. This particular question puts a pain in my stomach. My parents seem to be okay, talking on the phone all the time, but they're still apart and there's no reunion happening any time soon. *"Nothing's certain, Isla,"* Mama said just this morning, hovering in my doorway as I got ready for school. *"But don't worry about me and Daddy. We're not broken."*

"No." My gaze wanders to the football blanket folded on the edge of my bed, the one my father snuck in with my boxes when we moved. "He'll be here for my graduation, but then he's gotta go back for work stuff. He's getting an apartment."

"So you'll get to see him when you move back," Rigel says. "For college."

"Yeah, I will." The thought of it brings a smile to my face, and I can appreciate, not for the first time, the silver lining.

He tugs on my Adventuretime sleep shorts—a birthday gift from Sage—and slides them down my legs. I catch a glimpse of Finn and Jake as they go sailing off the bed, wishing I'd shaved earlier. Rigel wiggles out of his grey sweatpants and then we're kissing, all bare skin and tangled limbs.

And then the words that have been tickling at the edges of my mind slip out. "Do you think we'll stay together?"

He pauses, pinning me with his gaze. "You mean in college?"

Nodding, I press my thumb to the wrinkle between his brows, smoothing it. "There's a pretty good chance we'll end up at different places."

"Haven't really thought about it."

"Really? I think about it all the time." It's easier, admitting this, than I thought it would be.

"I guess I just thought we would." He shrugs. "We can make it happen if we want to."

"I want to." I kiss him, deciding to just go for it: "I really, really want to."

"So do I."

Camille's the first to get a response from a college. It's a rejection letter from Columbia.

"That was my reach school, anyway," she says, but it's apparent the letter's shaken her. She crumples it into her backpack, stone-faced.

I want to be supportive, but her dismay is contagious. Who knows? This could be me tomorrow. Letting my bag slide to the floor, I give her a hug. "One down, four to go, right?"

"Five."

"Five?" I pull back, looking at her. "I thought — "

"I applied to UCF at the last minute," she blurts. "Just in case. Jasmine convinced me."

Rigel's back to two-a-days in swimming, so I've been driving myself to school. After picking up dry cleaning for my mother and lottery tickets for Grandpa Harry, I head home.

"How was school?" Mama asks, taking her glasses off. Piles of paperwork are fanned around her laptop.

"Fine, I guess." I drop my backpack and make a bee-line for the fridge, hoping there's still soda somewhere back there. "Camille got her first letter...she didn't get into Columbia."

"I know," sighs Mom. "Greta told me."

Gratified to find one can of Coke left, I grab a glass from the cabinet. "She was pretty bummed out."

She smiles slyly. "You have a couple of letters here, too, and they look pretty official."

"What?" Whipping around, I nearly drop the glass in my haste. Riffling through the pile, I quickly find two fat envelopes. One is from Georgia State, the other, a tiny liberal arts school in Savannah. Neither school is my first choice, but my hands shake all the same as I open those envelopes.

"Well, what do they say?"

Not expecting her to be so close, I jump. "Mama! You're making me nervous."

"Sorry." She smiles sheepishly, squeezing my shoulder.

Both letters start similarly:

We are pleased to inform you...

"Isla!" Mama, who's reading over my shoulder, claps her hands. "You got in! "

I can't believe it. I read and re-read the letters until the words blur, overcome with relief that when all is said and done, at least someone wants me. The school in Savannah is expensive, so their financial aid package would have to be the stuff of miracles to afford my entrance, but that's okay. Knowing it's an option feels really good.

Mama yanks me into a hug. "We have to call Daddy," she sings, whipping out her phone.

Later, over Facetime, I show Sage the letters. "Now I'm just hoping for UGA."

"Isla girl—that's great!" Beaming, she gives me two thumbs up. "You can rest easy now. Morgan hasn't gotten any letters back."

"You've gotta be kidding. She's in more extracurriculars than the two of us combined."

Sage nods, chomping down her Twizzler like a rabbit with a carrot. She's already been accepted into a couple of schools—mostly in South Carolina, where her mama went to school—but also Juilliard, her dream. Part of me is sad we'll be apart, but mostly I'm just glad she's happy.

400

We've come a long way since freshman year, plotting and planning twin futures at the same colleges.

We'll always have Inman Park.

On Easter weekend in St. Croix, thousands of people go camping. I'm blown away at what a big deal this is, at how many people go—at how fancy some of the equipment is. Our diminutive bonfire on New Year's Eve is nothing compared to the patchwork of tent cities that bloom overnight as entire families descend upon the island's beaches. A bunch of Rigel's family head to the North Shore early Thursday morning to claim the Thomas family's usual spot, a little beach called Columbus Landing.

"You'll come, right, Isla?" Diana asks, pausing her cooler-packing and food prep to slide me a glass of passion fruit juice. "It's just family."

"You guys have a big family." I laugh, taking a sip. It's so sweet I shiver.

"There's always room. I can call your mom, if you'd like."

Mama's already made plans with Aunt Greta and Uncle Isaac, though. Even Grandpa Harry's going, per tradition, though he insists we attend church as a family on Easter Sunday. I'm in my room, considering the logistics of this, wondering if I'll just yank a dress on over my bikini, when Mama ducks in.

"I'm going to the store to grab a few supplies. You coming?"

"No, I'm okay."

She glances down the hall. "Grandpa's pissed I tossed out that other tent."

"It was moldy and gross," I mutter, wrinkling my nose.

"I know." She rolls her eyes, and we share a laugh. "I'll be back. Keep an eye on Alex, okay?"

I text Rigel, letting him know our family's camping down at Sprat Hall, and then do some packing of my own. Filling a smaller bag with toiletries, I make sure to grab the slim purple disc on my desk. They're my new birth control pills. I'm not sure what was worse: my mother's face when I told her I'd become sexually active, or the awkward drive to the gyno the next day after school.

She hasn't tried to murder Rigel, but we haven't told Daddy, and never, ever will.

Rigel messages back, and we lose time, chatting until the front door slams and Grandpa Harry yells something about his "frigging tent!" Alex darts into my room, jumping on my bed with relish until I sweep his knees from under him, making him collapse with an giddy shriek.

Where's Nando staying? I type.

heavenly bodies

They go to Cramer's Park. he's staying by me tmrw
night tho. We'll break you and Cam out ;)

By the time Mama, Grandpa, Alex and I join the others at Sprat Hall on Good Friday, the sun is setting over
the water. The mood is mellow, as most people have been
here all day. After a meal of fried fish and johnny cakes,
we take a dip down shore and then change into dry
clothes. Camille and I are hanging in one of the tents,
watching videos on our phones and munching on chips,
when Rigel messages me.

Hey. what are u up to?

Chilling w/Cam. you?

Nando's here. Want us to come get you?

"Tell him yes," Camille says, from right behind my
shoulder.

"Jeez, creeper." I snicker, shoving her out of my personal space.

She shoves back. "Tell him!"

Shouldering the assault, I return to my text conversation. **Yeah. when?**

Half hour

Camille and I visit The Moms, who have finally
stopped fussing over Grandpa Harry's sleeping arrange-
ments and are nursing thermoses of something steam-
ing. I suspect hot toddies with extra rum.

"Where's Alex?" I ask. Last I saw of him, he was running through camp with another little boy.

403

"Asleep, as of..." Mama looks at her watch. "Fifteen minutes ago."

"Everything all right?" Aunt Greta asks.

"Yep." I nod, pointing my toe and drawing shapes in the sand with it. "Is it okay if we go with Rigel and Nando for awhile?"

Mama purses her lips, like I knew she would. "For a couple of hours, Isla. You know this is a family thing. I'm surprised the boys aren't with their families."

Camille jumps in, which is good because not responding to my mother's judgemental undertones is taking monumental effort on my part. "Oh, it's cool. They've been doing the family thing since yesterday."

"Hmm." Mama sips her drink, sharing glances with Aunt Greta. I can imagine the years' worth of non-verbals these two have perfected.

"Go ahead," Aunt Greta says, waving us off. "Not for long, okay?"

"Thanks." I hug her, and then my mother, sharing a glance of my own with Camille. "We won't be late."

Weaving between tents, we duck back into ours long enough to grab flip flops and bags. After briefly discussing the ethics of drinking (and stealing) on Easter weekend, we liberate four Heinekens from Uncle Isaac's cooler and wait beneath a tree by the road. People are milling around, coming and going, the mood turning lively as night establishes itself.

heavenly bodies

At first, we startle at every thundering bass that passes, squinting at the headlights that sweep across the road. I look around, making sure I didn't miss something—did Rigel mean he'd park and find us? Will they pluck us up from the side of the road?—but as the minutes tick by, a half hour turns into forty five minutes, and I'm feeling as irritable as Camille sounds.

"What the hell?" she huffs, for maybe the eleventh time.

Rooting impatiently around my overstuffed bag—it's a beach bag doubling as a purse—I grab my phone. "I'm texting him right now."

"Only now?" She holds up her own phone. "I've been texting Nando for twenty minutes already!"

I peck out a quick message: *everything ok?*

Fully expecting a prompt reply, I sit with my phone in hand, waiting for it to vibrate. But it doesn't. Not when I wait, and not when I send two, three, four more messages.

My annoyance shifts to concern, though, when we hit the hour and a half mark. "Cam, what if something happened?"

"Like what?" she asks, rolling her eyes. "They probably went to another party."

"Come on."

"I'm serious! Everyone's out tonight...I can so see those two getting caught up."

"But they wouldn't ignore all these messages," I say, tapping the phone's screen. I'm not dating Nando, so I don't know how he and Cam roll, but Rigel's always been pretty good about getting back to me.

"First time for everything," she mumbles, already back on her phone.

Cam might be more experienced when it comes to guys, but that doesn't mean she's right. Although maybe it's better if she is.

Because the alternative is that something bad happened.

I wake up around dawn, eyelids prickly from a lack of sleep. Camille's knocked out beside me, her soft snores just audible over the perpetual push and pull of the tide. My phone's still clutched in my hand, and I stare at it now, confused.

But then it vibrates again. Someone's calling.

Rolling to my side in the stiflingly hot tent, I bring the phone to my ear and answer, knowing it's him. "Rigel?"

"Hey. Hey, I'm sorry—"

"What happened to you guys? Are you okay? We waited all night, Rigel." I know I sound slightly hysterical, but I've been anxious all night and it's got its claws in me.

"Long story," he rasps. "Are you up? Can I come now?"

"I'm up. Come." I'm so anxious, I agree before I mean to. I want to see him, but I'm exhausted. "Is Nando coming?"

"He headed back up east."

"He should probably call Camille. She was really pissed."

"Yeah, well, shit went down."

I blink at the edge in his voice, wondering what the hell happened. I'd known, though, hadn't I? Last night?

"Isla?"

"I'm here."

"I'll be there in twenty minutes. You're at Sprat Hall, right?"

"Yeah."

He pauses. "I'm sorry you waited all night."

Swallowing, I turn toward the water. It laps gently at the sand, gleaming dully in the early light. "Okay. I'll be waiting by the road."

When the black truck pulls up, sans music for once, I run to it barefoot. I see Rigel's face the second I clamor in, swollen with a split lip and a black eye. Gutted, I'm across the seat and in his arms before he can even take the truck out of park.

"Please, please tell me what happened." Eyes burning, I press my face into the side of his neck.

He squeezes me, kissing the top of my head. "I will. Come on," he whispers, reaching for the gear shift.

I scoot over to give him some room, but my eyes are glued to his face. He drives further down the road, past an endless line of parked cars. Everyone's camping. On any other day we'd have our pick of beaches, but today most of them are occupied. Even the private cove we go to sometimes is taken.

We drive far enough west, along the coast, that we begin to curve north. Rigel finds a secluded place right as the faintest glow of pink permeates the gray sky. There's no tree line here, just open access to a little inlet. No one's here, probably because the beach is so small. And rocky. I wince, stepping over broken shells and bits of driftwood.

Rigel ties his hair back and drops to the sand. He's barefoot, too. Even roughed up like this, he's beautiful. My throat tightens, like I might cry if I say anything.

"I told you about those guys from William's Delight," he says, turning his face to the water. "They've had beef with my brothers and their friends since way back. Nando and I were by the pier with some people when this dude comes up and asks where Orion is. He was drunk and in my face...but Nando was drunk too, so he pushed him away from me."

Picking up a small stone, he hurls it at the ocean. "That was it. The kid threw a punch and his friend jumped in and then there were five, six of them. They didn't know we had people with us though, so it evened out real quick."

"All because they were looking for Orion?"

"Yeah." He brushes sand from his shorts. "They recognized me, you know? I used to roll with my brothers a lot back in the day."

"How'd you break it up?" I'm glad I wasn't there. I don't know how I'd deal with Rigel fighting. "Did someone call the cops or something?"

"Eventually. It got broken up before that, though." Rigel touches his mouth, wincing.

"Why didn't you call me?" I ask, drawing my knees up and resting my chin on them. "Or text? I sent you a bunch of messages."

"I know; I saw them." He shakes his head. "I haven't stopped all night, Isla. I'm sorry."

My heartbeat starts to even out. Easing onto my back, hands beneath my head, I decide to drop it. He's already had the world's worst night. "I'm glad you're okay." He doesn't say anything for so long I touch his shorts. "Are you okay?"

"I'll be all right," he says.

"Are you going to tell him?"

409

"Orion?"

I nod.

"No." He shrugs. "He finally got off St. Croix...last thing I need is him coming back on a vendetta."

"He might hear about it anyway, though."

"I'm sure he will." He unfolds his legs and stands, stretching. "Let's swim."

The sky's a soft, dreamy pink now, clouds the color of cotton candy. Rigel wades into the calm, glassy water, passing his hands over top of it. There are cuts on his back and a bruise purpling his shoulder blade, making me wonder how much of his fight he's censoring from me.

How much of his life.

27.

Rigel's not at school on Tuesday. It'd be easy to write this off as nothing, but there are only a few weeks left and we generally spend our days prepping for finals and graduation. Besides, we're coming off a four day weekend.

No; considering what went down over Easter weekend, I suspect Rigel's absence hints at something unsavory. I try texting him around lunch. He responds with a prompt, "*stuff came up. I'm w/my dad*", so I drop it. He contacts me again during last period when I'm elbow deep in photo chemicals. Washing my hands thoroughly, I sneak into the yearbook office to check my messages.

You going home straight after school?

Maybe. Going to practice?

Yeah.

411

I'll stop by and say hi.

～ぁ⌒

Hot sun on metal seats can make the bleachers insufferable during the afternoon, but the far right corner is shaded thanks to a cluster of palm trees. That's where I sit, watching the members of the swim team as they splash and swim pre-practice.

Rigel comes over, goggles dangling from his fingertips. Even though I see him like this all the time, there's something about the swim gear I find sexy. Then I see his bruises, and my heart sinks. "Hey." I scan his face. No new injuries, thankfully.

"Hey." He leans close, brushing his lips against mine. "Everything okay?"

"I should be asking you." I wait until our eyes meet. "I missed you today."

"I know." He shifts closer, resting his hand on my thigh. "I was going to stop by later."

"Later when? Before dinner, when it's decent, or later when everyone's sleeping?"

He shrugs, tickling my knee through the hole in my jeans. "Before."

"So your dad doesn't mind you skipping?" I pull back, looking him over. "You've got the most lenient parents on the planet, I swear."

"Some things are more important than school." He ties his hair back. "It's not like I missed anything. The year's practically over."

I side-eye him, wishing he'd just tell me what he and his dad were up to. Coach Archer blows her whistle. She and her assistant are calling names as they round up the team. Rigel gets to his feet. "I gotta go, but I'll be by later."

I stand, too. "You and your dad...did it have anything to do with what happened over the weekend?"

Our eyes meet. "Yeah."

"So he knows everything?"

"You can't keep stuff from my dad," he says, staring out at the pool. "Even if it hadn't gotten back to him, which it eventually did, he saw me and Nando as soon as we got back to camp that night. He wanted to know what the hell happened to our faces."

I glance over his black eye, which has faded to a mottled purple. It isn't as bad as it was Friday, but it still hurts to look at. "What did he do?"

Rigel glances down at me, chewing the inside of his cheek. Archer calls for him, and he waves. "I'm coming."

He's really not going to tell me. Unbelievable.

"I gotta go," he says, bending to kiss my mouth. There's a smattering of applause from the sophomores sitting on the bottom bench. Archer snarks something about banning me from the pool.

Fights happen all the time, but I can't ignore the feeling that there's more to this story. Orion's involved in shady stuff; is their father, too? Scooping up my bag, I follow Rigel down the bleachers. "The longer I know you, the more I realize I know nothing about you."

Rigel grabs my arm, slowing me to a stop. "Don't be mad."

"I'm not mad." But I am, a little. I shake him off, walking away. "I just wish you trusted me."

"Isla." He comes around, blocking my path. "I do trust you. More than almost anybody."

"Like you trust Nando?"

He brushes my hair from my face. "Yeah, actually."

Archer blows her whistle. I shift, fiddling with my bag's zipper. "Really?"

"Mhm. And that's saying a lot. Nando's like...my Camille."

I smile, imagining Rigel and Nando having sleepovers.

"Look, I'll..." Linking his hands behind his head, he looks to the sky. "I'll pass by tonight. Catch you up on things."

"Want to come for dinner? I can ask my mama."

"What time?"

"Probably 6:30-ish, but I'll text you."

He nods, searching my eyes. "Everything's fine, okay? I don't want you worrying about my shit."

The sun goes behind a cloud, making it easier to see his face. "Maybe I want to worry about your shit."

"I know." He pulls me into a hug, resting his chin atop my head. "I kinda love that about you."

His words send a flush of pleasure through me. Disentangling myself from his embrace, I clear my throat. "Well, good. Because I love stuff about you, too." My face warms, but the look on his makes it worth it.

The assistant coach appears. "You have about ten seconds before Coach Archer makes you ride the bench at the next meet, Ri."

The mosquitos chase Rigel and me from the porch, driving us into the bright, warm, chaos of pre-dinner. Alex tends to grow increasingly hyper as bedtime approaches, so he's all over us, talking preschool, favorite songs, and the latest game on his tablet.

"Ok, Al," Mama says, smiling apologetically as she scoops him into her arms. "Come help mama in the kitchen."

"So what couldn't you tell me at school?" I ask, turning to Rigel.

"Can we..." He looks around, hands on his knees. "Go to your room?"

Mama's never explicitly told me not to have boys in my room, but that's only because she's never had to. Still, this is one of those times I'd rather ask forgiveness than permission. I make sure to leave the door open a crack, knowing she'll eventually show up.

I sit on my bed, Rigel settles into a chair in the corner. "So I used to be really close to Orion. I told you that. Everything he did, I did, and when he started doing things with Daniel, I did them too. Until we got in trouble that night, I was right at his side."

"Inseparable."

"Right." He takes a deep breath and lets it out slowly. For someone who's typically cool, he's pretty antsy right now. "Orion and Daniel went pretty deep, selling, but you should know I did it for awhile too. I wasn't just watching from the sidelines."

And there it is. I'm not as shocked as I should be. Logically, I get why he's kept this to himself, but I can't help but feel disappointed—not that he used to sell, but that I'm the last to know. Bits and pieces of conversations I've heard over the past months come back to me, and it all makes sense now. Rigel's not an angel. He never was.

I never wanted him to be. But I thought we were closer than that, especially after what we've shared. We talk every day. He taught me swim. We've had sex.

Our eyes lock, and I nod slowly. "Okay."

He sits back, chewing his bottom lip. "That's it?"

"I mean, Rigel, what do you want me to say?" I ask. Really, I've got a hundred things to say, but I don't know that he wants to hear any of them. "You don't do it anymore."

"No. But..." He stands, stuffing his hands in his pockets. "There's nothing you want to know? You'd just accept it like that?"

"Do I like that you did it? No. But we've all done stupid stuff." I stare at my hands. "I guess the only thing I want to know is why you didn't tell me before."

"I didn't want to scare you off."

My breath catches. "Oh."

"St. Croix's a small place. People know my family." He paces back and forth in front of me, his voice even. "But they know my brothers, too, on a different level. Remember what I told you, that one time, about our actions reflecting on each other?"

I nod.

"A lot of Orion and Daniel's enemies are also mine," he says. "Sometimes it's direct, like we had problems before. But sometimes it's just because of who my brothers are."

"Oh." Sighing, I scratch my leg. "So you weren't an innocent who got caught in the crossfire. You were on the same path at one point."

"Yeah. But the night they hauled us in was a serious wake-up call for me. I realized it wasn't a game, that it could really frig up my life." He stops in front of me.

"And it could've been worse, you know? It could've taken someone dying. That's happened. We know people who've died living this life. That's why I didn't call Orion. He finally got off St. Croix; I didn't want him getting sucked back in."

"I get it." I hold out my hand, and he takes it, sitting beside me. "But why did you miss school today? You were with your dad?"

"He and my Uncle Jimmy...know people. They're not into anything, but they know people who are." Rigel pauses, glancing at me. "They're afraid of retaliation. So besides family, and maybe Drew, no one knows where Orion is. No one even knows he's gone yet."

"But what exactly did Orion do?" I ask, horrified. "Why are people after him?"

"It's been escalating for a while. Someone from Orion's crew robs someone from William's Delight...they fight over girls, or turf...whenever they see each other in public, there's a fight. Last time they threw down, Orion really messed one dude up and I think it brought things to a head." He scrubs his hands over his face. "But now I'm having run-ins with these punks and I just...I thought I was past this. I'm so close to graduating, to getting out of here."

"You did move past it. It's just Orion didn't, and now it's affecting you."

"Or maybe my past is catching up to me."

Mama knocks on the door before pushing it open. "Dinner's ready."

"Okay, we're coming," I say, getting up.

"Keep this open next time, please," she says, disappearing back down the hall. "Wide open."

Well, that's that. Rigel and I look at each other. "Thanks for telling me," I say. "For trusting me."

We walk to the door. "It's not just about trust. It's about keeping you away from certain things."

"You don't have to protect me."

"Ah, Isla. Yes I do."

"Who protects you?" I poke his chest. I guess that's how it is sometimes. Old choices come back to haunt us, their consequences far reaching, and we have to ride them out.

"I'll be alright." Rigel follows me to the kitchen, petting Larry as Alex buzzes around our legs with his latest Lego creation. "I have family, remember? And unlike some people, I know how to stay out of trouble."

Feedback squeals across the crowded pavilion, triggering a wave of laughter. Mr. Randolph, Headmaster of the Palms, is at the podium, red-faced and harried as a gangly junior from the production team fiddles with his mic. Two weeks until graduation, and we're at another after-school dress rehearsal.

Thanks to alphabetized seating, no one's sitting with their friends. Our senior class is small enough that everyone knows each other, though, so it's no big deal. I'm signing Jasmine's yearbook when I detect a vibration from the shorts under my gown. Reaching beneath the satiny, gold material, I yank my phone out on the sly, not wanting it to be confiscated.

It's a text from Rigel. *Orion's back.*

For how long?

Don't know, but he's been here for days already.

???

Staying with Junie.

Junie? In the rainforest? I peek over at Rigel, who's seated in the T's between Amira Tehrani and Lucas Trudeau.

The one and only. And then, as if he can feel my gaze, he looks up at me and nods.

"Is it on?" Mr. Randolph's sonorous voice rings out, magnified by the now operational microphone. Startled back to reality, everyone quiets. I slide Jasmine's yearbook into my bag. "All right. Welcome!" With a perfunctory smile, he adjusts his glasses.

Your parents know he's here? I ask.

They do now.

After school, I walk down to my car, lost in thought. Why is Orion back? I'd like to think it's for graduation,

but he'd be a little early. I'm unlocking the door when I notice a folded white paper taped to my windshield. Careful not to tear it, I peel it from the glass and open it.

It's Rigel's acceptance letter to UGA. My heart drops to my shoes and I search the crowd, wondering where he is. He hugs me from behind, sliding his arms around me.

"Congratulations!" I say, twisting to kiss his cheek. "I can't believe you got yours first."

"You better get yours next," he says. "Otherwise, I'll have nothing to do but swim."

But I'm already there, thinking about fall in Athens, the leaves, and kissing Rigel in the cold.

"Here we go," I whisper, wiggling in anticipation. "Fingers crossed."

We're at the Sandbar, a popular beach bar in Frederiksted, watching the sunset.

Rigel folds his arms. "Don't stare too hard. It'll frig up your eyes."

The sun slips below the horizon, glinting green. "I saw it! I saw it!" I cry, letting out a cheer. Several of the people on the beach smile good naturedly at my excitement, raising their beers in a toast.

"That was a good one, too," says Rigel, as we make our way through the crowd.

It's a Saturday, so there's a cruise ship in Frederiksted. The pier and streets are jammed with passengers visiting jewelry shops and food vans; a steel pan band performs while ladies in traditional madras dresses hand out rum punch. The beaches are packed as well, as herds of tourists join the regulars. We did the beach thing today too, before stopping at The Sandbar for burgers. When it looked like we'd be there late enough to watch the sunset, Rigel waited with me to see the famed green flash.

Back at the truck, my cousin and Nando are rooting through the cooler. I climb onto the tailgate and Cam hops up beside me, her flipflops joining mine on the packed, dirty sand below. She's on cloud nine because she finally got accepted to one of her top schools.

Thankfully, I can relate. My acceptance letter to UGA was on the kitchen table when I got home last night. We've been celebrating ever since.

"So is your friend going to be able to make it down?" Camille asks.

"Once school's out. They're done before we are." Sage had wanted to visit during Spring Break, but Grady's vacation scheduled conflicted with ours. Summer turned out to be cheaper anyway, so she's coming for the second half of June. I'm so excited to share St. Croix with her. She'll fall in love.

heavenly bodies

Nando sidles over, whispering to Camille. Rigel's talking to some kid I don't know, so I sit back and people-watch. Rumor has it there might be fireworks at nightfall, right over the pier. As I think it, a high pitched whistle culminates in an explosion. Fireworks fill the sky like jewel toned confetti. Far away, in the housing projects down the road, there's celebratory gunfire; tell-tale *pop pop pops* between the glittery blooms in the sky. They did that on New Year's, too.

The cruise ship drifts slowly from the pier and out to sea. I wouldn't mind being a passenger right now, watching fireworks from the deck.

Camille leans close, resuming her story about Jasmine's pregnancy scare. "Anyway. She wouldn't have been able to keep it. Her mom told her when we were like, thirteen, that she'd make her get an abortion if she ever got pregnant."

I glance at Rigel to make sure he's not listening. "But she's not, though, right?"

"No, thank God. She got her period."

"And it was definitely Orion?"

"There's no one else."

"When did this happen, though?" I ask. "If he's been in Miami?"

"Right before he left, which made it even worse because he was even more absent than usual." Camille sighs. "I hate to say it, but I wish he'd just cut her loose."

I kind of agree, but... "That would break her heart."

"I know it would. But they've been doing this forever, Isla, and he's not gonna change."

As if summoned by our words, Orion appears on the fringes of the parking lot crowd. Thrown by the coincidence, I watch him. I haven't seen him since he's been back on island; his hair's longer than it was, starting to curl. Our eyes lock. Camille's voice, and most everything else, fades as he comes closer. I raise my hand in a hesitant wave, but something's up. He's walking funny...and he's got me trapped in a stare so intense I can't break it. He waves back belatedly as the fireworks' finale bathe his face in green, red and blue.

"Rigel." He's still talking to that guy, and he squeezes my foot in response. Orion's closer now, his face sallow even in the dim light. I shake Rigel's shoulder, not caring if I'm being rude. "Rigel!"

He turns abruptly, looking at me. "What's up?"

I point. "Did you see your brother?"

Camille grabs my arm, and then everything happens at once. Orion pushes his way through to us and starts to pass out, eyes fluttering shut. Rigel lurches toward him, Nando at his side, catching Orion before he falls.

"What happened?" shouts Rigel.

"It's okay," Orion says, letting them support his weight. "Just get me to the hospital."

"What the fuck..." Nando's lifted Orion's black t-shirt. There's so much blood it's hard to tell where the wound is. Together, we ease him into the truck bed and

lay him down, resting his head on my lap. Nando and Camille squeeze in on either side, bracing themselves against us to keep things steady. I focus on taking better breaths, shunning panic even as the overwhelm rolls over me in waves.

There's a break in the music up the beach. People are staring. Rigel slams the tailgate shut, looking at me. His eyes are wild. "Hold on to him, Isla."

Shouldn't we just call 911? I want to scream, but I just nod. He climbs up front and starts the truck. Beside me, Camille's on the phone to Jasmine, telling her what's going on. "She's meeting us at the hospital," she says.

"Okay." I'm unable to look away from Orion, from his face, from Camille's grasp on his bloody hand.

I scarcely remember the ride to the hospital. I stare into Orion's eyes the whole time, touching his cheek, making sure he stays awake. Rigel drives fast, but not crazy, pulling into the emergency bay as Nando runs in, calling for help. A team of medics rushes out with a stretcher, easing Orion on to it and wheeling him inside.

Rigel tosses Nando his keys and runs in after them.

Nando turns to Cam and I. "Go on in. I'll park."

Inside, it's carefully controlled chaos as the medics hustle Orion into a room for emergency operating. In the waiting room, Rigel paces. He can't even look at me, and when he finally does, his eyes are filled with tears. My own eyes spill over and he looks away, collapsing into a chair across the room.

425

Minutes melt into hours. Raymond and Diana came soon after we did, having left the younger kids with family. Jasmine's here now too, folded beneath Cam's arm as she cries.

Rigel, having gone outside with his father, comes back my way. I reach for him as he passes, wanting him to sit, wanting to comfort him—anything—but he ghosts past. He's not even here right now, not mentally, and wherever he is...I can't go. He's lost there.

I'm quiet for so long that when Camille leans into me, touching me as she asks about food, I startle.

"Sorry," she whispers, giving my arm a soft squeeze. "We're taking Ri's truck to Mcdonalds or something. You hungry?"

"Yeah." I nod, reaching for my bag, but she stops me.

"I got it. What do you want?"

"Just get me whatever. I don't care."

Nando walks over to Rigel, leaning down to speak to him. After a moment he comes over, offering me a hand.

Puzzled, I take it, letting him pull me to standing. "Everything okay?"

"Let's go eat."

I look at my phone—it's already past ten—and then over at Rigel, but his head's in his hands and he's staring at the floor. My heart is in my throat. There's nothing I can do right now, and that scares me.

"He asked me to bring you home," Nando murmurs.

I look down, wiping my eyes. "Okay."

426

Nando wraps his arm around me, but I shrug away and go to Rigel. "Hey."

Diana gives me a watery smile, patting my hand, but Rigel just looks at me with red-rimmed eyes.

"I'll go, okay? But I'll come back if you want me to. I'll have my phone right next to me." A sob works its way up and I clamp my mouth shut, swallowing.

He nods stiffly, hands clenched in his lap. Inconsolable. Out of everything that's happened today, this is what crushes me the most: to see this beautiful boy break, and to have him shut me out at a time when I want nothing more than to be at his side. I've known that I loved him for awhile, but in this moment, it strikes me so hard I'm left bruised.

"Thank you, sweetheart," whispers Diana.

I give her a small smile and turn to go. Camille and Nando are already waiting in the hall so I get my stuff and follow them out into the warm, humid night. There's a full moon and a gentle wind, and how can it be so lovely when such ugly things have happened? The fear and grief I tried so hard to subdue wash over me, and I stop, rummaging through my bag for a tissue.

The electric doors behind me whoosh open, and Rigel rushes out. Before I can say a word, he wraps himself around me and cries.

28.

Rigel doesn't call, and I hardly sleep.

When I close my eyes, I see Orion's staring up at me as we held on to him in the truck. It's a far cry from the cocky Casanova who danced with me last Halloween.

Finally giving up sometime around four, I flip my laptop on and browse through my portfolios. Photos from September remind me of how I looked I when I was new on St. Croix, skin lighter and hair darker. More makeup. I straightened my hair a lot back then, too, before giving up and letting my curls do their thing.

There are landscapes and classmates and swim meets and soccer teams. My mother, combing Alex's knotty hair. Grandpa Harry, dozing on the porch. My feet in the sand, shadows of palm fronds on my skin. Camille, on

Grandpa's lap. Camille, underwater. Camille, kissing Nando. Nando and Rigel goofing around on the soccer field.

Rigel.

My heart twists, and I sigh in the darkness, pulling my computer closer. The first photos of him are subtly stalker-esque, which is funny now. Rigel on the starting block, seconds from diving in. Rigel, running on the beach. Rigel, giving Phoenix a noogie. Rigel, trying to take the camera from me.

I send him a text, wondering if he's still at the hospital. There's no response, but then I don't really expect one. Exhausted, I shut my laptop and lie down.

When Mama shakes me awake a couple of hours later, it's to remind me it's laundry day. "Don't forget your pillowcases this time," she says.

I feel like death warmed over. "Okay."

"Any word?" she asks. She was up, reading in the living room, when I got home last night. I had called her from the hospital, but it felt really good to unload when I saw her. The stress of the day, coupled with the need to be there for Rigel, shattered me, and she held me while I cried.

I touch my face now, remembering how swollen it had felt before bed. "No...not yet. I'll call Jasmine."

"You think she's still there?"

"No, but her mother might be." Jasmine's mother pulls long shifts as a nurse in labor and delivery, so

430

there's a chance she's been able to keep tabs on Orion. Camille says Natalie didn't know about her daughter's relationship with him, but I'm sure she's figured it out by now.

Mama sits on the edge of my bed, touching my hand. "You okay?"

I rub my eyes. "Tired."

"When did you go to bed?"

"Late. And then I couldn't sleep."

Concern darkens her expression. "Take it easy today, baby. I have melatonin if you need it for tonight."

I sit up, stretching. "Are you still having problems sleeping?"

"It comes and goes. Usually happens when I'm stressed out, like when we first moved down here. I missed your daddy a lot."

I think back to those early days. I'd cried a lot, missed my friends, hated the lack of air conditioning. I'd been so consumed with myself that I'd missed things, like the depth of my mother's sadness and anxiety. Leaning into her soft, bathrobed side, I hug her with all I've got. "I still miss him a lot."

"Me too. You'll get to see him soon," she says, rubbing my back. "Lucky girl."

I close my eyes, inhaling her Mama-scent of coffee and cocoa butter. "But then I'll miss you."

There is something therapeutic about hard work, and, after stripping my bed and collecting every bit of

431

laundry I can find, I set about vacuuming and mopping my room, moving on to Alex's once I'm done. He protests loudly when the vacuum cleaner comes roaring in, but soon makes it a game, darting around it like a kitten.

After lunch, in an effort to occupy my mind, I join Grandpa Harry in the backyard. Alex trails behind with a beach bucket, amassing an armory of twigs and rocks. Just beyond Grandpa's lime grove sit several mango trees, branches heavy with ripe fruit. Alex won't allow me to touch his bucket so I grab one of my own to gather mangos, my mouth watering at the scent. Grandpa keeps a running commentary of the garden, explaining what blooms and bears fruit when. He's sharing it with me like he wants me to know, but I sense he's doing it for himself, too. To remind himself he still knows.

My phone burns a hole in my pocket. I check it all day, hating the knot in my stomach each time I realize there are no new messages.

Camille finally texts me. She's with Jasmine, whose mother finally forced her to leave the hospital.

I'm guessing Natalie knows now?

Yes. She was not happy, girl. But she said she'd keep Jas updated.

Anything new?

heavenly bodies

Orion's sleeping now. They're going to move him to another room soon.

That's good, right?

Yes. Want to come over?

I don't, though. Rigel's unexpected silence hurts, and I don't feel like being social—even if it is with just Cam and Jasmine.

By nightfall I'm fed up with my own restlessness, so I take Grandpa Harry to Mass. He likes the Sunday evening services at St. Patrick's, a historical Catholic church tucked into the hilly backstreets of downtown Frederiksted. We make our way up the aisle of the half empty nave, sliding into a row near the front. A lilting breeze blows through the open doors and windows of the chapel, wafting incense around.

Maybe I find it because I need it, but there's peace here. It's quiet, sacred. I sit still, listening to the priest and his patrons, and I pray for Orion and Rigel. And then, even though it's rude and possibly sacrilegious, I send a text from the pews.

In church with my grandpa thinking about you.

His response is unexpected, making my heart jump.

At the hospital with my mom thinking about you.

Rigel calls, finally, late in the night. Everyone but me is asleep, and I'm only awake because the book I'm reading has one cliffhanger after the next. And, maybe, because I'm waiting for a phone call.

Hoping my mother didn't hear anything, I answer on the second ring. "Hello?"

"Hey."

I close my door quietly, leaning against it. "How are you?"

He pauses. "I'm okay."

"Orion?"

"Better. Bullets missed vital organs and bone...he lost a lot of blood, though. Lots of tissue damage." Voices rise in the background. A door slams—his truck's, maybe. "He'll be in the hospital for another day or two. Maybe longer."

I have so many questions, but I don't know the right one to ask. "I've been praying a lot."

"It's helping," he says, voice dropping.

We're quiet for a moment. It sounds like he's driving. "Are you going to school tomorrow?"

"I don't know," he says. "But can I come see you?"

"Now?"

"I know it's late."

"Hold on." Leaving my room, I pad quietly down the hall. The strip beneath my mother's door is dark, so she's probably sleeping. Still, just to make sure, I peek in. Except for the fan, the room is still and silent. Tiptoeing back to my room, I return the phone to my ear. "Come through the kitchen door this time."

"Your bed's warm," says Rigel, touching the sheets. "Did I wake you up?"

"No." I lie beside him, looking up at my twinkle lights. "I was reading."

He nods slowly, closing his eyes.

"You okay?"

"Just thinking," he says, leaning against the head-board. His hair's so long it's almost always pulled back in a knot now. "About the past couple days."

"That's all I think about."

He shakes his head, scrubbing his hands over his face.

"It felt like you were blocking me out," I say.

"I wasn't." He pulls me close, and I rest my head on his chest. "I didn't mean to. I just couldn't see past my brother."

I get that. It's logical; it makes sense. There's nothing logical about feelings, though, and right now I feel insecure and clingy. It's different from when I wanted him, and different from loving him. This is needing him, and the thought of losing him does terrible things to my stomach.

"Isla."

"I understand. I just..." I close my eyes. "I wanted to be there for you."

"I know you did." He slides down so we're sharing a pillow. "Everything happened so fast. The worst case scenario happened. And I didn't know what to do."

I put my hand on his chest, feeling for his heartbeat.

435

"I've been angry at him for such a long time. Even when nothing was wrong, things just didn't feel right between us, you know? I felt like he was choosing that life over my mom, my family. Me." His voice cracks. "And then, just like that, I almost lost him. And none of that other shit mattered, even though it was the same shit that almost got him killed."

"Like it clarified things."

"Yeah."

"I was so scared," I say. "I don't know how you drove to the hospital."

"I don't either. I was freaking out." He lies on his back, staring at the ceiling. "It was that same crew, Isla. I should've been with him."

I freeze. "What do you mean?"

"That morning...he said he might pass by Rainbow while we were there. But he wanted me to come down to Dorsch Beach, too. He never said it, but I know one of the reasons he came back was to fuck up the dude who messed with me."

"Have you gotten to talk to him yet?" I ask. "Like, really talk?"

"Yeah. Soon as he woke up. We talked for awhile."

Larry barks from somewhere in the house, and we freeze. I wonder if Rigel's listening to my breathing the way I'm listening to his. "I'm so glad he's okay."

"Me too."

"And I'm glad you're okay."

"I should've called you," he whispers, easing on to me. "I'm sorry."

I don't want Rigel's apologies; I just want him. I wrap myself around him and then it's endless, soft lips and tongues, deep down and dark and good. These are the types of kisses that flow one to another, building until we're pulling at each other's clothes. There's no hesitation tonight, no discussion. We kiss until kissing isn't enough, and then we slip under the covers.

"I told myself I wouldn't do this," he says afterward, kissing the space between my breasts.

"Why not?"

Sighing quietly, he pulls the sheet over my chest.

"Isn't that why you came over?" I tease, trailing the backs of my fingers over his flushed cheek.

He grabs my hand. "You know it's not like that, right?"

"Sometimes I want it to be like that," I say, gratified by the renewed hunger on his face as I touch his man-bun. "I love this, by the way. It's sexy."

"It's a little out of control. I'll probably cut it before classes start."

I nod, because he'll be competing at a different level in college and little things like hair can be a nuisance. "I'll still love you." I don't mean to say it, not like that.

Maybe part of me does.

Rigel's eyes widen fractionally, and then he melts into a smile. Swear to God, even after what he just did to me, it's that smile that makes my heart thump. "Yeah. I love you too, Isla."

On Monday, at school, Orion's all anyone can talk about. The Palms is a tight-knit community of families, and the Thomas kids have been a part of it for years. Rigel's noticeably tight-lipped about it all morning, using his senior privileges to visit the hospital during lunch.

"How is he?" I ask, once he's back.

"Okay. In pain, still." He turns his attention to the window beside us. It looks like it might rain. "They want him to stay for another couple of days."

On Thursday, at final bell, Rigel finds me at my locker. "Orion's moving to Miami."

I twist the combination on my lock. "Miami, huh? Jasmine will approve."

"Why do you think he's going? She hasn't left his side since this went down."

I've heard as much from Camille. "Maybe he'll stop being such an idiot and treat her properly."

He adjusts his backpack. "I guess we'll see."

"Is he being released yet? I'd like to see him." The last time I saw Orion, he was bleeding out in the back of Rigel's truck. I need desperately to replace that memory with him healthy and whole.

"Yeah, my dad's bringing him home this afternoon."

I watch Rigel carefully, noting the faint smudges beneath his eyes. He's older than he was last week. "No more staying with Junie, huh?"

438

"Nope...the prodigal returns. Mom's making lasagna, his favorite." He pauses, yawning. "You should come."

Now that the yearbooks have been published and distributed, my afternoons are free. I leave campus the second last bell rings, impatiently joining the queue crawling out of the parking lot. On the way home, I stop at the bakery to load up on treats. I'm not sure what Orion likes best, so I buy a little of everything.

Several cars are parked in front of the Thomas house, Rigel's truck among them. Raymond and the kids are in the living room, watching TV and doing homework. Rory jumps up to hug me while Leo waves shyly. Rigel brings me to Orion, who smiles weakly from the couch. "Hey, Isla. Looking good."

"Hey, Orion." I bend to kiss his cheek, leaving a brown paper bag of sweets in his lap. Seeing him this way puts a lump in my throat. "Wish I could say the same of you."

"Ouch." He smiles as he searches the bag. "Coconut fritters? Guava tarts? Hold onto her," he says to Rigel, pointing. "Don't fu—mess it up."

"Watch your mouth, Orion," Diana says, passing by.

"I'm watching it, Mom," he says, winking at me.

Rigel snatches the bag, emerging with a fritter. The crinkling attracts Phoenix and Leo, who linger nearby until Rigel relinquishes the bag.

"I'd tell them not to ruin their appetites, but these kids eat like horses," Diana says wryly. "Anyway, we'll

439

be eating around six. You want anything, Isla? Juice? We have passion fruit."

"That would be great. Thanks."

She disappears again and I turn to Orion, studying him. "So. How're you feeling?"

"Like I been shot a heap of friggin' times."

Rigel sucks his teeth. "Ey," he says, jerking his head toward the younger boys.

Orion sighs loudly. "I'm sore. And very, very happy to be out of that damn hospital. You get no sleep in there. None."

I nod sympathetically, knowing from stories Mama has told that's true.

"Mostly," he says, serious now as he brings his eyes back to mine. "I'm just happy I'm alive."

After dinner, once we've helped clean up and Orion has been put to bed with plenty of pain medication, Rigel walks me to my car.

"I didn't want to ask in there, but, has there been any progress in the case? Do the police have any leads?"

He leans against the trunk of my car. "They have somebody in custody."

I lean beside him. "You didn't tell me."

440

"I just found out; I guess they brought him in this afternoon."

"Oh. Wow." I exhale slowly—relieved, but still unsettled. "That's good. Will Orion stay for the trial and all that, then?"

Rigel nods. "And then he needs to get the hell out of here for awhile. It's good he has Jasmine and Miami."

"Are you afraid of retaliation?" I ask. "Or just that he'll keep on living this life?"

"Either; both." He gazes up at the sky. "This is why I wanted out. The night I got caught with Orion, I had a choice. It would've been easy to stay on that path, you know? But I didn't want to live my life constantly watching my back, always having beef with somebody."

"And it's a small island."

"Too small," he says.

"It is too small, but...I'm really going to miss it when we're gone."

"Me too. But I need some distance from all of this." He pulls me into his arms. "And so does my brother."

29.

Daddy's been on island since graduation. We still haven't sold the house in Inman Park, but once we do, he says he wants to come to St. Croix. It's not clear if he, Alex and Mama would get a place close to Grandpa, or if Daddy would be in an apartment of his own. He and Mama are still Figuring Things Out.

Weird, but I'll take it. At least he'll be around for Alex.

The day before he heads back to Atlanta, we drive to the South Shore. Despite the rain we had earlier, the sky is clear now. In fact, the sunset looks like it's going to be spectacular.

"I was hoping it would be like this," I say, snapping a couple of shots with my Minolta.

"Rainy days usually have the best sunsets," Daddy comments, plopping down onto the sand beside me. "As long as it stops raining." I drag my fingers through the sand. It's still warm from the day.

"I wonder why that is?" I muse, gazing out at the horizon. A pod of pelicans drift past, skimming the surface of the water with their wings.

"Maybe it clears the air," he says.

"That makes sense, actually."

"Good a guess as any."

Daddy reaches into the paper bag at his side, retrieving jars of cookie butter for each of us. He hands me a plastic spoon and we eat quietly, watching the sun sink.

"Might have a buyer for the house," he says.

"Really?" We've had a couple of potential buyers, but nothing has panned out.

He nods.

An ache settles into my chest, but then, like clouds on a windy day, it blows away. "I'm really going to miss it."

"Me too." He sighs, gazing out at the sea.

"Would you really move down if it sold?"

"I miss your Mama, Isla girl. And Alex. I need to be here for them."

"Yes. You do."

Sighing, he thumbs a tear from my cheek. "You'll be alright."

"I know." I stare at the sand, giving myself a second to pull it together. "I was afraid you guys might not get back together."

"I was afraid of that, too. But you know your mama's my reason."

The sun sets. I lean close to my father, bumping his shoulder. "Okay, watch for it...these conditions are perfect..."

"I'm watching."

"But don't, like, stare right at it. Rigel says you'll get retinal fatigue or something."

"Isla, honey. I—oh!"

Tonight's green flash sparks like a tiny supernova, the brightest one I've seen yet.

Five months later

"Isla?"

I know that voice. Looking up from my phone, I meet the surprised gaze of Benson Reid.

"Benny!" Grinning, I give him a quick hug. "Long time no see!"

"No kidding. You look good," he says, blue eyes soft as they take me in. I step back and he lets go, sliding his hands into his pockets. "You're so...tan. Wow."

"Well, I've lost some of it now, but yeah. Island life was good to me."

Looks like life has been good to him, too. He's even taller than he was, trendy and cute in a beanie, jeans and flannel. "Heard you're at UGA."

"Yeah. I thought Sage said you were too?"

"I was supposed to be, but..." He drifts off, staring at something behind me.

Or someone, rather. Rigel saunters over, handing me my coffee. "I got you extra whipped cream."

"Aw, thanks." I wrap my mittened hands around the cup, savoring its warmth. "Ri, this is Benny. I've known him forever. Benny, this is my boyfriend Rigel. He's from St. Croix, but he's at UGA, too."

I watch this sink in as they shake hands. They're about the same height; Benny's a little taller, but Rigel's broader in the shoulders.

"Nice to meet you, man," Benny says, eyes flickering between the two of us.

"Yeah, you too." Rigel's casual as he sips his hot chocolate, but I know he's sizing Benny up just the same.

"I was just showing Rigel around Little Five Points," I say, shifting. "We're gonna pass by my house."

"Did your parents sell it?"

"Not yet. It's taking awhile." Rigel's hand drops to mine, taking it. It's time to go. "It was good seeing you, Benny." I give him a smile, remembering what it used to be like between us.

446

"You too." He smiles too, wryly, as he walks away.

Rigel's parked on a side street, close to the coffee shop we just went to. We walk down the sidewalk together, leaves crunching beneath our feet.

"I remember that guy," he says, wrapping his arm around my shoulder. "From your phone."

"Mhm. We had a thing."

He side-eyes me, smirking. "He wishes there was still a thing."

That's probably true, but it doesn't matter anymore. I link my arm through Rigel's. "Come on, St. Croix. I want to drive down my old street.

ACKNOWLEDGEMENTS

I have always loved to write. Always. Publishing this book is a dream come true, a true mark off the bucket list.

Enthusiastic, gushy, super-special thank you to:
- Anna B for reading my stuff and getting me off my butt and pushing me to just DO IT.
- Lauren for my beautiful, dreamy cover.
- Jessica B, Mary Foster, Joy DiPaola, Christina Gibbins, Michelle Collins, Grisell Cano and the ISoGs for reading, inspiring and encouraging me.
- April Salter, Beth Bolden, Mary Elizabeth, Jada D'Lee for your practical advice, encouragement, time and shared resources.

To my pre-readers and the Twi Fandom: I love you and appreciate you. You have grown me into the writer I am today and I hope only to become better and craft wonderful tales of love and kisses for you.

To my best friends, Caleigh, Kelley and Amanda. Many of my characters over the years were written with you in mind. You are the sisters of my heart.

To St. Croix, for being the most magical place a girl could grow up.

To my Mom, for believing in me and loving me so unconditionally. (And for loving everything I ever wrote...even the crappy stuff!)

To my husband, for giving me (gorgeous kids but also) the gift of time. For believing I could do this. I love you. You're the ultimate love interest.

And to God, for giving me this precious gift. I give you all the glory.

ABOUT THE AUTHOR

Rochelle Allison has been living, and thriving, in her imagination since she was a little girl in the Caribbean.

A true lover of words (books! thesauruses!), she can usually be found crafting stories, inspired by people, conversations and the world around her.

A wife of one and mother of two, Rochelle lives just outside of Atlanta. She's a lover of the beach, hiking and the outdoors, music, photography and baking.

And...she loves love. More than anything, she loves love.

Facebook: facebook.com/rochelleallison81

Twitter: @roglows

Amazon: amzn.com/Rochelle-Allison/e/B01H29KSSA/

Goodreads: goodreads.com/author/show/6545655.Rochelle_Allison

Made in the USA
Columbia, SC
20 June 2018